Buffy barely had time to channel her revulsion at the horrible images in her mind, for outside the house an engine roared and tires skidded to a halt and car doors opened and slammed closed.

For a moment she stared at Spike, then her gaze fell upon the Moruach Queen. The monster reached out and dragged its talons along the line of Spike's jaw as though she might tear his head off any second. Then the Queen gazed at Buffy, that dark intelligence commanding and brutal, and she slithered toward the Slayer on her powerful serpentine trunk.

The Queen waved toward the door and the Moruach cleared away. Buffy hesitated only a second before moving swiftly to the front of the room and peering through the open door. In the moonlight she could see five figures walking up toward Talisker House from an SUV parked sideways across the drive. They were silhouettes only. Two female and three male.

And she recognized the walk of one of the females.

Faith, Buffy thought.

All of them were armed.

They had come for war.

Buffy the Vampire Slayer™

Buffy the Vampire Slayer (movie tie-in)
The Harvest
Halloween Rain
Coyote Moon
Night of the Living Rerun
Blooded
Visitors
Unnatural Selection
The Power of Persuasion
Deep Water
Here Be Monsters
Ghoul Trouble
Doomsday Deck
Sweet Sixteen
Crossings

The Angel Chronicles, Vol. 1
The Angel Chronicles, Vol. 2
The Angel Chronicles, Vol. 3

The Xander Years, Vol. 1
The Xander Years, Vol. 2
The Willow Files, Vol. 1
The Willow Files, Vol. 2
How I Survived My Summer Vacation, Vol. 1
The Faith Trials, Vol. 1
Tales of the Slayer, Vol. 1
The Journals of Rupert Giles, Vol. 1

The Lost Slayer serial novel
Part 1: Prophecies
Part 2: Dark Times
Part 3: King of the Dead
Part 4: Original Sins

Available from ARCHWAY paperbacks and SIMON PULSE

Child of the Hunt
Return to Chaos
The Gatekeeper Trilogy
Book 1: Out of the Madhouse
Book 2: Ghost Roads
Book 3: Sons of Entropy
Obsidian Fate
Immortal
Sins of the Father

Resurrecting Ravana
Prime Evil
The Evil That Men Do
Paleo
Spike and Dru: Pretty Maids All in a Row
Revenant
The Book of Fours
The Unseen Trilogy (Buffy/Angel)
Book 1: The Burning
Book 2: Door to Alternity
Book 3: Long Way Home
Tempted Champions
Oz: Into the Wild

The Watcher's Guide, Vol. 1: The Official Companion to the Hit Show
The Watcher's Guide, Vol. 2: The Official Companion to the Hit Show
The Postcards
The Essential Angel
The Sunnydale High Yearbook
Pop Quiz: Buffy the Vampire Slayer
The Monster Book
The Script Book, Season One, Vol. 1
The Script Book, Season One, Vol. 2
The Script Book, Season Two, Vol. 1
The Script Book, Season Two, Vol. 2

Available from SIMON PULSE

The Wisdom of War

Christopher Golden

An original novel based on the hit television series by Joss Whedon

SIMON PULSE

NEW YORK LONDON TORONTO SYDNEY SINGAPORE

Historian's note: This story takes place in the second half of the fifth season of *Buffy*.

First Simon Pulse edition July 2002

SIMON PULSE
An imprint of Simon & Schuster
Children's Publishing Division
1230 Avenue of the Americas
New York, NY 10020

The text of this book was set in Times.
Printed in the United States of America.
2 4 6 8 10 9 7 5 3 1
The Library of Congress Control Number: 2002104217
ISBN: 0-7434-2760-2

This one's for all my friends in the United Kingdom. You guys throw a hell of a party.

And for Sally.

Acknowledgments

Thanks, as always, to Lisa Clancy and Micol Ostow at Simon Pulse, and to Debbie Olshan at Fox. I'm always grateful for the green light, but this time even more than most. What a rush.

Thanks are also due to my wife, Connie, and my boys, Nicholas and Daniel, who I hope when they're old enough will be able to look beneath the lunacy in these pages to see what the story is about. And thanks to the irregulars—Tom, Jose, Rick, Stefan, and Meg. You guys help keep me sane.

Finally, a special thanks to U.S. Coast Guard Petty Officer Jaimie Browne, who came through in a pinch and helped me face the monsters.

PROLOGUE

Buffy Summers was the town skank.

Not really, of course, but on this night she had chosen to play that role. When patrolling as the Slayer consisted of spending all her time trawling cemeteries for the latest accountant or high school student to rise from the grave as a vampire—just so she could put them back there again—Buffy could wear whatever she liked. Comfortable clothes: sweats, jeans, boots, even sneakers. Some nights she grew bored with the practical look and attempted to be a bit more fashionable in her war against the forces of darkness.

But tonight was different.

She wore torn low-rider jeans that showed her hip bones and felt as though they might slip that last precious, strategic inch at any moment. Her half shirt revealed a fake navel ring and Celtic patterns henna-tattooed around her belly button. Black fingernail polish, too much makeup, and hair in a wild tangle that fell across her face finished the picture.

More than anything, she looked as though she had raided Faith's closet.

But if she was going to go unnoticed in Docktown, get people to talk to her, she was going to have to fit in. As a rule, Buffy's detective work generally consisted of pummeling secrets out of demons and their disciples. Woman of a thousand faces she was not. Yet three nights of patrolling Docktown in the usual fashion had yielded no leads on the trio of violent murders that had taken place there in the last three weeks and so she had been forced to endure two extremely difficult trials. The first was to disguise herself in this fashion—she felt like an advertisement for Sluts "R" Us—but the second trial was even more challenging.

In order for her to discover what was killing people in Docktown, Buffy was going to have to be *patient.*

"Hey, darlin'," drawled a stout, brutish man with shaggy hair and thick, dark sideburns. He had moved up next to her at the bar with elephantine stealth and waited for her to notice his Popeye-size biceps, complete with anchor tattoo.

The music of The Black Crowes poured out of the throbbing sound system, and at the other end of the bar a pair of stringy-haired girls danced suggestively with one another, to the whooping delight of the men around them. In the back sailors and fishermen played pool and swore loudly each time money was lost or won. Tables were jammed full of people drinking beer and eating fried clams and the catch of the day.

It was a typical night in the Fish Tank. If you lived in Docktown, chances were your family made its living on or from the sea, on a fishing boat or a merchant ship or at one of the transport companies or warehouses that lined the waterfront. And for young people in Docktown, filled with blue-collar pride but not yet old enough to be worn down by their work, the Fish Tank was what passed for clubbing.

There had been three mutilation murders in the past three weeks in Docktown, all between the Fish Tank and the wharf. It was possible that human beings had done the killing, but not likely. Not here in Sunnydale, where the Hellmouth—a place where the barrier between Earth and the demon dimensions had worn thin—drew monsters like moths to the flame. That meant Buffy had to look into it. It wasn't her job exactly, but it *was* her responsibility. She was the Slayer, the one girl in all the world Chosen to receive a gift of power, power with which she must combat the forces of darkness.

Not fun. Of course if it had been fun, the Powers wouldn't have had to *choose* someone to foist the duty on, would they? There'd have been a line around the corner. But no line. Nobody actually wanted the job.

So it was down to her.

Tonight that meant making herself fit in at the Fish Tank, trying to overhear some conversation that would give her a clue as to what was killing people down here, or better yet, chancing to see some behavior that was even more suspicious than the usual. Sherlock Holmes she was not, but she hadn't been getting anywhere by skulking in the shadows.

Instead, here she was, humiliating herself by putting on a costume many months before Halloween and dealing with morons like this stumpy little muscle head in need of a shave, a shower, and a lesson in manners.

"Snap out of it, babe. I'm talkin' to you."

Buffy flashed him her best faux cheerleader smile. "Oh, I'm sorry, did you not realize I was ignoring you? Wait, is this better?" She tossed her blonde hair back and spun away from him so that her back was to him completely.

Stumpy sputtered, rendered incapable of human

speech by the depth of his offense. Buffy figured he was used to being rejected by women, but that the average girl in the Fish Tank would have spent more energy on that rejection. Her focus was elsewhere. She tipped back her virgin screwdriver—a glass of orange juice—and scanned the bar again over the rim of her glass. Under normal circumstances she would have been watching for someone a little shady, perhaps somewhat edgy and suspicious looking. At the Fish Tank, that description covered all of the regular clientele.

Yet there was one patron there in the bar that had drawn Buffy's attention. He was a slim, well-tanned man in a business suit and bright green tie. In every way he was ordinary looking. There were many women who might have thought him mildly handsome, but few who would later be able to recall his face. The graying hair at his temples perhaps, and the verdant brightness of that tie, but not his face.

Not for the first time he caught Buffy looking at him. Rather than smiling uncertainly, intrigued by the attentions of a woman—skanky barfly chick or not—he glanced away and loosened his tie. This guy wasn't a dockworker and he wasn't a sailor. He wasn't skipper of some fishing trawler and he wasn't a factory worker or warehouse security guard. And it wasn't only the suit that gave him away; he might have been any of those things and just come from a funeral or a day in court. No, it was everything in his presence, in his carriage, that cried out to those around him that he was out of place. He was jittery, his forehead slick with sweat, and he glanced nervously around as though terrified to be noticed but somehow yearning for attention as well.

At first Buffy had wondered if he was waiting for someone, some rendezvous with a secret lover in this place where they could be sure no one they knew might see them. But an hour and a half had passed since he had walked in—ninety minutes in which she had fended off enough unwanted advances to begin drawing more attention that she wanted—and it seemed clear now that the jittery man with the bright green tie was not expecting company.

But those eyes seemed to pale as the minutes passed, and they opened wider as he looked around again. A smile flickered at the edges of his mouth as though he held some secret he was certain the others in the Fish Tank would wish to share. The smile was replaced by a pained look, and the man's eyes narrowed confusedly. He clutched at his stomach and it seemed to Buffy that his suit jacket fluttered slightly, as if in some unseen breeze.

"Hey."

Buffy felt a finger poke the base of her spine.

"I'm talkin' to you, honey. Maybe you better think about your attitude."

Slowly she turned to regard Stumpy again. His nostrils had begun to flare almost like an animal's, and he seemed to stand a little taller. There was a dangerous light in his eye and menace in his stance; his muscles tensed as though he might strike her.

Now that he had her attention once more, Stumpy leered at her. "Not so uppity now, are you, sweets? Gotta learn some manners if you want to come round here. Startin' with an apology. Right now."

Buffy glared at him, uncertain if she'd heard him right over the music and laughter and the clinking of beer mugs.

"An apology?"

The smile went away and only the danger and cruelty in the man's gaze remained. "I'm not walkin' away from here without one."

Buffy tossed her hair back but there was no flirtation

in it. Slowly, very purposefully, she stepped in closer to Stumpy, holding her breath so that she would not have to inhale the reeking stench of him. He was barely taller than she was, and Buffy nearly bumped against him now, the two nearly nose to nose.

"Then maybe," she said slowly, carefully enunciating every syllable, "you're not walking away."

His arrogance had been roiling off him as though part of his body odor, but he hesitated now beneath her furious stare. Uncertainty flitted across his eyes, but for nearly a full minute he withstood the intensity of her nearness and her anger. At last, though, he faltered and lowered his eyes. He paused as though he might have some final word, but then slipped away along the line of patrons at the bar in silence, sparing her only a single, anxious, backward glance.

Several women who seemed to know him snickered and hid sly smiles as he passed. One of them raised a beer mug toward Buffy, toasting her. Buffy nodded at her and flashed a small wave, both pleased by the other woman's gesture and self-conscious, as though she had let slip the mask of normalcy she had worn into this place. It made her wonder as well, this brief contact, if she was not more than a little prejudiced about the people she had found in this place. Most of them, she was sure, were honest and hardworking. But there could be no denying that the Fish Tank was an establishment where things regularly spun out of control.

Now, she thought, *about the guy with the ferret.*

As she turned, however, she bumped into a tall, slender figure who stood so close she could not at first see his face. Wraith-like, he had somehow managed to sneak up behind her and must have been standing only inches away.

"Hey!" Buffy protested, brow furrowing as she took

a backward step and glared up into blue-green eyes eyes like the ocean. "Not big on personal space invasion."

The man's face was weathered and sallow and his hair cloud-white, so that only those bright eyes provided color to his overall appearance. The rest of him from head to toe, including his gray pea coat and dark pants, seemed bleached and faded.

When he bent and spoke to her it was in a hoarse whisper as though he'd shouted his throat raw. The look upon his face was that of utmost gravity and it seemed to Buffy that he was about to impart to her all the dark secrets of the universe, or at least *he* thought so.

"They're coming back," the old sailor rasped, for certainly his dress and complexion spoke of many years at sea.

"Sorry? Who's coming back?"

Ocean-green eyes twinkled even as salt-and-pepper brows knitted together.

"The Children of the Sea," he whispered grimly, and she could barely hear his words above the music. Then he glanced around as though suspicious others might be trying to listen in. "The shadow of Leviathan surges up from the depths, and the spawn of Kyaltha'yan—the lords of the endless fathoms, the orphans left behind by the Old Ones—they're coming back. I hear them in the crash of the surf on the sand. They whisper to me."

Buffy arched an eyebrow. "Uh-huh."

"The Children of the Sea return."

"This wouldn't have anything to do with the Sunnydale High swim team, would it?" she asked, regarding him carefully. Freaky, to be certain, but she'd dealt with wigged-out old men spouting gibberish before. There was no reason to believe it had anything to do with the mutilation murders that had brought her here tonight. In another town it would have demanded her attention, but this was Sunnydale. The town was a hotbed of evil and weirdness, and that meant it was possible that mutilation murders in the same neighborhood with strange old guys babbling about monsters might be just a coincidence.

Might be.

But it bore looking into.

"I'll hate myself for this later, but maybe you could be a little more specific?" Buffy suggested.

Bright eyes narrowing almost sternly, the old man nodded. "You hear them as well."

"Sorry," she replied. "But no. Maybe if I put a seashell to my ear?"

"They rise and they must feed."

"Don't they always?"

Yet even as she said it, Buffy's attention was drawn elsewhere. It was as though the music grew louder, volume increasing to an almost deafening pitch. The rhythm of motion as people moved around the bar changed as well—people stumbling into one another, getting up from tables so quickly that chairs toppled, waitresses dropping trays—and soon she saw that they flowed in a steady current of surprise away from one spot.

The ferret guy, she thought.

And it was. The people in the Fish Tank scrambled to get away from him, bottles and mugs shattering. Men cursed loudly. The old man with the cloud-white hair did not even turn around to seek out the source of the shouts and the chaos, but instead continued to stare expectantly at Buffy.

"Hold that thought," she told him, and then she shoved past him.

The rush of people away from the man in the bright green tie was like some mad exodus. Even as she shouldered and elbowed her way through, Buffy knew that she would really have to hurt someone to reach the man, whom she could only make out through the crowd now by the top of his head.

Adrenaline rushed through her and she leaped up on top of the bar. One of the waitresses actually yelled at her to get down but Buffy ignored her. She ran swiftly along the wooden bar but had not gone three steps before she saw what had sent the people scurrying. Her stomach churned with nausea and she hesitated.

That slender man in the business suit had not been carrying a ferret.

In one of his hands he held the ragged corpse of a redheaded waitress in a black apron. Her body had been torn and mutilated in seconds, but what had been done to her was clearly only the beginning of what would have happened. The man was no longer a man. His hands were scaly and green, and thick leathery webs connected his fingers, each of which ended in a long claw. His eyes were wide black things too large for his face, and they appeared to have burst out from within, so that his human eyes still hung on ropy muscle tendrils from their sockets. His face was sloughing off, revealing gray-green scales behind, and fins had torn out of the side of his neck, protruding through the skin.

But the worst were the thin, spiny vines that had erupted from his upper chest and now wavered in the air like tentacles, like some horrid combination of ravenous sea creature and deadly plant life. Even in the heartbeat that Buffy had paused, one of those thin, deadly appendages lashed out and wrapped itself around the throat of a man who brandished a table leg and dared to step nearer.

The snap of his neck resounded loudly in the bar. When the tentacle came away, its spines tore the flesh from the man's throat.

Then no other sound could be heard from the horrible creature as the room was awash in screams. People stampeded toward the doors at front and back. An alarm went off as someone crashed out the back door into the alley beyond. Windows shattered.

The tentacles lashed out at those nearest, and the thing began to follow after them.

"I don't think so." Buffy ran down the bar and, crouched on the countertop, snapped a kick out that connected solidly and wetly with its head.

"Let me guess," she said. "Ate a bad piece of fish?"

More bits of that ordinary face it had once worn sloughed off, and the creature turned, hissing, toward Buffy. Its thin tentacles were faster than she expected and they lashed out at her. One tore through her pants and ripped a gash in her left leg. The Slayer swore loudly, but when the tentacles swept toward her again, she jumped over them. The thing's spines gouged the wooden bar.

The last thing Buffy wanted to do was get any closer to this thing. The people had scattered and were shoving and shouting at either end of the Fish Tank now. When the tentacles lashed out again and the thing rushed at her, mouth now a circular, repulsive maw, she flipped backward off the bar and landed behind it, where she nearly stumbled over the corpse of the bartender. There was a large hole in his forehead where the creature had apparently driven one of its tentacles through his skull.

"Sorry," she muttered, though the word was lost in the roar of the music.

The Slayer turned to the row of liquor bottles beneath the mirror behind the bar. Her few flirtations with alcohol had ended badly, but she knew the difference between eighty-proof whiskey and one-hundred-fifty-proof rum—mainly that the former was just sticky while the latter was, more importantly, flammable.

Out of the corner of her eye Buffy saw a tentacle lashing at her. She ducked as the appendage tore the air just beside her and shattered liquor bottles and the huge mirror. But she had not moved quite fast enough and the needle-spines on the sides of that ropy tendril gashed her shoulder. As the shards of mirror and bottles showered around her, she swore, snatched the unbroken bottle of rum from the rack, and launched it at the creature.

It lashed out at the bottle, which shattered on impact, spraying this thing that used to be a man with alcohol. It shrieked as if the spattering rum had stung it, and the cry of pain seemed to come from somewhere within it, rather than from the last remnants of human face that hung from its bulbous-eyed, scaly brow.

Buffy's gaze ticked along the bar. Ashtray, ashtray, peanuts, ashtray. No matches. Ropy tendrils sliced the air toward her again, and she leaped over the dead bartender and started back, deeper into the Fish Tank. She saw what she needed at the end of the bar, an abandoned pack of Camel Lights and a little cardboard box of wooden matches from someplace with more class than this.

She got the box of matches open, took one out to strike, and then looked up in alarm as the creature lunged for her again. So intent had she been upon her goal, Buffy had trapped herself in the corner. The thing stank of the ocean and rotting fish and something like hot tar, and when she saw the gleaming wetness off those huge eyes there was a malign intelligence in them that she had not noticed before. This wasn't just a mindless monster. It was a thinking, contemplative beast, and it wanted her dead.

Its grotesque, round mouth gaped as it lashed at her with all of the appendages that jerked and swayed from its abdomen. Buffy leaped onto the bar and then into the air—tendrils just missing her as she somersaulted above the creature.

In midair she lit a match and let it drop.

Fire roared up behind her as she landed in a crouch and then tumbled away across the floor, the heat from the sudden blaze searing her arms and exposed midriff. Buffy sprang to her feet and grabbed a chair, raising it to ward off the scaly beast even as she turned to face it.

The creature shrieked loudly, an ear-piercing cry that seemed a combination of squeaking dolphins and grinding metal gears. It had turned on her and shambled toward her, engulfed in flames that spread to consume it as though the thing were made of oil. Fiery tendrils grasped for Buffy, but she batted them away with the chair.

"Fall down!" she shouted.

And it did.

Whatever had worn the body of that man with the bright green tie, it stumbled and collapsed in a heap of burning, acrid, stinking black flesh and pooling gray fluid. It twitched once, twice, and then was still. Flames licked up from the dead, charred thing and Buffy felt her stomach churn with nausea.

The overhead sprinklers erupted in a shower of cold rain that doused the flames and kept them from spreading any farther. Buffy strode across the now empty bar and went out the back way, hoping to avoid answering any questions from the people who had run from the place and spectators who were sure to have gathered.

She had found what she was looking for, but there was no satisfaction in that. Buffy only hoped she never met another one.

Chapter One

Aside from the occasional miracle, winter never really visited Sunnydale, California. More accurately, mild fall simply flowed into warm spring and lingered until sparkling summer arrived again. Even so, this particular spring day was stellar by comparison. Though early, it was already in the high seventies . . . the sort of spring day that seemed like a gift, or a stolen secret, best taken advantage of before some higher power realized it had been given in the first place and took it away.

Buffy squinted and raised a hand to shield her eyes from the harsh sunlight streaming in through the open car window. It had been a long Friday night and an early Saturday morning—too early, and without cartoons as a reward. Salty air blew through the open window and wrestled with the few strands of her blond hair that weren't caught up in the ponytail she had hastily tied back this morning.

Bubblegum pop played low on the radio and behind

the wheel Xander sang along, sort of unconsciously, in that way he'd deny having done later. Buffy's mother had lent them her car for the day, and now the six of them—Xander and Anya, Willow and Tara, adn Buffy and her little sister Dawn—were jammed in tight along with a football, Frisbees, a cooler the size and rough shape of a mausoleum, and a stack of towels.

Xander took another turn, and the sun shone even more directly upon Buffy's face. A low groan emitted from her chest.

"Bright light," she muttered.

Beside her, trapped in between Buffy and Tara, Dawn rocked against her big sister. "Wimp," she said. "Suck it up. Beach day. You remember beach days, don't you? It's like half the time you forget we live in a town that has a beach."

Buffy squinted over at her. "I've been to the beach plenty of times."

Tara raised an eyebrow. "When?" she asked innocently.

For a moment, Buffy hesitated. Then her eyebrows knitted together. "Plenty."

In the front seat Anya fidgeted around from between Xander and Willow and glanced back at them. "I don't remember you ever going to the beach unless it was to kill something."

Anya gazed at her the way she did at everyone and everything, with an almost scientific scrutiny, as though she were constantly attempting to make sense of the world around her. Which pretty much made sense, given that she had spent a thousand years—give or take—as a vengeance demon. Now she was trying to find her way in the world. She had fallen in love, and had friends—or at least, had Xander's friends. Anya had a habit of saying exactly the wrong thing at exactly the wrong time—mainly generated by her rampant self-interest and a total lack of social skills—that Buffy sometimes found endearing.

Not today.

"That counts," she muttered, slumping her head backward against the seat and closing her tired eyes.

"No it does not," Anya sniffed dismissively. "Xander, does that count?"

A weak smile played at the edges of Buffy's lips and she let her eyes flicker open again. Behind the wheel Xander fidgeted under the pressure of the question, yet again caught in the middle of his loyalty to his friends and his girlfriend's passion for speaking aloud what others politely maintained silence about.

"Well, without the fun and, y'know, the sun, that contributes so much to the beach-going experience . . . which isn't to say there isn't *mucho* fun to be had with the sand and surf after dark . . . in other towns than this one," he rambled charmingly. Then he glanced up into the rearview mirror and saw Buffy watching him and his eyes lit up in that way only Xander's ever did. "But, hey, there was loads of beach-going in high school. We went all the time."

Willow turned a doubtful, ironic gaze upon Xander. "Yeah, *we* went all the time. Buffy went, what, twice?"

She turned around in the seat as well, and now the attention of everyone in the car was upon Buffy, who sighed and sat up straighter.

"More than twice."

"Three times?" Dawn suggested helpfully.

"I went tons of times. In high school," Buffy insisted.

Tara pushed her long, light brown hair behind her ears. Always the empathetic one, she was obviously uncomfortable even with the fond ribbing the others were giving Buffy. "Well," she said, "the important thing is that we're going now. After the workout you've been getting lately, you deserve a day off."

Buffy brightened considerably. "I do, don't I?"

Willow shared a sweet smile with Tara and then craned around to glance back at Buffy again. "Yup. You keep up with the big ol' sunlight aversion and soon, yikes, no telling the Slayer from the Slayees."

A not-so-serious frown crinkled Buffy's features. "That would be bad," she said, truly waking up at last, letting herself enjoy the morning and this time with her friends—this time when she could be a part of something that didn't involve death and dismemberment. Her mother had recently been hospitalized, and she and Dawn had panicked for a while. Both of them had been on edge, but now their mom seemed to be recovering nicely, and half the reason Buffy had agreed to a beach day was because Dawn seemed to need it so badly.

And she was smart enough to realize that maybe it wasn't just Dawn who needed it. Though she vowed to herself that next time the Summers sisters hit the beach, they'd bring their mother along with them. Joyce might not be up to it yet, but she would be soon.

Xander swung the car left, and they all pressed even further against one another. The sunlight splashed in through the windows, and Buffy squinted against its glare again.

"Still bright," she said. "Shouldn't there be a way to control that?"

Anya snatched a pair of sunglasses off the dash and snaked an arm into the back seat to hand them to Buffy. They were too big, too red, and very much too her mom, and Buffy handed them back.

"I'll suffer."

"As long as it's in silence," Anya replied.

Properly chagrined, Buffy sat back and let herself bask in the wind and the sun. Dawn started chattering about a new boy at school named Spencer whom she thought was, as she put it, "a sugar cookie." Willow and Tara politely inquired about him and about her classes. Xander started asking about Spencer's family—what they did, where they lived—in a surprisingly paternal speech-before-a-date way that Dawn dismissed. Spencer was cute, she said, but he hadn't even noticed her yet.

"He will," Anya insisted. "They do. Boys. It's what they do, I mean. Notice. Then they get your hopes up and you start to think they're different, and then they cruelly and heartlessly disappoint you, after which you're forced to make them suffer in some horrible, physical way so that they can feel just a fraction of your pain, because they can only ever really understand the physical."

Silence reigned in the car.

"You're the expert," Dawn replied awkwardly.

"Yes!" Anya said happily, as if it were a moment of wonderful epiphany. "Yes I am."

"And we're having oodles of fun!" Xander declared.

"We are, actually," Willow said, nodding once to punctuate the words. "There aren't enough days like this."

She didn't elaborate, but she did not have to. Everyone in the car instinctively knew what she meant. So much of their lives these past few years had been spent in crisis. Buffy felt a certain amount of guilt for that, because she had been the one to bring that chaos into their lives. But she was profoundly grateful for the way they stuck by her.

So much had changed since Buffy had first come to Sunnydale, first met Xander and Willow and forged with them a powerful, enduring friendship. They had all been through so much. Xander had gained stability and direction since he had fallen in love with Anya, her history and her awkwardness with her newfound humanity seeming only to endear her to him all the more. And with Tara in her life, and the love and warmth she had found with her, Willow had blossomed into a far more confident person, a change that showed most obviously in the extraordinary surge in her proficiency with witchcraft.

And Buffy was just Buffy. The Slayer. Doing her job, trying to figure out why she could never make it work with a guy, and trying to keep Dawn out of trouble.

So much had changed, but as she sat there in the car with her closest friends and the women they loved, Buffy thought that maybe change wasn't all that bad. Some R&B diva grooved in a throaty rasp on the radio now, and Dawn poked Xander in the back of the head for some off-color remark he had made, and Willow focused on the yellow traffic light up ahead, trying to use magick to keep it from turning red.

This is good, Buffy thought. *This is magick, right here.*

Xander slammed on the brakes. "What the hell?"

It had taken Buffy all morning to ease into accepting the gift this day was. Out of the darkness that usually enshrouded her life she had captured a moment of bliss. Now the moment shattered. Everyone in the car sat up straighter, more alert, and peered out the windows.

They had turned onto the street that ran alongside the beach to find it jammed with cars. News vans were bumped up onto the curb and long cables snaked out of them, following after camera operators with heavy rigs on their shoulders. Police vehicles dotted the beach, and men and women in the uniform of the Sunnydale P.D. stood around monitoring the activities of a group of grim-faced people with signs in their hands. Buffy could make out a big PETA banner, but couldn't read any of the signs from this distance.

The parking lot seemed very far away.

"PETA?" Buffy said. "What are they protesting?"

"They're not the only ones," Willow noted, hanging her head out the window. "Greenpeace and the ASPCA are here too. It looks like a rally or something."

"For what?" Xander asked, frowning.

"For our inconvenience, I'd say," Anya replied. "It's awfully thoughtless of these people to create such a spectacle here, where they're in the way."

"Yep," Buffy agreed. "Though spectacle, pretty much the point of a protest."

"It's probably about the sea lions," Tara suggested.

With the car now firmly entrenched in traffic, even Xander turned to look at her.

"How's that again?"

Tara blinked several times quickly, uncomfortable being the center of attention. "California s-sea lions. They're all over the place."

"Haven't they always been?" Buffy asked, confused.

Dawn sighed and shot Buffy that look only little sisters could. "Don't you ever watch the news? Maybe read the paper?" She glanced around at the others. "For something other than weird cattle mutilations or whatever, I mean."

"The sea lions are new?" Willow suggested helpfully. "New sea lions?"

"Not new," Tara explained. "There are just . . . a lot of them. The people are probably p-protesting because the shipping companies won't stop work, even though they're killing sea lions. The last few days there've been so many offshore that the fishing boats and even the m-merchant ships and stuff are having trouble getting out to sea without hitting them."

Xander nodded appreciatively. "That's a lotta sea lions."

And there were.

When they had finally found a place to park and

made their way through the chaos and onto the beach, they discovered that the local authorities had cordoned off areas to the north and south where there were more rocks and less actual beach. On the long stretch of bleached sand where most people swam and sunbathed and played volleyball, there was an occasional sea lion sighting in the water. But beyond the cordons, where only the antisocial and the die-hard surfers wandered, there were dozens of sea lions on the rocks and in the surf, more than Buffy had ever seen in one place at one time.

It was sort of cool and somehow unnerving all at the same time. And the commotion up by the road didn't help much either. After a while, though, the warmth of the sun and the salty ocean breeze washed away the tension that the protesters and media people had brought with them. Buffy and her friends debated the rights of the sea lions versus the rights of corporations to conduct their business, and the chances that some rescue organization could clear the animals out of the area safely and quickly. But they talked about other things as well, and sometimes nothing at all. That was the point of a day like this, after all: to relax and think about nothing, to completely let go of their concerns.

So there seemed to be an inordinate amount of vampire activity in town lately. For a few hours, Buffy wasn't going to let herself think about that or anything else that resembled responsibility. She had dealt with something truly horrifying the night before and had a particularly gruesome nightmare about it. But she had destroyed it. Buffy had earned this day and she wasn't going to let it be ruined by a plethora of cute sea mammals who had inexplicably decided to congregate on the shores of Sunnydale and the shipping lanes on its coast.

Dawn, on the other hand, wouldn't let it go.

They had been on the beach nearly two hours—radio

on a little too loud, half-full water bottles twisted down into the sand, sneakers and sandals holding down the edges of towels, partially eaten chicken-salad sandwiches returned to the cooler after a breeze swirled up the sand so that they tasted like grit—but Dawn seemed incapable of focusing on anything but the plight of the sea lions.

Even as Buffy settled back and closed her eyes, enjoying the feeling of the sun on her, Dawn started in again.

"It just doesn't seem right," the younger Summers said. "I mean, here we are, just hanging out like nothing's going on."

Buffy did her best to ignore it, hoping Willow and Tara would pick up the other side of this conversation Dawn seemed so intent upon having. They had set up an umbrella and sat under it together, almost entirely out of the sun. To Buffy's surprise, however, it was Xander—momentarily shaken from his reverie as bikini spectator—who replied.

"Only a possibility, Dawnie," Xander said, "but could that be because *nothing* is exactly what's going on?"

"Okay, if you're *blind,*" Dawn sighed. "Or do you not see all those cute little guys in, like, prison camps on the rocks over there?"

Reluctantly Buffy lifted her head and stared at her sister. Dawn was propped up on both arms, long hair sweeping down her back, big eyes hidden behind stylish shades. As uncomfortable as Buffy was in her own bikini, the suit that her Dawn wore seemed more daring, though Buffy was willing to admit to herself that this opinion might just be a case of big-sister-itis. One of the reasons she had tried to keep her mind off the beach was to avoid seeing guys ogling Dawn. The last thing Buffy wanted to do was have a bunch of TV cameras record her beating a bunch of teenage guys bloody on the sand.

"Have you considered that maybe they *like* the rocks?" Buffy asked.

Dawn slid her glasses down her nose so her sister would be sure to catch the dismay in her gaze. "Did you miss the point, or did you not realize there was one? We should be over there protesting instead of over here drinking imported water and getting cozy with the slippery lotion."

Under the umbrella Willow had been smoothing sunblock onto Tara's shoulders. She shot Dawn a look, obviously taken aback.

"Just gonna say, hey!"

"No offense," Dawn said. "But how are we better than the fishermen and the guys who own the tankers and freighters and stuff? Sure, the boats stopped going out at first. But then the grumpy old men who run the companies decided that it was hurting business too much to care about a couple of sea lions, so they started sending ships out again. Now lots of sea lions are dying."

"Dawn," Tara said gently, "we went for a swim and threw the Frisbee around a little. We're not killing anything."

"But we're not helping either," Dawn persisted. "The beach patrol or whatever are keeping the sea lions back so we can be here. Instead, maybe they should be figuring out why all the sea lions are hanging out in the first place. Maybe they're afraid to stay in the water. Maybe it's poisoned or something."

Anya rolled her eyes as she sat up. "Can we please talk about something else? Anything else? It doesn't even have to be sex. The stock market, Japanese cartoons, ritual murder, anything else?"

Buffy ignored her, attention still on Dawn. "So, you're thinking what, they should close the beach while they investigate the mystery of the sea lions?"

Dawn's eyebrows shot up. "Ye-es. We shouldn't just sit here. It feels wrong."

"You know what?" Xander said suddenly. "When you're right, you're right." He stood up and brushed sand off his legs.

They all looked at him in surprise, Dawn perhaps most of all.

"You're not leaving," Anya said, staring at him in astonishment.

"Nope," Xander replied, smiling amiably. "I'm going surfing."

"But . . . but what about the sea lions?" Dawn asked meekly.

Xander gave her a sheepish grin. "Sorry, short stuff. This is the Scooby Gang. Those aren't the kinds of mysteries we solve."

With that, he picked up his surfboard and headed toward the ocean. Buffy felt a bit bad for Dawn when she saw how disappointed her sister seemed, but considering that it made her drop the subject at last, figured it was a small price to pay.

Content, Buffy lay back down to relax. If the past was any indication, it would probably be a very long time before she got another day at the beach, and she wanted to enjoy it as much as possible.

Bliss.

Xander straddled his board, hands trailing in the water, salt ghosts swirling around his wrists in constantly shifting patterns. He felt the sun baking his back and didn't care. The surfboard rose and fell gently with the waves that rolled beneath him. Further in toward shore he watched as a couple of guys—traditional California surfers with too-long blond hair set off by their dark tans—rode the crest of a huge white-cap and then slid into the curl in opposite directions. A moment later they were lost from sight as both tumbled into the water.

All right, so they're not perfect, Xander thought. It was cold comfort, though. He had always liked to surf, but even though he certainly spent more time at the beach than Buffy, he had never put in the hours to get really good at it. Especially post–high school, what with having to work and shoulder actual responsibility in addition to the Scoobying.

"Ahh, no, no," he whispered to himself, bending forward over the board and splashing some water onto his face. "Tainting the bliss."

He took a breath and glanced around again. Sun. Waves. Forty or fifty feet to his left there were a trio of older surfers—thirtyish guys doing the weekend warrior thing. Off to the right was a pair of girls in sporty zip-up one-piece suits that by no means made them less attractive. He might have been anxious about looking foolish in front of the curvy redhead and her fit and trim blonde friend if he hadn't already taken a couple of really lame spills with them looking on.

Didn't matter.

Bliss.

No work, no monsters, no worries.

He took a deep breath and glanced behind him. Squinting against the glare of the sun, he found what he was looking for. A distance back, rolling toward shore, was a perfect wave. It was tall and gently sloped with the barest ripple of white at its crest.

Instantly, his heartbeat sped up. Xander bent low on the board again and began to paddle toward shore. He cast another quick glance behind him, trying to gauge the exact moment the wave would break, the distance he needed to be from shore. As best he could he adjusted the angle of the board's nose so that he was aligned with the wave instead of the shore.

Somewhere off to his left the three weekend warriors were calling to each other, also racing to catch the wave. The roar of a boat's engine reached him, along with the distant chant of protesters up on the beach and more than one radio engaged in a kind of musical combat. Xander blocked it all out. He could be a bit scattered at times, sure, but no matter what his father said, he was perfectly capable of focusing when he had to. And surfing required a great deal of focus.

Damn, he thought as he glanced back again. He wasn't going to catch it. He was too far back. The wave swept in, rising even higher above the level of the ocean, but it was going to pass him before it started to break.

No way. Anya would be aggravated if he left her on the beach for too long, and he could go the rest of the day without getting another wave as perfect as this one. No way was Xander going to miss it. He cupped his hands and paddled, hauling himself forward as quickly as he could, the nose of the surfboard jerking back and forth with the shifting of momentum.

A final look back and he saw that the wave was almost upon him. In his peripheral vision he saw that the blonde girl had missed it but the redhead was already pulling herself up to stand on her board. Xander did the same, hurriedly hauling his legs out of the water, balancing precariously on top of the surfboard, and nearly tumbling into the ocean before he had even gotten started.

Just as he regained his balance, the wave was upon him. He felt the spatter of seawater as its crest turned white and began to break. The ocean swelled up beneath him, he held his arms out as though on a tightrope, and his toes gripped the board as the rush of the wave thrust him forward.

"Yes!" he shouted, mainly to himself and to the gulls that circled above.

Xander caught the wave. He applied precise pressure with his feet, shifted his weight ever so slightly, and he surfed the crest as the swell tumbled and broke and rushed toward shore. With a surge of triumphant adrenaline he cut across the face of the wave, feeling its power as he sliced into it, threatening to drive him over and pound him under at any second. But he was in control, he was going to pull it off, he was praying that Anya and the weekend warriors and the two cute girls were all watching—hell, that the TV cameras up on the beach were all trained on him.

Focus! he snapped at himself.

He rocketed along in front of the wave even as it lost some of its momentum. Xander had done it. It was the best he had ever surfed in his life.

Which was when he spotted the slick, dark forms arcing through the water, just beneath the surface of the wave. Four of them, maybe more, and others beyond them, like some strange, swift army attacking from beneath the sea. Only they weren't attacking. Just swimming. Just being.

Xander twisted his body, trying desperately to adjust the angle of his board to avoid a collision. But he was too late. When the surfboard struck the sea lions he was contorted into a bizarre position. The board hit soft, oily fur and fatty flesh, and Xander flew off the board, limbs flailing, water rushing up toward him.

Just before he hit the ocean, the wave rolled over him and his surfboard shot into him with an impact that took his breath away. It struck his shoulder so hard that he felt bone break, heard it crack inside his head. The pain tore through him, and then the water dragged him down, the wave pushing. him under.

With one arm he pulled for the surface. The saltwater stung his eyes as he looked for the light, trying to see which way was up. He swallowed seawater and his stomach churned. He felt like he was going to puke, panic racing through him. *What if I die? What if I drown?*

Black, oily shapes slid past him in the water. A sea lion bumped him, slamming into the shoulder where the board had struck and he nearly passed out from the pain, swallowing another mouthful of ocean. Weakly Xander reached upward through the water and felt his hand break the surface, clutching air.

He tasted something else in the water. Something awful.

Blood.

Through the discolored water, he saw something move away too fast to be more than a blur. It left behind something ragged and still, something drifting, trailing dark blood into the sea. A sea lion, torn in half . . . but where was the other half?

In horror, he tried to get away, to swim away, and his feet hit the ocean bottom. A shudder of relief went through him and he stood up. Xander clutched his shoulder as he glanced frantically around him, searching the water for the dead sea lion, for the half-corpse he had glimpsed beneath the waves, hoping whatever had torn it apart wasn't still around.

Something splashed off to his left, and he spun that way but saw nothing. Further off there were dozens of sea lions in the water, moving toward the shore, joining the others that had gathered there. Fleeing something.

Maybe Dawn's right, Xander thought. *Maybe they're afraid.*

Then the pain in his shoulder made him wince again, and he forgot all about sea lions, dead or alive. He spotted his board, washing toward the sand, and started in that direction, knowing he was going to have to go to the hospital and dreading it.

Xander had no illusions about his injury. It was going

to be a while before he could go surfing again. But given what could have happened if the board had struck him a few inches higher—in the neck or the head—he figured that was a small price to pay.

Chinese food and Japanese monster movies with Anya could be bliss too. And much safer bliss at that.

But first, the hospital.

Buffy had never seen the cemeteries so quiet. In most places, she supposed that was how graveyards always were, the places where high-school kids could go and have a few beers or grope in the dark beneath the outspread wings of marble angels and the crypts of the dead. Real romantic. In Sunnydale, though, teenagers learned pretty quickly that partying was best kept to an indoor sport. There were things in the darkness that were interested in a different sort of intimacy from the average seventeen-year-old.

Vampires.

Other things as well, of course. But in the cemeteries, you mostly had to watch out for vampires. Buffy had been doing the watching for longer than she cared to remember, patrolling the boneyards and the back alleys trying to keep her city—and a couple of times the world—safe from Evil. With a capital *E*.

The last few nights she had been so preoccupied with the mutilation killings that had apparently been perpetrated by Tentacle Boy from the night before that she had been distracted from her usual patrols. It seemed as though the vampires had somehow sensed that she was otherwise engaged, for there had been a rash of vampire attacks, ranging from minor bloodletting to full drainage murder.

Given the number of reported sightings and the "grave robbings" reported in the paper—more likely a few new vampiric resurrections—she supposed she ought to be grateful that only three of those attacked in the past week had died. On the other hand, Giles suspected that the survival of the other victims indicated that the vampires were in a hurry. While she went about searching for their nest—or nests—she was also in search of answers.

Something had the vampires agitated, and Buffy wanted to find out what. Before she could do that, however, she had to find herself a vampire. And despite how omnipresent they'd been the past week, that was proving to be very difficult indeed.

Sunnydale had more than its fair share of cemeteries, and she had been through more than half of them already tonight without a single sighting. The moon shone brightly in the clear sky and the air was heavy and warm, more humid than it usually got in Southern California, especially in spring. The day had gone from perfect to perfectly nasty. Even in the thin, blue cotton T-shirt she had worn, she was uncomfortable. Worse yet, she was bored. Xander had a broken collarbone and was at home being nursed by Anya, and Willow and Tara had their own plans for tonight, but she figured she ought to be able to find *something* else to do.

"Hell-ooo," she called as she strode swiftly through Edgegrove Cemetery. It was on the outskirts of Sunnydale and not part of her usual patrol route, but her more frequent stops had turned up nothing, and so she had thought to try some places where vampires might not expect her to turn up. Maybe, she had thought, they had smartened up enough at least to put a nest somewhere she wouldn't look *first.*

"Anybody home?"

There was no answer save for the distant rumble of a passing car in need of a new muffler. Not even the rustle of night birds in the trees or rodents in the grass.

"It was quiet," she muttered to herself, doing her best impersonation of bad hard-boiled detective dialogue. "Too quiet."

But it *was.*

Halfway across the graveyard, amidst a group of headstones that were old by California standards, Buffy simply stopped.

"Oh, the hell with this."

The night was ticking away and her search had taken her too far from downtown and the residential neighborhoods of Sunnydale. She turned and began to jog back the way she had come. *A car. A car would be nice right about now. You can take Mom's car to the beach, but not out hunting vampires.* But Buffy didn't drive and her patrols usually did not take her this far afield. Frustrated, she picked up the pace.

Just shy of a half hour later, she walked in the door of Willy's Alibi Room. It was a dive bar without even the character that separated the Fish Tank from other sleazy joints in town. There was nothing special about the building unless you counted the smell from the alley next to Willy's, where the Dumpster looked to have gone unemptied far too long. But it wasn't that edgy, cool inconspicuousness that underground clubs thrived on. It was just a dive. The stink of beer. Drunks playing darts. Guys avoiding going home.

The only thing that separated Willy's from a thousand other pit stops on darkened corners in American cities was the clientele. Most of them weren't human. The Alibi Room was a hangout for demons and vampires and the occasional human hanger-on or wannabe sorcerer. Which meant that, as its proprietor, Willy often overheard things. Secret things.

Over the years since she had moved to Sunnydale, the Slayer had found that with the proper prodding—a little cash or a motivational beating—Willy could be induced into telling her just about anything she wanted to know.

Buffy pushed through the door and scowled in disgust at the way her shoes stuck to the floor. A pair of Tarquel demons played pool at the back of the room. Other nasties were arrayed at several of the tables, and at the bar a human male flirted with a massive female Borqwa. Buffy shuddered in revulsion.

The ceiling fans whirred, pushing the warm air around while doing very little to cool the bar down. Her hair was tied into a ponytail but several tendrils of hair had come loose, and Buffy paused to pull it back together, slipping off the rubber band she had used and then sliding it back on again, tighter this time. *It's too hot for this,* she thought, and she fondly remembered the beach earlier that day. It had not been this sticky, and at least there had been a breeze.

Even before she started across the room toward the counter, Willy had spotted her. Behind the bar he stiffened and a false smile stretched across his weasely face.

"Slayer!" he said, too loud, by way of both greeting and announcement. "What brings you here?"

The exodus was immediate. Warned by the proprietor, his customers glanced up anxiously and then started for the door, keeping their eyes straight ahead, not daring to look at Buffy for fear that she might have come for them. She barely registered the departing creatures. Most of the demons that drowned their sorrows at Willy's were harmless losers, and those that weren't ended up on the business end of something from Buffy's arsenal eventually.

She wasn't there for any of them.

"Where are they?" she demanded as she approached the bar.

The human who had flirted with the Borqwa hid his face as he and the object of his desire edged away and then moved toward the exit. Buffy thought she recognized him as a local politician, but if his taste in dance partners skewed toward smelly, bovine, horned demons, that wasn't her concern at the moment. Unless the Borqwa ate him.

Buffy rolled her eyes and turned her attention back to Willy.

"Well?"

He showed her a nervous grin while he poured a shot of whiskey. Buffy was confused until Willy drank the shot himself. If he needed to steady his nerves, obviously he had information she could use.

Buffy sighed and placed a hand on her out thrust hip, glaring at him. "Willy, haven't we had the conversation about how much I hate to repeat myself?"

The little man slicked back his oily hair and poured another shot. His beady eyes would not focus on her. "You have any idea how bad you are for business?"

"You have any idea how little I care? Where are they?"

"Who's they?"

The slow churning of the fans was the only motion in the bar. Some old rock song played on the sound system. Buffy leaned on the counter and shook her head.

"It's too hot for this. I figured with this place empty I wouldn't have to hurt you to keep up appearances in front of your customers. But I can if you want me to. The vampires, Willy. We've been swamped with 'em lately, like someone bought in bulk, and tonight, nothing. Where. Are. They?"

The grin was back. Willy glanced at the clock on the wall behind the bar, and then raised the shot glass up, whiskey trembling and sloshing over the rim. "Did you see that big truck outside on your way in? Couldn't miss it. Screaming yellow moving van?"

Buffy frowned. She had seen the truck, but there had not been anything remarkable about it.

"You know in movies how they smuggle illegal immigrants across the border?" Willy went on. "The vamps've been coming out of the woodwork the last few days 'cause they're emptying their nests, Slayer. You should be happy. They're leaving town."

"What?" Buffy asked, the words sifting through her mind, not making any real sense. "What do you mean they're leaving? All of them?"

Willy knocked back the second shot. Then he shrugged as he wiped whiskey from his fingers with a bar rag. "All or nearly all. You don't look thrilled."

"Where are they going? And why?" she asked, biting off the words, alarmed by how improbable and therefore suspicious this development was.

"No idea where," Willy said, his smile gone. He seemed cowed by her obvious agitation. "As to why, maybe they finally wised up, figured to try a town without a Slayer. Every few weeks a new batch comes to town, tourists looking to set up camp near the Hellmouth. You dust them. Then more come. Had to figure they'd run out of stupid eventually."

Buffy's retort was cut off by the sound of an engine turning over outside the bar. A truck engine. It sputtered and choked to life.

"I'll be back," she promised the little man.

"I'll be here," Willy replied reluctantly. "But I've got nothin' for ya."

The Slayer ran from the bar, the soles of her shoes slipping on spilled alcohol so that she nearly lost her balance. When she burst out through the front door, she was just in time to see brake lights like demonic red eyes in the darkness as the yellow moving van turned a corner at the end of the block and disappeared out of sight.

She stared after it in astonishment. The vampires had left Sunnydale. Buffy knew she ought to be happy about that, and part of her was. Mostly, though, she was worried. Willy gave them too much credit. Vampires weren't very bright. Either they had something nasty planned elsewhere, or they were running away. Since most of them had known the town was protected by a Slayer before they ever came here, it wasn't Buffy that they were running from.

Despite the heat, she shivered.

If something had scared all the vampires out of Sunnydale, Buffy was not at all certain that she wanted to know what it was.

Chapter Two

The parade of cameras had come and gone. The beach patrol made an occasional pass along the sand, keeping close to the sidewalk to avoid running over any wandering sea lions. Cars went by up on the shore road, many slowing to get a look. A few hundred yards up the sand a group of teenagers sat together drinking beer and shouting profanities at one another.

Jillian Biederstadt was disgusted. Not merely with the fact that the beach patrol hadn't done a damn thing about the drunken teens, though that was bad enough. What bothered Jillian was that other than Ian, she was alone. The two of them were all that remained of the day's protest, of the vanguard that had set itself the task of protecting the forlorn creatures who were still cluttering the water and gathering on the beach in ever-greater numbers.

They sat on the sand perhaps twenty feet from the gently rolling surf and a handful of yards from the barricade that had been put up between the public beach area and the rocky stretch where most of the sea lions were. The moonlight gleamed off the animals' coats and Jillian marveled at how beautiful and innocent they are.

Someone had had to stay behind and make sure nobody did anything to them. That was just the kind of thing big corporations did in secret. She had read enough books to know that much. In the middle of the night they might try to drive the sea lions off the beach—even kill them—if no one was there to see, to bear witness. When everyone else left she had known it was up to her. Though she had met Ian only that day, when he realized she planned to stay behind he offered to stay with her, seeming genuinely concerned that she might be alone out in the dark all night.

It was kind of him, but Jillian wasn't thinking much about the nice man who had stayed. Rather, her mind was on the people who had abandoned the sea lions.

"I can't believe them," she huffed, for perhaps the hundredth time. She knew it must be getting monotonous, but she couldn't help herself.

"Seriously," Ian replied, in a tone that twisted the word to mean he agreed. "What a bunch of poseurs. The minute the cameras are gone—"

"Exactly."

Jillian paused and glanced at him, then let the glance linger. He really wasn't a bad-looking man. A bit gawky, she supposed, and his brown hair was in need of a serious trim. But he had nice eyes and a strong nose and seemed to be in excellent shape. And polite, Ian was that if nothing else.

Sea lions barked off to the north, past the barricade. Several of them had emerged on the public beach, south toward the rowdy teenagers, but they were still and quiet.

Ian's eyes were on hers, and Jillian smiled shyly and

pushed her long, straight blonde hair behind her ears.

"I know I've said this already," she told him, "but it really was nice of you to stay. I *so* appreciate it."

A certain playfulness lit up his eyes, made his lopsided grin all the more charming. "My mother's from England. She taught me well. Chivalry isn't really dead, just a bit anemic."

They watched each other for several seconds longer before Jillian looked away, out to the sea. When Ian let his hand slip down to rest upon hers on the sand, Jillian did not move it away.

"How long do you plan to stay out here, standing watch?" Ian asked.

That same playfulness was in his voice, but it was so gentle that she knew he wasn't teasing or criticizing.

"Until morning at least, or until someone else comes."

"All night," he said.

"All night."

Ian stood abruptly and brushed sand off the back of his shorts. Surprised and disappointed at the thought that he might be leaving, Jillian looked up at him. But Ian was still smiling.

"I've got a cooler with water, juice, and some snack-type things in the car. A couple of blankets as well. If we're going to be out here all night, we might as well get comfortable."

For the first time since the rest of the protesters had departed, Jillian forgot why she was angry, forgot even—for a moment—why she was sitting on the beach in the first place.

"No argument," she said.

As Ian turned and walked up the beach, she watched him go, wondering if he was all he appeared to be and marveling at the possibility that she could have met a sweet, smart guy in a situation like this. She thought that when he came back, she might just have to kiss him.

When he had reached the sidewalk and started across the street, Jillian couldn't see him anymore but she kept watching just the same, lulled and comforted by the sound of the surf and the breeze off the ocean.

After a moment her reverie was disturbed. Something had changed around her. A deep frown creased her forehead as she tried to figure out what it was. Then she had it.

The sea lions had stopped barking. They were completely silent. Even the playful splashing from the shore had disappeared. Curious and strangely troubled at the idea that her fears about the fishermen or shipping companies might be true, Jillian turned to peer into the night across the barricade.

There were dozens, perhaps hundreds of sea lions on the other side. The ethereal light of the moon glistened not only upon their sleek coats, but on their eyes as well.

Their eyes.

All of them were staring at her.

A chill ran through her. Jillian's mind raced. This was unnatural. So very deeply *not right.*

Then she noticed that the creatures weren't really looking at her. They were staring, it seemed, at something behind her. A sound came to her then, something wet sliding across the sand.

Jillian turned.

Her scream was cut off with her breath as it coiled—cold and sharp and damp—around her throat.

The sea lions were very quiet, as if loath to draw attention to themselves.

Jillian felt the sand beneath her toes as she dangled just above the ground in its grasp. And then she felt nothing at all.

* * *

Long before dawn had lit up the eastern sky, the crew of the *Heartbreaker* had been at the wharf in the Docktown section of Sunnydale, pulling snags out of nets, checking the lines and the supplies of bait. The sky had barely begun to lighten when the fishing trawler set out carrying the five seasoned men, who always worked together in silence this early in the morning. Not because they were tired, for they had long grown used to rising in the wee hours of the morning, nor because they did not like one another, for the truth was that they were like family with all the love and conflict that implied. They worked in silence, these men, because they had always done so.

Until the sun came up.

Until the day came to life.

Then there was coffee and good-natured ribbing and laughter. The captain of the *Heartbreaker*—Richie Kobritz—was not opposed to having a bit of fun as long as the job got done. His first mate, Dan O'Bannon, had seen a lot of crews fall apart in Docktown over the years because their captains had run things a little too heavy-handed. It was a lot of pressure, that was for sure, being responsible for the catch and the income not only of the entire crew but of the boat's owner as well. But Dan had never known anyone who handled that pressure better than Richie. The captain was as steady as they came.

As they had set out that morning, though, Dan noticed that the atmosphere among the crew was a little off somehow. They were slower to wake up, slower to laugh, and it seemed, impossibly, that the dawn was slower in coming. The early morning light had a strange hue and cast a kind of sickly yellow light across the waves before the sun rose in full and burned it away. Even Richie seemed agitated, and that bothered Dan more than anything else.

Everything just seemed . . . off.

Dan thought the others had sensed it too. The bags under Gordo's eyes were darker than ever. Sima—whose Scandinavian parents had refused to name him something that wouldn't invite the ruthlessness of his schoolmates—always looked pale despite the long days they spent in the sun, but today his face seemed almost ghostly. Of all of them, only Lucky Corgan seemed unaffected, and that was mainly because once they got going, Lucky never shut up.

As Richie killed the engine and they began to set the nets out, Dan watched the others carefully. It was still early morning and the sun threw an array of colors across the Pacific, gold and red and orange. This time of day always seemed surreal to him, but now more than ever. It had the texture of his dreams, in which he always found himself in familiar surroundings that had somehow become unfamiliar.

It was getting under his skin, the way everyone was behaving, the silent sort of unacknowledged tension that had seeped on board the *Heartbreaker.* Dan wanted to shout at them. They were doing their work, though, and so he figured it was best to wait until the end of the day. The problem was, things kept getting worse. For hours they trawled the best spots, miles off the coast, but the nets kept coming up empty.

Not light. Empty.

Three hours into it, Richie just snapped. "What the hell is this?" he shouted, slamming a fist into the bulkhead.

The others were startled, even skittish, as they glanced up at him and then back down at the empty nets.

"You know," Gordo began hesitantly, eyeing Dan instead of Richie, trying to avoid looking directly at the captain. "Morning like this, you know the day's shot. Probably we should just head in."

"Head in?" Richie said, his face ashen. "Are you high?"

Dan put a hand on Richie's thick bicep. In the history of this crew there had never been an actual fight—lots of arguments, but nothing physical. Given that he himself was half the size of most of the other guys—Lucky being the obvious and scrawny exception—Dan was not keen on the idea of stepping in to stop any of them from belting the other. But this was too much.

"Cap," he said to Richie, "he's just freaked. We're all a little off today." Then Dan shot Gordo a hard look. "You know we can't go in empty-handed. Light, okay. But we've got nothing on ice, Gordo. Nothing."

Sima was on his knees playing out the net, readying it to be dropped again. At this, though, he just stopped. Just stopped working and knelt there like a little kid whose father had just cussed him out. Only Sima was six foot four and pushing two fifty and could probably have snapped his father in two.

"Maybe that's best," Sima said.

Lucky snorted. "Oh, come on!" The little guy was on the other side of the net, but now he stood and flapped his arms up and down as he spoke. "You guys just give me a freakin' break. I got kids, you know? You hear some crazy talk, drunk talk, down on the docks and you start actin' like freakin' babies, I swear to God!"

Dan stared at him, then glanced at Sima and Gordo. He got it then. Understood. "This is about Baker McGee the other night, isn't it? That thing he says he caught?"

As first mate, Dan had a certain sway with the crew. But Richie was captain, and now that he had cooled down, he took control of the situation again. He did not even have to move toward the other guys. Richie just took a breath, crossed his arms, and gave them a look. When he spoke again his voice was steady.

"What *thing?*"

"The other night at the Fish Tank," Dan explained. "Baker said they'd had a light catch yesterday, partially because of this thing they'd pulled up in one of the nets. Said it was like something you'd see on the Discovery Channel—like one of those blind, freaky fish that live at the bottom, way down deep."

"Not a fish," Gordo muttered, scratching the back of his head. "He said it had flippers like hands and feet and tentacles where it's mouth oughta be. Said it was alive when they hauled it up. And he said it . . . that it *looked* at him. Like it really saw him, y'know, and was pissed off."

"Uh-huh," Richie grunted, rolling his eyes. "And where is this thing?"

"They cut it loose," Sima said, standing up straight now and meeting Richie's eyes. The big Scandinavian lifted his chin defiantly, not backing down. "Baker gave up that whole haul just to be rid of the thing. That was why he was light."

Richie shook his head sadly. "For God's sake, you guys, they're called fish stories for a reason, you know? You never heard that kind of thing before? Maybe Baker just didn't want to admit he'd had a bad day."

"You didn't see his face, Cap," Gordo said softly. "You didn't see his face when he was telling the story."

The boat rocked gently on the Pacific swells and Dan noticed for the first time how calm the water seemed today. Unnaturally calm. They were all silent for a moment.

Then Lucky laughed. It was too high and forced, not like the way he usually laughed, and to Dan it was like nails on a chalkboard. A shiver went up his back.

"Crap," Lucky said. "It's crap. The Fish Tank was closed yesterday. You guys know why? Somebody offed Jimmy Kelso."

"Jimmy?" Dan said, feeling as though someone had

just sucker punched him in the gut. He'd always liked Jimmy and could not believe none of the other guys had mentioned it before now. "You're kidding?"

"I look like I'm kiddin'?" Lucky asked. "Sometimes when people laugh, it ain't 'cause anything's funny. It's 'cause nothing is. So some crazy twit kills Jimmy, hurts some other people, then sets himself on fire in the Fish Tank. Sprinklers go off. All that stuff. But the drunks who ran out of the place? They start spouting garbage about how the guy who did it was a carnival sideshow freak or something, had scales and extra arms or something, his face fallin' off. I mean, it's tragic, Jimmy getting killed, but you gotta know where to draw the line with what you believe."

They all looked at Richie then. The captain took off his baseball cap. His gray hair was thinning on top and he kept it buzzed close to his scalp. Dan was stunned to see the look in Richie's eyes, like something had crawled into his head and he was trying to work it out.

"Lot of folks gone missing lately. Ben Varrey. Lainie Bloomberg. And Hank Kresky was murdered. Ripped up, I heard."

Dan stared at him. "Cap, it happens. All over the place. And Ben Varrey's a loon. This isn't the first time he's gone missing. He'll turn up."

For a long time the five men stood on the deck of the *Heartbreaker*. The cool breeze off the ocean was a blessing under the hot sun, but when an errant cloud passed overhead he shivered. The water seemed too dark suddenly. The boat rocked softly. After a while Richie Kobritz fitted his cap back onto his head.

"Drop the nets," he said. "We've got work to do."

Then he turned and headed into the cabin. The guys all stared after him for a few seconds until Dan clapped his hands.

"Come on, boys. You heard the man," he said, as upbeat as he could manage. "We go home with nothing, there'll be hell to pay."

Lucky nodded and turned back to his work, singing some country song under his breath like the whole scene had never happened. Gordo and Sima hesitated a second before Gordo nodded and the two men joined Lucky. Dan swallowed and found that his throat was dry. He smiled to himself; *water, water everywhere and not a drop to drink,* he thought. It was something his father had said anytime they were out fishing, but Dan had no idea where the quote came from.

Taking a short breath, he forced himself to stride across the deck and began checking the lines. Within minutes Dan waved to Richie and the engine roared the life. The nets were in the water, dragging behind them, and he allowed himself a small measure of relief; he closed his eyes and let the sun warm his face.

The *Heartbreaker* rocked hard to port, then rolled back to starboard. Dan had been at sea for years and immediately set his legs to keep from falling. He glanced quickly around and saw baffled expressions on the faces of the other men, knew they must only be reflections of his own.

Richie shouted to them from the cabin. "Where'd that swell come from?"

But Dan couldn't answer him. The sea was still as calm as it had been, the weather perfect, the waves barely large enough to be called such.

"Snag!" Lucky called.

Dan spun around just in time to see the little guy pulling his heavy gloves more tightly onto his hands. Lucky braced himself at the aft end of the boat and reached down. Somehow one of the nets had gotten tangled upon itself. It wasn't going to drag right if he didn't loosen it.

Any other day, Lucky would have waited for them to pull the net up. They could set it out again, start over. But with the hold empty, they hadn't a moment to spare. And it looked like a simple snag. One strong tug might put it right.

Lucky grabbed the net. His fingers twined in that tangle for a heartbeat, maybe two, and then his eyes went wide and he stood there bent over the rail staring into the ocean.

"God," Lucky muttered. "What's th—"

Then the *Heartbreaker's* engine screamed. If Lucky also screamed, Dan did not know, but there was terror etched in his features as the lines played out with a squeal and the net was yanked away from the ship, drawn down into the water, and Lucky with it. His fingers were clutching the net, and though he did let go—Dan saw that much—it was too late. Lucky went over and fell into the net. He was fighting it even as he went down, even as he went under.

The ship's nose raised into the air and the aft end dipped down into the water, and they began to move backward, the engine coughing and whining. Dan shouted Lucky's name. Even as he ran toward the railing a little voice in the back of his head registered the irony. Gordo and Sima were there as well, trying to reverse the winches, too busy to pay much attention to the water where Lucky went under.

To the blood there.

And the dark, misshapen things that moved beneath the surface.

White-knuckled, Dan gripped the railing. He could hear Richie roaring from the cabin, demanding to know what they were caught on. Then something shot from the ocean—green-black and gleaming with sliver edges like razors—and a shower of saltwater sprayed off it as it whipped toward his face.

Pain ripped through him, so excruciating that his mind overrode it, shut it down. When Dan hit the deck of the ship, he did not even feel his skull crack. He heard the screams of his shipmates, but they were so distant, so far away. His eyes were open, seared by the brightness of the sun high above.

Then the sun began to fade.

It was almost noon when Buffy arrived at the Magic Box. It was warmer than it had been the day before, but the unusual humidity from last night had dissipated and she had enjoyed the walk from home. Troubled by the developments at Willy's, she had found it difficult to fall asleep but once she had drifted off, she had been practically comatose and not woken until nearly ten o'clock.

Now, though, she felt happy and well rested as she strode toward the shop, the hem of her summer dress swaying around her legs. Not the preferred attire for vampire Slayers, but given the sudden dearth of vampires, she couldn't see any harm.

The bell above the door jangled pleasantly as Buffy stepped into the Magic Box. It surprised her how much it felt like coming home, how easily they had all adjusted to new circumstances after high school had ended so . . . explosively. Giles had always looked very busy and very capable in the school library, but Buffy wasn't certain she would have called him content. The magick shop had flourished under his proprietorship. Previous owners had let it remain a dingy little place. Giles had expanded it, cleaned it up, made it an appealing place to walk into.

In so many ways it was a job more suited to him than his other occupation as her Watcher. The Council of Watchers was an international organization of individuals with an interest in the supernatural—the study of it, the use of it, and the thwarting of its darker elements. As part of their efforts, they had guided the Slayers ever since the Council's formation. One Slayer, one Watcher.

Giles had been Buffy's Watcher until the Council had fired him for caring about her too much. Which was pretty twisted logic, from her point of view. When the Council had refused to save Angel's life, Buffy had quit, which had put a severe dent in the Council's rep in the supernatural espionage community. Once she figured out that they needed her, it had been a simple thing to coerce the Council into rehiring Giles. The tables had turned.

That was nice.

It was Sunday morning and according to the sign in front, the shop didn't open until one o'clock. So Buffy was not at all surprised to discover the place empty save for Giles, as well as Anya and Xander. Anya helped run the place, but from the pitiful look on Xander's face and the sling his arm was in, Buffy suspected he was only there for sympathy.

"Good morning!" she said breezily.

Giles raised his eyebrows and glanced at the clock. "Yes, well not for much longer."

Buffy cocked her head and paused on the stairs. "Sunday, Giles. Ever heard of it? A day of rest."

"What I've been telling him," Xander agreed with a nod.

"You hush," Anya chided him. "You're supposed to be home resting yourself. On a day of rest. You're supposed to have several Sundays in a row."

As usual, Giles paid no attention at all to the couple's exchange, not even glancing back to where they stood behind the cash register. His focus was split rather evenly between Buffy and the small stack of books he had out on the table in front of him.

"Something odd is happening, Buffy. Something I don't quite understand," he said.

Buffy arched an eyebrow and shot a meaningful glance at Xander and Anya. "I don't get it either, but live and let live, I figure."

"That isn't what I meant," he said dryly. "Did you see the paper this morning?"

"The news is always bad." She strode over and slid into a chair across from him. "And anyway, Mom's still getting her strength back, so she had me helping her move furniture around the living room for two hours this morning. Dawn had already taken off to see some friend's baseball game. By the way, the furniture? Pretty much back where it started."

Giles stared at her for a moment. Then he nodded curtly. "Lovely. Perhaps we could have a bit of focus now that your redecorating is done?"

"Day of rest," Buffy reminded him.

The gravity in his tone and expression dissolved. He allowed a soft, apologetic smile. "I'm afraid not."

"Darn. Do you think it's a myth? The day of rest."

"Buffy."

She sighed. "Oh, all right." Buffy leaned back in her chair and crossed her arms. "I patrolled for hours last night and did not see a single vampire." The story unfolded as she told him about her visit to Willy's and the revelation that most if not all of the vampires in Sunnydale had suddenly left for parts unknown.

As she spoke, Giles slipped off his glasses and set them on the table beside the books.

"Gone?" Xander asked, perking up. "The vamps are gone? You're sure?"

"Not entirely. But no reason to think otherwise. The cemeteries were like ghost towns last night," Buffy noted. "Even more than usual."

"Does this mean retirement for you?" Anya asked with apparently genuine concern. "Or just more travel in the job?"

"Neither, I'm afraid," Giles said. He slipped his glasses back on, studied the book that lay open before him, and then tapped a finger on the page. "It's only more troubling. Another mystery we could do without."

"Another?" Buffy asked. "Why do they always come in bulk?"

Giles slid back his chair and strode to the counter. He picked up the newspaper and returned, laying it on the table. The banner headline on the front page, somehow garish even though it was simply black and white, read SAVAGE SANDS! Then, in smaller type, the less tabloidy SEA LION PROTESTER SLAIN, MUTILATED ON BEACH.

"The reason I asked if you had seen the paper, Buffy, is that it appears that whatever you killed the other night at the Fish Tank was either not responsible for the recent mutilations, or—"

"Or it wasn't the only one," Buffy finished for him.

She picked up the paper and scanned the first few lines. Jillian Biederstadt had been murdered late at night, very messily, not far from the barriers that had been erected to try to keep the sea lions away from the beach-goers. A group of teenagers down the beach had run to try to help when they heard her screaming and saw someone diving into the water, but by the time they got there, the woman was dead. A man who had been with her—Ian Poston—had identified her.

"Poor guy," Buffy said, glancing up from the article. "He walked away for a minute."

"Lucky guy," Xander replied. "If he hadn't gone to get something to eat from the car, he would've been chum too."

Buffy frowned. "Chum?"

"Chopped-up fish used as bait to catch larger fish, including sharks," Anya said helpfully. "He used the same analogy when Giles showed us the paper before, then had to explain about *Jaws* and someone named Grody."

Xander sighed and shook his head. "Brody. It was Brody."

"Okay, honey. Rest your arm."

He smiled, but Buffy could see it was his way of placating her. Xander sat on the counter and slid his legs over, careful to keep his arm tight against his body so as not to jostle the broken collarbone.

"Does no one remember what I saw in the water yesterday? You know, when I was nearly drowning? Sea lion bitten in half. Blood in the water, all that happy stuff. Creature from the Black Lagoon was swimming away."

Giles glanced at him. "The *actual* Creature? You realize it was only a movie?"

Buffy frowned. "You were injured and . . . and babbling about sea lions and movie monsters. We thought you were in shock."

"Hello?" Xander said with a shake of his head. "I *was* in shock. Broken bones. Underwater terror. But I still saw it."

"Ooh," Buffy said quickly, waving her hand in the air. "Maybe it was one of the guys from the swim team."

"I considered that, actually," Giles admitted. "Though Xander did say he wasn't certain what it looked like. It was too dark and too fast, and he was too close to passing out."

The Watcher cast an admonishing look at Xander, who shrugged sheepishly, then winced in pain.

"I've discounted that possibility for the moment, mainly because—"

"The sea lions," Buffy interrupted.

Giles crossed his arms. "Yes, precisely. Perhaps you should sleep late more often."

Buffy glared at him a moment, then turned to Xander

and Anya. "We were wondering what was driving the sea lions up onto the shore. Now we know. Whatever's been mutilating people up on land isn't averse to a little sea lion appeteaser."

"What about the vampires?" Xander asked. "Ya think they're running away from these things too? Don't think I wanna meet the monstrosity that could clear the Hellmouth of vamps just by coming to town."

"There's nothing to indicate that any vampires have been killed by whatever these . . . sea creatures are. But we must consider that possibility."

"Maybe they didn't leave because they were afraid of being eaten," Anya said. "Maybe they were just . . . *afraid* afraid, y'know? Whatever these things are, the vampires might have been creeped out by them."

All through the conversation, the good feeling Buffy had had that morning had evaporated until now there was nothing left but a grim anxiety, an edginess that was all too familiar to her. Suddenly she felt out of place, even silly, in the dress she had worn. Buffy stared at Giles, and then gestured toward the stack of books. "What have you got?"

"Not much, I'm afraid. The description you gave of the creature in the Fish Tank the other night matches nothing I've found thus far. His physical description matches that of David Trebor, the vice president of a San Diego computer software firm, who has been missing since setting off from the marina there last Tuesday in his yacht."

"Did he have Gilligan with him?" Xander asked.

Giles ignored him and continued. "Either something took on the appearance of Mr. Trebor, or he was somehow transformed into that . . . thing. There are a dozen oceanic species of demon that might be responsible for these murders, though I don't think any of them can disguise themselves in human flesh. We'll need a better description before I can pinpoint exactly what it is we're up against, and how to stop it."

Buffy looked at him gravely. "Fire worked pretty well."

She stood up, the legs of her chair squealing as she pushed it back. "Keep researching. See if there's some kind of tentacle-guy repellant or something. I'm going to hit the beach and Docktown. See if I can't get that description you need. If there are enough of these things that every sea lion in Southern California's out sunbathing, someone has to have seen them. They may even have come ashore already. Could be a lair or a nest somewhere."

"Wait, let me come with you," Xander offered.

Buffy glanced at his sling. "Not with a broken wing. Sorry." She opened the door and the sun splashed in upon her, though somehow it did not seem quite as warm now.

"If you find anything—," Giles began.

The Slayer turned, hand on the knob, standing on the threshold of the Magic Box. "If I find them, I'm going to ask them what they want. Why they're here. Then I'll politely ask them to go away."

"And if they want to stay?" Anya asked.

Buffy felt a cold smile spread across her face.

"Then they're chum."

Chapter Three

When Geoff, Slade, and Moon had loaded their scuba gear at the marina that morning, the guy in the slip next to them had advised them not to even bother going out. Word was there were so many sea lions in the water it was hard to navigate around them.

Geoff had heard about the sea lions, of course. It had been all over the news. Nothing better for local news than a few dead animals and a bunch of screaming protesters. For half a second when the guy had tried to warn them off, he'd considered just hanging out, working on the boat, tossing back a couple of beers. But Slade and Moon looked at him like he was nuts. They'd lugged their gear; they meant to do some diving. Geoff had not been about to argue. He wanted to dive too. He felt bad for the little critters, sure, but there was a limit. Besides, his boat was a hell of a lot smaller than some freighter or even a fishing trawler so he figured he could maneuver around them. And if there *were* a couple of sea lions down there, that would actually be kind of cool.

So they had taken the boat out, strapped on their gear, and gone under.

Geoff had seen more than just a couple of sea lions. In the warm Pacific water, he had spotted dozens of the things. Even before they dove, the things had been swimming around the boat. He had been careful not to hit them, but he could easily see how a larger boat might have. The weirdest part, under the water, was that he could tell they were all heading the same direction.

Toward shore.

Toward the beach.

But sea lions weren't the only thing he and the guys had seen in the ocean. As he sat in the boat now he shuddered, wondering if his face was as pale as he thought it must be. In the back Moon was helping Slade bandage his ankle where something had grabbed at him just as he was getting out of the water.

It had tugged on him from under the boat. Slade had pulled his foot loose, but whatever had snagged him slashed his ankle, cut right through the wet suit. The bleeding was pretty bad. Probably wouldn't kill him, but Geoff still thought they ought to get Slade to a doctor as quickly as possible so instead of heading back to the marina he had turned the boat toward the beach. They could slide up onto the sand the way the boats that hauled water-skiers did, flag a lifeguard or the beach patrol, and Slade would get attention much faster than if they went all the way down the coast.

The motor whined as they skipped over the waves. Geoff knew that there were probably sea lions in the water, that he might even be skating over some, but at the moment he didn't care all that much.

"Jesus," he heard Slade mutter behind him. "What the hell was that down there?"

"Shark," Moon replied calmly.

"That was no shark, man. No way was that a shark," Slade insisted.

Geoff turned halfway so his words would not be taken by the wind and the roar of the boat. "It had to be," he said. "It had to be a shark.

"What else could it have been?"

Neither of the other guys had an answer for that. Geoff didn't either. But he knew one thing. Whatever had been under the water, it wasn't any shark.

They zipped across the water past waterfront homes worth millions, and then Geoff saw the beach ahead. But there were no colorful umbrellas today. Nobody in the water. No surfers, no sailboards, no WaveRunners. The beach had been replaced by an undulating mass of brown and black.

He let up on the throttle, fingers feeling almost as numb as his brain. The engine purred as the boat slowed, and Geoff stared at the shoreline. They slipped through the water, moving closer to the beach.

"You gotta be kidding me," he whispered to himself.

Moon came up behind him. "Geoff, what are you—"

His words were cut off in midsentence and Geoff understood exactly why. Moon had just gotten a look at the beach.

"What . . . what is that?" Moon asked.

Geoff could not tear his eyes away. "Sea lions," he said. "It's all . . . they're just sea lions."

"It looks like the beach is closed," Moon said.

But Geoff had already seen the bright orange bathing suits of several lifeguards and a beach patrol Jeep, not to mention the dark shapes of two police cars parked on the sidewalk above the sand.

"Geoff! What are you slowing down for?" Slade snapped, more than a little panic in his voice. "I'm bleeding here."

Anxious, Geoff spun to see that there was a lot more blood in the bottom of his boat than he had expected to find there.

"Okay, okay, we're going in," he said, and he pushed up on the throttle again. Geoff tried not to think about whatever had tried to pull Slade under, whatever had cut him, or about the other things he had seen under the water. Especially those things. He wished he could erase the images from his mind forever.

Geoff tried to avoid the sea lions as he guided the boat in, but there were three or four soft bumps against the hull before the small craft finally slid up onto the sand. He hoped he had not killed any of them, but even if he had, that would be better than the other possibility—that what he had hit with the boat had not been sea lions at all.

A whistle blew, loud and shrill. A lifeguard who had been trying to corral the sea lions, shooing them toward a barricade that had been laid across the beach, had turned and was now stalking across the sand toward the boat with the whistle to his lips. A pair of cops was also stumbling down toward the water. All three of them moved carefully among the sea lions, which barked at them but made no attempt to attack. Geoff thought sea lions were supposed to nip or something, but these guys just stared and didn't bother to get out of the way.

No respect for authority, Geoff thought, and felt a little jolt of hysteria pass through him.

"What do you think you're doing?" the lifeguard shouted at him. "Are you blind? You can't beach that thing here."

The lead cop—an older guy with no chin and a thick gray mustache—was more direct. "Beach is closed, son. Take her back out immediately."

Geoff jerked a thumb over his shoulder toward Slade and Moon. "My friend's hurt. We were diving, and something—something grabbed him, cut him bad. He needs a doctor."

The lifeguard glanced over at the cops who gestured for him to go ahead and check inside the boat. After all, the policemen weren't going to wade into the water in their shiny black shoes. The lifeguard stared at the tiny waves that rippled on the sand as though he had never seen water before. Gingerly, as though he were walking on hot coals, he edged along the beached portion of the boat and went into the water shin deep. No farther.

It was almost as though the guy was afraid to go in the water. *Maybe you're in the wrong job, buddy,* Geoff thought.

Then the lifeguard craned his head to look in the back. Geoff turned around to see Moon crouched down in the boat, feet stained with blood. Slade had slumped back, his mouth wide open, his still-wet black hair wild. He looked as though he had passed out from drinking.

Moon looked up, clearly spooked. "He's unconscious."

The ambulance arrived in less than ten minutes. Geoff had left Moon with the boat and stood up at the sidewalk to watch as their friend was loaded into the back. The paramedics seemed more than a little concerned by Slade's blood loss, but assured Geoff that he'd be all right. When the ambulance pulled away, Geoff stared after it a long while. Then he turned to go back down the beach.

The girl was standing right behind him.

She wore a light summer dress that danced around her knees in the ocean breeze. Not dressed for the beach, unless she had a suit on underneath, and Geoff did not think she did. He put her age at twenty, but she might have been three years older or younger. She was a petite little thing, and yet there was something in the way she carried herself, a kind of weariness about her, that made her seem much older than she looked.

"What happened?" she asked. Her gaze shifted to watch the ambulance as it disappeared along the shore road, then moved back to study him again.

Geoff was very shaky but he tried to stand up a little straighter, pushing his hands through his hair.

"A friend of mine got hurt. Cut pretty bad. They had to take him to the hospital."

The girl's blonde hair blew across her face, and she tossed it away so that the wind made it bloom out behind her. She was pretty, no question about that, but it was the intensity in her eyes that made her beautiful.

"You were diving?" she asked, her gaze sliding over his body, wrapped tight in his wet suit.

Self-conscious, Geoff glanced down the beach to where Moon had taken a bucket and was washing blood off the floorboards of the boat.

"Yeah."

"So what was it that attacked him? What did it look like?"

Geoff stiffened. A sudden chill rippled through him as he turned back to the girl, and now the intensity in her eyes was almost too much for him.

"I didn't say he was attacked."

"No," she said with a sad smile. "No, you didn't. I'm sure he's gonna be fine. Really. I was just—he isn't the first person to get hurt. A friend of mine was attacked, and I just wondered what you saw."

His eyes were locked on hers now. "You wouldn't believe me if I told you."

Her gaze did not waver. "You'd be surprised what I'd believe."

For a long moment, Geoff continued to stare at her. At last he looked away. "Maybe," he said, and then his voice dropped low, almost to a whisper. "Mostly sea lions. Not a lot of fish, which I thought was weird right away. Then, in with the sea lions, I thought I saw something else. First I thought it was another diver, with the fins and all . . . but it had a tail. And all these things were growing out of its chest, like . . . like sea anemones or something."

He threw up his hands. "I know, nuts, right? I only saw it for a second. Probably my imagination. Another diver, maybe carrying something, harvesting seaweed or whatever." He gave the girl a nervous grin and shrugged.

But she was not smiling. "But then what cut your friend? What attacked him?"

Geoff's mouth went dry. "I don't know."

She put a hand on his arm, very gently. "I'm sure he'll be all right." Then she started to walk away.

Words were stuck in Geoff's throat. He glanced around, saw that the cops and the lifeguard were far enough away. There was no one else around except Moon down in the boat and the beach patrol a ways up the shore.

"Hey."

She glanced back at him. *It's the eyes,* he thought again. If not for those eyes she might be any pretty California girl in a summer dress. But then he saw that it was not just her eyes. It was in her every motion. She moved as though she were ready for a fight.

"When we were surfacing, after I saw that—that thing—right before I came up, I thought I saw something else."

The girl only waited.

The images swam back into Geoff's mind and he blinked several times, trying to get rid of them. They would not go away.

"Bodies," he said. "I thought I saw a couple of dead guys, all . . . all broken, twisted up."

That was it. He could say no more about it. The girl only stared at him another moment. Geoff felt sick. He turned away from her and headed down the sand, moving through the sea lions as though they were a leper colony. He just wanted to get the boat back to the marina and go home, watch a movie, maybe play video games or something.

Not sleep, though. The last thing he wanted to do was dream.

Buffy walked to Docktown as quickly as she could without breaking into a run. She barely noticed her surroundings, her feet navigating the path with nary a conscious thought. The beach gave way to exclusive oceanfront property and then to clusters of cottages, after which there were several blocks of townhouses that overlooked the water. For a while the road swung so close to the ocean that there was nothing but sand between them. When the road moved inland again, the sand was replaced by warehouses and a factory or two, and soon enough Buffy was surrounded by gas stations and dive bars and row houses and the wharfs were up ahead.

Docktown.

The sun had moved farther across the horizon and was now out over the ocean. Buffy had walked the entire way in a kind of fugue state, a haze of frustration surrounding her. The kid in the boat had looked about as spooked as anybody she had ever seen, and an idea was forming in her head that it wasn't just the things he had seen under the water or that his friend might die from loss of blood. Something was getting under his skin, some unnamable feeling of unease and dread.

She understood, because she felt it too.

Whatever this new horror was that had descended upon Sunnydale, it had brought this dread with it. A general malaise had fallen over the entire area, and Buffy wondered if the creatures gave off some pheromone that was causing the feeling, or if it was something simpler, some instinctive, primal reaction to their presence.

As she strode toward the docks, she tried to shake it off. The solution to all of these problems—the killings and the attacks and that creeping ominous feeling—was the simplest and most direct. Find the sea monsters and kill them.

Buffy passed a bunch of dockworkers loading up a freighter called *The Sargasso Drifter.* They paused to glance at her—this girl in a light cotton dress—but none of them whistled or shouted obscenities. Any other day she would have been relieved, but today it unnerved her even further. For whistles and catcalls would have been the norm; the men's silence was unnatural.

She ignored their quiet stares, however, for these were not the men she wanted to speak with. Farther along the docks the air grew redolent with the smell of fish. It seemed like an invisible cloud that insinuated itself into her nostrils just as she knew it would her hair and her clothes. But up ahead Buffy spotted her objective, a whole expanse of smaller slips and docks where the fishing boats brought in their catch. Half a dozen boats were moored there now. In their midst, a group of deeply tanned men were unloading huge metal buckets filled with ice and fish from the deck of a boat called the *Bottom Feeder.*

Buffy strode directly toward them, but it was not until they paused in their work and looked at her curiously, taking in exactly how remarkably out of place she seemed there on the dock in her dress, that she realized she had no idea how to broach the subject with them. With the kid on the beach it had been easy. His friend had been hurt. This was different. How weird would it be if she just asked them outright if they'd seen anything peculiar? Would they just brush her off?

"Hi," she said. She cataloged a dozen ways to start the conversation in her head, but none of them seemed right.

Then one of the men closest to her frowned, lines crinkling on his dark face, gray-and-white beard stark against his skin.

"I know you," the man said, his voice a dry rasp from too many cigarettes or too long at sea.

"Kinda doubt that," Buffy replied, still trying to figure out how to break the ice, dilute the awkwardness of her approach.

"No, I do," the old fisherman said. Then he laughed, low and throaty. "You're that girl from the Fish Tank the other night. The one who fought that—"

He cut himself off in midsentence, mouth twisted up as he remembered exactly what it was she had fought. The older man—who really might have been as young as forty-five and simply been weathered by his occupation—had seen her, even though she had not noticed him in the exodus of patrons from the club that night. And he recognized her, but now that he thought about it, it seemed he was loath to discuss what happened at the Fish Tank.

Buffy couldn't blame him. But she needed him to talk.

"You're right," she said. "That was me."

The attention of the other members of the crew was even more focused on her now. From the looks they gave the older man, Buffy suspected he had told them the story but they had not really believed it.

"It was . . . pretty freaky," Buffy offered.

The old man took a rag from his pocket and mopped his brow with it. "You can say that again. But you weren't afraid."

"I didn't *look* afraid. Big difference."

"I thought you died in there. Didn't see you come out. Then with the fire and all . . ." His words trailed off and he studied her even more closely. "Just a little slip of a thing, ain'tcha?"

"That's me. Slip."

Buffy moved closer to the fisherman, and his crew—for she did think now that it was his crew, and his boat, that he was the captain—went back to their business. Though she suspected they were still listening.

"I'm Buffy Summers," she said, offering him her hand.

He took it and shook, his own flesh calloused and dry, his grip strong. "Baker McGee. Captain of the *Bottom Feeder*."

For a second she just looked at him. Then she plunged into it. "What do you think it was, the other night?"

Nervous, Captain McGee shouted a couple of orders to his crew as they off-loaded more fish. He replied to Buffy without looking at her. "Looked like a man to me, maybe hopped up on something. Wouldn't be the first time."

She grabbed his wrist. Surprised, perhaps, by the strength in her grip, he frowned deeply and gave her his attention again.

"We both know it wasn't a man," Buffy said, growing even more agitated, more frustrated. She stared at the man, forced him to meet her gaze. "Look, I know you can feel it, 'cause I can too. Something else is going on here. I'm willing to bet that isn't the only weird thing you've seen lately, or even heard."

The man gazed at her doubtfully. "What do you think you can do about it, girl?"

"You thought I was as good as dead the other night," she replied. "But I'm still here."

"All right, then," he said, straightening up a bit. Then McGee told her about the horrible thing his crew had hauled up in their nets two days before, and as he spoke those same men ceased their work again to listen.

When Buffy looked at them, the men glanced away, but she had a feeling it was not because their captain was lying. It was because what he said was true.

"And we're not the only ones with a story like that. Keep asking around and you'll find others. The owners and the companies may be squawking about the sea lions, fighting to keep sending us out. But there're some of us who'd have no complaint with waiting a week for all this to blow over."

"What if it doesn't?" one of the crewmen asked.

No one had an answer for that.

Baker McGee ignored the comment. After a moment, though, he turned away from Buffy and went back to his work. "You want to figure out what's going on, girl? Ben Varrey's the man to talk to." He paused and glanced up at her as he bent to pick up a tub of ice and fish. "You'll remember him from the bar the other night. Old fella running off at the mouth about sea monsters and such."

As though ashamed, the captain lowered his gaze. "Always thought he was full of it, myself. Just another crazy. Every port has its share." Once more he looked at Buffy. "You'll have to find him, though. No one's seen old Ben since the night before last, right before all hell broke loose at the Fish Tank."

Buffy thought about it, and she did remember the old man. With the chaos that erupted afterward and her horror at the man who had torn his face off, who had suddenly become something monstrous, she had forgotten all about him and his babbling. Now she tried to remember what he looked like, what he had been talking about. A ghost of a man in a faded pea coat, his hair incredibly white, raving about somebody coming back and the spawn of something-or-other.

She realized now that it might be important and was furious with herself for not being able to remember. But that night she was focused on something else entirely, and like Captain McGee had said, there were always plenty of crazies to go around. Most of them didn't turn out to be prophets. And maybe this Ben Varrey was no prophet either, but then, where had he disappeared to?

The Children of the Sea, she thought, the memory of his words coming back abruptly. *He said the Children of the Sea were coming back. Whatever that means.*

But hard as she tried, Buffy could not recall any more of the old man's ramblings.

Her thoughts were interrupted by the shouts of McGee's crew. Some of them were pointing. McGee himself had moved toward the edge of the dock and was shielding his eyes from the sun, staring farther along the wharf and past it, to where a fishing trawler had drifted in to a stretch of rocky coast, listing badly to one side.

"What are they, drunk?" one of McGee's crew asked.

For a moment they all just stared. Several fishermen had already started along the wharf and word must have traveled fast, for some of the dockworkers passed by the *Bottom Feeder* on their way to help. Buffy stood beside Baker McGee and watched the drifting trawler as the waves dragged it against the rocky shore.

"That's the *Heartbreaker,*" McGee rasped in his gravelly voice. "Kobritz's boat. No drunks on board."

As if he had forgotten he had any other responsibilities, McGee started along the wharf, following the other men who had gone to the aid of the foundering ship.

"Keep at it, boys," McGee said absently. The rest of his crew, instructed to continue with their work, made no attempt to argue.

Buffy fell into step beside him. "What's going on?"

"Not a clue, little girl," the old man said, his voice edgier than before. "You might want to run on home now, though."

Buffy bristled but did not challenge his dismissal. She simply ignored it. "It looks abandoned."

For a second, Baker McGee slowed, an anxious eye cast toward the boat he'd called the *Heartbreaker.* Then he shook it off and resumed his hurried pace. Buffy noticed that he glanced at her once from the corner of his eye, as though remembering she was there, recalling how he had first seen her in the Fish Tank, and the circumstances of that night.

"If she was abandoned during a run, do you have any idea of the chances of her beaching here, a hundred yards from her mooring?"

"Slim?" Buffy suggested.

McGee's jaw was firmly set. "None. Or near enough. Someone guided her back in."

They moved in silence after that, hurried to the end of the wharf, and dropped down off the edge to a rocky expanse of unappealing coast. The men who reached the *Heartbreaker* ahead of them had already begun to wade to the boat, calling out to one another to be careful of the lines and torn nets that dragged in the water behind it. The railings at the aft end of the trawler were torn and mangled, metal jutting at odd angles. The windows in the cabin had been shattered and a portion of it collapsed completely.

Buffy and Captain McGee caught up with the others at the shoreline where the *Heartbreaker* slid and twisted on the rocks, in the surf. Buffy kicked off the sandals she was wearing and stepped into the water, but McGee laid a hand on her shoulder.

"This isn't yours to do," the old captain said.

She stared at him a moment before she understood. Theirs was a kind of subculture, filled with its own rules of pride and honor and respect. It wasn't her business. It wasn't her place. The Coast Guard, certainly, but not some college girl in a sundress. Much as she hated the thought, she understood it. Buffy had spent years trying not to draw extra attention to herself, attempting to keep her status as the Slayer a secret. McGee had seen her at the Fish Tank the other night, but these others had not. She could wait. Just wait until they searched the boat or called the Coast Guard to tow it to its moorings.

Buffy nodded to McGee, who returned the gesture and then waded into the water himself, the waves rolling in around his legs as he moved deeper. At the edge of the *Heartbreaker* two men were hoisting a third up out of the water and onto the deck of the ravaged vessel while others tried their best to steady it.

The man on the deck was a burly, bearded dockworker Buffy had noticed when she walked past them before. From where she stood on the rocky shore she could see the man look around the deck of the ship curiously.

"Nothing!" he shouted. "Not a damn thing."

"Check the cabin, Holly!" McGee called up to him.

The burly man with the unlikely name of Holly nodded and went carefully to the partially destroyed cabin. The door hung off its hinges, glass shattered, swinging with a creak. Holly poked his head inside and froze for just a second before jerking backward and scrambling away from the cabin.

When he turned around Buffy saw that his face was etched with terror.

Holly jumped from the starboard side of the *Heartbreaker* without any hesitation, plunging into the chest-deep water. When he stood up, the waves washing over him, he was already shouting. "Get back!" Holly screamed wildly at his companions. "There's . . . just keep away from it. We should burn it. Someone burn it."

Buffy had already begun moving. She waded into the surf, headed for the trawler. Farther out, in the shadow of the *Heartbreaker*, Baker McGee turned to glance at her and she could see the fear in his eyes. He had seen too many strange things of late.

But Buffy had gotten only knee-deep in the water before something stirred up in the cabin of the fishing boat. Broken glass grated as it moved, and then it rose into view through the broken windows. Buffy paused. It was a man.

"Lucky?" she heard Baker McGee call. "Lucky is that you?"

Holly was rushing toward the shore and was nearly even with Buffy now. When he heard McGee's voice, he turned back to the men still in the water and started shaking his head so fast his whole body seemed to move with the urgency of it.

"No!" Holly cried. "You didn't see! Keep back. Get some gas, anything that'll burn."

Which was when Lucky stepped out onto the deck into full view. Buffy swore under her breath. The man on board the *Heartbreaker*—the last survivor of the trawler's crew, she assumed—was no longer a man at all. Like the man with the bright green tie in the Fish Tank, his skin had begun to slough off. Thin, barbed tentacles had erupted from his chest and they danced in the air, lunging and swaying as though each had a mind of its own.

"Its eyes!" the thing that had once been called Lucky cried. The voice was like an agonized wail, not even human. "It's coming for all of you. And its eyes are huge . . . so huge."

Buffy rushed into the water, practically hurdling the

waves, trying to get the trawler before anyone was killed. The fishermen and dockworkers shouted and began swimming and wading and falling toward the shore. All save Baker McGee, who only stared up at the babbling monster who stood on the deck above him.

"*Lucky,*" McGee said. "Holy God. Aw, kid. Aw, no."

There was no doubt in Buffy's mind that McGee was a dead man. The water was slowing her down. No way could she reach him before those thin, razor-barbed tentacles. In a moment the thing would drop down into the water and McGee would be dead.

But when Lucky moved, it was not to leap into the water. The thing that had been a man raised its right hand, in which it held something fat and black. It took Buffy only a moment to realize what it was—the only thing on board a fishing boat that would accomplish what needed to be done. Apparently, there was something left of the man inside the monster after all, for Lucky held a flare gun in his hand.

The creature put the flare gun into his mouth and pulled the trigger.

"Lucky!" McGee shouted over the roar of the eruption of that flare.

The thing fell to the deck of the *Heartbreaker*, dead.

Buffy was speechless. It was the last thing in the world she expected to see happen. Whatever had gotten inside the young fisherman, whatever had infected and changed him, she knew it must have taken an incredible force of will for Lucky to overcome it enough to destroy it—especially when that meant destroying himself as well.

When she reached Baker McGee, she saw that there were tears in the old captain's eyes.

Sunday nights were usually quiet in downtown Sunnydale. There were people about, certainly, at the Espresso Pump paying five dollars for designer coffee or spiced tea, window shopping at women's clothing boutiques that closed at six as the weekend wound down. But overall, Sunday nights were quiet. If the Sun Cinema was going to do anything interesting or different, Sunday night was the time to do it. Recently they'd begun a program of giving over one of their theaters to classic double features every Sunday night.

Tonight's lineup was a double feature of classic horror from Italian auteur Dario Argento. *Suspiria* and *Tenebrae*. The only thing that would have kept Spike away was sunshine.

The vampire stood in the short line grinning like a schoolboy. Argento was the maestro. Nobody made messed-up stream of consciousness horror like he did. Not another filmmaker in the world could match him when it came to translating nightmares to the screen. Sure, some of them were rentable, but one didn't get to see these pictures in theaters anymore.

Sure, he had a taste for the odd soap opera now and again. He'd always been a romantic. But there was something so wonderfully perverse about Argento, and that appealed to the other side of him. So he queued up with the geeks and the diehards, and he didn't wear his duster to avoid people asking if he wasn't hot. Temperature changes didn't tend to bother his kind much, but he didn't want to draw a lot of attention. He stood there in his boots and his black T-shirt, and he rolled his pack of cigarettes up in the sleeve and fancied himself looking not a little like James Dean.

He had pulled one of the cigarettes from the pack and now he poked it between his lips, lit it, and slipped his metal lighter back into his jeans.

The kid ahead of him got his ticket and moved on,

and it was Spike's turn. The woman at the box office was a sour old broad, and as she took his money and slipped him his ticket she glowered at the cigarette.

"There's no smoking in the theater," she said sourly.

"Not to worry, love," he replied amiably, unwilling to let her ruin his night. "Wouldn't want to break the rules, now, would we?"

Ticket safely in his pocket, Spike walked away from the box office and past the theater. He stood in front of the broad windows of a bank and leaned back to enjoy the smoke. By the time the butt had burned halfway down, the line was gone. All forty or so people in Sunnydale interested in Dario Argento had already gone inside.

Spike took another long drag on his cigarette and blew the smoke out through his nostrils. He glanced around the mostly dark storefronts. Music came out of the open door of the Espresso Pump off to his left. There were a few people on the sidewalks here and there, going to and from restaurants and bars, he supposed. To the right, though, at the edge of the downtown area, all was quiet.

He drew smoke into his lungs and let it slip slowly out between his lips. Then he frowned.

The darkened buildings off to his right were quiet, but the street was not completely empty. Two crouching figures slunk through the shadows, keeping tight to the storefronts. He could not make them out in the darkness, but they moved awkwardly.

"Well, well, what have we here?" Spike smiled to himself. Whatever they were, from the odd way they moved he did not think they were human. The silhouettes of their heads had odd angles, and their arms were too long.

Glass shattered, and the two figures disappeared inside a building half a block up.

Spike glanced at the theater, then at his watch. Fifteen minutes before the first film began. Non-humans doing some breaking and entering in Sunnydale. He could have a little fun, and the Slayer couldn't say a word. They were engaged in criminal activity, after all.

He dropped his cigarette and crushed it underfoot. Quickly, with a bit of bounce in his step, he went along the sidewalk. In seconds he arrived at the place where the figures had broken a plate glass window to enter. He was surprised that no alarm had sounded, but then he saw the brass plaque beside the door that identified it as the Sunnydale Historic Society and he understood. Why would anyone want to break into this stuffy old place? Not like they had anything of real value, like an actual museum.

With a broad grin quite different from the one he had worn earlier—different and sharper—Spike began to climb through the broken window.

Then he caught the scent and he stumbled, cut his hand on broken glass, and swore under his breath.

But the pain was nothing. He brought the cut to his mouth and sucked on it, wide-eyed, as he backed out of the broken window and onto the sidewalk. Anxiously he glanced into the darkness of the building, then up at the windows of the second floor. No sign that anyone had noticed him. For that he was deeply relieved.

Spike hurried back along the sidewalk toward the theater. He fumbled for his ticket, went in, and found a seat near the front, wanting to be as far away from the entrance as possible.

The last vampire in Sunnydale had recognized their scent.

He only hoped they did not remember his.

Chapter Four

Shortly before ten o'clock on Monday morning Giles reluctantly left the Magic Box in Anya's hands and strolled to the Espresso Pump. It had been especially warm over the weekend, and he was pleased that it had cooled considerably. It felt more like spring. The walk was enjoyable, and Monday mornings were always a slow period at the store—at every store, he suspected.

Buffy had suggested that they meet at the Espresso Pump before her classes for the day began and Giles had agreed. It was nice to get out from behind the counter, and he didn't mind a cup of coffee now and again. Not espresso, of course, nor any of those confections that were more like dessert than actual coffee. The one time he had ordered simple tea rather than coffee of any kind in the Espresso Pump he had received very odd looks. It was that awful chai if one wanted tea, and that seemed nothing short of blasphemous to him.

It was just ten when he went through the open door

of the Espresso Pump, and Giles was surprised to see that not only had Buffy already arrived, but she had Willow and Tara with her. He had no idea if any of the three girls had Monday *morning* classes, but clearly if they did they were in no hurry to attend.

One of the waitresses, a pretty thirtyish woman with short blond hair and pixie-like features, waved to him as he entered.

"Hey, Rupert!"

"Tawny, hello," Giles replied, a warm smile creasing his face.

Her eyes sparkled. "You don't come in here often enough."

"That's true," he agreed.

A customer waved to get her attention and Tawny hurried away. Giles watched her go, raising his eyebrows in appreciation, and then went to slide into the booth with the three young UC Sunnydale students. All three girls were staring at him as he sat down.

"What?" he asked, suddenly self-conscious.

Willow and Tara smiled innocently. Buffy gave a little shudder. "Nothing, sorry. Just, well . . . we're not used to 'smooth, flirty Giles.'"

The Watcher brightened. "Smooth? Yes, well it takes a certain amount of style."

"It's disturbing."

Giles gazed steadily at her. "You know, Buffy, one day you'll be my age and some twentyish person will be horrified by how old *you* are."

"Not necessarily. I could get lucky and be eaten by some hell beast. Or the Earth could be swallowed by ancient dark gods."

Across the table, Willow snuggled closer to Tara, staring at Buffy wistfully. "The strangest things bring out the cheery Buffy."

Tara nodded encouragement to the Slayer. "She's just looking on the bright side. Which, as sides go, isn't very. But that makes it that much greater an accomplishment."

Obviously pleased, Buffy looked at Giles.

"Not that I don't enjoy these digressions—live for them, actually—but I quail at the thought of leaving the store to Anya for too long. Might I suggest we actually discuss business?"

Looking slightly miffed, Willow sat up straighter. "That's what we were doing before you came in, grumpy Mr. Smartypants. Maybe you want to tell us all what you've turned up on the icky sea monster front in the last twelve hours?"

All three of them gazed at him. Before Giles could respond, however, Tawny came over to their table. For a moment she looked at the three girls, obviously wondering what he was doing with them. But then Tawny smiled prettily and focused on Giles.

"I traded Aimee for your table," she said, her voice a hush as though it were meant to be a secret. Giles returned her smile before she continued, speaking to all of them now. "So what can I get you?"

All four of them ordered—the three girls had mochaccinos and Giles a simple café au lait—and then Tawny hurried away. When she had gone, the Watcher turned his attention back to the matter at hand.

"Now then, I confess I've discovered little that—"

"Never mind that," Willow said, a very precious expression on her face. "That waitress has a crush on you."

"What?" Giles said. "Surely not. I won't deny a bit of flirtation, but—"

"Crush," Buffy said, nodding.

Giles looked at Tara for a rescue, but the quiet young witch only nodded slowly in agreement.

"Crush," Tara said. "She's smitten."

"It's sweet. Really," Buffy assured him.

"Now back to the part where your research turned up jack," Willow prodded.

Tara glanced sidelong at her girlfriend.

Willow made a small fist and waved it at her, and the two grinned in that secret, knowing way only lovers ever did. It amazed him now, looking back upon it, that he had not realized sooner that Willow and Tara were more than merely friends.

"Not 'jack,' precisely," Giles explained. "True I've nothing new on what's been happening to the men who seem to have been altered, or what may be causing it. However, I have begun to compile a database of oceanic demons and other monsters that might be capable of the attack yesterday on that fishing boat. I'm going to cross-reference that with this infectious metamorphosis phenomenon and other recent events, such as the fleeing of the vampires and the events at the aquarium last night—"

"Aquarium?" Tara asked. "What happened at the aquarium?"

Giles raised an eyebrow at Willow, pleased to have a bit of new information after all. "A security guard was killed and the facility's tenants are gone."

Buffy stared at him. "By tenants you mean fish?"

Tawny brought their order and the booth was quiet as she placed each glass and mug carefully on the table. She lingered a moment until Giles thanked her and smiled gratefully, then Tawny moved off.

"Fish, yes," Giles continued. "But not merely fish. Everything. Penguins, turtles . . . everything. Not a trace of blood. In a matter of hours, someone made off with all of the aquarium's collection."

Bent over her mochaccino, blowing on it to cool it down, Tara glanced up from behind the long, straight curtain of hair she so often hid behind. "Wow," she said appreciatively. "I'm guessing somebody saw *Free Willy* one too many times."

Willow lifted her chin. "Hey, no wows. We've been research girls all night, forsaking all else. We have . . . stuff. New stuff."

"It isn't a competition, Willow," Giles reminded her.

She pushed a lock of red hair behind her ear. "I know. But when you're working on just a few hours' sleep, sometimes one-upmanship is the only motivation that'll keep you awake." Then that secret smile returned as she glanced at Tara. "Other times—"

"What *did* you find out?" Giles interrupted.

"For starters, the aquarium wasn't the only place broken into last night. Nobody was killed, but someone did a little smash and grab at the Sunnydale Historical Society."

"You're watching those cop shows again," Buffy said.

Willow ignored the comment, but Tara smiled.

"They had some artifacts stolen," Willow went on. "Things that dated back to before Sunnydale was even a town, when fishing boats would moor here. Definitely not Native American artifacts, either, or so the Historical Society says.

"I haven't been much of the Net girl lately, but I'm searching for any reference to this type of transformation I can find. Also, I think I may have found the crazy old guy Buffy was looking for, Ben Varrey?"

Buffy wiped a bit of whipped cream from her lip and gazed at Willow. "Really? How'd you manage that? None of his Docktown buddies seemed to know . . . wait, you're not going to tell me he's in the cemetery, are you?"

"Nope, but that was the first place I looked," Willow admitted. "Turns out the night you killed icky-fish-man in Docktown, the old guy was raving so much out on the street that the cops took him to Charles Dexter."

"Who's Charles Dexter?" Buffy asked as she took another sip of mochaccino.

"Not a who, Buffy," Giles corrected, frowning deeply. "Charles Dexter is a psychiatric hospital not far from Crestwood College." The Watcher turned to Willow. "Well done."

Tara nodded in agreement. "She has magick fingers." Then, as though the words had just echoed back to her and sounded not at all right, she perked up and glanced around at the others. "On the keyboard."

Giles cleared his throat and removed his glasses, idly cleaning them with a napkin from the table. "Yes, Willow. Your attention had been so often diverted by magical pursuits of late, it's easy to forget your facility with mundane research. You've certainly trumped me."

He slid his glasses back on and regarded her. "Are you pleased?"

"Yep!" Willow said, nodding happily.

Unable to stop himself, Giles grinned and shook his head. "All right. I suppose I must get back to my own research then. Meanwhile, Buffy, a conversation with Ben Varrey may prove him somewhat less the lunatic than the authorities imagine."

The Slayer sighed. "Great. Send Buffy off to the nuthouse. I knew it was only a matter of time."

Tangled in the sheets of her sleigh bed, Helen Fontaine stretched lazily, unwilling to allow herself to come fully awake. Barely conscious of the world around her save the soft sheets that smelled of her body lotion and her husband, Steven's, aftershave, she burrowed her head deeper into her pillow, and then her breathing deepened as she dropped off completely again and dreamed of brutal men on horseback, clad in leather and fur. It was not a pleasant dream.

The phone trilled beside her head and Helen began to reach for it even before her eyes were open. At last, as she pressed it against her ear, she parted her eyelids slowly and let the daylight seep in, waking her fully.

"Hello?"

"Get out of bed, lazybones."

Helen laughed softly. "Steven. You should be in here with me instead of *there*. Where are you, anyway?"

"About to go into court in Brooklyn. I thought you might need some jostling to get out of bed this morning after how late you stayed up working last night."

She smiled to herself. "The phone is not the sort of jostling I would have liked. And anyway, I'm way ahead of schedule on this one. At this rate, I'll deliver months early. Terry won't know what to do with himself."

The night before, like so many nights, Helen had stayed up until the wee hours of the morning working on her book, *The Life and Times of Genghis Khan*. Terry was her oh-so-patient editor, who had waited far longer than he ought to have for her two previous books. Helen was determined to get this one in on time.

"As long as it's on time, hon," Steven said. "Don't kill yourself to get it in early. On time should make him just as happy."

"Ecstatic, more like, given my track record," Helen replied. "So when will you be home?"

Steven paused a moment and when he spoke again his tone was grim. "Well, if my client has been entirely truthful with me, probably in time for a late lunch. If he's the lying trash I think he is, possibly by nine."

They said their I-love-yous and Helen hung up the phone. The sunlight streamed through the open windows of the bedroom of the antique Federal Colonial where the couple had lived since their marriage six years before. The light spilled along the warped, uneven wood floor and onto the bone-white sheets and warmed Helen as she lay there. She stretched again and was tempted to fall back to sleep, but at length she rose and slid her legs over the edge of the bed. Today was a research day. She was going to have to head down into Manhattan again. The train ride from Dobbs Ferry wasn't bad, but she wanted to get started just in case Steven really did get home at a decent hour.

Helen rose and slipped her nightshirt over her head, walked to her dresser to turn on the radio, then went to the master bath and turned on the shower. Classical music swelled and filled the room, echoed in the hall. Helen Fontaine and her husband, Steven Gershman, liked all sorts of music. But in the morning and at bedtime, classical could be wonderfully soothing.

Always too serious, always too deeply entrenched in her work, Helen had rarely if ever relaxed. But Steven's success as an attorney brought a kind of freedom she had never known before, and she found her writing almost as soothing as Vivaldi. Only in the research was she as intense as she had always been before.

As Helen climbed out of the shower the phone began to trill again. She wrapped a thick white towel loosely around herself and rushed to pick it up.

"Hello?"

"And how is the new book coming?"

The voice on the other end of the phone was clipped and proper, and the speaker had a British accent. It took her a moment to place that voice, but only because he had never called her house before, never even spoken to her directly, only as part of a group at gatherings.

"Mr. Travers?"

"Hello, Ms. Fontaine. You're well, I presume?"

As if Travers were outside the window instead of all the way across the Atlantic, Helen pulled the towel tighter around her and sat down demurely on the bed.

"Yes. Yes, sir, and you?"

"A bit preoccupied, I confess. Did you tell me about the book? What's this one? Genghis Khan, yes?"

"Yes."

"Excellent subject. I'm sure you'll do a fine job. I hope you're well caught up Ms. Fontaine, because you'll be required to put your . . . secondary career on hold for a time. The directors have an assignment for you." There was a long pause on the line before Quentin Travers, a member of the board of directors of the Council of Watchers, added two more words.

"In Sunnydale."

All the wind went out of Helen for a minute. She could not breathe. *Sunnydale.* That was where the Slayer was. Of course she was completely up to date on the recent history of the Slayer—or Slayers, if she included poor Faith, the girl who was now in prison—but Helen had never imagined she would have any contact with them. She was largely untried in the field, and such activities were generally left to more seasoned Watchers, and those who worked out of the main branch in London.

"My . . . my husband—"

"You shall make your excuses, my dear. You're to meet with our operative Mr. Daniel Haversham at the Manhattan branch at noon. The other Watchers on hand there shall update you with recent developments, including some very curious reports in today's *Sunnydale Times,* reports which may relate to rather sensitive Council matters. You have a flight west at five thirty."

Helen's mind whirled. She had to pack. She had to hurry! A train to the city to meet Daniel—whom she had met several times at the branch office—and then out to the airport. Meanwhile, how to explain to her husband why she had to rush out to California at a moment's notice? It was going to rock the boat, that was for sure. And how long would it take? She could afford a couple of weeks, no more.

But her first duty was to the Council. They had trained her, paid for her education, helped her get connected in the publishing world . . . and her grandmother would never forgive her if she let the Council down.

The Slayer, Helen thought excitedly as she dressed. Difficult as relations had been with the girl of late, it was still the assignment every Watcher hoped for. Not that she had been assigned as *the* Watcher to the girl, but still . . .

At the very least, it would be interesting.

The shadows had grown long as Rosanna Jergens sipped from the tiny bottle of Coca-Cola the waiter had brought her. She sat at a small table in front of a restaurant at the intersection of two narrow alleys that passed for streets in the center of Seville. The old town area was a warren of such alleys, many of which were truly beautiful, with flowers overflowing from planters hung from windows. Huge wooden doors found only in Spain led into courtyards with fountains bubbling up in their midst. The Santa Cruz section of Seville was particularly lovely, clean and well kept, painted in bright colors. From time to time a horse-drawn wagon would rattle by.

Tourists flocked to these back alleys and the cathedral that towered over them. There were shops and restaurants every step of the way, but without a map it would have been simple for a newcomer to get lost for hours in the maze of Santa Cruz.

Rosanna Jergens was not a newcomer. Nor was she wandering.

The restaurant in front of which she sat had closed for two hours in the afternoon. She had been there when it closed and then when it opened again. Though she had a magazine open on the table in front of her, Rosanna paid little attention to it. Behind her sunglasses she watched only the intersection ahead, waiting.

A moped roared by, a girl in leather pants holding tight to the well-muscled boy who was driving. Tourists mingled with locals. Rosanna sighed and rotated her head to the left and right with a series of pops. The late afternoon sun had moved too far on the horizon, and now nearly the entire intersection had been thrown into shadow by the buildings that lined the streets.

She pushed her sunglasses up on top of her head, tucking her shoulder-length, raven-black hair behind her ears.

Then she saw him.

The demon Matteius entered the intersection from the alley off to Rosanna's left. He was dressed casually in dark pants and shoes and a navy-blue cotton jacket, and in his arms he carried a package wrapped in brown paper with thick string tied around it. Inside it was a book the Order wanted very badly to possess. Matteius was passably humanoid—enough to walk through the streets of a major city without anyone noticing the blue tint to his skin—but dark glasses hid the demon's burning eyes and an old-fashioned bowler hat covered his horns. The hat would draw attention, certainly, but not the sort that horns would have.

As Matteius approached, looking nervous, a young man—hardly more than a boy—stepped away from where he had been leaning against the wall. The kid dropped his cigarette and approached the demon, eyes darting about anxiously. He reached into his pocket and removed his pack of cigarettes. For a moment Rosanna thought he was going to light another, but then he handed the package to Matteius. For his part, the demon looked reluctantly at the brown-paper-wrapped package.

The kid stared at the package as well.

Rosanna lifted the collar of her shirt and spoke into the small phone receiver hidden there. "Green light."

A pair of tourists walking nearby turned abruptly toward the demon and the kid. The roar of a moped's engine rattled windows, and along the alley came the same muscular kid and his girlfriend in leather pants.

"You sure we don't need him for the lab?" a voice asked quickly, through the small black module in Rosanna's left ear.

"Not at all," she insisted. "I told you. Don't harm him if you can help it. That's not why we're here. We've dissected a dozen like him after death, and studied others in captivity. We only need the book."

A hand reached in front of Rosanna and she jerked back, heart thundering, but it was only the waiter removing her empty Coke bottle.

"Nada mas?" the waiter asked.

"Gracias, no," she replied without even looking at him again.

As Matteius reached out to hand his package to the kid, the two "tourists"—Valentin and Sato—rushed them, removing black plastic tasers from within the folds of their clothing. The kid went down instantly, jerking spasmodically as electricity surged through him. Matteius was too fast for them, however. The prongs that fired from the tip of Sato's taser shot past him as he dodged out of the way, and the demon lashed out with such ferocity that he tore off Sato's arm at the elbow. The man went down screaming, blood gouting from the stump of his arm. Rosanna knew he'd be dead in minutes.

So much for the taser.

Valentin dropped his—it would be useless for a couple of minutes anyway—and staggered backward, shouting "Deadly force? Deadly force!"

He wore a setup just like Rosanna's, and the way he shouted into the receiver in his shirt collar made her pull out her earpiece and hold it further away. "No!" she snapped. "That's final option. Got it? Final option!"

People were scattering now, some shouting, some merely running away. Waiters stood inside the doorways of small restaurants, and old Spanish women peered from within the open doors of bodegas.

Matteius clutched the book against his chest with one hand. The other suddenly sprouted long claws that gleamed like steel. The toes of his shoes were torn open as talons suddenly protruded out from within. The demon leaped six feet off the ground directly at the face of the building beside him and plunged his feet and free hands into the wall. Book held tight to him, he began to quickly scale it. One story. Two.

Valentin had his gun out. He took a single shot at the fleeing demon. The spectators scattered, running for cover wherever they could find it.

"We can't go back without that book, Rose!" the man snapped into her earpiece.

She felt sick, and her throat closed up as though something were stuck inside it. *Damn it,* Rosanna thought. Then she swore loudly.

"All right! Lethal force!"

The moped roared up onto the sidewalk and the girl in leather pants leaped off the back, a gun already held in both hands. She stood next to Valentin, shoulder to shoulder, and the two of them fired three or four shots apiece. Bullets punched through Matteius's back, spraying blood against the wall of the building, spattering a window.

The demon slowed. One last time he punched his talons through the solid wall. Then Matteius slumped backward, and the hand clutching the book slipped loose and dropped down at his side. The book fell end over end, cover and pages fluttering, and Valentin caught it, there on the sidewalk below.

Matteius hung there, nailed to the wall by his own strength and instinct for survival, a dead demon dangling by his talons from the second floor of a bodega building in the Santa Cruz district of Seville. No way could Rosanna's team get him down before the police came. The Spanish authorities were going to be all over the place trying to figure it out.

"Wonderful," she sighed. Then she spoke into the receiver in her collar. "Vanish."

Most people still had their heads down as Valentin took off running down one of the narrow alleys, leaving Sato's corpse behind in a pool of blood, several feet from where his arm lay. Valentin would find his way through that maze and end up back at the rendezvous point. Sato's body would be just another mystery for the locals. The two agents on the moped—Mira and Paolo—took off down the road at a good clip. There were so many damned mopeds in this city, they'd never be found.

Rosanna looked around and saw that most people were staring after the moped, or down the way Valentin had run. Only her waiter was staring at her as she fitted her earpiece back into the cleft of her ear. She smiled at him, offered a friendly little wave, and pulled several more bills from her pocket. She left the money on the table along with the magazine she had been so studiously not reading, and she headed off along the third arm of the three-way intersection.

"We're clear," she said into her collar receiver.

"Well done, Rosanna," said another voice, that of her supervisor, Astrid Johannsen.

"Not really," Rosanna replied sadly. "It shouldn't have had to go that way. That's not what we're about."

There was a long pause as she hurried along the

shadowed sidewalk in silence and then slid in the open door of a building that promised flamenco dancing at nine o'clock that night. She would exit through the front into the large square in front of the cathedral, a tourist mecca, and that would be that. Hidden in plain sight.

"Well, perhaps your next assignment will go more smoothly."

Rosanna frowned, wishing she could see the look on her supervisor's face. "Astrid, I've got two weeks coming up, starting today."

"Two weeks coming up, yes. But not starting today."

With a sigh, Rosanna paused on a street corner, not far from where a line of carriages waited for customers to approach.

"Where?" she asked.

"California."

Once upon a time—when people in America still called things what they were instead of labeling them with vague euphemisms—the Charles Dexter Institute would have been called an asylum. Colloquially, a nut-house, madhouse, or loony bin. Properly, perhaps a sanitarium or psychiatric hospital. The latter was still in use, but Buffy figured it was only a matter of time until the official name for an asylum would be that-place-where-they-take-you-when-(pause)-*y'know*.

The Institute—which she had discovered was referred to locally merely as the Dex—was situated at the top of a small hill on a gorgeous piece of property within sight of the grounds of exclusive Crestwood College. Though it was privately owned by a foundation created at the turn of the previous century by the Dexter family, the Dex did take in indigent patients from time to time as a service to the city and the state of California. In exchange, Buffy was certain they received certain tax breaks and other consideration. But at least it meant that people in need had a place to go.

Willow and Tara had gone back to campus to get to their respective classes. Her mom was still recovering but had gone into the gallery for a few hours. Giles and Anya were at the Magic Box, dealing with customers and research simultaneously. That left her no choice but to ask for a ride from the last person who should have been driving around.

Xander winced as he turned into the long driveway up through the well-groomed grounds of the Dex. Lawn sprinklers chattered as they sprayed water across the grass, and the roar of a powerful mower reached them through the open windows of Xander's car, though Buffy could not see anyone actually mowing.

"You all right?" Buffy asked him.

One-handed, he guided the car up the hill. "I'm really not supposed to be driving. If I can't go to work, I just think it's a little dishonest of me to be chauffeuring you around town."

Buffy cast him a doubtful glance. "You realize that HBO only shows *Real Sex* late at night?"

Xander sighed. "Please, Buffy. Yes, I know that." He shook his head sadly. "How little you think of me." He guided the car into a parking spot, then maneuvered it into park and shut off the engine before glancing at her. "So, any idea of the actual night and time, 'cause I'm having a heck of a time finding it in the *TV Guide*."

"No," she said pointedly. "And yuck. I knew I had to get you out of there before you got too stir crazy." Buffy reached out to touch his arm. "I appreciate it, Xander."

"Nah. My pleasure. There's only so much Emeril and *Behind the Music* one guy can take."

Buffy shut the door, glancing about her at the serene landscape and up at the plain white bungalow-style building. There was a fountain in front with a trio of waterspouts erupting from it. To Buffy it seemed more like a retirement home than an insane asylum, but at least it was a nice, sunny day without the heat they'd had over the weekend.

She leaned in the window. "You'll be all right out here."

Xander took a deep breath, put back his seat as far as it would go and closed his eyes. "You just wake me when you're done."

A smile flickered across Buffy's features as she walked over to the entrance of the Dex. Huge potted plants framed the doors and they slid open in front of her. Air-conditioning blasted her as she walked into the bright, sterile foyer that consisted of a small waiting area with expensive armchairs, an elevator, a stairwell that wound up to her right, and the reception desk dead ahead, behind which sat a short, thin guy with deep olive skin and a thick mustache. From his outfit, Buffy thought he looked more like a hotel concierge than a hospital receptionist.

"Hi!" she said brightly as she walked up.

The man put on his most professional smile—exactly the same one that the people behind the counter at Blockbuster wore. "Good afternoon. What can I do for you?"

Buffy allowed her own smile to flicker and fade to a quiet sadness and she glanced down as she spoke. "I'm . . . I just found out my grandfather's here. I hadn't been to visit him in a couple of weeks, and when I went by his place—"

Shamefaced, she put a hand to her forehead as if to hide her eyes. "I feel so bad. Maybe if I'd gone by sooner." Then she shook herself and stood up straighter, making a show of regaining her composure. "I'm sorry. This isn't what they pay you for, is it? I'd just . . . could I see my grandfather?"

To her surprise, the expression on the face of the receptionist seemed to hold genuine sympathy. "What's his name, miss?"

"Benjamin Varrey."

The receptionist tapped at the keyboard of a computer down behind the counter. After a moment he frowned. "We don't have any next of kin listed, Miss . . . ?"

"Summers. I guess I'm not surprised. My parents are divorced and he's my father's father. My dad . . . hasn't been around in a long time. I guess I'm the only blood relation who's visited him in years. And he's not exactly . . . all there, is he?"

The receptionist nodded. "We're going to need you to fill out some paperwork, Miss Summers."

Buffy realized that her charade was working and tried not to reveal her surprise. She had been certain she would be turned away because she had no proof she was related. Giles had suggested that if the old man had no other relatives, they might be relieved to have someone—anyone—show up to claim him because that meant they might get paid their usual rate instead of what the state would pay.

She forced the sadness back onto her face. "Sure. No problem. But do we have to do that right now? Can it wait an hour? I just . . . I feel like I abandoned him, y'know? Sometimes he loses touch with reality and I'm the only one who can bring him back."

The receptionist hesitated a moment, then smiled. "Sure. Let me get someone to take you to him, and you can see one of the nurses before you leave. I'm sure your grandfather will be happy to have company."

Yeah, she thought, *if he's not lucid enough to tell the nurses he doesn't have a granddaughter, or he does but her name isn't Summers.*

Buffy sat down and prepared to wait patiently, but

only a few minutes passed before a broad-shouldered orderly appeared from the stairwell and invited her to come with him. They took the elevator to the third floor. In her mind Buffy had images of padded walls and patients in straitjackets wandering around mumbling to themselves or to their imaginary companions. But when the elevator doors slid open the orderly led her out into a corridor that looked more like a five-star hotel than *Girl, Interrupted.*

"We've brought your"—the orderly glanced down at a clipboard in his hand as they walked—"grandfather to a visiting lounge where the two of you can speak privately, away from the treatment ward."

Buffy heard a TV blaring from inside one of the rooms. From down the hall somewhere came the sound of someone singing loudly. "Thank you," she said.

A moment later, the orderly pulled a ring of keys from his pocket. They were attached by a metal line to his belt. He fitted one into the lock of a thick oak door and pushed it open, then stepped inside and glanced around for any sign of trouble before moving aside to let Buffy enter.

The room was very dark, with narrow slashes of sunlight streaming in through the blinds that covered the large window on the far wall. Ben Varrey looked thinner than Buffy remembered, and his white hair had been cut short. In the pajamas and sky-blue robe the Dex had given him and now that he was well groomed, she would not have recognized him on the street. He no longer fit the image of the old man of the sea as he had when she had first seen him in the Fish Tank.

Varrey didn't turn around when they entered the room. The orderly paused a moment then glanced from the old man to Buffy.

"Ten minutes." He shut the door as he left.

Alone with this strange old guy, Buffy felt unnerved

in a way she never did when fighting demons or vampires. Those were physical monsters. She could knock them down and make sure they never got up again. But how did you combat mental illness?

"Mr. Varrey?"

His fingers were splayed between the blinds, spreading them open slightly so that a stripe of bright sun illuminated his eyes. The old man twitched and let his hand fall away, the blinds rustling with a metallic jangle. He shuddered as though cold and slowly he turned just his head to look at her over his shoulder. His eyes narrowed.

"You're not really my granddaughter, are you?" The old man's voice still had a rough edge, but he spoke more softly now, and with more focus than the mad ramblings she had heard from him before.

Buffy hesitated a moment, then shook her head and moved further into the room. "No," she admitted, sitting down in a high-backed leather chair. "No, I'm not."

A dry chuckle issued from Ben Varrey's mouth and he rocked a bit from side to side. "That's a relief." His fingers spread the blinds open again and he returned his attention to the lawn outside. "I was afraid, y'see, that I might actually have a granddaughter and just forgot."

He shot her a quick glance, his expression grave now. "I'm in the booby hatch, y'know. Makes you wonder if you're as crazy as they say you are."

For a long moment the two of them were silent. Buffy was not quite sure how to begin. This wasn't roughing up Willy or staking a vampire, but it shared just as little in common with those activities as it did with visiting a sick relative in the hospital. She had never liked hospitals, not since she was a little girl, but this place was far, far worse. No matter how nice it seemed, what was on the inside seemed sinister to her. She knew she was being ridiculous, that it was exactly that sort of medieval thought that put such a stigma on mental illness for so many people, even now. But she couldn't help it.

Yet the old man did not seem as freaky as he had that night at the Fish Tank. He seemed contemplative, even sad as he stared out the window, and she could not tell if he was yearning for freedom or watching for trouble. Only the little twitches and shudderings were at all odd. As Buffy watched he did it again, this sort of parade of spasms that went up and down his body.

At last she could stand the silence no longer.

"So, do you remember me from that night? At the Fish Tank?"

"I remember," he answered without turning. "Know who you are, too. Or what. You're the little girl who fights the monsters. I had a dream about you."

Buffy frowned. *He's dreaming about me. Wonderful. What's that all about?* But all she said was, "That's me. You were pretty scared that night. You said somebody was coming back. The Children of the Sea or something. What was that about, Mr. Varrey?"

As Buffy spoke, the old man grew very still as though he had frozen in place. Then he slowly raised his right hand, fingers trembling, and pulled the chain that would close the blinds. Only a pair of dim yellow overhead lights illuminated the room now, and when Ben Varrey turned toward her, his skin looked jaundiced. His face was slack, and it occurred to Buffy that the man seemed somehow hollow to her. Empty.

The tremors spread from his hand up his arm, and his chin sagged forward so that he was staring up at her, head bowed. Drool began to slide off his lower lip, swaying as he twitched. Buffy was disgusted, but what truly upset her were the tears that spilled down his cheeks. She stood up from the chair but hesitated, uncertain what she could do for the old man.

"M-my house. Go to my h-house," he stammered, staring up at her balefully. A tremor went through him, and when it passed over the muscles of his face it looked almost as though something were moving there, under the skin, sliding along the bone.

His eyes began to fill with blood. When he spoke again his voice was a deep rasp as though something had torn down inside him. Bloody spittle shot from his mouth.

"They are the Children of the Sea, descendants of the Old Ones who claimed this world when it was young and were banished beyond time and space and who will return to walk the world once more. For all the ages of the earth their children, the Moruach, have always been here, deep beneath the seas, waiting for that moment.

"The moment has come."

From somewhere out in the hall there came the sound of breaking glass, and then the screaming began. Buffy shot a glance at the door, then gazed around the room for anything she might use as a weapon. When she looked at the old man again the front of his pajamas were soaked with blood and something had punched its way out of his chest, a long black tendril with gleaming spikes along its length.

"The Moruach are here."

Chapter Five

The old man fell to his knees, thick mucousy choking sounds coming out of his mouth. He gagged, heaved, and then retched loudly but what came out of him was not the last meal he'd had; it was a swarming nest of thin, spiny tentacles that lashed across the room as if they had eyes of their own. Buffy leaped up in a backward somersault, vaulting her chair, and landed behind it. The jagged tendrils tore the leather upholstery with a vicious ripping noise.

Buffy swore. No fireplace, so no metal poker. No floor lamps. Not even a table with legs long and thick enough to brandish as a weapon. And out in the hall there came a crash and more screams.

The thing that had been Ben Varrey staggered to its feet again, and she saw that the flesh of its face had begun to fall away, revealing the scaled thing beneath with bulbous eyes and a round mouth with a ringlet of razor teeth. Webs had ripped through the skin of the old man's hands, and it lifted its arms even as those tentacles lashed out at her again. She thought of Greek mythology, of the creatures that had hair made of snakes. Gorgons, they were called. The razored tendrils that struck out from its chest reminded her of Gorgons.

Buffy snapped a side kick up at the back of the chair she'd just vacated, drove it across the room where it collided with the creature. Varrey staggered slightly and went down on one knee, still changing, still becoming whatever it was becoming.

The Slayer didn't wait to see what that might be. People were screaming elsewhere and she had to figure out what was going on. Plus she figured there had to be something somewhere she could use as a weapon.

Turning her back on the thing that was quickly shedding the husk that had once been Ben Varrey, she ran to the door and flung it open. The handsome, hulking orderly who had walked her up here was just across the hall trying to calm a male patient who stood in the door of his room clad only in heart-patterned boxer shorts.

"Hey!" Buffy snapped.

The orderly turned to her. "Miss Summers, I'm not sure what's happening, but you have to get back—"

"Keys!" she demanded, hand outstretched toward him.

He scowled. "I'm not going to—"

Buffy heard a hiss in the air behind her, saw the orderly's eyes glance past her and widen in horror. Without pause she spun, ducked low, and reached up for the doorknob. The thing was almost completely changed now; still humanoid, but its body was covered with scales, and where flesh and fabric had been torn away she could see at least three extra mouths, all round and ringed with tiny little vicious teeth.

Tendrils reached for her. One raked the skin of her neck, cutting her deeply. A second shot at her leg and tore through her pants and her skin, puncturing her flesh. Buffy hissed in pain as she hauled the door closed so hard that the tentacles caught in it were severed and fell twitching to the floor. The one that had cut into her leg dangled from the hole it had made, and she tore it out with a shout of blinding pain as the razor barbs on it ripped flesh.

Snarling, Buffy turned to the orderly and thrust her hand out again.

"Keys!"

Wide-eyed, the man reached out to hand her the keys, indicating which one would lock the visiting room door even as he stayed well clear of the still twitching tentacles on the floor.

"What the hell is that?" the orderly whispered.

Buffy shot him a dark look. "My grandfather."

The patient in the boxer shorts looked at her sympathetically from his open doorway and clucked his tongue. "Poor girl. He doesn't look too good, your grandpa."

Buffy raised an eyebrow. "I know. It's a shame. It's also contagious."

Insane or not, the man stepped back into his room and slammed the door. Buffy turned to the orderly and tossed his keys back to him.

"That oughta keep him in there for a while. Stay here. Keep your patients in their rooms. Anything comes down the hall, hit the stairs. Whatever you do, don't open *that* door." She pointed at the door to the visiting room.

Even as she did, something collided with it from within, shaking it on its hinges. There was a sound like splintering wood but the door held.

"Do I look stupid to you?"

Buffy did not answer. She did not want to hurt his feelings. Instead she turned and ran down the hall toward where the screams were coming from. Not just screaming now, but a kind of running babble of voices all talking at once. She saw as she went that there were a number of bathrooms along that corridor, a lot of private rooms, and two more visiting rooms with their doors open, but otherwise it was all very sterile, very much the same. Nice carpets, nice paintings on the wall, but now that she was in it, the Dex did not look like a hotel after all.

It was a hospital. Prettier, cleaner, but still a hospital.

She hated hospitals.

Up ahead the corridor turned right, through a pair of steel doors that led into another wing. The doors were propped open and had only small square windows in them. On the other side the floors were linoleum, the walls were plainer, and the patients were cowering in nothing but pajamas or nightgowns on the floor, or inside their rooms screaming and muttering to themselves. A skinny old woman batted at the air around her as though the screams were mosquitoes she might swat.

Twenty feet away was a patients' lounge. Blood had sprayed all over the floor, and a young girl in flannels had fallen in it and was curled into a fetal ball. Buffy could not tell if any of the blood was hers, but she knew not all of it was. Most of it belonged to the orderly whose head lay on the floor next to the girl, and whose shattered body was sprawled across a fallen chair at the edge of the lounge.

Buffy paused and for a second she could not breathe. Two other terrified orderlies were trying their best to make sure nobody else died. They each held an eighteen-inch electrical prod. Buffy did not want to know what orderlies at a mental hospital would be doing with such devices, but given what they were up against, Buffy doubted those weapons were going to do much good.

Moruach, she thought.

This monster was nothing like the creature Ben Varrey

and that fisherman, Lucky, had become. This was something completely different. It had four almond-shaped amber colored eyes, two on each side of a flat head. When it reared up, hissing, and lashed one of its long arms out at an orderly, webbed talons barely missing his face, the thing gnashed its jaws and all Buffy could think about was a shark, for its mouth was huge and it had three rows of dark teeth. A pair of ribbed, dangerously sharp-looking fins began on its head and ran all the way down its back. The Moruach had gills, of course, but obviously it could breathe out of the water as well.

It had no legs. Its body was serpentine, but as Buffy looked at it standing up on its trunk, only a few feet of long flat tail supporting it, she thought of a moray eel she had seen at the aquarium once.

And it stank to high heaven.

"Gahh!" she said, wrinkling her nose. "What sewer did you crawl out of?"

Before she could stop them, the orderlies tried to attack it together, reaching in with their electrical prods. The Moruach ducked its head down and slammed it into the chest of the one nearest him, and Buffy heard the man's rib cage shatter. The other orderly was successful, his prod touched the Moruach's flesh and the thing flinched as thousands of volts of electricity zapped into it.

Then it batted the prod from the orderly's hand and sunk down lower so that it could swing its tail up. The tail struck the man across the chest, and Buffy heard bones snapping as the man slammed into a chair and then slid to the ground.

"Okay, watch the tail. Good to know," Buffy muttered.

All around her, patients screamed. Those who were more lost in their own minds than the others had retreated into some internal world and were whispering or just rocking back and forth inside doorways or on the floor. One of their orderlies had been slaughtered, probably in front of them, and the injuries these two had just sustained might cost them their lives as well.

Buffy circled the outer edges of the open lounge. She wasn't going to let the monster get to anybody else. *But what the hell are you doing here in the first place?* she thought. *And how did you get in?* The Moruach seemed to pause, gills undulating as it glanced around.

"What are you looking for?" she asked aloud.

It lowered itself down, eel-like body sliding along the floor toward her slowly. Its black eyes seemed to shrink as it studied her, and Buffy knew as she stared into those eyes that this wasn't some mindless beast. The monster was primal but intelligent.

The Moruach lunged for her, too fast to evade. Buffy ran at it, leaped into a spinning kick, and connected with its head. The Moruach squealed in a pitch so high Buffy shouted in pain and clapped her hands to her ears even as she landed. The monster was knocked backward but was too strong, too fast. It righted itself immediately and came at her again, more slowly this time, wavering back and forth, looking for an opening. It lifted its tail up behind it like a scorpion and waited for her to come closer.

After a few seconds, when she did not attack, it seemed to forget about her and glanced about again, its four amber eyes finally focusing on a place further down the hall, back the way Buffy had come.

It started to move, sliding its body past her. Buffy ran at it again. Beyond it in the hall she had seen what she wanted. Getting past that tail was the hardest part.

As Buffy ran at it the Moruach turned and lowered into a defensive crouch again, shark teeth gnashing as its tail flashed up and swung at her. The wound in her leg made her grit her teeth and wince, but she dove through the air above the Moruach. It tried to bite her and to strike with its tail at the same time and succeeded in doing neither.

It was the last time she would be able to pull that off. The thing was too fast and too smart to fall for it again. Not that it mattered. She was past it.

A fire extinguisher was displayed behind a small glass door set into the wall. Buffy smashed the glass with her elbow and tore the red canister out of the clips that held it there. She turned just as the Moruach lunged at her again. Her fingers found the trigger for the extinguisher, and she cracked it across the face with the bottom of the metal tank. Teeth cracked in the Moruach's mouth.

The thing's flat, muscled tail came down at her, and Buffy could not avoid it. It struck her on the shoulder, and she went down hard on the linoleum floor, canister still in her hands. The Moruach was slinking low, practically on its belly, and its huge jaws opened as its body thrust toward her.

Buffy rammed the fire extinguisher into its throat. The Moruach started to withdraw, but she was not about to let that happen. She reached out and grabbed its head—upper jaw in one hand and lower jaw in the other, rows of teeth puncturing her hands—and she pulled them apart, breaking its jaw.

It flailed on the ground, choking on the fire extinguisher, and seconds later it died.

Buffy stood over it, breathing heavy, and then she scanned the hall and the lounge, stared at the patients. She remembered the way the thing had been searching for something.

"Where did it come from?" she asked, trying to get one of the patients to meet her gaze. "Come on, people. Hello? I killed the big bad monster, okay? Can anyone tell me where it came from."

The teenage girl in the bloody flannel pajamas unfolded from her fetal ball on the floor and pointed across the lounge at a small foyer where there was a single elevator. It was dark inside and Buffy had not noticed it in the chaos, but the doors were open onto nothing but an elevator shaft and cables.

"Where does that go?" she asked the girl. "Basement? All the way to the basement?"

It smelled like sewer, she thought, frowning.

"Two," the girl said, grinning broadly with blood streaked on her face. "Two basements. One and two. Two and one. One-B. Two-B."

Sub-basement, Buffy thought. *Pipes down there, gotta be maintenance tunnels. Who the hell designed this town? They came up through the sewers to stay out of sight. Or out of the sun? They live in the ocean, they're not gonna be real morning people.*

A loud banging echoed down the hall from back the way she'd come. Loud footsteps pounded toward them from around the corner.

"Hey!" shouted the hulking orderly she had left in front of Varrey's room as he rounded the corner and ran into the bloody hall. "Hey!"

Buffy stared at him. She'd almost forgotten the creature Ben Varrey had turned into and now she wondered what it was, 'cause it certainly wasn't the same thing as a Moruach.

Beautiful. Two totally different species of slimy demon to deal with.

"It's breaking loose?" she asked, anxiously looking around for a weapon. As vicious and nasty as the Moruach were, whatever it was that had erupted out of Ben Varrey's body was just that much more disgusting.

The orderly shook his head. "No. There's something else. Something banging around inside the elevator. The doors—something's smashing at the doors from inside."

Buffy sighed and steadied herself. "My kingdom for an ax," she said, wondering how many more there would be.

Then she looked at the orderly. "Get the patients out of here. Pull the fire alarm. Get as many people out of here as possible."

"Where are you going?" he asked, staring at her as though she was completely out of her mind, looking at the wound on her leg and the other on her neck, which had dripped bloody stripes down the front of her shirt.

Buffy ran across the lounge, darting around corpses, and bent to retrieve both of the electrical prods the orderlies had tried to use. They had had an effect. Not much, but something. And it wasn't like anyone was going to hand her a broadsword any time soon.

Without another word she sprinted back into the other ward, then down that sterile hotel-like hallway. At first she heard and saw nothing out of the ordinary, but just before she reached the locked door to the visiting room, a thundering blow rattled the elevator doors. She stood in front of them, only a few feet down the hall from the visiting room, and saw that there were massive dents in them and one of the doors had begun to tear. Clawed talons scrabbled at the torn metal, and it shrieked as it tore further.

More Moruach. Great. Some of them had come up from the elevator shaft in the next wing, but that had not been *all* of them.

Now that they had gotten a handhold, this fresh batch of Moruach would be through in moments. In her mind's eye she saw them crawling up the elevator cables, clinging to the inside of the shaft. From the ear-splitting screeches coming from inside the elevator shaft she knew that there was more than one of them, probably more than two.

With a grin, she pressed the up button to call the elevator and heard it rattle into motion. Inside the shaft the screeching became louder, and she heard a bang and loud thump. She imagined one of the creatures had been thrown off-balance and she smiled.

"Going up," she said.

It would take them a few extra seconds to deal with that. If they got down inside the elevator, though, that was another story. Because then the doors would just open.

As if on cue a clawed talon thrust through the opening in the doors trying to pry them further. With a pop, they separated and spread two more inches. But the number two above the elevator was lit, and a second later there were several loud thumps and a squeal as the elevator pushed the Moruach upward.

Buffy stood back in the hall, glanced both ways to make sure no other patients had come out—there was no time to evacuate the people on this ward—and held an electrical prod in either hand, waiting.

Which was when the door to the visiting room exploded in a shower of broken wood, tearing off its hinges as the horrible thing that had once been Ben Varrey crashed out into the hall. Its round little mouths gnashed the air as though searching for flesh, and its slick black tentacles massed at its chest, waiting to attack, razor barbs gleaming. Unlike the Moruach, this thing was humanoid—had once *been* human—but it was just a perversion of humanity now, like it had been wearing Ben Varrey's flesh as a costume at some monstrous masquerade and was now tearing off that disguise.

"You couldn't have waited a few more minutes?" Buffy asked. "I was gonna get around to you."

The elevator dinged and the doors slid open. Inside the elevator the ceiling was already being torn apart, Moruach hauling themselves down inside it with powerful talons. Their scaly flesh rasped on the metal surface. One of the slithering things spotted Buffy, glaring at her with its quartet of tiny amber eyes. Any second they'd be in the corridor.

Buffy was trapped between the Moruach on one side and the nightmare creature that had once been Ben Varrey on the other. Varrey lurched toward her, razor-sharp tendrils whipping the air.

"All the boys want to dance with me," Buffy sighed. "Where were you all when I was in junior high?"

Behind her the elevator dinged again and she heard the doors begin to slide closed. The Moruach banged around in there, sliding heavily to the floor. Buffy could feel how vulnerable her back was as she turned to face Ben Varrey.

The tentacles that had burst from his chest reached for her, and Buffy held the two electrical prods up in front of her as though they were battle staves or billy clubs. Effortlessly she slipped deep within herself, to a place where combat became instinct alone. Slick black tendrils whipped at her face, but Buffy acutely felt the pain in her throat and leg and was not going to be cut by the monster's barbs again. In a blur of motion she moved forward, one arm flashing down and the other up, blocking each tentacle's attack individually with a speed that was far greater than human. With each tap from one of the prods, the creature would jitter and that singed tendril would retract.

A barb tore at Buffy's shirt; another slid along the prod and barely scratched the back of her hand.

She felt as though she had entered a kind of hyper-reality where her every nerve ending was attuned to changes around her. The sound of rending metal came from the elevator doors behind her, and she knew the Moruach were finally coming through. But she had Ben

Varrey on the retreat, some of its tentacles smoldering, held close to its trunk, and she pressed the advantage. It continued to back up under her onslaught, under the *tap-tap-tap* of the electrical jolts she sent through it with every blow.

"Never been a sushi girl," Buffy revealed as she forced it back into the visiting room where it had undergone this horrible transformation. "If it comes from the ocean, it needs cooking."

Even as she spoke the words she saw an opening. The thing stumbled slightly, tentacles wavering, some crippled and dangling uselessly. Buffy tried not to remember the eccentric old man it had been when she arrived. She risked an attack, ducked in, and thrust both electrical prods right into the nest at its chest from which all those tendrils protruded.

In a gurgling voice the thing let out an anguished scream and staggered farther back, right in front of the broad window and its closed blinds. It reared up in agonized fury, but Buffy was already in motion. She could hear the screeching of the Moruach coming into the room and knew at any second those talons would rake her back.

With a soft grunt she leaped off the ground and snapped a solid kick up into the monster's jaw, shattering teeth in that round, vicious maw. Remnants of Ben Varrey's flesh tore off under the impact of the blow as the tentacled creature crashed backward through the blinds, shattered the window, and fell through a shower of glass shards wrapped in a shroud of metallic blinds that tore off their moorings.

Sunlight flooded in and Buffy blinked at the brightness of it, holding up her hands to ward it off as the entire long window vaporized. The monster fell three stories, shrieking and struggling against the blinds in which its tentacles and limbs were caught. She stepped to the massive window—fresh air and warm light suffusing the whole room, evaporating the darkness—and took a quick peek outside. The monster that Ben Varrey had become lay motionless where it had hit the ground.

Buffy heard loud hissing behind her and spun around quickly to see the eel-like tail of a Moruach fleeing back into the corridor. Hoping the Ben Varrey-creature was dead, she turned to go after the Moruach, afraid they would kill anyone who got in their way. When she rushed into the corridor, however, she saw them retreating through the torn up elevator doors and up through the trap door in the elevator's roof.

She was fairly confident that they were headed back down—down into the sewers that made them stink so badly. She wrinkled her nose at the stench in the hall as she strode over to the elevator. For a moment she stared at it, and then she looked around for the sign that would lead her to the stairs.

The Moruach are afraid of the sun, that much is obvious. When the window had shattered in the waiting room, they had not dared come after her. But she did not think that was why they were leaving. They could have waited for her in the hall, after all. No, Buffy believed now that all of the Moruach that had infiltrated the Dex and torn their way up through two elevator shafts had been there in search of Ben Varrey . . . or at least, to destroy whatever it was he had become. With Ben dead, the Moruach had no more reason to stay.

So she had some answers.

And a great many more questions.

Outside, she made sure that Varrey was truly dead, watched a crowd of gawkers begin to form, then she walked to the car and tapped on the window.

Xander was sleeping with his mouth wide open, a thin line of drool on his chin, snoring softly. He looked sort of adorable, and Buffy smiled and shook her head as she climbed into the passenger seat. Embarrassed, he sat up and wiped his chin with his good hand. Then he noticed the blood on her clothes and the gathering crowd.

"Things get out of hand in there?"

"Not for long," she replied as she pulled the door closed.

"We'll just keep the drool thing between ourselves, right?" Xander asked.

"But I can talk about the snoring?"

As he started the car, injured arm still held tightly against him, he shot her a hard look. "People snore. People who are asleep. Snore. Sometimes."

"You looked so peaceful I almost didn't want to wake you. And then I could have studied the pattern of drool in greater detail."

"Oh, right, 'cause Slayers don't drool."

Buffy smiled. "Only with the proper inspiration."

Xander shook his head. "I'm a pitiful human specimen, but also remarkably self aware."

"There's that," Buffy agreed.

"So how'd it go? Find what you were looking for?"

"Maybe," she said, frowning.

"And we can go home now?"

"Nope," Buffy said. "We need to go to Docktown first."

Xander glanced at her as he guided the car one-handed out of the long drive in front of the Dex. Buffy smiled sweetly and batted her lashes in a mockery of innocent persuasion that made Xander chuckle.

"Your wish, as ever, is my command."

Even with the address Willow had provided them with earlier, it took Buffy and Xander nearly forty-five minutes to drive from the Charles Dexter Institute and locate Ben Varrey's home, a little shack on a side street in Docktown, two blocks from the ocean. There was a small row of run-down cottages between a large dilapidated apartment house and an old factory building that had probably once leaked whatever chemicals it used right into Sunnydale harbor. The factory was abandoned and probably had its share of squatters, but Buffy was not interested in anything at the moment but the contents of the old fisherman's house.

They were both surprised by how tidy the man's home was, and, though he was dead, they attempted not to make it too much of a shambles as they pulled it apart looking for anything that might help them. Varrey had said there was information about the Moruach here, and indeed Buffy found some yellowed papers, a journal, and chunks of what seemed ancient pottery, as well as a few other artifacts that piqued her curiosity. With his broken collarbone and his arm in a sling, there was a limit to how helpful Xander could be. But it did not take long for Buffy to put them all in a box and carry it out to the car.

As she stood and peered back inside the small, musty cottage, with the faded photographs and maritime paintings on the walls, a burden of deep melancholy fell over her. Something had infected old Ben Varrey, taken his life away. He had been an odd, lonely old man, but much loved by the other old-timers in Docktown. Buffy had seen his death as horrible, but now, here in his house, she also saw it as tragic.

The shadow of that tragedy hung heavy on her as Xander drove them back to the Magic Box. Xander drove in silence, also affected by this visit to the dead man's home. As they parked not far from the shop, Buffy cast a sidelong glance at him. She had met people who knew Xander only superficially, and almost without fail they thought of him as a clown, as the kind of guy who couldn't take anything seriously. *How blind do you have to be,* she thought, *not to see how totally wrong that is?*

Xander took *everything* seriously. He just dealt with it his own way.

"Hey," Buffy said as they got out of the car.

Xander was trying to retrieve the box of Varrey's things from the backseat one-handed and he glanced up at her over the car roof, eyebrows raised.

"Thanks. For playing chauffeur."

A playful twinkle sparked in his eyes. "It's my life's ambition." He maneuvered the box out and bumped the door shut with his hip. "Gonna go to L.A. and be a limo driver. That or a valet-parking guy. I'll be discovered. I'll be a star. Or just another wide-eyed country boy whose hopes and dreams got chewed up and spat out by a cruel city."

"Country boy?"

Xander shrugged. "It seemed to fit."

Buffy grabbed the handle to open the door of the Magic Box, but it was locked. She frowned at the closed sign on the door and glanced at Xander. It was very late in the afternoon, but the shop was supposed to be open until seven o'clock on Monday nights. Hours yet to go.

"Back up," Buffy told him.

Xander nodded and stepped away from the door, concern etched on his face. Buffy did not blame him. Anya worked at the store. If anything bad had happened, she would have been at ground zero.

Cautious, ready for a fight, Buffy knocked hard on the door and stepped back. From inside she heard footsteps and a moment later the sound of the lock being turned. The door opened and a grim-faced Giles peered out cautiously. When he saw them, he visibly relaxed.

"Buffy," he said as he stepped back and opened the door further. "Please come in. We've been waiting for you."

There was a gravity in his voice that Buffy did not like at all. But when she entered—Xander following with the box under his arm—she saw Willow, Tara, and Anya sitting around the table in the midst of the shop, stacks of books before them. The sight was so familiar—that of her friends deep in research mode, trying to figure out what she needed to do to stop the latest crisis—that she began to relax a little.

But as Giles closed the door behind her, Buffy saw that they weren't alone. Two strangers stood near the checkout counter, and from the look of them Buffy knew immediately they were not customers. The woman was maybe thirty, her long hair dyed blacker than black, dressed well. Even from across the shop Buffy admired her shoes. What surprised her the most, however, was the amiable smile on the woman's face. It seemed oddly genuine, as though the woman was happy to be here.

The man was another story. His blond hair was buzzed short enough to be unflattering, his blue eyes icy and almost as cold as the expression on his face. His arms were crossed, and he watched her as though she were some sort of experiment and he the scientist who was expecting results.

"Hi," the woman said warmly, striding across the room, hand outstretched. "You must be Buffy. We've been intruding, I'm afraid. Waiting for you, when it looks as though you're all in the middle of something."

"Hi," Buffy replied doubtfully, shaking her hand.

"I'm Helen Fontaine," the woman said, as though it had been a secret up until now. Then she shot a quick glance back at her companion. "This is Daniel Haversham. We were asked to pay you a visit by—"

"The Council," Buffy finished for her.

Helen smiled. "Exactly." Then her face grew serious. "I know your relationship with the Council hasn't always been a positive one, Buffy, but I hope you'll keep an open mind. I'm just glad that we're all working together again."

Buffy looked past her at the cold blue eyes of Daniel Haversham, whose face remained expressionless.

"Where's Travers?"

Helen flinched, backed up a step or two. "Mr. Travers assigned me personally to—"

"I already have a Watcher."

Realization dawned on the woman's face then. She shook her head. "Oh, no, Buffy I'm not here to be your Watcher. There have been numerous signs and portents that lead us to believe something big is happening in Sunnydale right now. You've seen them yourself, I know. Strange killings, the disappearance of the marine life from the zoo, the massing of the sea lions on the beach . . . the attack upon that fishing boat. We're here to help."

Still doubtful, Buffy glanced at Giles, whose eyes were narrowed. He was clearly just as dubious as she was. The Council never just showed up to help unless they had a vested interest.

"Why?" she asked.

Helen Fontaine shook her head. "I'm sorry, what?"

"Why?"

The woman glanced away, then sighed before looking back at the Slayer. "Listen, Buffy, let me break ranks for a second here, okay? I have another life outside of this one, just as Mr. Giles had before he became your Watcher. But this is important to me, the Council and its efforts. To know the truth about what really threatens us from the darkness and be able to help fight against it. That's a noble cause.

"Now as I said, I know your relationship with the Council hasn't always been a rosy one. Your methods are considered pretty unorthodox to say the least. But you've managed to stay alive this long so obviously you're pretty good at what you do. Hopefully one day things will be smoothed over enough that this sort of tension doesn't exist. But for now, is it such a great deal to ask that you take me at face value and just believe I want to help?"

Buffy frowned. "You did say you work for the Council. Is this the same Council that helped me celebrate my eighteenth birthday by trying their best to get me killed and then *fired* Giles?"

The woman blinked, obviously baffled. It was obvious she had no idea what Buffy was talking about.

The Slayer sighed. "Face it, Helen, you're the sacrificial lamb. Travers is a jerk, but he isn't stupid. He knows we're not going to trust him on anything. So he sent you. And all the really crappy things the Council has done to me and Giles and everyone else? Not your fault. So I'll bite. What are we up against?"

There was silence in the shop. Willow, Tara, and Anya were watching as though they were at a tennis match. Xander had gone to sit with his girlfriend, sliding the box they had taken from Ben Varrey's onto the table. For his part, though, Giles stood only a few feet away from Buffy, his arms crossed, glaring balefully at Helen and her silent companion, the grim Mr. Haversham. Under other circumstances, it might have been almost comical, the two men quietly staring each other down.

Buffy raised an eyebrow. "Well?"

The young Watcher hesitated. "Mr. Giles said that you were out investigating. Did you—"

"I said no such thing," Giles interrupted, lifting his chin as he looked down at Helen. "I said that we had been researching demon species who might be responsible and that Buffy had run out on some errands. Now why don't you get to the point, Miss Fontaine and tell us what you know? Something is killing people, and we haven't time for a scrimmage."

"Surely a sharing of information—"

Buffy turned her back on Helen, walked across the shop to sit on the edge of the table near her friends. "Sharing? Doesn't sound like you want to do much sharing," she said.

With a burst of energy and a frantic tone to her voice, Anya interrupted, jumping up from the table and gesturing toward Haversham.

"Does he talk at all? It's kinda creepy, him just standing back there doing that eyeball thing."

Helen softened. "Actually, he doesn't. I'm afraid Daniel hasn't spoken in years."

All attention was on Haversham now.

After a moment, Giles cleared his throat. "He can't speak, or he won't?"

The woman glanced at her silent companion. "I'm not certain, really. Some trauma, I guess, but I've never felt it my place to ask."

Haversham nodded his chin toward her, very slightly, as if to thank her for her courtesy.

"Anya, sit," Xander said.

"It's creepy. He's making me nervous!" she said, but reluctantly returned to her seat.

They were at an impasse built from mistrust. Buffy glanced at Giles and then back to Helen Fontaine, both of them waiting on the woman to make the next move. At length, the younger Watcher nodded.

"The creatures who are doing the killing are from a race called the Moruach. They're truly ancient, children of the Old Ones, left behind millions of years ago, making their homes in ocean trenches and caves. We don't know what's brought them here, but they're savage, practically mindless. Your mission is simply to track them and kill them, eradicate them completely from Sunnydale before more people are killed."

Buffy bristled but Giles spoke up before she could.

"Aside from the Council issuing orders or demands," Giles began, looking at Helen sternly, "I'm afraid there's nothing 'simple' about this situation at all. Whatever these Moruach are—if indeed that's what is doing the killing—they're not alone here. The monsters we've dealt with thus far have been transformed humans, people infected with some dark curse that changes them into sea monsters. Do you have any explanation for that?"

Helen blinked and glanced at the ground. She looked quickly up at Haversham before shaking her head. "No idea. That's certainly not something the Moruach have historically been capable of. But I assure you that they are the real danger you face. Eradicate them, and you'll solve your problem."

Or maybe just your *problem,* Buffy thought. There was no doubt in her mind that, however genuine she might be, Helen Fontaine was holding something back. Quentin Travers had given her her marching orders, and they did not include letting Buffy or Giles in on what was really going on around here.

Buffy turned on her heel, walked over to open the door, and held it wide. "Thanks for dropping by. We'll look into it and get back to you."

Past the two Council representatives, Buffy could see the smiles on her friends' faces.

Willow tsked loudly. "In that file you read on Buffy, doesn't it say anywhere that she doesn't like to be told what to do? It's all in the approach."

Realizing she was getting nowhere, Helen grew anxious and angry. Giving up on Buffy, she turned to appeal to Giles instead.

"Mr. Giles, you really ought to reconsider. You know the work the Council does. Whatever your misunderstandings with them, you are a member, you are a

Watcher, as your father and grandmother were. The battle against the darkness is greater than just one girl."

Giles walked to her, staring down into her eyes until she was forced to look away. "How dare you speak to me of my family, as though you know anything about me or my life."

Then he looked up at Haversham, though it was clear he was speaking to both of them.

"Get out."

With a sigh, Helen Fontaine strode red-faced out of the magick shop with the mute Mr. Haversham in her wake. At the door she turned to glance one final time at Buffy.

"The Council of Watchers is officially taking control of this situation, Miss Summers," the woman said stiffly. "With or without your participation."

"Next time you drop by, be prepared to buy something," Buffy told her. "This is a place of business, y'know?"

Then she shut the door in the woman's face and turned to face the others, all of whom were gazing at her expectantly. *With or without your participation,* the woman had said.

"Hunh," Buffy mused. "Do I even wanna know what she meant by that?"

Chapter Six

Nothing felt right to Willow. It was as though a shroud of malicious intent suffused the air around them. Too much death, too many mysteries, too many questions all at once with no time to catch their breath and find the answers. As Buffy closed the door to the Magic Box, shutting the two visitors from the Council out, Willow slid a bit closer to Tara in her chair and reached out for her hand. Tara let her chin fall slightly, her hair spilling over to cast her eyes in shadow, retreating.

She feels it too, Willow thought.

The two girls twined their fingers together and watched as Buffy came back down the steps toward the table where they sat with Xander and Anya. The Slayer looked up at Giles and shrugged.

"Nice of 'em to drop by, don'tcha think?"

"Should've seen it before you got here," Willow told her, trying to lift the mood of the room. "It was a big ol' tension fiesta."

Beside her, Xander nodded emphatically. "Wow, yeah, so sorry we missed that. Maybe it's not too late to get them to come back?"

Anya looked at him sternly. "Stop that. Every minute of meaningless banter is another minute during which customers are prevented from giving me their money."

"My banter is not meaningless," Xander corrected. "It's—"

She shot him a withering glance.

"—also not always welcome or well-timed."

"We could move to the training room so you could reopen the store," Tara suggested.

"Another few minutes won't break us," Giles replied with a quick glance at Anya. Then he gestured toward the box Xander had slid onto the table. "Buffy, what did you and Xander discover?"

As Buffy told the story of her visit to the Charles Dexter Institute, Willow felt Tara's grip on her hand tighten. Her own throat was dry, and though it was warm in the store, a chill ran through her as she listened. They had faced a lot of horrific things since the Slayer had come to Sunnydale, learned a great deal more about what really lurked in the shadows than they had ever wanted to know, but times like this it was much worse. It was bad enough when vampires were stalking human prey in town, but this was just so much stranger, so profoundly weird, that Willow could not help but be disturbed by it.

The light outside the few windows at the front of the store had dimmed completely, with only blackness beyond, and as Buffy spoke of the thing Ben Varrey had become and the creatures he prophesied, these Moruach, Willow once again moved closer to Tara. She saw that Anya and Xander also seemed to be almost huddled together. *We're like little kids telling ghost stories around the fire,* Willow thought.

Why?

Certainly they had dealt with mysteries as unfathomable as this? Monsters as hideous? A sudden certainty solidified in her mind, but she kept silent about it as Buffy finished telling them about the events that had unfolded at the Dex.

"So, now we're trying to ID two species of water demon?" Tara asked.

"And what the heck are they all doing here at once?" Anya added. "Is it water-demon carnivale or something? I can never remember the dates of the big feast days."

Xander regarded her with horror. "Sometimes I really don't want to know if you're kidding."

But Giles was already in motion. He strode to the table and began sifting through the large pile of books they had all been using for research. The Watcher lifted first one, then a second, and finally a third before flipping through several pages and finally punching a finger at the open book.

"Here we are. *Moruach.* 'A legendary race of sea creatures purported to have had the physical attributes of mythical sea serpents but on a humanoid scale. Several accounts exist that imply that these beings were more than legends and might actually have existed, indigenous to the Pacific islands and perhaps more widespread Pacific Ocean locales. However, the most recent such account dates back to the late sixteenth century, and as such, the Moruach may be presumed to be either extinct or purely mythical. If they ever truly existed, they may have inspired more than one legend of creatures from the sea.'"

While Giles was reading, Buffy had opened the box she and Xander had brought back with them and began to remove small artifacts and old, crumbling documents. Willow leaned forward and saw that on both the parchment paper and the artifacts—shards of broken pottery—

there were crude images that most people would assume represented traditional sea serpents. But the artist had given them arms. Swirling lines wove in and out among the images on the pottery.

"So where have the fish guys been hiding out for five hundred years?" Xander asked.

"Hibernating, perhaps," Giles suggested, surveying the artifacts and picking up one of the parchments. He peered down at it through his glasses.

But Willow was paying attention to the broken pottery. She reached out and fingered one of the pieces, its shattered edges worn smooth by time.

"Maybe they never went anywhere," she suggested. "Maybe they've been down there all this time and just weren't all that sociable."

"So why now?" Buffy asked. "They just decided to pay us a visit? And don't tell me it's the Hellmouth, 'cause that's been sending out the oogy-vibe for ages. Something had to set these guys off. They show up, start attacking fishing boats, drive the sea lions out of the ocean, the vampires out of town, kill a bunch of people, and take all the fish and animals out of the zoo, sharks and all? Somebody or something broke into the Historical Society and stole artifacts from Sunnydale's early days. I'm guessing they were a lot like this stuff. And what about what's happening to these people, like Ben Varrey and that guy on the *Heartbreaker*?"

"Jeez," Anya protested, "one thing at a time."

Buffy put her hands on the table and leaned over, looking now at the pile of research books. "All I'm saying is, Lagoon Boys? Not here on vacation."

Tara had picked up a piece of the pottery and sat back in her chair, away from the others. Willow glanced over and saw her girlfriend's brow deeply furrowed. As Tara gazed at the thing, she tucked her hair behind her ears and gnawed slightly on her lower lips. Ignoring the others for a moment, Willow leaned over to her.

"What is it?"

With one finger Tara traced a curling line that wove in among the painted Moruach. "This." She glanced up at Buffy. "The Moruach don't have tentacles, right? You said this other thing did, the thing that Ben Varrey turned into?"

Buffy nodded. "Yep. Only the humans have tentacles. Which, okay boy, sounds weird."

Tara tapped the pottery shard and looked around the room, suddenly more self-conscious. "Then what's th-that?"

Willow stared at it. That feeling of dread she had earlier had returned and her earlier certainty along with it. She took the shard from Tara's hands and stared at it a long moment, and when she looked up she realized that everyone else was looking at her.

"What?" she asked.

"You've got *hmm*-face," Xander noted.

Giles still held the book where he had found the Moruach reference in his hand. Now he set it down atop the others. "Yes, Willow, by all means if you've got an observation let's have it."

"Okay. But it might sound a little freaky."

Buffy raised an eyebrow. "Compared to what?"

Willow smiled, but it didn't last. A chill ran through her again and she shuddered. "Do you guys feel weird? Different, I mean. With all the stuff we've dealt with . . . I guess what I'm saying is, are you more—"

"Afraid," Buffy finished for her, and her voice sounded hollow.

With a quick glance at the others, Willow nodded. "Though maybe *afraid* isn't the right word. It's just giving me a major wiggins—and I haven't used that word in forever, but it just so fits—like I've only ever had a couple of times before."

"Like now that the sun's gone down, it's never going to rise again," Tara said softly.

Willow nodded. "I don't think it's natural."

Xander's free hand fluttered up. "And what was your first clue? Fish guys, octopus people, what gave it away?"

"There's no need for sarcasm, Xander," Giles admonished. He removed his glasses and slowly sat down in the nearest chair, a contemplative look on his face. "Willow, you think that the presence of the Moruach has exaggerated whatever normal feelings of fear or dread we might have? That they exude some sort of pheromone that's causing it?"

She shrugged. "I don't know. But I think something is making us feel this way. And probably everyone else in Sunnydale too."

"And the sea lions!" Anya said quickly. "Don't forget the sea lions!"

"The hell with the sea lions," Xander muttered. "Or didn't we all see my broken collarbone?"

Willow was glad Dawn wasn't around to hear him talk like that. Buffy's little sister had taken a particular interest in the problems of the sea lions and the protests against the shipping and fishing companies who were not cooperating in efforts to keep them from being struck by boats in the waters off Sunnydale. Willow could relate—she'd gotten involved in similar wildlife and environmental issues in the past when she'd had time—but she understood Xander's point as well. All the better, then, that Dawn was home curled up watching a movie with Mrs. Summers.

Giles leaned forward and picked up two pieces of the ancient pottery. He seemed to weigh them in his hands, and Willow wondered if he was thinking the same things she was: Who had made them, and how old were they? At length, Giles shook his head.

"It does seem likely that the Moruach and these . . . infected humans . . . these mutations, are somehow connected. Yet given the savagery of their attack on the Dexter Institute and that Buffy's description of those events suggests their sole purpose there was to reach Ben Varrey, I believe it's likely the Moruach were trying to destroy him. Or this mutation he had become. I may be proven wrong, but I don't think the Moruach are responsible for what has befallen Varrey and that fisherman Buffy saw. In fact it may well be that the people infected with this 'virus,' if we can call it that, are the natural enemies of the Moruach.

"If that hypothesis proves correct, it would appear that somehow the Moruach can sense the presence of this infection, these human monsters, and are preying upon them."

Buffy tapped the table. "But what's making these people change? What's infecting them in the first place?"

Giles glanced up at her. "I don't know."

"Great," Buffy sighed. "When are the giant man-eating crabs going to show?"

They were all silent, none of them meeting Buffy's gaze as she looked around. Then the Slayer began to shake her head.

"No, no. Do not tell me there are giant—"

"Not exactly," Willow offered, trying to sound hopeful.

"But there have been a few developments you ought to be aware of," Giles added.

The atmosphere in the Magic Box had grown too warm suddenly, heavy and stagnant. As if she had sensed it at the same time as Willow, Anya rose and went to the back to turn on several more lights and turn up the air conditioning. It hummed to life instantly, but Anya did not come back. She puttered behind the counter and cash register, obviously anxious for the meeting to be over and the store to open again.

"Such as?" Buffy prodded.

Giles glanced at Willow. "Would you?"

"Sure," she said, and focused on Buffy. "There were three more mutilation murders in town last night. One in Docktown, but two up the coast on Whitecap Drive."

Buffy frowned. "Ritzy new development? All those huge new money McMansions?"

Willow nodded. "Plus at least six people have gone missing. Four of them were protesters who had been picketing one of the shipping companies over the sea lion thing. The other two were members of the crew of the *Bottom Feeder.*"

"That's the fishing boat Baker McGee's captain of?" Buffy asked. "The guys who dealt with the *Heartbreaker* when it drifted in?"

"The very same," Giles told her.

"There's more," Willow added. "A freighter from Hendron Corporation carrying imported electronics has gone missing."

Buffy stared at her. "Missing? You don't lose a boat that big. They're assuming it sank?"

Giles cleared his throat. "Not yet. The Coast Guard are searching for it. If it did sink, it obviously wasn't inclement weather that caused it."

With a faraway look in her eyes, Buffy reached out and picked up one of the parchments she had brought from Ben Varrey's house. She stared at the drawing of a Moruach for a long moment, then let the paper float back to the table. She pushed back her chair, its legs scraping the floor, and glanced over at Anya as she stood.

"I guess you can open up again."

"Yay," Anya said dryly. "Just in time for it to be almost time to close."

Buffy ignored her. "Xander, go to my house and pick up Dawn. She was having some quality Joyce-time today, but I don't know what she's got planned for tonight and I'm pretty sure she was hanging around at the beach earlier with the protesters. Whatever's going on with these murders and disappearances, I don't want her going near the water alone anymore. Bring her with you. Go talk to someone at the Coast Guard station and see if you can find anything out about the missing freighter.

"Willow, you and Tara talk to Baker McGee. We need to nail down the locations of the rest of his crew and the other guys—the dockworkers—who helped pull in the *Heartbreaker*. They should all be checked out for signs they might be . . . changing. I don't know if there's anything magical you two can do to stop that from happening, but think about it. Otherwise, I guess a regular doctor'll have to do for now."

Buffy turned then and looked at Giles. Her gaze was cold and grim. "I need to know what we're fighting here. Not just my Lagoon Boys. We know what the Moruach are called, but there's gotta be more. I'm thinking maybe I sent the Fontaine babe packing a little too hastily. But whatever. Call in some favors. Find an expert. We need to know what the story is on the Moruach. And we better find out what this infection is, what's spreading it, and how to stop anybody else from sprouting tentacles."

Giles nodded. "Of course."

Willow glanced at Tara and the two of them stood. The Slayer turned and strode purposefully up the few stairs to the exit. She turned the sign around to OPEN.

"Where are you headed?" Willow asked.

Silhouetted against the night, Buffy stood in the open doorway and glanced back into the magick shop.

"Seems to me the vampires wouldn't have skipped town based on bad vibes alone. If they're afraid, I'm guessing they know what they're running from. Maybe the one vampire left in Sunnydale can tell me."

* * *

In the cold stone crypt that was his home, Spike slept the sleep of the dead and dreamed fearful dreams. They were strange visitations for a vampire, dreams. The mind of one so long upon the earth was a treasure trove of memories, of passions and delights, of obsessions and horrors. Some days, with the hated sun high above, he lay in the darkness, and the dreams and nightmares that visited him were far too real, far too familiar. There were times when sleep transported him not to some unknowable realm of subconscious fears and desires, but backward through time. For an immortal, falling asleep sometimes meant reliving events of years long past, disinterring the bones of things better left buried deep.

This day, as the last glimmer of sunlight burned off and dusk fell deeply into evening, Spike's sleep was troubled. On the tomb he had made his bed, he curled in upon himself and it might have been that he growled just a little.

And he dreamed.

Dreamed . . . and remembered.

Cairns City. Europe grew boring for Drusilla, as it does so often. There are times when she craves a rougher trade, when she wants to get dirty. Her cravings have brought them to the frontier towns of the United States more than once, but that's become almost trite to her.

Tame.

And if there's one thing his Dru hates most, it's tame.

Now their ramblings have brought them to the other side of the world and a different sort of frontier town. Cairns City lies on the northeastern edge of Australia and it amazes Spike to find that the king's reach extends so far. How can one rule a land and a people so far away it might as well be another world?

It's a fascinating country, unlike anywhere else in the world. Spike wants to explore Australia.

Drusilla is already bored.

Though the river that impales it carries new people to it every day, and the sails of fishing boats and traders rise on the horizon, she expected more somehow. She'd heard this was a land of mystic tribesmen colonized by British thieves and murderers, and she expected a crueler people. Spike could tell her just from the weeks they've spent here that in Australia it was the land that was cruel, but Dru won't listen.

Cairns City is rough and tumble, with dank pubs and bare-knuckled brawls, frustrated men who hoped to strike it rich on the inland goldfields, only to find they'd worked their way to the bottom of the world for a dream few would claim. Twenty years after the city's founding, it is already changing. Its wildness is slowly eroding and will someday soon rot away leaving only civilization behind. Drusilla senses this and wants to flee from it.

She's had enough of civilization.

It occurs to him, not for the first time, that she is always leaving, growing tired of everything almost as soon as it has struck her fancy. And he wonders how long before he himself is too civilized for her to stay. The thought is a passing one and he banishes it quickly, sloughing it off, but somehow he knows it will return.

This night they are drunk on the whiskey-blood of a pub whore, and Drusilla is grinning suggestively as they stagger-stroll down toward the docks, running her fingers through his hair. He is pleased because she has not smiled in days, wrapped in a blanket of melancholy that had begun to worry him.

Ironically it is only now, when she seems lighthearted again at last—the pirouetting, whispering, mad beauty he loves—that Spike feels his resolve to explore this hard, marvelous realm begin to crumble.

Yet it isn't Dru's wanderlust, for she is fickle. It is

something else that drives him, some unknown dread that makes his skin prickle and the hair rise on the back of his neck. For the past two nights he has felt it and it has only grown stronger. Now the closer they get to the water, the worse it becomes.

"You win, love," he tells her. "Next ship out of here, we're on it."

It is as though a weight has been lifted from him.

In sight of the docks and the ships moored in the river and the ocean beyond, Spike stops and spins Dru toward him. Her smile is infectious and he grins back at her, laughing softly. She nuzzles his neck, whispering to him of the songs sung by shadows and the buzz of blood and whiskey in her brain. And then she stiffens and her eyes widen and her pale flesh seems all the more so, that little-girl pout turning fearful as she glances out toward the ocean.

"They're coming up from the deep, Spike. The serpents are rising. They felt us here, all stomach and instinct, and they're coming. They want to suck the marrow from our bones."

Another time he might have brushed her off, but Spike's learned that there's a dark prescience to Drusilla's ramblings, and this night she is not the only one who feels something. In a back alley the feeling would make him turn, certain that he was about to be attacked. It is the feeling, the certainty, that he is being hunted.

A scream tears through the darkness and curiously they look down toward the docks. It has come from a trader ship, a proud two-masted vessel. It is followed by a shout of alarm and then another scream, this one not of pain but horror. In the light of the moon they can see the shape of a man stagger across the deck clutching his gut, and then he stumbles off the deck and falls into the water and is gone.

Spike begins to walk along the dock. He is drawn by the violence and his own curiosity and strangely driven by his fear. Every instinct within him tells him to turn and flee, the bone-deep dread trying to force him away. But he is a dead man, and ever since the night he died he has feared nothing but the loss of his love. Where logic tells him one thing, he will do the other. Where only a fool would stay and fight, he cannot wait to taste the blood, whether it be his own or his enemy's.

Drusilla loves him for it. It arouses her, the recklessness in him, the wildness.

But not this night.

Her hand clamps on his shoulder. "Spike. No."

He turns to glance at her, surprised, and he flinches at the strangeness of her gaze. It takes him a moment to realize what it is in her eyes that staggers him so.

It is sanity.

In that moment, Drusilla looks completely sane.

Spike pulls away from her, angry with himself for his fear and with her for her caution. He strides to the end of the dock and narrows his gaze, peering at the trader ship moored out in the water. In the moonlight he sees something shift against her hull, and, like a painting that only comes into focus after a time, now that he has seen it he cannot unsee it. There are things there, clinging to the hull like leeches. Things with long flat bodies ending in serpents' tails, and clawed hands with the strength to let them climb though they are legless.

And on the deck, carved from the darkness in a frame of moonlight, one of the creatures stands tall upon that serpent's trunk. Still and motionless it faces him, and Spike knows it is watching him. He can smell the scent of the things, salty and dank, slightly rotten.

From behind, Drusilla darts her head forward and her fangs sink into the flesh of his neck. He cries out in pain and turns on her, slaps her away, sees that her face has changed, contorted with the inner beast, the true countenance of the vampire.

"Bloody hell, Dru!" he snaps.

She quails like a battered child, grotesque and beautiful with her fangs and her savage eyes and that pout. "They'll have our guts for garters, Spike. I can feel it, can feel her up inside me, and behind my eyes."

And then Dru stands and she comes to him and lays her sharp-nailed fingers upon his cheek. She won't meet his gaze, ashamed. But she speaks.

"We're going now."

Before he can reply—before he can agree for that is what he must do, Drusilla holds his heart so completely—something splashes in the water behind them. A second and third splash follow, and Spike turns again and stares as a fourth creature drops off the hull of the boat and slips beneath the surface of the water.

The thing on the deck has disappeared.

"They're coming," he whispers.

And though he knows it means his death, part of him longs to stay. To let her touch him.

Spike tears his gaze away from the ocean and he takes Drusilla's hand and together they do something they despise.

They flee.

And they never speak of it again.

In his crypt, Spike shuddered beneath his single sheet and his arms reached out once, grasping at nothing, as though trying to pull himself out of this dream. Then he turned over and settled down again, and the past swallowed him.

Venice. They have come here again and again over the years, though more than once it has nearly cost them their lives. Spike and Drusilla cannot get away from this city for long. It calls to them with its narrow alleys and waterways, these eerie passages where even during the day the sun does not reach. Away from the broad Grand Canal and its main tributaries, the labyrinth of smaller canals that twist through the heart of the city are nearly always in shadow, the daylight struggling to slip between the buildings before night falls again.

The people of Venice are intimate with the shadows, then, for they have lived with them all their lives. The bright public squares are exulted in, celebrated, but most of the people live in the shadows of the city, overlooking the dark water that rolls beneath each bridge.

An hour before dawn he has left Drusilla, sated on his own body and the blood of a gondolier, sleeping in the huge bed in their hotel. And he walks, and he relishes the shadows, wondering where her cravings will take them next.

Yet as he walks all the joy of Venice is drained from him and an unease grows in Spike unlike anything he has felt in fifty years. He remembers the last time he felt this very clearly. It pains him.

Cairns City.

As he walks through an alley so narrow he could stretch his arms out and touch the walls on either side of him, he pauses, lip curling back in dread and anger. But he goes on.

Step by step Spike walks the stone alleyway until he comes to a bridge that crosses a canal. It is like a courtyard here, the canal turning left on either side, as though the architects of this city let the water in because it desired to flow here and not by any design of their own. Nothing picturesque here, and any gondolier poling through this canal would have to shout ahead at each corner, as they so often did, to warn others of their approach.

But there are no gondolas here at this hour. Perhaps ever.

Spike walks up the stone steps of the bridge. His flesh is cold, frozen it seems, and he has never felt so very much like a dead man. That old feeling has returned so intensely that it feels as though it never left, so familiar, so intimate.

Run, it tells him. Run back to Drusilla.

But in his mind's eye he can see the deck of that ship in Australia, where things unknown swam around the Great Barrier Reef. He can see her standing outlined in the moonlight, this horrible, hideous sea beast, this perfect predator.

And there on the crumbling stone bridge in the forgotten heart of Venice, he looks down into the river and he sees her, staring up at him from the water, her body outstretched, long and thin and slowly moving to keep her still and steady. Her maw is open and he stares at her teeth, a terrible, hungry grin.

He is frozen.

It is impossible. The Moruach—for he has found out what they are in the intervening years, he most certainly has—they live in the waters of the Pacific, rarely if ever straying.

But then she slides from the water, powerful talons clinging to the stone wall, and she slithers up onto the bridge and drops into his path, belly low to the ground, four black eyes gazing up at him, darker than the deepest shadow.

Slowly she rises, wavering as though she is a snake charmed from her basket by a beggar in a Cairo marketplace. Yet it is not the Moruach queen who is charmed.

And she is their queen.

He does not know how he knows this, but it lingers in his mind, entangled with the dread, the terror that tears him up inside, drives him to flee. But he does not, and he can feel her confusion over this as well.

At her full height she is far taller than he. The strange protrusion atop her flat head scratches at the air as if it smells him. Propelled by moving only the base of her long serpentine body she slithers close to him. Spike cannot move, locked in place by fear and wonder, as she encircles him with her body, with her embrace.

Her maw opens and he feels the chill of her breath, smells the stink of rotting fish from her belly, and he knows he is dead. Truly dead. She has captured him without a fight.

From her mouth slithers her thin black tongue; Spike feels it drag across his cheek as she tastes him. He stiffens, wondering what the queen—what this monster—wants of him.

He grows warm.

But it is not her frigid embrace nor his own cold blood. It is the dawn, which has snuck upon them with stealth worthy of its sister night and dipped down into this strange gash in the city whose construction sets it apart from so many other narrow Venetian passages.

The sun rises on the horizon and it sears them both.

Spike shouts in pain and the queen of the Moruach hisses and brings up her claws to shield her eyes. Even as the vampire's clothing begins to smolder, he feels himself released from the strange hold she had on him, set free of both dread and allure. She wavers there, stunned and vulnerable.

"You filthy bitch!" Spike snarls.

Hatred and shame surge up within him, and, though his hand bursts into flame and he can feel the fire eating his flesh, still he lashes out at her, grabs the queen of the Moruach by the throat. The fire from his hand licks at her, and Spike shoves her off the bridge into the water, want-

ing to hurt her but wanting even more for her simply to be away from him.

Then he runs from the bridge into an alley, into blessed darkness, quickly putting out the flames that threatened him. Cleaving to the shadows he rushes along alleys and over canals still untouched by dawn, weaving his way back to Drusilla.

At dusk they will leave Venice.

Never to return.

In his restless dreams Spike turned fitfully, muttering to himself, the salt smell of the ocean in his nostrils or perhaps only in his mind. Though his dreams changed, skittered off into other shadowed corners, less linear thoughts, and images that came not from memory but from imagination, still the queen of the Moruach lingered. The feel of her tongue on his flesh, her serpentine form folded around him, her throat in his hand, that quartet of black eyes cutting him deep, they stayed in the back of his mind, tainting his dreams, a dark thing lurking even deeper than his subconscious.

Again and again the image of her returned to him—on the deck of a trader ship in Australia at the twilight of the nineteenth century, face up in a Venetian canal five decades later.

Her jaws open. She lunges for his throat.

"No!" Spike shouted as he woke, chest rising and falling quickly in the pantomime of breathing most vampires perpetuated, a disguise of life meant to fool the world, and often themselves as well.

He stopped breathing then. In total silence he peered around the crypt, gazing into every crevice and shadow, worried despite the foolishness of it that the horrors of his dream, of his past, had followed him into the waking world.

Then he remembered that she had. That the queen of the Moruach was here, in Sunnydale.

And what the hell are you still doin' here then, you stupid git? he asked himself. *Why not blow town like the rest of the local vamp population?*

Angry, jaw set in a determined line, Spike threw off his sheet and stalked across the crypt to pull on his pants and a shirt.

"Sod that," he said aloud.

There was nothing he wanted more than to run away, but the first time he had run from the Moruach it was because Dru had dragged him, and the second time the dawn had ended things before he and the queen could find out how things were going to finish up between them. She had sought him out in Venice, he knew that. It was the only explanation. She must have figured he wasn't the type to run away, and that intrigued her enough to look him up again.

Well he wasn't going to run away this time. This time he'd find out what the old girl really had in mind. If she wanted a mate, well, he'd have to disappoint her—he just didn't swing that way. And if she wanted to have him for supper, well then they'd go at it fang and claw and be done with it.

Spike paused as he slipped his jacket on. *'Course,* he thought, *wouldn't hurt to have a bit of an insurance policy along.*

Which was when, as if on cue, Buffy kicked the door in. They shared a quizzical look and when they spoke it was in unison.

"We need to talk."

Chapter Seven

It was a vacation Andre Peters had been planning for more than a year—captaining his own yacht on a trip all the way up the coast from L.A. to Vancouver—and nothing was going to keep him from following through. He owed it to Barb, who'd been waiting more than four years for him to take time off again, and he owed it to himself. Today they had gotten underway at last, but the burden of what the trip was costing him hung heavy on Andre's shoulders and he wondered when that weight would ease.

As an entertainment lawyer in L.A., his career was made on his reputation. Taking this time off had cost him a client who'd been with him almost ten years—through the collapse of his first marriage and his wedding to Barb—not to mention potential new business from a major box-office attraction who had been considering him.

He should have stayed home, should have kept working. But Andre had not taken a vacation since his honeymoon with Barb and they had waited long enough. One day he was going to have the heart attack he knew was inevitable. He could picture it in his mind. He'd be driving down Santa Monica Boulevard with a latte in his hand, talking on his headset, rushing to a meeting at one production company or another. The sun would hit the windshield just right and he'd be temporarily blinded, and he'd tap the brakes and lose his train of thought, and suddenly the coffee would be falling from his hand, spilling onto the upholstery, pain spiking through his chest and up his arm, and he'd smash into the BMW in front of him.

It was perverse, he knew, that he had imagined it in such detail.

Andre hadn't told anyone about these thoughts, not even Barb. But it was his vivid imagination that had convinced him to take this vacation, no matter what. One never knew when one would get another chance. What was he working so hard for anyway if he couldn't do this sort of thing?

But still the knowledge of the business he had lost and the things that might happen in his absence haunted him.

With a laugh that was half-forced he tried to shake it off. Andre breathed in the salt air, letting it fill his lungs and expand his chest. He glanced to the east, toward the shore, and could see lights far off in the distance. He knew how long they'd been out, how many nautical miles they had traveled, but he wondered how far up the coast that worked out to. Whose lights was he seeing now? What town was he passing?

Inside the cabin of the *Intellectual Property,* he took another deep breath and sat back in the comfortable leather chair from which he piloted his yacht. There was a ship on the far edge of his radar to the west but not much more than that, save for the eastern shoreline and the boats docked there. The radio played low, a soft rock station that had sifted through the static to replace the jazz he'd been listening to out of L.A.

He peered out through the windshield again and marveled at how dark the ocean could be. It was mostly clear tonight, but there was a thin veil of cloud cover that passed across the moon from time to time, and when it did, only the yacht's running lights cut the darkness.

"Honey?"

Andre glanced beside him to see Barb coming up the steps from below decks. The smile on her face was enough to lift his spirits, to dispel some of the burden on his heart.

"I thought you might like some coffee," she said, offering him the rubber-bottomed travel mug he used in the cabin.

"Love some. And some company," Andre replied.

Barb came over and bent to kiss the back of his neck. Then she slid into the seat next to him. Her blonde hair was tied back with a single dark green ribbon that matched the color of the ribbed cotton shirt that clung to her curves. Earlier she had been in a bathing suit, but it had grown cooler at nightfall and she had put on the shirt and a pair of faded blue jeans. She put her feet up on the instrument panel and Andre saw that his wife was barefoot. He smiled. There was something precious about her like this, out on the ocean just the two of them. Their marriage had been smooth so far, and he loved her dearly, but he had a feeling that this trip was only going to bring them closer.

"I'm so glad we're doing this," he said.

Barb turned toward him, face illuminated by the lights from the instrument panel, tiny crinkles of amusement around her green eyes.

"Me too. I don't want you to think about anyone but me for three weeks."

With the moon behind some clouds, the moment seemed as intimate as any they had ever shared together. It was truly just the two of them. Andre leaned forward and slid his fingers behind her head, pulling her toward him. When they kissed, the softness of her lips took his breath away.

This is what it's all for, Andre thought. *This right here.*

He rested his forehead against hers. Andre could see her skin gleam golden as the moon appeared once more from behind the clouds and its light cascaded through the windows of the yacht's cabin.

Barb glanced to the right, looking out at the ocean, perhaps looking up in search of the moon. Her face contorted in horror and she screamed.

"Andre! Turn! Oh, Jesus, turn the boat!"

He whipped his head around and his eyes widened. The moonlight had revealed a massive vessel dead in the water just ahead. Its gray hull gleamed dully, but Andre had no time to examine it for identifying marks. He swore loudly, heart trip-hammering in his chest—and maybe he was wrong about where he'd have that heart attack after all.

But no, there was no pain. Just panic. He had been running the boat slowly, and now he cut the engine down to almost nothing and cranked the wheel hard to starboard. The yacht listed to one side and drifted in the water, bobbing on the calm sea toward the massive freighter.

"Oh God, oh God, oh God," Barb was muttering over and over, hands clapped to her eyes.

"Hey," he said softly.

She pulled her hands away, saw the ship looming above them and let out a sigh of tremendous relief. Barb grabbed him and hugged him close, and together they stared out through the glass at the freighter. They had stopped short of hitting it by no more than fifty feet.

"We almost—" She cut herself off and looked at him. "I can't believe we didn't see that."

Neither could Andre. The freighter was completely dark, no running lights to be seen, and no illumination on board as far as he could tell. With the moon behind the clouds and Barb to distract him it was easy to imagine he would not have noticed the darkened vessel ahead.

But the radar didn't need the moonlight and it couldn't be distracted by his wife. It should have picked up the ship, but it had not.

"I don't get it," he told Barb, shaking his head. He tapped the radar screen, but knew it was an idiotic thing to do. "It's picking up a ship to the west and now two smaller objects up north, and the coastline. But this?" he glanced up at the freighter. "Nothing."

"That's impossible," Barb told him.

Andre swallowed hard and stared at the darkened ship. "Yeah. Yeah it is." Then he shut the engine down completely and went to the door of the cabin.

"What are you doing?" Barb demanded, an edge to her voice he had never heard before.

"Taking a closer look."

She stared at him as though he was out of his mind. "Like hell you are! What you're going to do is move the yacht a good distance away from that thing, radio the Coast Guard with our location, and when they show up, we're getting the hell out of here. We're on vacation, Andre. We are not 'taking a closer look' at ghost ships that don't show up on radar."

His heart still beating a little too quickly in his chest, Andre laughed nervously and stepped back into the cabin, shutting the door behind him.

"Sweetie, you know there's no such thing as ghosts."

But after he had stepped in closer to hug Barb tightly,

breathing in the scent of her hair, he moved the yacht away from the dead freighter and radioed the Coast Guard.

Jim Laurence was twenty-three and planned to make the Coast Guard his career. There was so much about it he loved. The ocean, for starters, but more than that, he was proud of what the USCG stood for. They protected the shores of the United States of America, they spent their days aiding people in trouble at sea, and they were a vital part in the nation's war on drugs.

It was the greatest job Jim could imagine. He wanted to do this for the rest of his life.

But tonight something just didn't feel right. And if he allowed the thought to sneak into his mind, there had been a lot of nights since that weird feeling had first hit him. Out on the water was usually the only place in the world he felt happy, free. But in the past week it had become the last place he wanted to be. Jim kept it to himself, but he thought he saw a similar anxiety in the eyes of some of his fellow sailors.

Now this.

Michelle Browne was the captain on board the hundred-and-ten-foot Island Class patrol boat. At forty-two, she still had to deal with crap from some of the older guys who didn't think women ought to serve, but Jim idolized her. She represented everything he wanted out of the Coast Guard.

Michelle was scared.

Which terrified him.

The crew of the Coast Guard cutter manned the searchlights, which passed back and forth over the length of the huge Hendron Corporation freighter. It had been missing for days. No sign of it on radar, no sightings at all. The Coast Guard had told the CEO of Hendron it had in all probability been sunk.

But here it was. Solid enough that the metal hull rang hollowly when Jim had thrown a quarter at it, but the damned thing did not show up on radar. Not at all. When the call had come in from the yacht with the coordinates, nobody had believed the guy. It wasn't on radar, so how could it be there?

How? Unless something out here—or on board the freighter—was screwing with their instruments. Their searchlights played across the deck, but there was no sign of life, no sound at all. It was a huge, silent, floating tomb.

Tomb, he shuddered at the word. But Jim would have been lying to himself if he denied that was exactly what he figured it was. He was trying not to picture what they might find inside, trying to figure out what had happened to the crew and why, without allowing his imagination to run wild. It was difficult.

"Over here!"

Spence Jewell had cranked his spotlight around so it shone on the surface of the ocean. Captain Browne started to snap at him as she strode across the deck, but she must have seen the same thing on Jewell's face that Jim did, because she shut her mouth and hurried toward him. Jim was right behind her.

The three of them stared down into the water at a length of polished wood that could only have come from another boat.

"Search the water!" Captain Browne shouted.

The crew was nervous, turning the searchlights away from the freighter, but they did so. For fifteen minutes they scanned the waves but found nothing. Not a single sign that anything else had happened here except for that piece of wood.

When they had arrived at the coordinates, the yacht was gone. The guy who had called it in had said he was headed up the coast on vacation and didn't want to wait. He told them to hurry. Captain Browne had told the crew she figured he had gotten bored and gone on.

Jim stared down at the piece of wood bobbing in Jewell's spotlight and knew where it had come from. The searchlights had been put back to work studying the abandoned freighter. Captain Browne was on the radio with the base. Jim shook his head and went into the cabin to talk to her.

"Michelle," he said, quietly so the guys outside the cabin could not hear him.

She turned, face drawn and pale, and held up a finger to silence him. After she had signed off she looked at him again.

"Captain," she corrected. "When we're on duty you call me Captain."

He nodded. "Sorry." Then he looked out at the freighter, dark and imposing. Jim shuffled his feet a bit before breathing deeply and speaking his mind. "I think we should wait for morning. Wait until dawn. And get another clipper out here."

Michelle covered her mouth with an open hand and stared at the ominous vessel, and he thought he could see her shiver.

"I agree. But we have our orders."

Dawn Summers sat slumped down in the passenger's seat of Xander's car with her arms crossed and glared grumpily out the window. Streetlights flickered across the hood and strobed the windshield as they rolled along the street. They were on Route 24 headed south, but despite its designation it had always looked to Dawn like just another two-lane highway. The only thing that made it a highway in her mind was that there weren't very many stoplights.

Above the houses to the right of Route 24, a thin layer of clouds surrounded the moon. Dawn shivered as she watched it, waiting for the clouds to pass and the moon to shine fully down upon Sunnydale again. For some reason the eerie feelings that had been bothering her the last couple of days were worse without the moonlight. She pursed her lips in annoyance. Sunnydale had always been Creepsville. So why was it bothering her all of a sudden?

Shaking it off, she turned her pique on Xander instead. Once upon a time—back when she had had a crush on him—this turn of events would have had her giddy. A moonlit drive with Xander, him all funny and tousle-haired and charismatic and her all nervous, just like it was a date. But she was over that crush—at least mostly—and with the creepy factor and the knowledge that she was only with him because Buffy had asked him to take her, well, giddy would definitely not be the word for her mood at the moment.

She turned in her seat and shot him a hard look. "So let me get this straight. You're pretty much taking me along so you can keep me from turning into an octopus?"

His free hand firmly on the wheel, Xander cast her a sidelong glance and nodded. "Pretty much. Turns out standing up for the rights of sea lions? A possibly perilous exercise of social consciousness."

Eyes back on the road, he chuckled softly. "Say that five times fast."

"Isn't that all the more reason someone should be with these people?" Dawn said, shifting in her seat and throwing her hands up. "Seriously. If people down on the beach or at the Hendron Corporation are in danger from the Humanoids from the Deep or whatever, we should go down there. Keep them from getting hurt. Isn't that what we do?"

Xander slowed the car and when he glanced at her again there was no humor in his eyes at all, only deep concern. "No, Dawnie. That's what *Buffy* does."

Dawn dropped her eyes and scowled slightly. "But we help."

"Yep. We help," Xander agreed, shooting her quick looks as he tried to keep his eyes on the road. "But that's all we do. We're the backup. The Scooby Gang. The Slayerettes. She's the main event. Giles may be mucho mojo with the knowledge, but Buffy's the Chosen One. She's got the instinct and the skill."

Dawn slid even lower in her seat. "And she's my sister and she wants to keep me out of trouble. No matter what happens to anyone else."

"Pretty much, yeah," Xander nodded. "Why is that bad? You're not a little kid anymore, Dawn-atello. You get this stuff, so why pretend you don't? Buffy'll do whatever it takes to stop the big evil from hurting anybody else, but you're her priority. She needs to be able to think straight, and she can't do that if she's worried you're gonna go all *Little Mermaid* on her."

Reluctantly, Dawn sat up straighter in the car. She looked out her window again for a few seconds before turning back to Xander.

"I guess."

"Good," Xander said.

He started to take a turn in the road and the steering wheel slid slightly in his one functional hand. The other, in its sling, twitched as though to grab for the wheel and he cursed and cringed. His broken collarbone must have hurt him badly.

"You okay?" she asked, more gently now.

Xander slowed the car again and settled his grip. Through gaps in the houses on their right Dawn could see the ocean.

"Peachy," he told her. After a moment he glanced at her again. "Don't worry. You're probably not missing much. My guess is after what happened to that woman on the beach and the people who've gone missing, you're not gonna see a whole lot of sea lion sympathizers out right now."

That saddened Dawn, for she immediately began to wonder what would happen to the sea lions if nobody stood up for them. If the monsters didn't eat them, the boats would hit them or the sea lions would get caught in their nets or propellers. But if she was honest with herself, she knew that most people weren't going to risk facing demons for a bunch of sea lions, no matter how cute they were. The truth was, the sea lions were depending on Buffy just as much as the people were, and neither group knew it.

Dawn didn't mind so much, after all, just hanging with Xander. With her mom on the mend she had spent a lot of hours eating popcorn and watching movies in the living room. Though there were worse things, like turning into a gross, tentacly sea monster and having her face slide off.

The headlights picked out a sign for the Coast Guard station, and Xander slowed and put on his turn signal before taking a right down a short road toward the squat building surrounded by a chain-link fence, with the ocean and the tops of several boats visible beyond. Xander killed they engine and they climbed out.

"Come on, Dawn Corleone. Time to get to work."

"I'm coming," she said, jogging lightly around the car to match step with him. "But quit it with the kid nicknames or I'll totally blow your cover story."

With an easy grin Xander bowed to usher her up the steps in front of the building. "Whatever you say, Dawn Quixote."

"You are *so* dead." She punched him lightly in the stomach and Xander doubled over, expelling a pained breath.

When he stood up again, he shook his head once and shot her a resigned look. "I get a lot of that." Then his expression became grave. "Seriously, Dawnie, I don't think you're going to become an octopus."

Her hand on the door, she paused and stared at him, trying to bury the anxiety that was bubbling up inside her. "Well, good," she said. "'Cause that would totally suck."

They went into the reception area together. A sailor in a white Coast Guard uniform sat behind a desk wearing a headset telephone. His eyebrows went up as he spotted them, and he excused himself to the person with whom he was speaking before putting them on hold. Then he focused on them again, first glancing oddly at Dawn and then addressing Xander.

"Can I help you?"

From the look on the Coast Guard officer's face, Dawn was just glad he had not asked them if they were lost.

"I hope so," Xander replied, very serious and professional. "My name is Alexander Harris. I write for the student paper at UC Sunnydale, and I was hoping to speak to the officer-in-charge about the bizarre things that have been happening recently. Especially about the freighter that's gone missing from the Hendron Corporation."

The sailor's expression changed. All of a sudden he was taking them seriously. Dawn was impressed that Xander was capable of behaving so much like a grown-up. It was easy to forget he wasn't really just an overgrown kid.

But then the eyes of the man at the desk ticked toward Dawn again and the sailor looked doubtful.

"And you are?" he asked Dawn.

She rolled her eyes. "His sister. Look, it wasn't my idea to come along. Blame my mother for not coming home from work earlier."

The sailor laughed and turned his attention to Xander again. "Look, there's no way the commander's going to talk to you right now. But let me see if the executive officer will talk to you. Just hold on."

He clicked back into the conversation he'd been having on his headset, transferred the call to someone else, then rang up someone else to explain their presence and ask if the XO was available. When he finished the call he slid the headset down around his neck and stood, stretching like he'd been in that chair all day. He was a good-looking guy and completely buff, and his uniform was pressed and perfect.

The guy caught Dawn looking, and she blushed and glanced away.

"What happened to your arm?" he asked Xander.

"Surfing accident."

"Yeah," he said. "Been a lot of those lately. The XO will give you five minutes. Compared to the last few days it's been slow tonight, with one big exception."

"What's that?" Dawn asked.

The sailor smiled. "Looks like that freighter isn't missing anymore."

They took a seat on the other side of the reception area and waited until a female officer with her hair pinned up tightly came out to fetch them. Dawn disliked her immediately. The woman was cold and distant and prettier than the female naval officer on *JAG*. It was always annoying to her when a girl had beauty *and* brains, but was so ungrateful about it she could march through her day with a huge attitude problem.

Not that I'm judgmental or anything, Dawn thought in amusement as she and Xander followed the woman up a set of stairs and down a long corridor.

A moment later her thoughts dissipated, replaced by one big mental *wow* as the woman led them into an enormous room with an electronic radar map of Southern California on one wall and perhaps a dozen people at computer stations and in cubicles. They could hear loud, static-filled communications that were apparently going on between boats and from boats to this very room. To Dawn it looked more like an air-traffic-control center at an airport than what she had expected, or even a smaller version of Mission Control in movies like *Apollo 13*.

"Cool," she whispered.

Beside her, Xander smiled. "Very."

"Wait here," the woman said, her tone and the look on her face making it very clear she had no idea why the XO was bothering with them.

She strode across the room to a trio of officers who were clustered together. The man she spoke to was balding and wore thick glasses, and his uniform didn't fit him the way the reception guy's had, but when he looked over at them, he had a warm smile that Dawn liked.

Then one of the officers he was standing with said something to him that Dawn couldn't hear over the noise of the many bursts of communication going on. The XO—for that was who Dawn assumed the balding man to be—snapped off a quick reply, a sort of shadow falling over his face. A moment later he strode across the room toward them. The woman who had escorted them here began to follow him but the XO waved her away.

"I'm Gavin Teller, the group's XO," he said as he reached them, extending his hand. "I hear you've got some questions for me, Mister . . .?"

"Harris," Xander replied, shaking his hand. "And this is my sister Dawn."

The XO smiled at her. "Do you have questions too, Dawn?"

"Loads," she said dryly, arching one eyebrow.

"No," Xander said quickly. "Nope, she doesn't. Sir." He scratched at the back of his head with his free hand. "I'm doing a story for the paper at UC Sunnydale about some of the strange things that have been happening recently. The sea lions and what happened to that fishing trawler the other day. I also wanted to ask about the missing freighter, but the officer at the front told us it wasn't missing anymore. Anything you can tell us about that?"

The man frowned at them through his glasses. They were so thick they made his eyes look bigger than they were.

"He said that, did he?" Teller clucked his tongue. But then his smile returned and he glanced around at the room. "Well, it's true. In fact we've got a cutter out there right now. The freighter's drifting. Obviously we're worried that something's happened to the crew, but I've just given an order for several sailors to board her."

Dawn's throat went dry. Nervously she glanced at Xander and saw that he didn't like the sound of that either. With the Moruach and whatever else was going on, and what happened to the crew of the *Heartbreaker,* the last thing she would want to do was go on board that boat right now.

"Um, is that a good idea?" she asked softly.

The XO frowned and peered down at her through those freaky glasses. "What do you . . . it *is* our job, miss. No offense, but maybe you should let your brother ask the questions after all."

He forced the smile back onto his face, but it wavered and looked hollow to Dawn. The XO looked to Xander as if to say maybe-you-should-have-left-her-home.

But Xander was not paying any attention to the XO, Dawn saw. Instead he was staring at the huge radar screen on the wall. There were plenty of ships up there and

Dawn noticed that a couple of them were Coast Guard vessels identified by name on-screen.

"Where's . . . you said you found the freighter?" Xander asked.

Teller's expression hardened. "It's not showing up on radar at the moment."

"Why?"

"I think the important thing is that we've located it, don't you?" the man said sharply. "Now we can determine what happened to it and verify the condition of the crew."

Dawn was staring across the room at the same group of officers who had now been joined by several others. They were bent over a young guy with a headset who stared at his computer, then up at the large screen and back at his computer. Voices were rising, and now she could separate the communications from each other. Some of them, at least.

She very clearly heard someone in the midst of static say, "There's nobody on board. It's totally abandoned."

XO Teller heard it as well. It was one of those moments when an entire room falls silent at once. Other communications continued, but the people in the room were quiet as they all looked up at the massive radar screen . . . all looked up at nothing, for the freighter was not there. It was invisible. A ghost.

"No, no," another voice crackled over the radio. "Someone's still here. I just saw . . . did you hear that?"

Dawn grabbed Xander's arm, whispered his name. Her heart had begun to beat so fast it hurt, and she bit her lower lip. She felt like crying. Xander gazed at her, and she could tell just by looking at him that he was holding his breath.

Teller had looked at them again, seen the expressions on their faces. "What?" he demanded, obviously very agitated. "What's with you two?"

Xander let out a breath. "Maybe you should have towed it in. In the morning." He shrugged. "Just, y'know, a suggestion, but then, I'm pretty much a coward so—"

He was interrupted by static-filled screams that filled the room.

When the XO turned to run back over to the others gathered around the young communications officer, Xander took Dawn by the hand and they hurried back the way they had come.

"This is getting out of hand," he muttered.

Dawn could barely hear him over the screaming.

The cell was ten feet square, exactly like the others she had been in during her tenure here. Concrete and steel. But it was clean and empty—about as spartan as life could be—and that was good. It kept her head uncluttered.

She hung backward by her legs—hooked at the knees—from the top bunk. Her cellmate, Carrie, sat on her shins to anchor her, keep her from slipping off the bunk. Carrie was a big girl.

Hung upside down like that with Carrie gazing down at her, she pulled her body upward in curls that would have been sit-ups if she had been on the cold cement floor. She huffed with the effort of each curl, elbows behind her head, twisting alternately to the left and right as she pulled her body up. This was good. Becca had been the cellmate before Carrie and had been barely heavy enough to keep her anchored. With Carrie—who wasn't really fat but an absolute Amazon of a woman—she could get a real workout.

"One twenty-seven," she counted, grunting. "One twenty-eight."

"God, you're incredible," Carrie said, gazing at her in admiration. "I can barely do a sit-up. I don't think I've ever known anyone with half your discipline."

"One twenty-nine," she huffed, paused with her body bent upward. "If you make me lose count, I'll break your face."

Carrie giggled girlishly, a sound that seemed strange coming from a woman so physically imposing. "Yeah. Uh-huh."

Her cellmate did not take her seriously. Carrie had no idea what she was capable of, and that was all right. Whatever she might say, she was trying to put all of that behind her, violence for its own sake, forcing the world to conform to her image of it with her fists. Carrie was right about one thing, though. The body curls she was doing weren't about getting into shape or even staying in shape. In fighting form, yes, but she didn't really need to exercise.

It was about discipline.

That was something she had to teach herself. Even as she opened herself up to the world and the possibility that not everyone was against her, that she could find a new destiny for herself, she had to simultaneously pull herself inward, focus her energy on getting through her imprisonment day by day, controlling her temper, preparing for life *after.*

Discipline. Without it, she would not have lasted here a week.

That's what it took for her to focus. For her to allow herself to hope. To believe in herself.

"One thirty-four," she grunted, feeling the burn in her abdomen and relishing it. "One thirty-five," as she curled her body upward, rejoicing in the work of every muscle.

An abrupt clanging upon the bars of the cell interrupted her next body curl. Again she paused halfway through the motion and looked up to see Bridwell, a thick-necked guard who seemed to have been born with a permanent scowl on his face.

"Hey. Tough broad. You got visitors."

Bridwell was never physical with the inmates unless they got out of hand, but he needed a lesson in manners. He had been one of her greatest challenges; if she could hold back the urge to rearrange his face that was a step in the right direction.

"Visiting hours were over a long time ago," she said, finishing the body curl. Then she tapped Carrie's knee for her cellmate to move, grabbed the upper bunk with both hands, and let herself gently down. She faced Bridwell, arms crossed, one hip jutting out. "What are you playin' at, Bridie?"

The guard reddened. "Told you not to call me that, girl."

With a flirtatious grin, she blew him a kiss. "So bring 'em in, these visitors."

Bridwell motioned to someone out in the corridor, and a moment later two people entered the cell. The woman was thin and attractive, and would have looked professional in her stylish brown suit if not for her hair, which was dyed so black she looked goth. The guy was grim-faced and square-jawed, and his cool blue eyes and buzz cut made him look imposing. He seemed out of place without a uniform.

She stared at her visitors, lifted her chin defiantly. "So who are you two supposed to be?"

The woman looked nervous, like she wanted to be anywhere else in the world except here, but after a quick glance at her companion she took a step further into the cell and crossed her arms.

"Quentin Travers has made an arrangement with the state for you to be temporarily transferred into our custody. That is, if you'd like to get out of here for a while."

"You're American."

The woman's brow knitted. "Yes?"

"Quentin Travers tried to have me killed."

Now the woman's silent companion turned to glare at Bridwell, who was attempting to get closer, to hear more of what was being said. The guard shot the man a petulant look and made an obscene gesture. Up on her bunk, Carrie watched the entire exchange intently.

"If you're expecting an apology, you obviously don't know Travers very well," the woman said. Then she shrugged. "I thought you were supposedly all about redemption now. You could break out of here any time you like, yet here you sit. Why, if not to make up for the sins of the past? Well maybe you can take a more active role in that. At least for a while."

"You're asking me to help you?"

"Yes."

"Where's Buffy?"

The woman stiffened, then exhaled, letting her arms fall to her sides. "She's out of it."

Faith smiled.

"All right. Let's get it on."

Chapter Eight

Headlights appeared over a rise at the far end of the street. Buffy and Spike sprinted across the road to avoid being seen, and she held the heavy battle-ax down at her side. They were keeping to backyards and empty lots for the most part, but it wasn't easy to cross Sunnydale unnoticed with an antique weapon in her hands. Stakes were so much simpler and easier to conceal, but she had left the Magic Box empty-handed, planning to head back there before going out on patrol.

Probably still should have checked-in first, she thought as the two of them ran in a crouch through the shadows beside an aboveground swimming pool. A few doors down a dog began to bark. People in their backyard—barbecuing, from the smell of it—shouted at the mutt to be quiet. It continued barking until they had slipped through two more backyards and out onto Dolphin Street.

Turned out Spike not only knew what the Moruach

were, but he'd had a couple of run-ins with their queen.

"Color me stunned," Buffy had muttered when he had told her. "You sure got around, didn't you?"

Spike had grinned broadly. "Yeah. Guess I did at that."

"And now you're housebroken," she'd replied.

It had wiped the grin from his face and now his mood was sour. But he was determined to help her track the Moruach, and so she did not really care what his mood was. Cranky Spike she could take if it meant helping her locate the lair or nest where the Moruach had set up shop. The thing was, according to Spike, he had the Moruach's scent. He had no idea what the other things were—what was causing humans to mutate—but Buffy figured if she found the Moruach, that would be good enough to start.

At the intersection of Dolphin and Gaudett they paused. Gaudett was a main road and there was plenty of traffic on it, both locals and trucks rumbling through town. There was a more direct route for them to have taken, but that would have brought them right through downtown, and once again there was the matter of the really obvious implement of death in Buffy's hands.

A lull opened in traffic and they hurried across the street to the parking lot of a strip mall that was closed and dark by this time on a Monday night. That was helpful. Buffy switched the ax from behind her to in front of her, hoping the metal didn't catch a glint of headlight and bring attention to the blade.

They passed through the lot in front of the darkened storefronts and Buffy looked over at Spike. He'd put his black duster on, and even this close to him she could not see the ax he carried, a twin to the one in her own hands. They had come from his private collection—which she was certain he had stolen from someone *else's* private collection. It had made sense at first not to take the time to go back to the Magic Box, but as soon as they had left the cemetery and started on the trek to Docktown, Buffy had thought better of it.

Too late to turn back now, though.

"Would've been nice if you could kill these things with weapons that were a little less obvious," Buffy muttered.

Spike chuckled. "Yeah. Well, you could try to stake the giant eel-creatures, Slayer, but I'm not sure how much luck you'd have. Just 'cause they're afraid of the sun, that don't make 'em vampires."

"Says the guy with the long jacket handy for hiding lethal weapons. It's a little hot for that outfit, don't you think?"

"Hot's a relative term. Doesn't bother you so much when you're . . . cold-blooded."

"And that's you to a tee," Buffy noted.

They turned left alongside the strip mall, moved between a pair of blue Dumpsters, and scaled a chain-link fence. There was an incline that led up to a broad circle at the end of a residential road Buffy did not know the name of. With a quick glance to make sure no one was around they started quickly down the street toward another busy main thoroughfare at the other end.

"So you told me about your adventures with the sea monkeys," Buffy said, though she was certain Spike had been holding something back from his account. "But you still haven't explained why every other vampire in Sunnydale took off like it was dawn in the Sahara."

Buffy held the ax at the top of the shaft, just under the blade, and picked up the pace. Spike kept pace, falling in right beside her, though she sensed a certain hesitation in him. As they ran he glanced at her.

"You're jealous."

"What?" she scoffed.

"Yeah," the vampire said, smirking. "The mighty Slayer is ticked off because a nasty's come to town that's scarier than she is."

"Are you serious? I'm just pissed they got out of town alive. Like I care about the rest."

"I think you do. I think your rep means more to you than you'll admit," Spike said happily.

"And your opinion matters because?"

"Maybe it doesn't," Spike allowed. "But you're still jealous."

"You were saying?" Buffy said, putting a little snarl in her voice, letting him know the subject was closed.

Spike did not reply at first. They were both silent as they hurried across another busy street, then started alongside the fence that surrounded what had once been the Sunnydale High School football field. Buffy glanced through the fence and across the field, where she could barely make out the black, jagged silhouetted of the burned-out remains of the high school. It was eerie, standing like that, a corpse filled with the ghosts of decades of teenage angst.

If it isn't haunted yet, it's bound to be eventually, she thought. *They don't tear it down soon, I'm gonna end up having to blow it up again.*

"So," she prodded as they hurried along beside the fence. "What's so scary about the fish guys?"

Spike was staring across the football field as well, a deep frown creasing his forehead. He reached inside his jacket and retrieved his ax, letting it hang at his side as Buffy was doing.

"There aren't a lot of natural predators for my kind, y'know? There's you, o' course," he said, a crazy kind of smile on his face as he glanced at her, keeping pace.

He stopped, turned to face her. For a moment he looked down at her, only inches between them, and the blades of the two antique axes gently clanged together. Buffy took a step back.

"Watch the personal space," she warned.

His gaze skittered away, across the field again and then up at the moon. "Right. Well, the Moruach, they eat pretty much anything. So the way I heard it, the Moruach don't hunt humans."

"They killed—"

"An orderly at the nuthouse. Yeah, you said. And tried to have you for a nibble as well. But it doesn't sound like they started it. The orderlies tried to stop 'em, so did you. Maybe you didn't give them a choice. I'm just telling you what I heard, which is that they don't prey on humans. Don't like the flavor or some such, if you believe that. Anything in the ocean, near enough. Some land animals too. But what they like best is anything with a little magick in it, a little darkness. They've got a particular taste for vampire, maybe with a little tartar sauce on the side. They go back a long way, understand. Back to the first vampires, in the days when the curtain was fallin' on the demons' reign over this world.

"But we remember. Vampires, I mean. Humans talk about ancestral memory, instinctual things passed down genetically. Think of it like that. Even if a vampire never heard of the Moruach, he catches that scent and instinctively he knows it's trouble. Some vamps got a better sense of it than others."

"Like Drusilla," Buffy said.

Spike narrowed his eyes. "Yeah. Like Dru."

Buffy hesitated a moment. Spike began to turn away and she grabbed his arm. "The rest of us, we've all been feeling something. But that doesn't make any sense if the Moruach don't hunt humans. And, okay, not even mentioning the mutilation murders in the last week."

"Can't help you there," he said with a shrug. "But

you said yourself there's somethin' else going on around here. Could be that's what's got your knickers in a twist."

Buffy let go of his arm, her lip curling in disgust. "Leave my knickers out of this." She rolled her eyes. "And I can*not* believe I said that. Can we move on, please? It's gonna take all night to search Docktown with you as my bloodhound."

But Spike wasn't paying attention to a word she said. Once again his gaze had traveled across the football field. Buffy looked to see what had distracted him so much, but all she saw was the charred remains of Sunnydale High.

"Hell to Spike? Come in, Spike."

She would have thought it impossible, but he looked even paler than normal. He looked like he was going to throw up, and as she saw the way his lips pressed together, saw the look in his eyes, Buffy realized that Spike was terrified.

His nostrils flared angrily, as though fear was the first enemy he had to conquer. When his lips curled back, she saw that his fangs had begun to elongate. He shook himself, threw his shoulders back, and glanced back at her as he started for the fence.

"Looks like we won't have to go as far as Docktown."

Willow had been surprised to find that Baker McGee's address was listed in the phone book, not because it meant he owned or at least rented his own place—he captained a successful fishing boat after all—but because he was listed as *Baker* McGee. She had been certain it was not his real name but rather some salty old sailor's nickname he'd been given. But no, there it had been, at 15 Chesbro Street.

Given that Xander was otherwise occupied, Giles had grudgingly allowed Willow and Tara to borrow his car on the condition that Tara do the driving. Willow had been offended, but Giles had insisted, explaining that while he had no reason to think that Willow herself was a poor driver, he suspected that Tara might be a more cautious one.

There was no arguing that.

Though it was noted on the map of Sunnydale they had dug out, it had turned out to be more difficult to find Chesbro Street than they would have imagined. There was a warren of small streets, many of them dead ends, in this part of town. Several times they found themselves turned around and back on a street they had driven down before, or taking a turn prescribed on the map to discover that it was not the street the map promised it would be. In some strange way it felt like there were streets missing—as though there were a couple of small narrow roads that one simply could not get to by car.

That was impossible, of course, unless there was some supernatural influence. But as Willow and Tara were witches, they quickly attributed it to bad map-making and signage and eventually realized that one of the roads they had been on several times had three different names, depending upon where you entered it.

"There it is," Tara said, both hands tight on the wheel, the car rolling along at less than walking speed. She tapped the brakes.

Willow peered through the windshield and sure enough there it was, a sign that very clearly said CHESBRO STREET. A sign they must have driven by three times already.

"Thank the goddess," Tara whispered.

"We just won't mention getting lost," Willow said. "Kinda ruins the image of the big bad witches."

"Deal," Tara agreed as she turned the corner.

A moment later Willow spotted number fifteen on

her right. If she had been expecting some sea shack with a boat on a trailer being worked on in the driveway—which was not that far off—the reality of Baker McGee's home came as an utter shock to her. It was in a blue-collar neighborhood where most of the houses needed a paint job and someone to pay attention to the landscaping. Baker McGee's house was a small cottage painted off-white, but with its shutters and trim and front door a robin's egg blue. The house was lit up warmly from the inside and the small porch had a wooden swing that moved gently in the wind, along with the wind chimes that hung near it. The lawn was perfectly manicured.

"It's so . . . pretty," Willow said.

"You sound disappointed," Tara replied as she turned off the engine and unlatched her seat belt.

Willow nodded slowly. "'Cause I'm thinking we got the wrong place."

Tara shot her a quizzical look. "Why?"

"From the information we turned up online, we know he's not married. No children. He's the captain of a fishing boat and he lives alone, Tara. Take a look at the place. This can't be Baker McGee's house."

A soft smile crossed her girlfriend's face, and she tucked a strand of hair behind her ear. "Again, why? Don't be so judgmental, Sweetie. And trust your detective work. This is the address. It's his place. Maybe he's one of those men that likes to putter, take care of things? Just because he works on a boat, that doesn't mean he has to be a slob."

Willow opened her door and began to climb out. "Guilty as charged. Given the men I've been exposed to, though, I'm thinking I can pretty much be forgiven thinking only British men are capable of neatness."

"Not to worry," Tara said as she pocketed Giles's keys. "Forgiveness can always be earned."

They walked together up the path to the front door, where a pair of outdoor sconces lit the three steps. Willow rang the bell, and then the two girls paused there and listened to it echo inside. It was quiet in there, despite the lights gleaming through the curtained windows. Though the possibility that McGee might be infected had occurred to her, only now in the silence after ringing the bell did the reality of it strike home.

"Back up," Willow said warily.

She and Tara moved to the bottom of the steps, eyes on the door. When after half a minute there still had come no response, Willow glanced at Tara and shrugged. She was tempted to walk away, but they could not. Baker McGee was their starting point. He would be able to identify the other men who had been at the wharf that day.

Willow started back up the steps.

"Be careful," Tara whispered, and when Willow looked back she saw that the other girl had a kind of purplish glow around the fingers of her right hand.

"Hold off," Willow said.

Tara nodded, the magickal glow dissipating. They both knew it would be hard to get McGee's trust if they started doing magick in front of him, and were certain that before the night was through they'd need every ounce of magickal power they could muster, and it would be a bad idea to waste it.

Willow reached out to pressed the bell again and the door opened. She gasped lightly, for there had been no sound of footsteps or movement from inside and it surprised her.

But then she saw the man within the house and she relaxed. With his gray-and-white beard, weathered face, and kind eyes, he looked like Santa's thinner brother. There was a sort of bemused expression on his face and Willow did not blame him. He was an older, single man in a residential neighborhood and was probably unused to having attractive college girls show up on his doorstep in the middle of the night.

"Let me see," McGee began. "You're too old to be Girl Scouts. Not dressed conservatively enough to be Jehovah's Witnesses. Not delivering me pizza, which I didn't order anyway."

"I'm Willow, Mr. McGee," she said. "And this is Tara. We're friends of Buffy's."

His eyes ticked right and left and then he gestured for Willow to continue. "And Buffy is . . . running for mayor? Raising money for charity?"

Willow paused. The man was either avoiding the subject or he had simply never gotten Buffy's name.

Tara joined her on the steps. "She's the girl from the Fish Tank. The one who helped you when the *Heartbreaker* drifted in."

All the humor went out of Baker McGee's face then. His tanned features paled and his eyes narrowed. But he nodded.

"Right. Buffy. What can I do for you?"

Willow glanced at Tara, took strength from her presence. It felt sometimes as though they were one person, and when they acted together, Willow felt capable of almost anything. That extended to their magick as well. Together they were more powerful than they were separately; greater than the sum of their parts.

And so she stood there on the stoop and explained to McGee why they had come, that whatever happened to Henry "Lucky" Corgan might have been contagious, might have passed to all of the people who were there when he killed himself on the deck of the *Heartbreaker*. Willow told him that they feared that might account for members of his crew who were missing, and that McGee himself needed to get to a hospital. But not before he helped them track down the rest of his crew and the dock-workers who had been there that day.

The man seemed to age before their eyes, the weight of every word exhausting him further. He seemed to be digesting everything Willow had said and had not noticed the awkwardness of having the conversation at the threshold of his home rather than inside. Willow could forgive him that. It was a lot to take in.

"I know it's hard to understand," she said.

"It's hard for *us* to understand," Tara added.

"But we should kinda hurry . . . if we want to keep anyone else from getting killed."

At this McGee winced. Then he sighed and reached to one side of the door to grab his keys from a hook there and stepped out onto the stoop with them. Willow and Tara moved out of his way as he locked the door and pocketed the keys, then turned and raised his hands to them.

"Let's go," said Baker McGee. "And don't worry about my understanding things. I saw what happened to Lucky and to that fellow in the Fish Tank that night. No way am I gonna let that happen to me. Or anybody else, if I can help it."

Willow smiled. "Then maybe we *can*. Help it, I mean."

They drove all over town and it seemed wherever they went, Baker McGee was known and welcomed. Their first stops were the homes of the members of his crew who had not gone missing. Two were at home and agreed to see a doctor first thing in the morning for a complete checkup. A third man, Frank Austin, had been in an argument with his wife, who had told him to get out. But McGee expected to find Austin at the Fish Tank.

Once they reached that dive, Willow and Tara stayed near the door while McGee worked the room. The Fish

Tank was not the sort of place either one of them would have hung out, and Willow suspected that some of the other people in the bar sensed this, for many of them glanced her way and muttered to one another.

"T-tell me I'm not paranoid," Tara said, her eyes roving as she tried to look at the mirror behind the bar or the windows or the floor or anything but the people who kept staring at them.

"Nope. Feeling more than a little self-conscious myself," Willow admitted.

A strange smile passed over Tara's face, and she turned to whisper to Willow. "They're looking at us like they think we're gay or something."

The two girls laughed softly and Willow covered her mouth to hide her laughter. It was a relief to have that release to the tension they were feeling. But underneath it all the reason for it still remained. When she had realized what she really felt for Tara and not only admitted it to herself but embraced it, Willow had known that there would be times when ignorant people would not accept her, or welcome them. Those times had been mercifully few, but they'd happened. The vibe in the Fish Tank was much the same; they were being shunned because they were different.

When Baker McGee made his way back through the bar to them, the girls shared a sense of relief. Willow slipped her arm through Tara's for comfort and didn't give a damn who saw her. For his part, McGee seemed not to think anything of it.

"Austin's not here," the captain said, deeply troubled. "I talked to a couple of the guys who'd been working on the dock that day. Turns out one of their buddies, turned up missing this morning. They're gonna go see a doc tomorrow, and they gave me addresses for the rest of the boys who helped with the *Heartbreaker*. Plus a couple of bars where they might be. We hit them, we're likely to come up with Austin as well."

"Maybe we sh-should try the bars first, then," Tara suggested. "We can probably get to more of them faster that way, eliminate some of the other stops."

The three of them agreed and soon they were rolling again. Though she was certain he was a tough old guy, Willow sat in the back out of deference to McGee's age. They got lucky at their first stop, a pool hall called Felt Up, where two of the dockworkers were hovering around a table shooting eight ball with their girlfriends. It was almost funny the way they looked at McGee and then glanced at Willow and Tara, wondering what the old fisherman was doing with these two college girls. But Willow didn't smile and neither did Tara. They wanted to be certain the men understood that there was no joke involved in this.

Eventually, McGee convinced them to see a doctor, though like the others before them the men insisted upon waiting until morning. Willow would have been happier if they'd all agreed to go right away, but she knew that pushing would not help. At least they would go. She would have to be satisfied with that.

When they left Felt Up, they hit a pair of bars named after the men who owned them, and one without any name at all. In the latter they turned up a huge, bald, thick-necked dockworker with the unlikely name of Dazy. Neither of the girls asked where Dazy had gotten his nickname, nor how it was he didn't mind people calling him by it. In that no-name bar, the seediest, filthiest place they had been inside yet, they were the only women and subject to the watery stares of tired, drunken men whose collective and indefinable despair made Willow want to cry. They left before McGee had finished speaking with Dazy, and waited for the old man on the sidewalk in front of the place.

He emerged at last a few minutes later, and they were silent as they climbed back into the car. Tara started up the engine and glanced over at the man. "What's next, Mr. McGee?" she asked.

"Call me Baker," he said. "Mr. McGee makes me feel old." Then he laughed and glanced back at Willow, then at Tara again. "I know, I know. I *am* old. But let's just say 'Mr. McGee' reminds me."

"Baker, then," Tara agreed.

McGee nodded. "All right. Next stop's Hollywood Lanes."

Willow frowned. "The bowling alley?"

"Sailors can't bowl?" McGee asked as Tara put the car into gear and turned the car around, heading out toward Route 16.

"No. I mean, yes, of course," Willow replied. "I just . . . haven't been there in a long time."

Behind the wheel, Tara glanced into the rearview mirror. Willow saw her girlfriend looking at her and smiled sheepishly.

"You bowl?" Tara asked. "You never told me you bowl."

"Bowled. Past tense. Past as in my eleventh birthday, being the last time I bowled. And, say hello to the memory of disaster and embarrassment involving the confession of my massive crush on Jimmy Gorka, the assistant manager, and the wild gutter ball that knocked him down two minutes later. It was all tears and mortification and not coming out of my room for days. Ask Xander; he'll tell you."

McGee had partially turned around in the seat to regard her with a grandfatherly smile. "You can wait in the car if you want. Don't want to dig up memories best left buried."

"Too late," Willow sighed. "Hollywood Lanes, bane of my eleventh year."

Tara's eyes once again found Willow's in the rearview mirror. "Don't worry. I've got your back. And Jimmy Gorka's loss is my gain."

Willow grinned.

The rest of the ride was mostly silent as each of them retreated into their thoughts about what was happening. Willow hoped that McGee was not dwelling too much on the possibility that he might be infected, but at the same time she was relieved that he had showed no signs. Not merely because she had taken a liking to the old man and did not want him to die, but also because if he was infected and contagious, there was nothing to stop her and Tara from catching it.

So far Giles's research hadn't turned anything up. Willow wondered if it had been premature, sending away the people the Council of Watchers had assigned. Too late now, though. As always, it was up to them. Together, they would figure out what was going on in Sunnydale and stop it before it got any worse.

She hoped.

Even as these thoughts echoed in her mind, she saw the tall HOLLYWOOD LANES sign glowing up ahead with its bizarre logo of a movie camera shining light on bowling pins that were inextricably behaving as though they'd just been struck by a nonexistent ball. Tara clicked on the turn signal, slowed, and began to make the left.

Tires squealed and an aging Corvette shot out of the parking lot, engine roaring loudly.

"Tara!" Willow shouted.

But Tara was already in motion, cutting the wheel hard to the right, swerving out of the way and skidding to a halt as the Corvette swung too far into their lane, back tires slewing sideways before the driver righted the vehicle. The 'Vette barely missed colliding with them. As it passed, Willow stared out the window and saw the driver of the car glance at them, his eyes wild with fright. Then the Corvette's engine roared even louder and it tore off down the road, the sound diminishing in the distance.

"Jerk," Tara muttered angrily.

"Probably drunk," McGee added.

Willow did not think the man was either. The dread that had been lingering within her changed now. Once she had realized that it was somehow being created externally, that everyone was affected, it had been easier to deal with. But this new dread was different; it was real. She stared at the parking lot of Hollywood Lanes and the front door, and she wondered what had terrified the man so. It might have been nothing strange, of course. He could have called home and found that his mother was ill or someone he loved had been in a car accident.

Somehow, though, she knew that wasn't it.

Tara parked the car in an empty space three rows from the front. Hollywood Lanes was rocking as they walked toward the entrance. The doors were wide open and music poured out. McGee led the way inside. Tara glanced at her inquisitively, and Willow could see in her eyes that it wasn't only sympathy for her eleventh birthday tragedy. She sensed it too, whether she had seen the fear on the 'Vette driver's face or not.

Side by side they walked into Hollywood Lanes.

Willow stood holding her breath as she stared around in astonishment. The place looked . . . normal.

The rumble of balls rolling down lanes, the crack as they collided with pins, could be heard over the music. The walls were painted with Tinseltown scenes and the faces of famous actors and lights flashed in synch with the music over each of the lanes. The place smelled exactly how she remembered it—a little stale sweat, popcorn, and a kind of metallic smell like a burnt fuse.

Normal.

About a third of the lanes were in use. There were several couples and a few small groups of teens, as well as a cluster of half a dozen guys laughing loudly and jeering one another as they bowled. They were down at the far end of the alley, and Willow suspected her group might have found some of the men they were looking for.

The only thing missing was Jimmy Gorka—not that she minded. Behind the counte,r where customers paid and could rent bowling shoes, there stood a woman with stringy black hair and a shirt with the Hollywood Lanes logo printed large on the back. She was turned away from them, watching the action in the lanes.

"Over there," McGee said, pointing to the six men at the other end of the alley. "The guy with the goatee is Shaw. One of the others is Troy something, works the docks. Don't remember if he was there that day, though."

Together they began to walk across the lobby toward the cluster of men. A clatter of pins and a howl of triumph told Willow someone had scored a strike. She smiled to herself. The dread she had felt must have been nothing after all. Of course that didn't explain the look on the face of the guy driving the Corvette.

As she passed the front counter, she glanced over at the woman in the Hollywood Lanes shirt again. From this angle Willow could see her face—could see the way she bit her lip and the black mascara tears that had painted streaks upon her cheeks. The woman noticed Willow staring at her and she motioned with her eyes and the smallest twitch of her head for Willow to go back, to leave the alley.

Her eyes were red and swollen and filled with terror.

Willow collided with McGee, who had stopped short in the lobby staring at the men.

"Baker, what's wrong?" Tara asked.

"The . . . the guy in the baseball cap," McGee stammered.

Down in the two lanes being used by the group of men, there was one among them wearing an Oakland A's cap. He had gray stubble that might have been carelessness or the beginning of a beard, and thickly muscled arms.

"What about him?" Tara asked.

Willow glanced back at the woman behind the counter, who had her back turned now, one hand up to her mouth as though she were covering it to keep from screaming. But she remembered the woman's eyes, insistently urging them to leave.

"That's Richie Kobritz. He's . . . he was the captain of the *Heartbreaker*. He went out with the boat and he didn't . . . he didn't come back. He can't be—"

"We should go," Willow said. "Right now."

Which was when another of the men, who had just launched a total gutter ball down the lane, turned to the others with a grin on his face. The front of his shirt was dark with blood and had been torn open. From inside the ragged fabric a mass of dark, thin tentacles coiled and uncoiled.

As one, all of the men in those two lanes turned to look at Willow, Tara, and McGee.

"Get out!" screamed the woman behind the counter. "Get out now!"

For it was not merely the men in that far corner who were staring, who had begun to hiss, whose clothes began to rustle with the presence of things beneath them, of sharp-bladed tentacles that began to slide out through holes and between buttons. The teenagers in the middle lanes were moving as well, and so were the couples scattered about the place.

Goddess, Willow thought. *Whatever's taken these people over, whatever they've become, they're starting to come together. They all came here tonight . . . like a swarm.*

But that did not make any sense. *If they're all these . . . things, why would they be standing around bowling?* And then it occurred to her that maybe they had gathered because they felt the metamorphosis coming, and they were just waiting for it to happen. Gathered together, waiting to become monsters.

Willow shivered.

Behind the counter another figure was rising up beside the screaming woman. He wore a Hollywood Lanes shirt just as she did, but the front of it was torn and bloody. The razor sharp tentacles that unfurled and grasped at the air around him caressed the poor, terrified woman. For a single moment Willow froze, certain that when he looked at her she would see the face of Jimmy Gorka.

But then she saw that he had no face, only rough remnants of skin remaining behind, replaced by a huge-eyed, horrible visage with a round maw filled with tiny sharp teeth. It raised its hand, this thing that had once been an employee of Hollywood Lanes. Upon its palm was another of those mouths, right in the middle of its hand, a round little hole that gnashed its teeth hungrily.

When the woman with the mascara tears began to scream again, it was this hand that clamped down over her face.

The screaming stopped.

And Willow knew what had sent the terrified man in the car racing out of the parking lot. Other than the woman behind the counter, he had been the only normal human left in the place.

"Run!" Willow shouted at McGee as she reached out to grab Tara's hand, and they fled toward the double doors, which still hung wide open, the brightly lit interior of the bowling alley spilling light out into the parking lot.

Those doors beckoned with a promise of safety. Willow

and Tara were witches, but they didn't have the kind of power it would take to destroy all of these things. That would take reinforcements. If they could just get to the car—

But the open doors were suddenly filled with huge forms, darker than the night outside, black silhouettes that made all three of them stop short.

"More of them!" McGee shouted.

Then the things moved into the light and Willow saw that he was wrong. Whatever the people in the bowling alley had become, these new arrivals were not like that. They had never been human. They were huge serpent-like creatures: shark, fish, and eel all in one, with long arms and sharp talons and mouths filled with rows of teeth.

The Moruach.

Willow risked a glimpse over her shoulder and saw the mutated humans spreading out, preparing for a fight, all of them hissing as they tore off their human skin and faces to reveal what they were becoming. The Moruach on one side, these things on the other.

And we're stuck in the middle.

Beside her, Tara whispered, "I love you."

The way she spoke the words it sounded like she feared it might be the last time she ever said them.

Chapter Nine

Rupert Giles was afraid.

There was always fear, of course. Living in Sunnydale, watching over the Slayer, he never lacked for anxiety. Anything could happen here at any moment, and the girl he had watched grow so quickly from teenager to formidable woman put herself at risk every single night. When he had been training to become a Watcher he had read dozens of journals by those into whose care had been placed the education of previous Slayers. They were all different—some stern and grim, others whose words echoed with the love they felt for their charges, still more who wished for simpler assignments. And yet among the scribblings of these Watchers—scattered across time and geography—one constant appeared, a deep and abiding melancholy.

They knew, as he did, that despite their greater age they were likely to outlive the Slayers with whom they worked each day. Giles was far from old, but he was not a young man anymore. He could see the horizon that represented the end of his physical life and was deeply troubled by it, wondering when it would come, how long he would have, what sort of difference he could make in the world—if he would be remembered.

Yet it was almost never for himself that he was afraid. Giles feared for Buffy, that she might be injured or killed, and for the pain that would bring to her family and friends, and to his own heart.

But for himself, well, the end would come when it came, and he would fight it until it did. He had faced vampires and demons and the ghosts of dead lovers, and they might terrify him in that vital moment when it was kill or be killed, but such events never made his resolve waver. From the moment he had truly dedicated himself to the life of a Watcher he had been committed to standing against the darkness, whatever the cost.

Yet tonight Rupert Giles feared not for his home or for Buffy, but for himself. He could not combat the dread that had settled deep within him this night. A constant chill ran up the back of his neck and his heart beat too fast. He stood in the midst of the Magic Box surrounded by books and artifacts and herbs and everything necessary for practitioners of magick—from witches to magicians to true sorcerers—to cast just about any spell imaginable. There were cases of weapons here and in the training room in the back. Everything he could possibly need to defend himself was near to hand, and yet a creeping terror stretched long fingers beneath his skin and threatened to push him into a panic at any moment.

All of the lights were on in the Magic Box. Any other night, after the shop had closed he would have left only the lights behind the counter and those upon the table where he was doing his research, flipping through books, searching for more information on the Moruach and these other creatures in Sunnydale. But this was not any other night.

He had sent Anya to fetch sandwiches from a shop downtown. It had been perhaps ten minutes since her departure, but those minutes had seemed infinite, the tick of the clock behind the counter impossibly loud.

Bent over the table, he tried to focus on the book he was now looking at—a dusty old leather-bound thing he had retrieved from a box in the basement, a box that had remained packed not merely since he had left his job as librarian at Sunnydale High, but since he had first gathered his things to move to California from London. Every sensation seemed acute to him, the feel of the thick paper between his fingers, the rustle of it as he turned the page, the smell of dust in the air.

A loud clack came from outside the shop, followed by shouting. He glanced nervously at the door until his mind had worked out the noise, realized he'd heard it before: some kid trying stunts on a skateboard, friends yelling to one another.

He stared at the page. His eyes couldn't focus.

"Bloody hell!" he shouted, and he slapped the table so hard the books jumped and began to slide.

Feeling foolish he reached for them, trying to catch them before they hit the ground. He blocked most of the pile from falling but could not stop the thick book he had been leafing through, which tumbled to the ground and struck on the edge of its binding. The binding cracked and tore, the book so ancient that the impact split it in two.

"Bugger!" Giles snarled, furious with himself and with this thing that was influencing him, the dread that had wormed its way into him. He snatched up both pieces of the book and pressed them together as though some magick might fuse them once more. Then he shook his head and paced a moment. "Get over it, Giles. You're acting like a complete prat."

He sighed, shook himself, and found that he did feel a little better. The yelling and anger had helped. Though he knew he was perceived as overly analytical, he did wonder if the surge of emotion had helped to filter the fear somewhat, to counteract whatever was influencing him, causing him to be so afraid.

He took a deep breath, calming down, his heart slowing. "All right," he muttered to the empty shop. "All right. Get ahold of yourself."

Now I'm talking to myself, he thought.

Rather than sit again, he paced across the length of the store several times, peering into the shadows, reassuring himself that he was indeed alone. Then he paused at the checkout counter and laid the two halves of the book open, side by side. Some of the pages were torn free and he tutted with his tongue as he realized it was going to take work to salvage the thing.

It had broken open in the middle of a section on Polynesian water demons. He had been reading up on water-based monsters and demons in general, trying to find correlations to the Moruach but had gotten lost, his eyes blurring over with all of the variations on mermaid myth, the merrows and roanes, selkies and havfrue, the Bonito maidens and the blue men of the Minch. Marine-based creatures ugly and beautiful, evil and benevolent, natural and supernatural, gods and devils and shape-shifting abominations. That did not even take into consideration the behemoths and leviathans, the huge sea serpents of ancient legend. It was an impossible morass of myth.

Idly he collected the loose pages, placing them carefully one upon the other so that he could restore the book later. And on the last page there was a drawing that matched exactly Buffy's description of the Moruach.

It was a crude rendering, drawn by an unsteady, childish hand. But it could be nothing else. The antenna or feeler was there atop its broad, flat head; its arms were long and its fingers were deadly talons. Its mouth was like a shark's, and it stood up on its serpent body, looking as though it would attack.

Beneath the picture, the caption read: *Eyewitness drawing of a "dragon-shark," one of a race of such things reported to guard the caves of the Aegir.*

"Dragon-shark," Giles repeated aloud. It was easy to see how people who had no name for such things might come to call the Moruach that. Their bodies and heads did suggest a combination of creatures both real and imagined.

But what is this Aegir?

Setting aside the back portion of the book and the loose pages, he set the first half on its face and gently turned pages backward, reading the subject headings in bold, scanning the entries on Polynesian island ocean myths. Several minutes passed. Again the dread began to build in him, light fingers playing at the back of his neck, spider's legs crawling on him. Out of the corners of his eyes it seemed to him that shadows shifted menacingly.

He shivered, but was determined not to look away from his work. And then he saw the name again. *The Aegir.* The entry was brief, less than a page, and he read it quickly. The Aegir was a mammoth creature that lived in a trench or cave deep beneath the ocean. In ancient times, according to legend, the peoples of many Polynesian islands worshipped it, or at least offered it tribute out of fear. Other parts of the world had similar legends about this sea monster. Over the centuries it had been considered alternately a wrathful god and an ancient demon, and the book drew parallels to myths dating back to before recorded history. Some suggested it might be one of the so-called Old Ones, the elder demons who existed on earth before humanity. Others passed it off—thanks to many reports of its huge, multiple tentacles—as nothing more than a giant squid.

But that was what they always said about sea monsters.

The Aegir. Giles shivered again, rereading the entry. It was offered human sacrifices as part of its worship on some islands. Those who claimed to have seen it described it as having masses of tentacles . . . that were edged with blade-like protrusions.

Giles could not breathe. He stared at the page. Reached over for the one with the drawing of the Moruach on it.

The phone rang.

He bolted upright, heart thundering in his chest, eyes wide. Then he sighed and shook his head, angry at himself again. With a finger in the book to mark the page with the passage on the Aegir, he snatched up the phone.

"Magic Box," he said, snappishly.

"Hello, Rupert. Not taking you away from your customers, am I?"

Travers. Giles leaned against the counter, holding the book against him. "We're closed for the night. What can I do for you, Quentin? Quite late there, isn't it?"

"Not so late. I'm here. In Sunnydale," the other man said.

Quentin Travers was a member of the board of directors of the Council of Watchers. He could be an officious son of a bitch and quite callous as well, but Giles tried to believe the man was still in it for the battle, rather than the glory. Still, Travers had coerced him into taking part in a test of Buffy's skill that had nearly killed her, had insulted Giles, disdained his methods and his emotional attachment to his Slayer, fired him, and only rehired him under duress. The news that he was in town again was unwelcome, to say the least.

"I won't be asking you over for tea," Giles told him.

"No. I didn't expect that you would," Travers replied. "I'm calling because I've had a report from my people. You met them, Fontaine and Haversham?"

"She's an operative, yes, not a Watcher?"

"True. But she's excellent. Published several books, in fact. A real scholar in her own right. We have great hopes for her. Just as we once did for you."

"Charming as always," Giles said coolly. "What do you want?"

"You sent them packing, Mr. Giles. That isn't quite in the spirit of cooperation we recently established, is it?"

"Buffy isn't going to be told what to do by one of your lackeys, Quentin. You still haven't learned that after all this time?"

Travers was silent a moment. Then he cleared his throat. "The Moruach must be hunted and exterminated. Immediately. All of them. Down to the very last. They represent a danger you cannot imagine."

Giles felt a queasiness in his stomach completely unrelated to the dread that had been affecting him before. This was typical of Travers and of the Council. They knew more than they were saying, as always, but wanted to control both the information and the action that was taken.

"Explain that," Giles demanded.

"Perhaps if the Slayer were a bit more cooperative," Travers replied. "We all want the same thing here, Rupert. Working together we can achieve it more quickly than working at cross purposes. More people will die. I'm staying at the Hotel Pacifica. Bring the Slayer to see me tomorrow afternoon. Otherwise you're on your own. The Council, meanwhile, has already begun to take measures of our own. If you choose not to work with us, I warn you at the very least not to get in our way."

Before Giles could even reply there came a click on the line. Travers had hung up. For a second he stared at the phone, and then he dropped it into its cradle. As he rolled the other man's words over in his mind he found himself staring again at the crude drawing of the "dragon-shark," the Moruach.

Knock-knock-knock!

Giles spun, startled, and stared at the door. Even as he did so he realized it had to be Anya. Perhaps her hands were full or she had forgotten her key. He let out a breath and shook his head. The girl drove him insane at times, but he would be glad of the company. Perhaps then he wouldn't be so jumpy. One thing was certain, though: They had to get to the bottom of all of this right away. His nerves were frayed.

He strode across the shop and turned the dead bolt, then pulled open the door. The bells jangled above his head.

The woman standing on the threshold of the Magic Box was not Anya. She had the most perfect, silken alabaster skin he had ever seen. She wore a light summer dress with spaghetti straps, black with the outlines of roses stitched in crimson thread. Her shoulder-length hair was a rich black.

She was stunning.

For just a moment, the whisper of time between heartbeats, he thought she was Jenny Calendar, returned from the grave. Jenny whom he had loved. Jenny who had ended up dead in his bed surrounded by scattered roses.

But no, this was not Jenny come back to haunt him.

Giles could not decide if what he felt was relief or disappointment.

"You're Rupert Giles?" the woman asked, and her slight English accent dispelled what remained of the illusion. Her eyes searched his face, took in the store behind him, business-like but not unkind.

"I am. And you are?"

She thrust out a hand and he took it, felt her warm, confident grip. Her fingers curled inside his, and she held on just a little too long as she looked up at him.

"Rosanna Jergens," she said, and the way she gazed at him he could not help but notice again how lovely she was. "I need your help."

The ax felt warm in Buffy's hand, almost as though it were a part of her. She raced across the football field toward the charred, crumbling structure that was all that remained—like some horrid tombstone—of the building where she had gone to high school. Spike ran beside her, black duster whipping softly behind him. Swift and full of grim purpose, they sliced through the darkness toward the figures moving swiftly through the black interior of the charred ruins.

Spike sniffed the air. "A few of 'em in there at least. Can't tell exactly how many. What do they want with the ol' place, do you think? Not the safest place to nest, is it?"

"No idea," Buffy said, keeping her voice low as they ran, closing in on the ruins and searching for the best place to enter.

But it was not entirely true that she had no idea. She did not know what the Moruach wanted with the old high school. But a flutter of suspicion had begun in her heart the moment she had realized they were in there, and it grew as she spotted a doorway that seemed relatively intact and clear of debris. Boards had been nailed over it but they now hung aside. The Moruach had torn them off to gain entry.

What do they want with the old place? she thought, her mind echoing Spike's question back at her. Buffy gritted her teeth together, a horrible certainty settling heavily upon her. *What do they always want here?*

With a quick glance at Spike, finger over her lips, she gripped the ax he had loaned her and slipped silently through the entrance into the remains of Sunnydale High. The entire structure creaked with every gust of wind. Buffy squinted, waiting for her eyes to adjust as Spike moved quietly up behind her. When she glanced at him she saw that his face had changed, become feral and ugly, long fangs showing: It was the visage of the vampire, and it told her more than anything else that he was nervous about facing the Moruach. Even afraid. Spike never needed an invitation to kill something, but Buffy sensed that tonight he was hunting out of self-preservation more than anything else.

The door through which they entered had been an emergency exit once upon a time, not far from the principal's office. The irony was not lost on Buffy as she walked carefully along the rubble-strewn hallway. Mangled pipes jutted from collapsed walls, beams and charred debris lay across her path, and she felt like she was stuck inside the corpse of some ancient giant beast. A tangle of shattered desks lay against one wall. They had fallen down through the floor above.

It was silent in the ruins save for the creak of steel and charred wood with the pulse of the night breeze. Ash and debris shifted with each step Buffy and Spike took. She narrowed her gaze and peered deeper into the remains of the school, and it occurred to her not for the first time that she had been hell on high schools.

Still, she'd been hell on high schools. So far, UC Sunnydale had gotten off lucky.

The skin prickled on the back of her neck and Buffy glanced around. What remained of the structure on either side of her could no longer reasonably be called walls, for only sections of them remained and there were holes in those portions still standing. It was a kind of perverse maze of concrete and steel and shadows within shadows. The floor was cracked and in places the crevices seemed to tumble off into some hidden abyss.

"Did a bit of work here, Slayer," Spike whispered.

She glared at him, but the vampire only nodded encouragingly. And the truth was, despite the glee he obviously took in the destruction she and her friends had caused, his words weren't too far off from her own thoughts of only moments before.

Something shifted in the darkness to her left and she froze, staring through a gap between wall fragments. A figure moved through the ruins on the other side of the wall, low to the ground and far more swiftly than any human.

Along the rudimentary path that remained of the main corridor she heard movement and her gaze ticked in that direction. At the far end two serpentine silhouettes moved through a hole that would take them to what was left of the Sunnydale High library. The wind blew harder ,and the building creaked more loudly than before. Buffy and Spike started forward again, moving toward the library. To the right they passed a stairwell and Buffy glimpsed a quartet of red eyes down in the darkness on the stairs, staring up at her.

In some places above her there was only the sky and stars, but in others portions of the second floor remained, leaving a crumbling ceiling in place. Ash and dust rained down upon them now as something moved across the floor above. Then it hit her, how foolish she had been. In his stories of his meetings with the Moruach queen, Spike had spelled it out for her. He had the scent of these creatures, but they had his as well. It wasn't just the Moruach queen who could track Spike from his scent, who would recognize him. . . . They hunted vampires. They had known Spike was here since he had entered the building.

A hissing sound began to build around them as though the long inert pipes were leaking steam after all this time. But it wasn't the pipes. She couldn't even be angry with Spike, for it was her own fault. Not that she would have avoided coming in after the Moruach, but she might have done things a bit differently.

Had a plan, for instance.

A creak came from the ceiling above them, but this time Buffy knew it was not the wind. Along the ravaged corridor she saw another Moruach slipping into the library.

"They know we're here," she whispered.

"Well, yeah," Spike replied softly. "What was your first clue? Us being surrounded like Butch and Sundance in Bolivia?"

"You don't see a problem with this?"

Spike shrugged, lips curling back from his fangs, yellow eyes gleaming in the dark. "Thought it was all part of your master plan. Typical Slayer scheme, ain't it? Get yerself neck deep in it, kill your way out?"

Buffy glared at him. "I hate you."

He only smiled that horrible smile.

Through holes in the walls on either side of them, Buffy saw the Moruach moving. Instantly she was in motion as well. She snagged Spike's arm and propelled him forward, and then they were leaping debris and hustling along the ruined hall, no longer making any effort at silence. There was no need, after all, for the Moruach were upon them. The ceiling collapsed above the spot where they had been standing a moment before, and two of the slithering things crashed down to the floor. Others darted up from partially blocked stairwells and in through holes in the walls. Her gaze flashed around, taking in flat heads and rows of gleaming teeth, long eel bodies and deadly talons, and red eyes, too many eyes.

"I make it seven," she said as she and Spike leaped a

beam that had fallen across the corridor in front of them, barely staying ahead of the Moruach.

Then the sea monsters began to scream in that high-pitched wailing that sounded to Buffy like dolphins being murdered.

"We're goin' the wrong way, Buffy! The exit's back where we came in!"

"The whole place is an exit," she snapped. "But we're not leaving until I see what they're doing in there."

Even as she said it, a pair of Moruach slithered out of the hole in the wall ahead, then zeroed in on her and Spike. They were blocked in now. That was fine with her. Maybe Spike was right after all about her usual MO.

Huge pipes hung down from what remained of the ceiling overhead. She shot a look up there to be sure there was no sign of more of the monsters, and whipped around, back to back with Spike as the Moruach slithered closer, some of them standing high up on their flat serpent trunks, some sliding low along the ground.

"What now?" Spike demanded. "Buffy!"

"Kill your way out," she muttered.

Then she shoved Spike hard against the wall and backed away, pointing at him. "Here you go, boys. Fresh vampire! Get your fresh vampire right here!"

There were nine of the sea monsters in the corridor altogether. All but two went after Spike. He shouted obscenities at her and brandished his ax, baring his fangs at the Moruach as they moved in. Then Buffy wasn't looking at Spike anymore. One of the Moruach who kept after her slithered low over the debris while the other kept tight to the wall, watching for an opening.

Buffy did not wait for them to come to her.

She ran at the one slithering along the ground, ax held tightly in her right hand. Its head and torso rose up, talons lashed at her, and Buffy spun around and brought the blade of the ax down, lopping off one of the Moruach's arms. It opened its huge maw and that deafening shriek pounded her ears. In that moment of distraction it whipped its tail around and struck her in the head. The blow was fierce, so much force behind it that if she had not seen it coming, had not rolled with it, it would surely have broken her neck.

But she did see it coming. It struck her and she moved with the force of it, spun around, letting the ax handle slide in her hand so that it was at its greatest length, and as she turned she stepped in toward the Moruach that had struck her. Its mouth was open in some combination of vengeful screech and primal hunger, and the ax blade went into its mouth and cut off its head from the tongue up.

The one that had slunk along the wall lunged at her from the side before the dead one had hit the ground. She was off balance, a perfect target and she did the only thing she could do. Buffy fell forward, tumbled into a somersault across the floor and immediately she regretted it. Down low like this was the Moruach's territory. They were belly-draggers, built to fight down here.

As she spun up to face it the thing was already gnashing its huge shark's jaws as it came for her. Its arms were out, talons reaching for her, and she had no time to bring the ax around.

Buffy snapped a sidekick up into its gut, then smashed it in the face with the haft of the ax. It lashed at her and caught her shoulder with two talons, slicing her skin. She didn't even feel it, adrenaline coursing through her. Behind her was the beam that she and Spike had leaped over, but most of the Moruach had slid under it.

Perfect, she thought.

In one swift motion she turned and dove under the beam, ax in hand. She heard the Moruach choke off what must have been a snarl for their kind, knew it would follow her any second. Buffy pulled herself up and leaped on top of the beam.

When the Moruach slid under it she brought the ax down, cleaving its head right down the middle between those two sets of red eyes.

Spike was roaring at her, fury making him almost rabid.

"You stupid Slayer bint, what are you playin' at?" the vampire screamed.

Buffy launched herself over the beam again and saw that the fight had moved closer to the hole in the wall that led into the library. That was good. The actual entrance was barricaded with fallen debris, and she wanted to see through that hole, into what was left of that room.

First, though, she supposed she ought to help Spike.

He had killed two of the Moruach already, the ground slick with their dark blood. Five left to go, and they had already slashed him badly. Somehow he had eluded further injury, but now they had him cornered and even as he swung the ax, lodging it in the chest cavity of another of the creatures, one of them raked his face with its claws.

Ax still clutched in her right hand, Buffy leaped up and grabbed a thick exposed pipe on the ceiling, threw her legs over the shoulders of one of the Moruach, closed its head in a scissors-grip, and twisted hard. The crack of its neck snapping echoed in the ruined school. The Moruach had noticed her now, several of them turning away from Spike.

Buffy pulled her body up, hooked her legs over the pipe, and let herself swing down with the ax held in both hands. She cut the face of another Moruach in two. Then she pulled her legs free and flipped over, landing on both feet in the debris. The Moruach were on her instantly and she felt claws slash her back and leg, but she buried the ax in the shoulder of another of the monsters. It let loose that piercing wail and she thought her ears might be bleeding.

The ax came away from her hands, but she threw lightning punches and leaped up into a high kick that drove one of them back toward the library. Spike had killed another, and so there was only this one remaining at last.

It glared at them with those red eyes, and then it fled, serpentine trunk twisting on the floor and propelling it with remarkable speed through the hole in the wall.

Spike rounded on her. Blood dripped from a gash in his forehead, and his clothes were torn in half a dozen places revealing wounds beneath. When he moved toward her, he was limping slightly.

"What are you playin' at, Slayer?" he snarled again. "Nearly got me killed."

Buffy raised an eyebrow. "I thought you were a big boy, Spike. Figured you could handle yourself. Besides, you were what they wanted. If I hadn't used you to distract them, we might both be dead now. Or did you miss that there were a lot of sea monkeys?"

"So I'm bait now?" he asked, still infuriated.

"Pretty much." Buffy hurried away from him, toward the hole in the wall.

Behind her, Spike wasn't through. "Look at me!" he cried. "I'm a mess, Slayer. Got blood all over me. These clothes are ruined. Look at this coat!"

Buffy had seen the damage to the coat already. It was in shreds. It seemed to her, however, that Spike did not fully appreciate the protection the coat had afforded him. If not for it, he would have been wounded far worse than he was now.

"You're a vampire," she said. "You'll heal. So, are you gonna just stand there and whine or are you coming?"

He muttered under his breath, and she glanced back

just in time to see him whip off the tattered coat and leave it behind in the rubble. Bloody slashes on his right arm had already begun to heal.

Just beyond the edge of that hole in the wall Buffy paused, took a breath, and leaped through it with the ax in her hand. She landed in a crouch on blackened, pitted concrete that seemed to have melted and then hardened again. It was not completely dark in the ruined library, however. Moonlight streamed into the ruins from above and she could see that the room was empty. There had been other Moruach here, she was certain of that, but they had fled when she and Spike had turned the tables in the fight out in the corridor. Fled in too much of a hurry to bother putting out the torches.

And they had left behind traces of their presence.

There were two corpses in the room. One had been a human being once upon a time, a police officer or security guard from the look of what remained of his uniform. The other corpse wasn't human. It was a sea turtle, an absolutely huge thing with a shell the size of a small bureau. The turtle lay on its back, the soft underbelly of its shell had been torn open and its innards strewn around the room.

Spike whistled appreciatively. "Someone's been havin' a grand old time."

Buffy frowned and moved past the dead to where Spike now stood in the center of the room. A large area had been cleared of debris, and an enormous symbol had been painted on the rough concrete in slashes and spatters of blood. It was not the sort of pentagram or druidic runes she was used to; this was a strange design that looked almost like a madman's geometry, created not from swirls and circles but from hard edges and straight lines and weird configurations. Around it were strings of tiny figures that might have been letters or symbols or hieroglyphics.

Spike inhaled deeply. "Blood's fresh."

Buffy nodded, pointing to the scrawl on the floor. "Looks like we interrupted something. I don't think they finished."

"Finished what?" Spike asked. "They tryin' to summon something, then?"

She shot him a look that she hoped made him realize how dense he was being. "Where are we, Spike? Think about it. They're trying to open the Hellmouth."

His lips parted in a sort of pout and he stiffened. "Well, yeah." He sneered. "'Course I knew that. Just wanted to see if you were on your toes."

"Yeah, thanks. Good thing I've got you around."

"That's the truth. Here now, though, Slayer. Isn't there a way to close the bleedin' thing forever? Just shut it down, turn off the magnet that keeps pulling all the loonies into town?"

She raised an eyebrow. "What brought *you* here?"

"Well, sure, but I didn't try to end the sodding world, now did I? Helped you save it at least once, in fact."

Buffy regarded him a moment and then stared back at the strange markings on the floor and the mix of human and turtle blood. "We do what we can. But there are just places in the world where the stuff that separates us from them gets worn down. Thin. Guess it doesn't help that there's so much of that kind of traffic around here."

Once more she glanced up at him. "Go find a camera."

Spike narrowed his eyes. "What for?"

"If this spot is part of whatever they're doing, I'm gonna bring the place down. The roof, the walls, make it harder for them to get at. We'll have to keep watch over it too. But I want pictures of this for Giles before I do that."

"And there's a reason you can't get your own camera? 'Cause maybe you didn't notice, but I'm the one with the limp and you've got a perfect pair of legs on you."

She stared at him. "You want to stay here by yourself? Now that they've got your scent, know you're here? Be my guest."

"On second thought, I'll just go, shall I?"

"Thought you might."

The outer wall of the library was riddled with holes where portions of it had either collapsed or been blown out by the explosion that had destroyed the school. The Moruach had not had any difficulty finding a way out when they decided to retreat. Spike paused cautiously before leaving, sniffing the air until he was satisfied there were no Moruach in the immediate vicinity. He slipped out without another word.

Buffy settled down to wait on the concrete, arms resting upon her knees. Her gaze drifted around the circle, ignoring the dead man and the eviscerated turtle. Something kept drawing her eyes, however: A large chunk of debris that gleamed in the flickering torchlight. It wasn't concrete.

She got up and went over to it, picked it up, and realized that it was a broken piece of pottery, inscribed with strange images. With a start she knew that she had seen other pieces of the thing—it had to have come from the same bowl or plate or whatever that she had found pieces of in Ben Varrey's house.

The break-in at the Historical Society, she thought. Supposedly the only things stolen had been artifacts dating back before the founding of Sunnydale. Buffy turned the thing over in her hands. The crude engraving showed long lines that might have been tentacles, just as the other one had. But this one also showed part of the thing to which the tentacles were attached.

It was hideous, with too many eyes and a massive

round mouth filled with jagged teeth, tentacles jutting from almost its entire surface. A huge pseudopod extruded from beneath it almost like a tail or a single leg. There was no head, simply a fat body with strange, unnatural contours. Buffy made the connection immediately to the horrible metamorphosis of Ben Varrey and Lucky and the man in the green tie at the Fish Tank.

But that wasn't the worst of it.

The worst part was that there was a Moruach engraved right beside it. Several of them, in fact. And in comparison to this thing, they were tiny. Lilliputians.

"Oh," she said dryly. "Marvelous."

She wondered how quickly her mother could sell the house so they could move somewhere—anywhere—else. But it was an idle thought, a mere bit of whimsy. Buffy Summers wasn't going anywhere. She was the Slayer.

But how the hell do you slay that? she thought, staring at the broken pottery again.

Buffy sat in the ruins of her past and waited for Spike to return. The torches began to burn lower and the shadows shifted around her, and the dread crept back into her bones, slid under her skin.

In the gathering dark, Buffy shuddered.

Chapter Ten

Willow felt Tara's grip tighten and the two of them stood close together. A wind kicked up around them from out of nowhere—or nowhere on Earth—and it blew their hair across their faces. Instinctively they drew on each other, magickal energy coursed through them and from one to the other, and that familiar verdant light glowed around the place where their fingers were twined together.

When they were joined like this, the magick flowing through them, it was the most intimate connection either of them had ever known. Sometimes they could cast spells jointly, without communicating their plans with words or even thoughts but with feelings.

Baker McGee shouted at them to come away, to run.

Willow and Tara stood their ground, a preternatural calm falling over them both. Tara used her free hand to push the hair away from her eyes, and Willow could feel the motion all through her.

The Moruach rushed at them, huge horrifying nightmare beasts with bodies dripping wet and exuding a sewer stench, leaving a trail of slime behind. There were two at first and then four and finally a total of five.

Together the witches raised their hands and they were bathed in that green light; the wind inside Hollywood Lanes swirled around them now as though they were the eye of the storm. And of course they were. Perhaps it was instinct or intuition that allowed them to work together so seamlessly or perhaps Willow truly could feel Tara's mind touching her own, but at that moment they opened their mouths simultaneously and shouted the spell.

"Emptum articulus!"

Willow felt as though something had been torn out of her chest and she shouted in pain only to find that Tara cried out beside her. The wind turned hot and flashed past them, blowing at them from behind, their hair flying around and their clothes whipping against their bodies. The spell was difficult, something they had talked about but never tried before. But the power of it surged across the room, and a bright blue light engulfed the serpentine sea creatures and it flashed . . .

And the Moruach were gone.

Baker McGee shouted the Lord's name. "How the hell didja do that?"

Weak-kneed from the effort, Willow could barely stand, but somehow she and Tara stumbled toward the door. Far enough to see the Moruach emerging from an open sewer grating in the parking lot and heading for the building. That was the gist of the spell . . . it did not teleport an enemy, but rather turned back the clock around them, bought the witch or sorcerer time.

"But not enough time," Tara rasped, clutching her chest.

"We won't be doing that again," Willow said.

Still holding hands they gestured together at the front doors, which closed and locked. They couldn't get out that way.

When they turned around, the mutated humans were slowly moving toward them, all hissing from their many vicious mouths. Tendrils whipped the air, the sharp nodes along their lengths whistling like a thousand tiny scythes. The dockworkers and sailors and the teenagers and the middle-aged couples were converging behind the creature in the Hollywood Lanes shirt, which had come out from behind the counter. All things considered, Willow would rather have to face the Moruach than these infected, transformed people. The Moruach were just monsters, probably demons. These other things had once been human.

"The woman . . . the woman behind the counter," Tara said, voice quavering.

Willow remembered the sight of the horrible mouth on the palm of the other employee's hand as the monstrous creature grabbed the woman's face. She shook her head. The woman had fallen down behind the counter now. It was too late to save her. Tears threatened the corners of her eyes and she bit her lip to fight them back. There was Tara to think of still and Captain McGee as well. If she thought the spell to turn back the clock would have affected a dead woman, she would have tried it, but it simply didn't work that way.

"Back up," Willow told Tara.

Baker McGee had stepped up beside her and he acted as though he might try to shield her with his body as the three of them all moved backward toward a corner where a huge air hockey table and several vending machines hummed low, their electricity slightly audible even over the music and the hiss of the creatures.

"No windows," Tara said. "Willow, there aren't any w-windows back here."

Willow glanced around and found that Tara was right. But there were a pair of restrooms side by side, men's and women's. Tara saw where her gaze was going and nodded, but in that moment the tentacled man in the torn, bloody Hollywood Lanes shirt and a thing with ravenous mouths on its forehead and cheeks—a thing that had once been a teenage girl—began to circle around to their left, cutting off access to the bathrooms.

The front doors shook as the Moruach arrived again, the eel-like sea creatures hammering against them. One of the doors cracked. The locks creaked, wood splintered, and, like a battering ram, the head of one of the Moruach smashed a hole right through the metal door. Its quartet of eerie amber eyes scanned the interior, and then it opened its mouth and screamed in a voice that chilled Willow to her core.

"Up for more magick?" Tara asked breathlessly. Her nose had begun to bleed from the effort that one difficult spell had taken.

"Can you?" Willow asked.

Grimly, Tara nodded.

Willow let her hand go and they separated, standing apart from one another. McGee stared at them, wide-eyed, and then at the monstrous humans whose flesh was molting off to reveal hideous forms beneath. With a flick of her wrist, Willow levitated a trio of bowling balls from one of the lanes. She had reached the point where it should have been easy, but the strain cost her now. Still she tugged them, using her magick to slingshot the balls at their attackers. Her aim was flawless. The balls struck a pair of dockworkers and a teenaged boy in the back of their heads and they all staggered. One of the dockworkers even fell down, head hanging at a disturbing angle.

But the tentacles kept moving like a nest of snakes on each of their chests, and Willow realized that they might no longer be thinking with whatever was left of their human brains.

Tara performed the same spell. Her aim was not as accurate, but it was enough to drive back a couple of the things. They'd bought a few more seconds, that was all. Which was when the front doors exploded inward under the Moruach assault and the creatures slid into the Hollywood Lanes for a second time. They all screamed now with that piercing wail and Willow cringed. Baker McGee swore and clapped his hands over his ears.

This time Willow, Tara, and McGee were not in the Moruach's way and the creatures did not even glance at them. They swept in, terrifyingly fast on their long, flat eel bodies, and they attacked the other monsters, the ones who had once been human. The Moruach began to tear them apart.

Willow glanced over at the bathrooms and knew that it was now or never. There were two of the creatures still in the way. She grabbed Tara's hand and they stared at the monsters, and Willow wondered if the one in the Hollywood Lanes shirt really was Jimmy Gorka. She decided she didn't want to know.

"Exussum!" they shouted.

The two creatures began to shriek as they burst into flames.

"Let's go!" Tara snapped, and she grabbed McGee's hand and hauled the old man with her as they ran for the women's bathroom. McGee didn't balk at the choice of gender.

Willow slammed the door open, held it so the others could follow, then glanced back into the bowling alley to see that their departure had attracted no attention at all. It was war there, in the lanes. Blood was being spilled, monsters were screaming, and she could not help grieving for both the humans who had suffered so and were now dying and for the Moruach themselves. Whatever had brought them to this savagery, it was tragic and ugly and it made her want to be sick.

"Good," McGee muttered behind her. "Let the bastards kill each other. Let's get out of here."

Flinching, Willow turned to look at him. Tara was already on her tiptoes opening the window on the other side of the bathroom. It would be just wide enough for McGee to squeeze through, and simple enough for the girls.

Tara glanced at her, silently urging her to hurry.

As they slipped out through the window one by one, McGee kept glancing at them, staring. Outside they raced across the parking lot to Giles's car, and Tara slid behind the wheel. The engine started easily and its growl was comforting. Willow remembered the driver who had fled the parking lot in a tire-squealing hurry and now she knew why.

McGee turned around in the front seat as Tara peeled out of the parking lot as fast as Giles's car would take them.

"I've seen some unbelievable things," McGee said. "But in all my life nothing like I've seen in the past week. First that other girl, Buffy, the things she can do. And these monsters. And now you two. What the hell *are* you?"

Tara reached around into the back seat to take her hand and Willow clasped it gratefully, comfort and relief in that contact. McGee had not said it cruelly or even fearfully, only in amazement. She considered explaining and then thought better of it. Willow smiled at the old man.

"Just a coupl'a girls trying to keep you alive."

The Talisker House had stood atop the bluff at Smuggler's Cove since before Sunnydale had come into existence. It was, in truth, the reason the spot was called

Smuggler's Cove to begin with. William Talisker was of Scots descent, though his family had been in America before there had been an America to speak of. The youngest of four sons, he had come west after the discovery of gold in California in 1848. Unlike so many prospectors, William Talisker had found a cure for gold fever.

He had gotten rich.

By the time the mandate had come down from the federal government to build a transcontinental railroad, he was in place to provide some of the services necessary on the Pacific end. With the outbreak of the Civil War, most of the railroad-building efforts were concentrated on the west, and in 1862 the northern government ordered a line built west from Sacramento. William Talisker only grew richer.

Upon his retirement in 1879 he went in search of a place to grow old in peace. A place where he could look out at the Pacific Ocean, a place where the same sort of growth he had thrived upon and even helped to foster had not yet reached. He found that place in a small hamlet in the southern part of the state where only a handful of families had settled thus far. Upon a bluff two hundred feet above the gentle surf of a narrow cove, William Talisker had a formidable home built of stone. From among the few families already settled nearby he took a new young wife, his third. The first he had left behind when he'd come west and promptly forgotten about. The second had died while he had been overseeing the construction of the railroad.

Sarah Talisker was nineteen when she married William, who was fifty-four and ailing, yet she bore him two sons before he died some years later. The Talisker boys—Billy and Sam—were a vital part of Sunnydale during the time when it officially became a township and elected its first mayor, Richard Wilkins. The boys were natural explorers, investigating every dusty corner of the sprawling house and the grounds around it, getting to know everyone in town, every hill and field of Sunnydale. They were heirs to a great fortune but as children they rambled the way boys often did.

At the edge of their property the Talisker boys discovered a crevice in the earth. Within that crevice—left there by the drift of continents or the passing of glaciers or some less tumultuous natural event they could not fathom—they found a cavern. A system of caves, in fact, connected by splits in the rock and earth that often passed for natural tunnels. For months they spent each day, every available minute, exploring the caves and tunnels with lanterns and inventing stories about monsters that must live inside them. Over time they found to their delight that if they were determined enough they could follow the path all the way down inside the cliff face to emerge only a few feet above the ocean, in that quiet cove where the coast had formed a cleft.

They grew up, of course, and they visited the warren of caves less and less. Sarah died eventually, but by then the boys were hardly boys any longer. They were men with wives and children of their own, with tastes and predilections that often led them into trouble . . . and debt. Their debtors—which included Mayor Wilkins and other influential men in the town—were not as forgiving as two boys who had grown up so loved, so favored by their neighbors, might have hoped.

Samuel and William Talisker Jr. were forced to find other ways to earn money, and they found that avenue of income when the American Congress passed a law prohibiting the sale of alcohol. Prohibition, it was called. Sam and Billy called it hitting the jackpot. They remembered the cove and the caverns, the tunnels that came up to the backyard of the house their father had built.

The house was expanded, a new wing built that covered the crevice, the entrance to those caves. It was simple enough then to make contact with Canadian businessmen whose whiskey profits were being decimated by Prohibition and to begin smuggling whiskey into southern California on boats that would anchor in the cove and bring shipments through the cave, up through two hundred feet of stone and earth via those tunnels, and into the Talisker home.

For nearly half a year Sam and Billy made the kind of money that they could only have dreamed about, but which their father would have remembered well from his Gold Rush days. They lived the high life, hosting parties that were talked about from Los Angeles to San Francisco and beyond. Stars of the burgeoning film industry, senators and governors, and foreign diplomats were all in attendance.

Those golden days lasted right up until the FBI broke down the front doors and took the operation apart . . . and the Talisker boys off to prison. They had received a tip, they said, from concerned citizens of Sunnydale. Though they had no proof, in retrospect Sam and Billy knew that among those concerned citizens had been the now reclusive Mayor Wilkins. It would have been wiser, they realized, to have cut the Mayor in on the action. But by the time they understood their peril it was too late.

The house was sold out from under their wives and children, and the Talisker boys both died in prison, as paupers. Sam was killed in a brawl with a guard. Billy died of cancer two years later. Their widows, Eileen and Bernadette, were often heard to say to one another and whomever would listen that it felt like they were cursed. A ridiculous notion, the residents of Sunnydale thought. It was bad luck, that was all. The boys had been a bit indulgent, but really, it was just plain bad luck.

The property had changed hands half a dozen times since then. While many of those owners had only a vague idea of the house's history, they continued to call it the Talisker House because it had a plaque beside the front door declaring that to be its name and noting the date of the completion of its construction. The current owners, Rick and Polly Haskell, wanted to know more. The Haskells had thoroughly investigated the house's history, had been fascinated by such things in the same way that people who showed up on the Home & Garden Channel on cable always were.

In addition to its colorful history, Rick and Polly loved the atmosphere in the old house, the size of it, and the view of the Pacific from the top of the bluff. Rick had inherited sizeable wealth from his father and was an attorney himself, and though they had been married seven years they had decided only now that it was time to settle down to the business of having children. What an extraordinary place this house was.

They would have to be careful about the bluff, of course, perhaps put a fence up to keep their someday children from getting too close and falling by accident. Also the basement of the wing that jutted oddly from the back of the house had been let go to ruin for more than fifty years, had even been boarded up, and they would have to take care that it was safe back there. Maybe even restore it, though of course if there was any truth to the stories about smuggling they would make certain any secret passage through the cliffs was filled with cement and sealed up. It was too dangerous to leave open.

Soon, they vowed to each other. They would take care of that wing just as soon as possible.

At the moment they Haskells lay sleeping in their mahogany sleigh bed, the TV droning on in the background because Rick had forgotten to set the timer. Even in the midst of a half-formed dream about her long dead grandfather, Polly could hear the television. When the ads came on they were louder than the regular programming and she would shift uncomfortably in bed, burrow more deeply into her pillows.

A loud clatter woke her.

Polly opened her eyes just a slit. They were heavy and itchy with sleep and she would have closed them immediately if not for the television. A soft groan escaped her lips. She was too warm, too comfortable there in the bed to possibly move an inch, but her eyes cut toward the television. The sheet was tented above her and she could make out only the upper edge of the screen. Voices chattered in the flickering gray light of the bedroom. The television had woken her. She felt like shooting Rick an elbow in the ribs. Polly Haskell loved her husband, but sometimes he could be such an oaf.

A tired smile played on her lips and reluctantly she drew herself to a sitting position on the edge of the bed. She kept a glass of water on her bedside table at night and she reached out to take a sip from it. The TV wouldn't be nearly so troublesome if her forgetful husband would have simply let her have the remote control.

She dragged herself up and ran a hand through her sleep-bedraggled blonde hair, then tugged her nightgown down. It had ridden up and twisted around her hips while she slept. For his part, Rick was dead to the world. He was a wild sleeper and even now was splayed across more than his share of the king-size bed, twisted up in the sheets, one hand thrown across his face so that she could only make out his mouth, hung open in a little *O*.

The big goofball. Polly grinned and then sighed as she walked around the bed to retrieve the remote from his bedside table. It would take her several minutes to drift off to sleep again, and so rather then click the television off she set the timer so that it would turn off automatically in half an hour. Then she set the remote back down on his nightstand. He'd only grab it back in the morning otherwise.

Her side of the bed seemed awfully far away. Lazily she knelt on the bed near his legs and made to crawl over him.

The clatter came again, a slap of wood on wood and something rattling. This was the same noise that had woken her before, but for the first time Polly realized that it had not come from the television set. She froze there on the bed on her hands and knees, holding her breath. Her throat felt closed and tight, and her chest hurt where her heart did not seem to beat so much as convulse. A prickling sensation washed over her, every inch of skin bathed in this strange, eerie static. She cocked her head and she listened harder than she had ever listened in her life.

Something shifted deep within her house.

"Rick," Polly whispered, voice cracking.

He did not even move. A kind of anger flashed through her and she turned to him, gave him a hard shove, and hissed his name with more urgency though no greater volume, or so she hoped. Her husband began to stir and she shoved him a third time. His eyes flickered open.

"Polly?" he asked quizzically. With the back of his hand he wiped drool from his cheek. "What's the matter?"

You woke me up, she wanted to say. *You didn't set the TV timer.* Polly wished she could say one of those things. But she could not. What she said, instead, was:

"Someone's in the house."

One of his eyebrows went up and the corresponding eye opened just wide enough for him to stare at her a moment. Then he let it flutter closed again.

"Go to sleep, Pol. It's your imagination."

Before she could reply, there came a long creaking

noise from downstairs. Rick sat up, wide awake now. He looked doubtfully at her, then at the floor. Polly was somewhat relieved to see that her husband seemed more wary than frightened.

"That's not my imagination," she told him.

Rick nodded, head cocked just as hers had been, listening carefully for some other sound. But none came, the house was silent now. After a few seconds she crawled across him to her side of the bed and sat next to him, listening intently. As another minute passed without further incident she breathed more easily and let out a long sigh.

Her husband reached out and took her hand to comfort her. He smiled gently. "It's an old house," he said. "They make noise. If you heard banging, it was probably just the pipes. The heat, maybe." A mischievous grin illuminated his face. "Or rats in the walls."

Polly struck him in the chest. "Not funny."

Another muffled sound floated up to them, but this time it was indistinct. It could have been the pipes, or even rats, though she was loath to consider that possibility. But there was no way of telling.

"Should we call the police?" she asked.

At first this had seemed like the natural course of action, but, now that a couple of minutes had passed, even as she suggested it she felt like she was overreacting. They were new in town, living in a huge nineteenth-century mansion with the nearest neighbor half a mile away. The last thing she wanted was to call the local police over a raccoon or a skunk or stray cat in the house. The house was spooky, sure, but they were going to have to adjust to that—and the place was so beautiful, that was a small price to pay.

Rick took a deep breath. She could seen in his eyes that he wanted to go back to sleep, but he climbed out of bed and offered her a placating smile. He was a good husband, even if he hogged most of the bed.

"Sit by the phone. If it's anything to be concerned about I'll give a shout and you call nine-one-one."

"That's comforting," Polly said, mouth twisted into a mask of doubt. She grabbed the portable phone off her nightstand and hefted it. "I'm not sitting up here by myself."

Rick's smile softened a moment, and then he glanced around the room, hesitated, then walked out into the hall and into the guest bedroom, where he had left his new golf clubs resting against the wall. He pulled out a seven iron, gripped it in both hands, and then led the way down the stairs.

The foyer was dark save for the moonlight coming through the windows. Still, it was easy to see that nothing was moving there even before Polly turned on the lights. With that illumination she relaxed a little and her grip on the portable phone loosened somewhat. She had been holding it so tightly that her knuckles hurt. Following Rick through the house, from parlor to parlor, from living room to dining room to kitchen, from sitting room to study, she began to feel silly. The thump had been loud enough to disturb her sleep and that second one even louder, but it was an old house. They groaned with age just like people.

On the south side of the house was the vast family room, where the Haskells had put a pool table and a bar and a huge entertainment center. Not quite what Talisker had had in mind when he built it, Polly figured, but despite its age, this was their home now. A modern home.

At the center of the family room, Rick lowered the golf club and faced her.

"There's no way into the basement from outside. Tight as a drum down there. No way any animals—or prowlers for that matter—got in there. It was nothing. We're just not used to living somewhere so remote."

But Polly barely heard him. There was still one place they had not looked. She stared past him at the large oak door that led to the abandoned wing of the house. Her husband sensed that she was still agitated and turned to follow the line of her gaze. When he realized what she was looking at, Rick glanced at her.

"Come on, Pol," he said. "It's blocked off. There's nothing—"

"We don't know that," she interrupted. "There could be all kinds of animals in there and we'd never know. Anything could have gotten in."

"Fine, then tomorrow morning we'll call an exterminator and have them give it a once-over. For now, let's go back to bed."

She nodded but did not move. "Just look. Look to make sure nothing got into the hall."

On the other side of that door was a short corridor that provided both a back entrance to the kitchen, a narrow rear stairwell going to the second floor, and a boarded-up door that led into the abandoned wing. If something had gotten through from that wing, it could have gotten into the kitchen or even upstairs by now.

Rick nodded, realizing that she was resolved, and he strode over to the oak door, golf club hanging loosely in his right hand. He pulled the door open and stepped through. Polly was surprised to find that she was holding her breath.

"Nothing," Rick called back. "Now can we go to bed?"

Polly followed him into the corridor, which was lit only by a single, grimy fixture overhead. This was a forgotten little corner of the house, used only very rarely by them to travel from kitchen to family room, the back stairwell almost never utilized. She resolved then and there to get it cleaned up and start cleaning out the abandoned wing first thing in the morning, even if they couldn't afford to have it renovated yet.

"Polly?" Rick pleaded, looking sort of silly and foolish in his boxer shorts and white T-shirt, standing there in front of that boarded up old door. "Bed?"

She smiled at him, her silly man.

The monster burst through the splintering wood with a horrible screech, pieces of the door crashing all around. Its huge hands clutched Rick by the shoulders and threw him to the floor.

Polly did not even remember that she held the phone in her hand. She stared, wide-eyed, disbelieving, denying what she had seen. A single tear slipped down her cheek and the phone slid from her grasp as the monster whipped toward her.

Polly Haskell whispered her husband's name.

The Queen led her children into the human dwelling. It was crude and its geometry offensive, neither the smooth structure of the world beneath the waves, nor the perfect edges of the realm of the Elder gods from which they had been spawned during the long night that enveloped Earth before the first dawn.

One of her scouts had found the split in the cliff face in the cove down below, that wound in the rock face of the shore that provided shelter from the water and from the *Aegirie,* the pawns of their enemy, which hunted them. The Aegir, master of these freakish creatures, was coming, and its pawns were attempting to destroy them to curry the Aegir's favor. The Queen had fought back, rooting out the Aegirie and slaughtering them before they became too plentiful to overcome. They were multiplying quickly, but as long as the Queen and her followers could fulfill their purpose here in the human world before the Aegir itself—the Old One—reached the land, she would be able to get her clan to safety.

They would find peace at last.

It was fortunate that her scouts had found the ocean cave. The sea lions were also fleeing the evil of the approaching Aegir. Moruach had their own word for sea lions, and though the Queen and her followers had eaten such creatures many times themselves, she felt a sadness for them now, for the Aegir and its slaves, its Children, would feast upon them all. The terror the sea lions felt had permeated the ocean and the very air, was in every breath and every gust of wind.

The sea lions could not use this cave, but the Moruach could.

In the cave they had found the lingering scent of humans. The smell was very, very old, but it remained, and it guided them upward through tunnels and narrow cracks and one cave after another. It had led them into the house, the human dwelling, which at first had seemed abandoned. Only after they had entered and begun to move around did the Queen smell the humans elsewhere in the structure.

The scent of their fear had been strong.

She had waited. Listened. Breathed them in.

Now the dwelling belonged to the Moruach. The Queen slithered up stairs and through doorways, knocked over furniture and paused to gaze in mute wonder at the talking box in the bedroom. It had been many years since she had trucked with humans, and they had grown only more bizarre in that time.

As her children moved from room to room they closed the shades and curtains, and where there were none they stacked furniture to block the windows. It was vital that they be protected from the daylight. This would be their place now, the perfect place with its tunnels by which they might come and go from the ocean unseen by man and untouched by the sun.

Not for long, however. They could not afford to rest very long. In truth the Queen had hoped to leave this very night, but her will had been thwarted. The scouts she had sent to perform the spell, to open the way, had failed. Most had been killed and only a handful survived to return to her. They would have to begin again, but the way was shielded now. A human and a vampire, her children had told her.

Not any human, that much was clear. A warrior. A champion.

And not merely any vampire either, for she had caught the scent of him off the survivors of that melee, and it thrilled her. Even as she thought of him now the Queen shivered with anticipation. The vampire had not run from her that time long ago on the other side of the world. He had not wanted to run. He had not been afraid. And then later in the city with the ocean for streets, he had defied her. Even hurt her.

His ferocity intrigued the Queen. Aroused her. It would be good to see him again, to be near him. She eagerly anticipated the way he would smell and the soft, dead chill of his flesh. The Queen of the Moruach bared her teeth and thin black rivulets of drool slid out of her maw. After all they had been through and the desperation of this new undertaking, the world had turned to sorrow and grief. Never had she imagined that in all of that anguish she would find anything to ignite this passion within her.

She longed to taste him. To tear him with her teeth and drink his cold, clotted blood.

It was going on two in the morning by the time Buffy

came in sight of her house at last. A light still burned in the living room and in her mother's room upstairs. A twinge of guilt went through her; she did not want to think that her mom had waited up for her. But another part of her was grateful to see that light, that warmth, and secretly hoped her mom was still awake. Dawn had probably gone to bed already, and Buffy thought it would be nice to have a few quiet minutes just for her and her mother before she had to hit the sack.

Spike had taken his sweet time returning with the camera, but eventually Buffy was able to get photographs of the bloody designs on the floor of the abandoned school's library. She had the broken pottery in a small paper bag she had retrieved from a trash can, and she kept it clutched in her fist, banging against her leg, the way she had done with her lunch in grade school.

Her muscles ached and her eyes burned with the need for sleep. With Spike's help Buffy had collapsed some of the remaining walls of the library, demolishing the unstable remains of that room so that the spot where the Moruach had attempted to open the Hellmouth would be buried in debris. But now she was weary and dirty, with a dozen little cuts and scrapes that had come not from the fight with the Moruach but from her own efforts at destruction.

Even so, despite her need for rest, her mind was crowded with plans for the following day. It seemed to her that the crises that presented themselves in Sunnydale came in two varieties: those that stuck to the shadows, slinking about with quiet menace that built to a kind of crescendo, and others where everything hit the fan at once and the whole world seemed about to crash down on her. The last couple of days had proven to her that whatever the Moruach were up to, and whatever else was going on in Sunnydale, it was happening all at once.

Now.

There was no time to fiddle with solving mysteries. Terrible things were happening and she felt certain that they had yet to see the worst of it. In her mind she could see the monster painted on the pottery she had in the paper bag, and she shuddered.

The minute she got inside she would call the Magic Box. Giles was likely still there, asleep on top of his reference books. If he wasn't, she'd try him at home. She had to catch him up on what had happened and what she had found. They could get the film developed first thing in the morning and maybe he would have something solid to work with at last.

Meanwhile, she would have to have someone stake out the school. Spike had remained behind with instructions to come find her if any more Moruach showed up, but he would have to leave his post shortly before sunrise.

If he lasts that long, Buffy thought. For she knew that despite all his bluster, Spike was nervous about what would happen the next time he faced the Moruach Queen, and he might well have retreated to his crypt the minute Buffy was out of sight. He wanted to kill the Moruach, no question, but she had a feeling he was not enthused about the possibility of facing them alone.

Buffy yawned, more exhausted than ever at the thought of how early she would have to rise in the morning to see to all of these things. She wanted to find out how Willow and Tara had fared with Baker McGee and the others who might have been exposed to the evil that was transforming people into monsters. Xander and Dawn had been out doing a little detective work, and Buffy wanted to find out if they had learned anything.

In the morning, she reminded herself. *First thing.*

Her heart heavy with worry and lingering dread, Buffy strode up the walk toward her front door and slipped a hand into her pocket to retrieve her keys. In her peripheral vision she saw something move, and she spun to her right to see a dark figure step into the light that glowed from the living room windows. Black low-rise leather pants and a cropped, beige cotton T-shirt at least a size too small. Buffy stared at her and her mind flashed back to the night she had gone undercover at the Fish Tank. Suddenly she realized exactly who she had been masquerading as that night.

Faith.

"Hey, B. Long time no see."

Chapter Eleven

Buffy stared at Faith, shook her head to make sure she wasn't seeing things. "What are you doing here?" she demanded.

"Yeah, great to see you, too." Arms crossed in defiance, Faith offered her a playful grin. "You look like hell, by the way."

The other Slayer was almost ghostly in appearance, bathed in that dim light from the house and the glow of the moon above. Buffy stared at her for several seconds, too tired to know how to deal with this turn of events. Her feelings about Faith were complex, and her arrival was the last thing Buffy had been expecting. Once upon a time, Buffy had died—only for a moment, for Xander had used CPR to revive her—and whatever cosmic mechanism controlled such things had called a new Slayer to replace her. The girl's name had been Kendra, and though she had been tough and earnest, she had not lasted very long at all.

Upon Kendra's death, Faith had been called. But to Buffy's mind, whatever higher power did the choosing, they had made a mistake with Faith. The girl had pretty clearly been damaged goods even before she was made a Slayer. The details of her growing up were vague—Faith kept them that way—but it was pretty clear she had led a difficult life and dealt with a lot of issues of abandonment and acceptance before the Council of Watchers rounded her up and started training her.

From what Buffy knew, Faith had liked it. A lot. Her Watcher had become like a surrogate mother to her; she finally had found someplace she belonged. But then they'd gotten into a melee with an ancient vampire running his own little dictatorship in the swamps down South somewhere, and the vamp had killed Faith's Watcher. Faith hadn't been able to do a thing to stop him, and she had done the only thing she could think of: she'd run to Sunnydale and hooked up with Buffy.

Faith hadn't had anywhere else to go.

At first Buffy had been skeptical. Faith was different, a wild girl, and she embraced the gifts that being a Slayer provided, the enhanced physical abilities and the permission to pound the hell out of the bad guys. But over time Buffy had come to appreciate that there was someone else in the world who was like her, a sister of sorts. For a time, Buffy had even embraced Faith's more visceral attitude toward being a Slayer. Faith had started to become a part of the family, so to speak.

But Faith wasn't built for that. Even when she had first arrived, the new kid in town, she had tried too hard to impress, to be cool. She had rubbed almost everyone the wrong way—except maybe Xander, and Buffy didn't like to think about Faith and Xander and rubbing.

She began to be jealous of what Buffy had. Family, friends, a Watcher. She tried to trust, and through a series of unfortunate incidents came to believe that it was foolhardy to trust anyone, that Giles and Buffy would never truly accept her. Faith became reckless as a Slayer, and one night, she had killed a man.

A normal human man.

It had been an accident, of course, but Faith had shown no remorse at all. Buffy had thought that was the worst thing that could happen. Then Faith betrayed them all, switching sides to become a pawn of the mayor of Sunnydale, a wannabe demon who had been manipulating the town for a century. The mayor had offered her yet another parental figure and the kind of acceptance she had never felt from Buffy or Giles.

Faith had become the enemy.

In a way it seemed a long time ago now, though it was not really. Still, much had happened since then. They had nearly killed each other. Buffy had put Faith in a coma for months. Faith had woken and tried to destroy Buffy again, but this time when she failed she set off on a self-destructive rampage. It had seemed like she had a death wish, wanting to end her own misery.

Buffy hadn't cared. Once she had felt close to Faith, had let the other Slayer into her life. But because of whatever had twisted her up inside, Faith had turned it all around, had hurt people Buffy loved, lashed out at everyone who offered her a hand. Faith had ended up in Los Angeles where she tried to kill Angel, Buffy's ex. Angel was a vampire, but one with a soul, with a conscience, trying to atone for the sins of his past.

Angel forgave her. He comforted her. He understood.

All her life, Buffy now realized, Faith had been searching for nothing more than that. Someone who understood. She had thought she had found it in Buffy, but Buffy could never understand what her life had been like and why she had done the things she did. But Angel could, and he did, and through his example Faith realized that it was possible to start again.

To atone.

She had given herself up to the authorities for the crimes she had committed, and gone to prison.

Prison.

In the front yard of her home, the home that Faith had defiled with her betrayals more than once, Buffy stared at the other Slayer, completely numb. How was she supposed to respond now, after all that had happened? If Faith was trying to atone, why was she not still in a cell somewhere?

Faith tossed her silky black hair back and strode forward, then waved her hand in front of Buffy's face. "Hello? Anybody home? What's up with you, B? You look like you've seen a—"

Buffy slapped her. The sound of it echoed across the lawn.

"You've got a short memory, coming here, to my house."

Eyes dangerously narrowed, Faith stared at Buffy and gingerly rubbed her cheek. "All right. I'll give you that one." She shook it off, did a little twist of the head, all attitude. "But I didn't come here to fight."

"Fine. I just want to make sure you don't have any illusions. Maybe you're trying to turn your life around, Faith. I hope so. But you and me? We're not okay. Five by five, that's what you always say, right? Well we're not."

Faith's eyes burned into her, the other girl's lips pressed tightly together. After a long moment she nodded. "I'm good with that. And just so you know, what I'm up to now? Doing my time? It isn't about you. Get over it or don't."

Nearly a full minute passed as the Slayers faced off with one another. A lone car passed by on the street, but neither of them even glanced at it. Eventually Buffy nodded.

"You didn't answer my question. What are you doing here? How did you get out?"

Faith chuckled softly and shook her head. "Don't worry. I'm going back." She strode to the front porch and sat down on the steps. "Our friends at the Council *borrowed* me from the state of California. You believe that crap? They've got friends in high places. Pulled some strings. Bam, I'm out for a bit, and going back when they're through with me. But that's okay, right? I mean, I get a little fresh air, maybe start scoring some points for the Home Team in the war against the darkness. I can use the exercise."

Buffy glared at her, not bothering to hide the doubt in her heart. "I'm surprised they'd do that. You and the Council, not exactly a mutual admiration society. Last I knew they wanted you dead, and you felt pretty much the same about them."

"Funny world, ain't it?" Faith shrugged. "Funniest part of it is, they came to get me 'cause you won't play ball. They explained the situation. Got these Moruach things slaughtering people in Sunnydale, Council wants an exterminator, but you're getting all People for the Ethical Treatment of Demons. Doesn't sound like you, B. Isn't that what we're supposed to be about? Protecting people from the monsters?"

Buffy studied the other Slayer a moment. Would Travers really have brought Faith into the situation after all that she'd done, just because Buffy would not cooperate with his agenda? *Of course he would,* she realized. There was probably little that was beneath Quentin Travers when it came to getting his way. Well, Buffy didn't answer to the Council and she sure as hell didn't answer to Faith, but if the other Slayer really was here to help, for both their sakes and for Sunnydale's, Buffy figured she should at least lay it out for her.

"That's what I *am* doing. I'm just not going to blindly follow orders. There's more going on here, and I think the Council has answers they're not sharing. The Moruach aren't the only monsters in town, and I'm not even sure they're the ones who are doing most of the killing.

"There are three deaths I'm sure they're responsible for, but you could make an argument that those were self defense. Overall I'm thinking the others are more vicious. I've killed ten or so Moruach in the past twenty-four hours. If that's what needs doing, fine. That's the job. But right now I'm more concerned with the big picture, figuring out what's really going on here, than I am with searching every basement in town for monsters that might not present any real danger.

"Come by the Magic Box in the morning if you want the full run-down. I'm not going to play it the Council's way, but if you're gonna be here, I guess you should at least know what you're dealing with."

Faith stared at her thoughtfully a moment and then stood up. She strode several paces from the steps and turned back to look at Buffy.

"Thanks, but I don't think so. You're puttin' too much thought into this, B. So you've got kinda dangerous killer sea monsters on the one hand, and really dangerous freakish mutants on the other? Let the Watchers figure out what's the what. Giles and Travers can do that. It isn't what we do. We're the hunters. We're the warriors. We go out and kill the nasties so nobody else dies."

Faith frowned deeply, obviously troubled, and shook her head. "I'm staying at the Hotel Pacifica with Travers and some others. You decide you want to do the right thing, come by." The she smiled. "Weird. In my wildest dreams I never figured things'd come full circle like this."

"Like what?" Buffy asked.

"Me the good girl," Faith replied with a chuckle, "and you the rebel."

She turned to leave but paused one last time and glanced back at Buffy. "I waited for you, by the way. I wouldn't have gone inside. You and me, we got a lotta baggage, figured things might get physical. Joyce didn't need that. She's a class act, and I messed with her bad last time I was around here. I'm sorry about that."

Buffy stared. It was the closest thing to a real apology she had ever heard from Faith, and she had no idea how to acknowledge, nor even if she wanted to.

After a moment Faith turned on her heel and walked off. Buffy went and sat down on the steps. She stayed that way for some time, paper bag still clutched in her hand, just looking out at the night. At the darkness.

Despite its picturesque location, the Sleepeasy Inn was the sort of place that appealed only to families, business travelers, and people looking for lodging on the cheap. Sunnydale was not a resort town by any stretch of the imagination, but it had its share of pretty coastline, and as such, also its share of charming bed and breakfasts and homey inns overlooking the ocean.

The Sleepeasy wasn't charming and it wasn't homey. It was a big pile of cinder blocks painted screaming flamingo-pink half a block from the ocean.

On the inside it did not look very different from the average Comfort or Holiday Inn, and the seventh-floor balcony that overlooked the ocean made it easy to forget the bright pink stucco exterior. Especially at night.

Rosanna sat in a plastic chair on the balcony and sipped from a five dollar bottle of lemon soda she had taken from the minibar. She looked out across the whitecaps and the gently rolling waves beyond and tried to imagine she could see all the way across the Pacific.

It should have been soothing, but it was not. In the back of her mind she was constantly aware that the ocean was not as benevolent as it seemed. It was vast, practically infinite by human reckoning, and it held ancient secrets unlike anything that could be found on land. Most of the mysteries that remained in this world existed beneath the waves.

The Order of Sages was dedicated to unraveling those mysteries, to uncovering the secrets of the universe in the hope that the shadows might be dispelled and the things humanity thought of as monsters might emerge to become part of a world that would no longer need to fear them. It was an enormous undertaking, one that most would find ridiculous. Even for those who were a part of the Order, it took time and a kind of psychological evolution to accept the sublime mission upon which they had embarked centuries before. Like the architects of ancient Egypt, they had to understand that what they had begun was unlikely to be finished while they still drew breath. The Order of Sages was made up of men and women of singular dedication, and led by those who understood that they were merely part of a process that would take many generations to complete.

To Rosanna, that was the fundamental difference between the Order and the Council of Watchers. The Order was patient and humble and accepted that they were merely—*what was that saying? Cogs in a wheel.* But the Watchers were swaggering and puffed with self-importance, believing themselves not merely to be taking part in the eternal combat between chaos and order, but vital to it, even in control of it.

Didn't any of them see that they were beneath the notice of the powers locked in that infinite struggle? Even the Slayer, the Chosen One, singled out by some higher power to be the light in the darkness, was little more than a cog in the wheel. What Rosanna admired most about Buffy Summers and Rupert Giles was that from all the reports she had read of their exploits and their conflicts with the Council, they seemed to understand this, to realize their limited roles in the overall scheme of things.

Rosanna sighed and sipped at her lemon soda, her gaze searching the dark surface of the ocean for some sign of the mysteries that lay beneath. Were the Moruach there, even now, beneath the waves? And what else lurked on the ocean bottom alongside them?

The phone rang in her room. Rosanna set her glass down and went inside, picking up the phone and lying back upon her bed.

"Hello?"

"You're all settled in?"

The strident voice on the other end of the line belonged to her supervisor, Astrid Johannsen. A pleasant enough woman between assignments, but when Rosanna was on the job Astrid was never anything but direct and to the point.

"Yes. But the Council's already been here."

"So fast?" Astrid asked, words clipped, frustrated. "I thought the Slayer was still estranged from them?"

"She is. So is her Watcher, Mr. Giles," Rosanna explained, staring up at the plaster ceiling. "Ostensibly, they're working with the Council again. That's the official word. Unofficially, the Slayer seems less likely to cooperate with them than ever. She was apparently suspicious about how emphatic they were in ordering the immediate slaughter of the Moruach."

Astrid did not reply immediately. When she did, Rosanna had the sense that her supervisor found the turn of conversation nothing short of delicious.

"Do you think she can be turned to our purposes?"

Now it was Rosanna who hesitated. After a long

moment, she sat up in bed and drew her knees up under her. "It's possible. But let me be clear. Buffy isn't against killing the Moruach. She just needs a reason. If the Council provide her with one, she isn't likely to balk. She's been their hunter too long."

"Perhaps she needs to be spoken with away from the influence of her Watcher," Astrid suggested.

"Giles may once again be in the Council's employ, but there's no love lost between them," Rosanna reasoned. "Any influence he may have over Buffy has to do with what he himself feels, not with the goals of the Council."

Another protracted silence ensued. At last, a soft sound on the other end of the line made Rosanna think that Astrid had actually chuckled.

"Well then," the supervisor said, "might I suggest you work very closely with Mr. Giles? If he can be made to see the value of the Order's philosophy, then the Slayer might also be swayed."

Rosanna stared out onto the deck and the formless dark beyond. "I'll do that, Astrid. But I'm here, if I'm not mistaken, to study the Moruach and attempt to open up communication with them and learn what I can about their culture. I'm here to try to prevent the Council from slaughtering what it doesn't understand. I'm not here to proselytize."

"Rose, don't kid yourself," Astrid replied, relaxing now. "What better way to further all of our aims than to have the Slayer on our side? You want to speed up the Order's long term goals? Steal the Council's thunder and our ranks will swell with new recruits, new Sages."

Though thought it seemed crass, Rosanna could not argue with the logic of it.

"Get some sleep," Astrid instructed her.

"I will. But hold on. You know the Moruach aren't

the only things here? There's something else coming out of the sea, killing people. The town isn't safe. We should be helping the Slayer to protect the area. How soon can you send a team?"

"We've got a lot of field operations in progress," Astrid replied. "Let me see what I can do."

But her voice had gone cold once more, and the two women quickly said their good-byes. After she had hung up the phone, Rosanna stared out into the dark again for several minutes before she rose and went to shut and lock the sliding door. She pulled the curtains as well, blocking the view of the ocean entirely.

Rosanna did not think any help would be coming. The Order, after all, was focused on a solution still generations away. What were a handful of human lives in the scheme of things?

They were nothing more than cogs in a wheel.

The world was gray. Nothing was ever truly black and white. Faith knew that as well as anyone; she'd spent so much time living in the midst of all that gray, swinging one way or the other along the scale between the dark and the light.

In Sunnydale, there was no place that represented the overall grayness of things better than Willy's Alibi Room. Behind the bar, the little weasel who ran the place never asked the demons and vampires who frequented his place where they fell in the war between light and darkness, between order and chaos. They were all just customers to him. Money spent the same, no matter where it came from. All of which meant that Willy's was host to vicious, anarchic demons as well as to those who had chosen to live peacefully among humanity. Throw in the occasional wannabe-sorcerer drowning his sorrows that he would never be Merlin and a handful of cantankerous vampires always spoiling for a fight, and that was a typical night at Willy's.

But tonight wasn't typical.

When Faith walked in the bar was empty except for a trio of X'ha Guila demons shooting pool at the back and Willy himself, who sat on a stool in front of rather than behind the bar reading a newspaper.

He looked over the top of the paper at her when she came in and then instantly hid his eyes behind it again. Faith caught the look of recognition and the fright in his gaze before the paper blocked her view. There was something delicious about how intimidated he was by her presence, but she could not halt the little ripple of guilt that went through her along with it.

"Slow night," she observed as she took the stool beside him, the newspaper a screen that separated them, like he was a priest and she preparing to confess.

Willy said nothing. Faith thought it was admirable that his hands were not shaking. The newspaper did not rustle at all.

"Eventually your arms are gonna get tired from holding that thing up, Willy," she said. In her mind she ran down the ways in which she could deal with him. The easiest was the most violent way, and probably that would also be the most gratifying. Even if she'd never seen the guy before there was something about him that just cried out for a beating. He was a snitch, a slug, not someone you could trust to keep his word, or even to give you back the right change from the till. With the clientele he had, Willy's life was ruled by fear.

Faith felt tired just thinking about it. She sighed.

"Willy, listen," she said, gazing at the newspaper as though she could see him through it. "Normally I'd just hit you right through the *Sunnydale Times*. But that'd get newsprint all over your face and my fist. Neither one of us wants to get smudged. You don't want me here. I don't wanna be here. Just tell me what you know about the Moruach. Where can I find them?"

A loud clack came from the back of the bar—the sound of a new game of pool beginning, followed by the soft thumping of balls as they bounced off the felt bumpers on the table. The X'ha Guila demons had noticed her—Faith had seen them in her peripheral vision, checking her out—but so far they'd kept to themselves.

Slowly Willy lowered the paper. There was a kind of resignation in his eyes that was pitiful. When he spoke it was in a whisper, hoping he would not be overheard by the X'ha Guila.

"You can give me a beating if that's what gets you off, but I got nothing. Swear to God. I know they're ocean demons. I know there's some here. But where, I couldn't tell ya. All the vamps skipped town 'cause they're afraid of the things. Most of my other customers are still around, far as I know, but they're keepin' a low profile till this whole thing blows over."

Faith frowned and slowly glanced over her shoulder at the three demons at the pool table. "Except them."

Willy looked at the floor. "Pretty much."

The Slayer patted him on the head, then lifted the newspaper up between them again, hiding Willy behind it, giving him back his fear and his ability to pretend to see nothing. Ironically it was then that his hands at last began to shake.

Faith turned her back on him and started toward the pool table. The X'ha Guila were on the less-hideous side of the humanoid bell curve, but they were still demons, still ugly. As a race the X'ha Guila were completely hairless. Technically they were also skinless, their bodies covered instead by a series of leathery plates that looked more like a tortoise shell than flesh. In the right light—or enough shadow—they might pass for human. But one close look at that outer covering would be enough to freak just about anyone out.

In the first weeks after she had been Chosen and had begun to train with her Watcher, Faith had run across a couple of X'ha Guila stalking a woman who had been pushing her infant in a stroller. Faith had stopped them, of course, but she still remembered the feel of their leathery touch on her skin and the revulsion she'd felt when her Watcher had told her it wasn't the mother they were after.

All of which meant that tonight, as she strode over to the pool table, her hands were already clenched into fists.

The X'ha Guila who was bent over the table about to take a shot was the first to notice her. His gaze ticked to the left, and then he lifted his eyes and began to stand. The other two had been focusing on the difficult shot he had been about to take and only noticed her approach when the player stepped back from the table and grinned lasciviously at her.

It had no teeth. Only a layer of smaller plates inside its mouth that must have served that same purpose.

"Well, hello there," said the player, his attention completely torn from the game now. He was the largest of them, and the way the other two stood mutely with their cue sticks in their hands, Faith judged him the leader as well.

Despite the bizarre nature of their appearance, the X'ha Guila seemed like typical males. All three of them looked her over like butchers trying to pick the choicest cut of beef.

"Come to play?" asked the one whose turn it was.

Faith tossed her hair back and put a hand on her outthrust hip. "Not much into games. There's a bunch of water demons in town. Moruach. I want to know where to find them."

She expected some lame come-on, something about how they could do things for her a bunch of sea serpents never could. Even if they knew where to find the Moruach, the X'ha Guila were scum. She didn't expect them to just tell her.

But the leader surprised her. He grinned with those vicious-looking non-teeth. "A different game, then. You ask your questions. For every answer you get, you take off a piece of clothing."

A cold ripple of disgust mixed with hatred went through her.

"Deal," Faith replied. "Where are the Moruach?"

Again that grin. "I don't know."

Faith shuddered, her gaze strafing all three of them. "Do any of you? If not, who would?"

"Whoa, whoa, honey, that's two more questions and you haven't even taken off the piece of clothing you owe us from the first one," the leader said.

Again he grinned, and this time, just beneath the other ambient noises in the room—the rotation of the overhead fans, cars going by outside, music tuned almost subaudible on the sound system—she heard a series of clicks, the sound of the creature's plating shifting and moving against one another as it changed its facial expression. Faith swallowed back her revulsion.

The leader reached out with the tip of his pool cue and touched her zipper. "I say you start with the pants."

Faith snatched the tip of the cue stick before he could draw it back. "Fine," she snapped.

Then she tugged it out of his hands and swung it in a long arc so that it whistled through the air. The X'ha Guila saw it coming, but he was too slow to duck. The thick end of the pool stick cracked across the bridge of his nose, and he staggered backward to crash into the wall beneath a dart board. The board fell off the wall and struck him on the head as he slid downward, several of the plates on his face shattered and hanging loose to reveal raw pink flesh beneath.

"You little—," one of the other X'ha Guila began.

Faith leaped up onto the pool table and kicked him in the face hard, driving him back. She dropped into a crouch, scooped up the eight ball in her left hand, and fired it at the third one even as the demon tried to grab her legs. It struck the thing in the temple and the X'ha Guila slumped onto the pool table and then slid to the floor, unconscious.

The one she had kicked came at her again. Faith dropped down off the table, shot a high sidekick at its face that broke its nose with a crunch of bone, then used the splintered cue stick like a stake. She rammed it against the demon's shoulder, pinned it to the wall, then worked it up and down until she had pried between two of its skin plates. The demon screamed as she staked its shoulder to the wall.

"Stop whining, ya big baby," she sneered. "You'll live. More than I can say for your victims."

Behind her, against the wall, the leader began slowly to rise to his feet. Faith could hear him groan. She spun, grabbed the seven ball and the thirteen off the table with one hand, and threw them so hard that they exploded to dust against the wall on either side of the demon's head.

"If I wanted to hit you—"

"Gotcha," he said quickly. "Gotcha."

She turned to the one she'd stabbed with the broken cue. "The Moruach. You got something to say you think is worth me taking my clothes off? Go 'head. Hell, tell me what I want to hear, maybe I'll give ya a little show right on top of the table."

Regret filled the demon's silver eyes. "I . . . we . . . No clue, babe. I swear. We just got into town. Don't even know what these Mor-ew-acks are."

Fury raged through her. Faith twisted the pool cue in his flesh, and she heard something pop. "You lie!" she snapped.

The X'ha Guila screamed. The leader called out to her to stop, and Faith turned on him, reaching for two more pool balls and advancing on him menacingly.

"It's true," he said, his voice a frightened whisper. "We just got here."

All the anger went out of her then with a single rush of breath, and she stared at them. A sadness welled up within her, bone-deep, the kind of melancholy she had rarely felt since the day she allowed herself to be locked in a cell. With a sigh she tossed the pool balls onto the table and turned to stride back toward the bar.

The newspaper was shaking in Willy's hands, but still he held it up as though Faith might have forgotten he was back there. She didn't even have the energy now to hit him.

"You didn't mention that they just got into town."

Willy froze. His voice came to her from behind the paper. "You . . . you didn't ask. I really, I don't know anything. If I did, I'd have told Buffy already. She'd have made me. When you came in, I figured you were set on handing out a beating, I just . . ."

"You just wanted someone else to get it," Faith finished for him.

A long silence came from behind the newspaper. Then, at length: "Pretty much."

With a scowl, Faith turned on one heel and stalked from the bar. She slammed open the door and walked out into the darkened street, blood boiling with anger. The problem was she was uncertain who she was angrier at,

Willy, the X'ha Guila, or herself. All she knew was that it could have gone differently in there.

"Faith."

The voice echoed across the street. She looked up just as a truck rumbled by, and for a moment it obscured her line of sight. When it had passed she saw the Mercedes parked on the other side of the road. The driver's window was down and blond, porcelain-doll Helen Fontaine was eyeing her quizzically from behind the wheel. Beyond her, in the recesses of the car, Faith could see the silhouette of Daniel Haversham.

But the voice had not belonged to Helen, and Haversham was mute. Her gaze ticked to the SUV behind the Mercedes. The driver's door opened and Quentin Travers stepped out. Almost simultaneously, the passenger door opened and out stepped Tarjik, the furtive man in the turban whose presence had not even been mentioned by Helen or by Travers, who had brought him along. If he was a Watcher or an operative, Faith had no idea. All she knew was that she did not like the way he looked at her, which was similar to the way the X'ha Guila had looked at her before she had taken them apart.

"Were you able to discover anything?" Travers asked as he strode over to her.

Faith glanced away a moment before dragging her gaze up to meet his. "No. Willy's clueless. A few demons in there. I thought they might know something, but I handed 'em a hell of a beating. Turned out they were playin' me. I took 'em down for nothing."

Travers smiled, even chuckled softly. "They're demons, dear girl. That's reason enough. If there are no answers here, we simply continue searching for the Moruach. It would have been convenient to get a lead here, but we can do this the hard way."

He clasped her shoulder with a firm hand. "You're

doing a fine job, Faith. It's a shame the way things went with your relationship with the Council. But if we continue to work well here, one day when you're free of your other . . . commitments . . . I see no reason why we could not repair that fractured association. Misunderstandings lead to estrangement. Yet I continue to hope that we'll grow to understand one another again."

But I don't *understand,* Faith thought. It made no sense to her at all, in fact, that she should feel guilty about unleashing a little violence on some demons from a race with a history of eating small children. Especially since Travers—who along with the rest of the Council had sat in moral judgment of her in the past—thought it was a perfectly reasonable way to spend her night. Okay, she had no idea if these X'ha Guila were predatory or not . . . *but it's a safe assumption,* she thought.

Isn't it?

And even if they weren't . . . she was doing the right thing this time around, wasn't she? Following orders.

"Go on with Miss Fontaine and Mr. Haversham, then," Travers told her. "There's still work to be done tonight."

As she walked over to the Mercedes and slipped into the back seat of the car, Travers's voice was in her head. *You're doing a fine job,* he'd said.

So why does it feel so much like before, like I just traded the mayor's agenda for Travers's? Why does it feel . . . wrong?

The word felt foolish, almost ridiculous in her mind. But in her time behind bars, Faith had done a lot of thinking about right and wrong, the light and the darkness, about living her life in the gray.

As the sedan pulled away from the curb, her thoughts returned there again and she wondered what it would be like to live in a world where things were black-and-white, where it was easy to figure out what was wrong and what was right.

She saw Travers's expression in the rearview mirror. He looked very pleased with her. That had to be good, right? That had to mean she was closer to the light than the shadows.

The parking lot outside the emergency room was quiet, but Willow had expected that. In Los Angeles they might get a lot of gang-warfare victims and car crashes in the wee hours of the morning, but this was Sunnydale and a school night. There might be a few domestic disturbances or a kid hit with a vicious stomach flu, but she imagined quiet was to be expected tonight.

Still, she had a terrible feeling that it was not going to remain quiet for long. Not if what had happened back at Hollywood Lanes was happening in other places as well.

"You can just drop me in front," Baker McGee told Tara, who was behind the wheel.

Willow saw Tara's frown in the rearview mirror.

"No, we'll come in," Tara said. "Really, it's no trouble. Just until you get checked in. And in the morning if you want a ride home you can call. I'll come get you."

The old fisherman smiled warmly at her, obviously touched by Tara's concern. In the backseat, Willow shook her head in amazement at how fortunate she had been to find such an amazing person for herself.

But as these happy thoughts went through her mind, something less pleasant was nagging at her. Every few seconds, Baker McGee scratched at the back of his right hand. He had started to cough a little also, as though he had something stuck in his throat. It had barely registered at first but now McGee began to scratch the back of his hand vigorously.

What's got him so itchy all of a sudden?

With only the dashboard light for illumination Willow could not see the man's hands clearly, but she feared she knew what she would see once they were inside. Papery, peeling skin, and rough, dark green underneath.

Willow said nothing as Tara parked the car. The three of them walked to the emergency room door together, the witches trailing slightly behind McGee. But as the electronic doors slid open the night was pierced by the sudden peal of sirens. Willow realized she had heard them from the moment they had stepped out of the car, but they had sounded distant and she had been occupied with other thoughts.

Now they all turned to see an ambulance roaring up the drive toward the emergency room. Red lights splashed crimson shadows across the parking lot and the hospital doors as the vehicle backed up to the building. Willow, Tara, and McGee stepped aside as the doors to the emergency room slid open and four hospital personnel came crashing out with a gurney. In the chaos of their shouts to one another Willow could not determine who was a doctor or a nurse.

The rear doors of the ambulance swung open even as the vehicle's driver leaped out.

"Give 'em room!" the driver shouted. "The guy's on something. Tried to rip his face off. He's doped to the gills and still thrashing back there."

From her vantage point Willow could not see inside the ambulance, but she did not need to. Seconds after the doors were thrown open a pair of EMTs jumped out. They waved away the hospital's gurney, prepared to use their own. Their reason was obvious a moment later when they hauled the contraption out of the ambulance and its metal legs dropped open, locking into place.

Strapped to the gurney was a man whose hands were dripping with his own blood. He struggled against his bonds and shouted unintelligibly and where the straps rubbed against his flesh, the skin was chafing away. Half of his face had indeed been torn off, revealing cruel amphibious features beneath.

"Jesus!" shouted one of the hospital personnel. "What the hell's wrong with him?"

"That's your department," retorted one of the EMTs.

Cursing and staring in amazement, the hospital personnel raced back into the emergency room with their patient. The EMTs followed, rattling off the man's vital signs and warning the doctors and nurses not to get anywhere near his hands.

When the doors had closed, Willow, Tara, and McGee were left alone in the parking lot with only the rumble of the engine and the silent strobing of that red light atop the ambulance for company.

Baker McGee scratched idly at the back of his hand.

"You girls were right," the old fisherman said. "It's spreading." When he turned to them, his eyes were moist. "And you don't have to look for Frank Austin anymore."

"That was him?" Tara asked.

McGee nodded. "Guess I'd better go and get myself checked out."

Willow gazed at him a long moment before she spoke. "Call us if you need that ride," she said. "Or, y'know, anything else."

Another silent moment went by, and then McGee turned and went into the emergency room. Willow wondered what the doctors would say when he showed them his hand, his flaking skin.

Tara stood staring at the doors. Willow touched her arm. "Hey. Let's get some sleep."

"If we *can* sleep," Tara replied.

"Yeah. If we can."

Chapter Twelve

The girl had long powerful legs and she strode confidently across the grassy lawn of the UC Sunnydale campus, eschewing the path for a more direct route to the dormitory ahead. Still, despite the way she held her chin high and her shoulders thrown back—broadcasting the certainty she felt in her ability to defend herself—she did not stray too far from the lampposts that gleamed with the promise of safety alongside the path. And why would she, this late at night with nobody else around?

Almost nobody.

Spike moved in the deepest of shadows, hanging back and sliding from the cover of one tree to the next, keeping out of the range of her peripheral vision. The girl was not as awake as she pretended. Her long chestnut-brown hair was tousled as though fresh from bed and she had yawned more than once, hiding her mouth behind a hand. She had come either from a long study session in the library or from a tryst, and the wrinkles in her shirt and the fact that she had missed a button while putting it on indicated the latter.

He was stalking her, and it warmed his cold heart.

A government collective of soldiers and scientists called the Initiative had set up shop in Sunnydale for a while, and he had been one of their captives for a time. And one of their victims. The Initiative had put a chip in Spike's head that prevented him from harming human beings. As a result, a kind of uneasy coexistence had been established between himself and the Slayer. He couldn't kill Buffy, was harmless by her standards, and so she wouldn't even *try* to kill him.

But a bloke has to keep in practice. Doesn't want to get rusty?

It rankled Spike more than he cared to admit that he could no longer prey on human beings, that the blood he drank came out of plastic bags he bought on the black market or from animals, instead of from the hot, pulsing veins of a sweet young thing with the just-got-shagged look he was trailing at the moment. Sure he entertained himself by getting in a demon-brawl now and again, downing a few drinks at Willy's, and playing cards—and truth be told there was a certain amount of entertainment value in helping Buffy and her mates avoid an apocalypse now and again—but it just wasn't the same.

Not like it had been once upon a time, whipping up some terror on the streets of Europe or that insanity at the World's Fair way back when. With Dru.

Spike comforted himself as best he could with the knowledge that there was still some thrill in the hunt. Maybe he couldn't go in for the kill, but the stalking was a pleasure all its own, got his motor all revved up.

Like now.

He slid from shadow to shadow, stepped up beside a tree, and rested his hand on a branch, watching her from between the leaves. She was a pretty one, this one, and her scent on the breeze was alluring. The wounds he had incurred earlier were already healing, dried blood crusting over and drying stiffly on his torn shirt and pants. He had left his ruined jacket behind. Even in spite of all he had been through this night, he could have caught up to the girl without any problem at all.

It was delicious, that knowledge. He could have stepped from the darkness and wrapped his fingers around her neck, run them over her body while she stared in horror at his true face—the face of the vampire—just before his fangs pierced the pale and tender flesh of her throat. He shuddered with the tactile memories of long decades filled with such moments.

As though she could feel his gaze upon her she shivered and ran a hand over the back of her neck, then looked quickly around, all the while trying to look as though she were not at all worried about walking alone on the campus at this time of night.

"That's right, love," Spike whispered. "Be afraid. Ya never know what might be waiting for you in the dark."

An urge came over him then that he could not control, and Spike ran swiftly from the cover of the trees. With an unnatural silence he sprinted through the night, his footfalls making hardly a rustle on the grass as he ran at the girl. He could not hurt her, could not *have* her, but he could terrify her, and that would feel good and right.

A jagged grin spread across his face as he sprinted toward her. The girl's pace faltered and she paused, perhaps sensing something. The front doors of the dormitory were fifty feet away.

Spike inhaled deeply the scent of her, and he froze. There was another scent on the breeze as well. He glanced nervously around, his motions unconsciously mimicking those of the girl he had been stalking. He did not even realize that his features had shifted again, the face of the vampire retreating beneath a more human countenance.

Moruach. They were around here, somewhere nearby. Or they had been recently. Were they hunting him? Spike didn't know. But he was not about to stick around and find out.

"Hey!" the disheveled girl snapped when she finally saw him there, perhaps a dozen feet behind her. "You got a problem?"

Spike's upper lip curled. He stood and stared at her and the girl brazenly stared back, probably afraid to turn and run for the door, fearful of turning her back on him at all. Spike wished for a cigarette but he didn't have any on him.

"Me?" he asked. Then he nodded. "Yeah. Yeah, I think I do."

The vampire turned and strode away, leaving the girl to stare after him. When he glanced back moments later she had already disappeared inside the dorm, and he picked up his pace, hurrying off the campus and away from that scent.

Or so he had hoped.

But when he arrived back at the cemetery he called home, the scent of the Moruach was there as well. It was a rich ocean smell, saltwater and a kind of oily odor, and beneath it a smell like rotten fish. Spike glanced around the street outside the wrought-iron fence that separated the cemetery from the road, and then he moved swiftly alongside it, walking the perimeter of the graveyard. Halfway around he climbed and then quickly vaulted the fence.

The scent was stronger here.

He clung to the shadows once more, but he knew that it was no longer the behavior of a predator. He hid in darkness, for he was the prey. And it burned his ass.

"Bitch," he whispered to the shadows. But even Spike wasn't certain if he meant the Moruach Queen, whose fascination with him was only flattering when he hadn't seen her in a decade or so, or the Slayer, for having turned in without seeing him home safely.

The thought made him angry. *Don't need the homicidal bimbo baby-sitting me,* he thought.

And he stood.

And when he walked through the cemetery toward the crypt he had turned into a sort of apartment, he swaggered just for the hell of it. The whole graveyard stank of the sea monsters, with a concentration of their scent outside his crypt. It was obvious they had come looking for him, tracking him by his own scent. Spike ignored this proof of their presence, strode to the door of his crypt as though daring them to attack him, if any of them had remained behind to watch for his arrival. Sure, it helped to have Buffy along to even the odds, but Spike was not going to run and he was not going to hide. If the Moruach Queen wanted to finish their little mating dance, she was more than welcome to come for him.

Once he was inside the crypt, however, he locked it up tight and slid a heavy marble casket in front of the door.

He was the Big Bad.

But he wasn't completely insane.

When Buffy stepped into her house she shut and locked the door behind her. Vampires needed an invitation to enter, but for everything else she had to rely on a dead bolt. She set down the paper bag with the broken pottery she had found at the high school. From the living room she could hear tinny voices coming from the television and she smiled. Exhausted as she was, the image that now popped into her mind—of her mother curled up on the sofa beneath a blanket in spite of the warmth of the night—let her breathe a little easier.

Faith's arrival had thrown her off, unsettled her even further, which was quite a feat considering the things that were going on in Sunnydale at the moment. The mysteries and murders she was dealing with had her head spinning already; the last thing she needed was a visit from the other Slayer, the girl whose presence never failed to complicate matters. There were a lot of reasons for this, not the least of which was that Buffy felt—and would probably forever feel—that she had failed where Faith was concerned. Not that she was responsible for what happened to the other Slayer, or anything Faith might have done . . . just that she could not help suspecting that somewhere, back in the days when Faith had first come to Sunnydale, there might be a moment where if she had done something differently, things might not have turned out the way they had.

See, Buffy thought. *She's doing it to me already.* Frustrated, she put thoughts of Faith out of her head and walked into the living room intending to wake her mother up and guide her half-asleep upstairs to bed. But her mother wasn't in the living room at all.

Xander sat sprawled in a wingback chair, head lolled to the side and drool slipping down his chin. He snored softly, the sound blending in with the late-night talk show audience's laughter that came from the television set.

On the floor in front of the couch, Dawn sat with an open bag of microwave popcorn and tried to chew what was in her mouth even as she waved hello to her sister.

"Hey. You're earlier than I figured."

Buffy gave her a dubious look. There were questions in her mind, including one where she'd ask Dawn what she was doing up so late on a school night. That sounded very Mom-ish, though, and since Mom had already gone to bed, Buffy thought their mother had probably sanctioned the little slumber party in the living room, including late-night Dawn-age.

She settled on the question that seemed to loom largest in her mind at the moment.

"Why is Xander drooling in the middle of our living room?"

Dawn shot a sidelong glance at Xander to confirm the accusation and emitted the requisite "eew" before leaning over and whacking him on the leg.

"What?" Xander barked, waking abruptly, bleary eyes trying to focus as he looked first at Dawn, and then at Buffy. "What happened? Crisis mode? We at Def-Con four?"

Buffy smiled and sat down on the sofa. "No. Wipe your chin."

Xander brushed a hand across his face and grimaced at what he found there. He brought up the bottom of his T-shirt and rubbed it quickly over his chin.

"Gross," Dawn observed calmly.

"Yep," Buffy agreed.

Sheepish, Xander shrugged. "It's late. Hack me off a hunk of slack."

Buffy sat forward on the sofa. "What's going on? I'm assuming you found something?"

"Nope," Xander replied.

"But the Coast Guard did," Dawn added.

Buffy listened as they described their visit first to the Hendron Corporation, where they were turned away, and then to the Coast Guard installation south of town. It was chilling, particularly when Buffy glanced over to see the look on Dawn's face as Xander described the screams of the Cutter's crew as they boarded the freighter.

"Sorry you had to be there for that," Buffy told her sister.

Dawn raised her eyebrows. “Me too. Especially considering I wouldn’t have had to be there for it if I’d been out protesting the shipping industry’s treatment of our local sea lions.”

She said it with humor, a jab at Buffy’s precaution, but also with an air that suggested she knew best, that she could take of herself. The sad part of it was that Buffy knew in any other town, Dawn probably would have had reason to be ticked. She was better able to manage herself, and protect herself, than the average high-school girl.

“If you’d been out protesting you might have ended up as one of the things on that ship, instead of just hearing them.”

The mischievous twinkle faded from Dawn’s eyes and her face paled. “Oh,” she said, her mouth a tiny circle.

“So you’re thinking the things on the freighter are the formerly-human, chest-bursting tentacle monsters, instead of the born-that-way sea serpent variety?” Xander asked.

“That was the thought that I had,” Buffy confirmed. After another moment’s thought she stood and went to the phone. “I’ve got to call Giles. Spike and I ran into some of the Moruach tonight, and I have a feeling I know what brought them here. No idea what’s going on with the others, why they’re doing the whole watery *West Side Story* rumble thing, but at least we can start putting this puzzle together.”

Xander ran his hands through his messy hair. “We already talked to him,” he said through a wide yawn. “He said something about the Council and Sage or something.”

Buffy paused with the phone in her hand. “Sage? The herb?”

“I was a little busy being completely freaked and hoping the Coast Guard would call in some reinforcements to pay attention to a recipe for one of Giles’s savory English dishes.”

"Maybe it was an ingredient he needs for a spell?" Dawn suggested.

Buffy nodded. That made sense. "What else did he say?"

"To meet him in the morning. His research turned up some stuff, but he didn't feel like sharing it with me, I guess."

"'Cause you weren't paying attention to his recipe," Dawn scolded.

"Oh, and he heard from Willow and Tara. They were taking that McGee guy to the hospital. I guess they found some of his crew and some of the other people who helped out with that lost ship the day you were down there and they'd already started with the Godzilla Acne."

"Did they say how many?" Buffy asked.

"Not exactly. But I got the impression it was more than a couple."

Dawn stared at Buffy. "You're not gonna turn into an octopus are you?"

"Nope," Buffy replied. "Got too much to do."

"Like sleep?" Xander asked hopefully.

"For now. But tomorrow morning the Coast Guard's gonna tow in that freighter. And we're going to have to be there."

Out on patrol.

It felt strange to Faith to even think those words. In fact, *strange* wasn't even the word to describe it. She had spent months behind bars trying to find a calm center within herself, which wasn't easy given the temper she'd had pretty much since birth. With very few exceptions, she was not making a lot of friends in prison. Other inmates—even the guards—seemed to live to antagonize her, as though put there by some cosmic force to tempt her to cross a line she had sworn to herself she would never cross again. That did not mean she was unwilling to hand out a few bruises here and there, but she wanted to stay out of trouble. To stay centered.

This was different. Completely different.

Here she was, the Slayer, out on patrol in Sunnydale, home of your friendly neighborhood Hellmouth. It wasn't like it had been back when she had first come to town. Too much had happened since then. But it was a charge, just the same. If she let her mind drift a little, it was possible for Faith to pretend that it was real, this illusion of things that might have been. But her illusions never lasted very long. She knew she was due to head back to prison when it was over, and she was okay with that.

Doing her time. No sweat.

And when it was done? She'd jump that canyon when she came to it. For now it was cool just to be free for a while. The last time she had gotten to Sunnydale—after coming out of a coma she didn't like to think about—there had not been much time for her to check out the town. Even when she had lived here, the tourist thing had not appealed to her. For instance, Faith had never been to the beach before tonight.

She was pretty sure the sea lions were new, though. The animals had massed on the sand, across the rocks and even up onto private property to the north of the public beach. The beach itself was closed, and barricades had been put up along the sidewalk to keep people away from the sea lions, and the animals from getting hit by cars. Every few minutes a police car would pass by on the Shore Road and Faith would stiffen up. Being out was great, but when she spotted a cop it felt like she was getting away with something, and she did not like the feeling.

Faith walked beside the concrete barricade with Daniel Haversham at her side. He wasn't a Watcher, but an operative in the Council's employ. That meant he was probably less educated about the supernatural than the average member of the Council, but it didn't mean he was less a part of the war effort. From what Faith had learned from her first Watcher, operatives handled most of the clandestine supernatural cloak-and-dagger crap that the Council was involved in.

Unfortunately, Faith had had her own experiences with Council operatives in the past. A couple of times they had tried to capture her and take her back to England so the Board of Directors could review her performance as a Slayer. When that didn't work, they just tried to kill her.

As part of her effort to find a calmer center, Faith was trying not to hold a grudge. At least, not against Haversham. Travers was a bastard, no question about that, but Faith did not have to like him to know that her future might be tied up with the Council's and for better or worse Travers was the man they sent when dirty work needed doing. Faith would have dearly loved to kick his ass, but that wasn't going to get anyone anywhere.

Haversham, though. The guy was a new face to Faith and had not been involved in any of the efforts to take her down in the past. They were all on the same team for the moment. And it didn't hurt that he was both easy on the eyes and mute. Faith didn't like her men to talk back. She had caught Haversham looking at her more than once, seen the gleam in his eye, and every time she had flashed him a knowing grin that said she didn't think he could handle her.

Even now the man at her side stole quick glances at her and Faith ate it up, extending her stride and putting more than a little strut into it. She felt energized by the attention, in control after so long without anyone looking at her that way.

Helen, the uptight Watcher who had sprung Faith from prison, was driving a Mercedes with blacked-out windows, trailing behind them as both backup and transport. Faith wondered if Helen had the hots for her partner.

The Slayer smiled to herself. *I've been behind bars too long.*

"What's up with them, do you think?" she asked, pointing to the sea lions on the beach.

She shot a quick glance at Haversham, then offered a mischievous grin by way of apology. "Forgot. Never mind."

The moon was bright but its light seemed not to penetrate the ocean at all, illuminating only a streak across its surface and the tips of each wave. Faith wondered what was down there, beneath the water. From her conversation with Buffy it was obvious that her "big sis" wanted to know what the Moruach were doing in Sunnydale, and what was causing sailors and longshoremen to turn into monsters.

Faith just didn't get it.

It was not that she did not care or that there was no curiosity in her. She wanted to know the answers, sure. But that wasn't her part of the deal. The Council did the research, figured out the whys and wherefores. Her gig was tracking down the nasties and making them dead until the answers to those questions just didn't matter anymore.

As long as those answers didn't impact what she was trying to achieve by staying in prison and doing her time. This was a war, all right, and she was just a soldier in it. Travers, he was the general. And that was fine as long as his agenda didn't conflict with her own.

Faith stopped short on the sidewalk and shook herself to clear her head. "Jesus," she muttered. "My brain hurts."

They had walked the length of the public beach from north to south, where Shore Road turned inland again.

Straight ahead there was a maze of little streets dotted with mid-range cottages, mostly seasonal rentals but some year-rounders from the look of them. Helen Fontaine pulled the Benz up beside them and let the engine idle. Time to move on, obviously, and see if they couldn't drum up trouble elsewhere, even though the night was rolling on and it was well on the way toward morning.

Reluctantly, Faith walked toward the car. When the sea lions began to bark she was stunned to realize she had not noticed their silence before. They had been moving, making low noises to one another almost like a flock of roosting pigeons. But there had been none of the loud barking that erupted from the beach now in a loud chorus that echoed across the sand and waves.

Faith ran back to the barricade and leaped up on top of it. From there she scanned north and south, looking for the source of the animals' distress. But there was nothing. At least nothing visible. In the water, maybe, but hard as it was to kill a Slayer, they drowned almost as fast as anyone else. She wasn't freakin' Aquaman.

"What is it, Faith?" Helen called, stepping out of the car. "What do you see?"

"Squat," Faith replied, dropping to the sidewalk again. "Let's get out of here. Make a sweep through Docktown, then you two can get some sleep if you want. I'm gonna start at the southern end of town and work my way north. Travers wants a look at a Moruach. I'll bring him one."

"Even if you start now that would take all night and probably all of tomorrow as well," Helen said doubtfully.

"Yeah, thanks for caring." Faith glanced at Haversham, arching an eyebrow. "I'll get to bed eventually. I'm just not tired yet. Or didn't you know? Slayers can go all night long."

The grim, muscular man blushed and averted his eyes, then climbed into the passenger's seat of the Benz. For her part, Helen wasn't stupid. She had obviously caught Faith's flirtation but chose to ignore it.

"Docktown it is," the petite blonde Watcher said. "Climb in."

Faith opened the rear door.

Somewhere to the south in that maze of cottages glass shattered and a scream tore through the night.

Faith grinned as she jumped into the backseat. "That's my cue. Drive the car."

Helen dropped it into gear, and they sped the short distance to where Shore Road turned inland. The Watcher stayed straight, guiding the car onto a narrow side street among cottages that were dark this time of night, whether they were occupied or not. The scream was sure to have woken some people and the roar of the automobile's engine might draw attention as well, but Faith noticed only a couple of lights clicking on as they raced into the neighborhood. The windows were open and she listened carefully for any further screams but there was nothing to hear.

"Stop the car," she said.

The tires skidded in the dusting of sand the wind blew up from the beach. Faith stepped out of the car and glanced around the darkened street. They had come to a stop in the midst of a narrow intersection, yet even here the roads were barely wide enough for two cars to pass in opposite directions. The pavement was rutted and the grass grew in clumps because of the constant intrusion of the sand. Some of the cottages were three stories high and others so small they looked more like woodsheds.

She closed her eyes and focused, shutting out the sound of the car engine. Her skin tingled and she stood in the road and got her bearings, figuring out by the closeness of the ocean and the sound of the surf the direction from which the scream had come. When her eyes opened Faith glanced to her left, where one of the intersection's branches led off to the southeast.

Haversham was standing right beside her. He was so very silent, not merely because he was mute, but in the way he moved. She had barely heard him get out of the car.

"I make it that way," she said, pointing. "You?"

The operative nodded. Faith bent down and looked in through the window at Helen, whose forehead was creased with tension. She looked skittish, like a gunshot would have given her a heart attack. Faith wondered how much time she had spent in the field before this, and guessed not a hell of a lot.

"Fontaine. Stay in the car. Don't move. Keep it running and pay attention. Oh, and just hope the trunk is big enough to fit a dead sea monster."

The Watcher started to argue but fell silent.

Faith started off along the road that led southeast out of that tiny intersection. Haversham trailed behind her by a couple of yards as backup, and she was surprised to find that she didn't mind. Not because she was interested in him, but because she had the idea that if there was a fight he might be good to have along.

Her eyes scanned the shadows beside each cottage and in the breezeways beside them where cars were parked. If the Moruach were out here they'd be sticking to the dark places out of any obvious line of sight, just like any other kind of vermin. But there was nothing in the dark that did not belong there, only the silhouettes of trash cans and bicycles and one hissing cat that hid beneath a rusted Chevy as they padded quietly by.

Faith faltered, then slowed. Something wasn't right. The fear she was supposed to be feeling, the manufactured chemical dread Travers had told her that the Moruach inspired, seemed if anything to have lessened since they had gotten out of the car. She had felt it in the air since her arrival in Sunnydale, but now instead of getting stronger it was weakening. That made no sense. But it was not as though she could ask Haversham about it.

Haversham had slowed as well so that the two of them were now moving at a quick walking pace. Abruptly the operative put out a hand to halt Faith. The Slayer shot him a glance, then saw that his own eyes were locked on something farther along the street. Faith focused on the darkness ahead, and then she saw what had drawn Haversham's attention. In the shadows on the other side of the road a woman stumbled toward them in a shambling run, one arm clutched against her as she stole brief glances back the way she had come. The moment Faith saw her, she realized she could hear the woman as well, breathing hard and whimpering.

"Hey," Faith said.

The woman looked up, wide eyes wild and too white in the ghostly moonlight.

"You screamed?"

"Oh, God," the woman gasped as she shifted direction, running toward Faith and Haversham now. "You've gotta get me outta here. They're coming."

"Cool. I was getting bored." Faith glanced at Haversham. "Take her back to the car. Open the—"

She was interrupted by a loud hiss from the shadows between two houses just behind the woman. Faith snapped her gaze up and peered into the darkness. The thing that moved out into the moonlit street was not human, but it also wasn't a Moruach, at least not the way Travers had described them. It was wearing clothes, for one, or at least the remnants of clothes. Its face was hideous, like a man wearing fish parts as a mask, with huge black eyes and a tiny little mouth. Thing was, it had more than one of those mouths. But that wasn't the worst part; the worst was the swarming nest of tentacles on its chest that moved around like each one of them had a mind—and an appetite—of its own. It moved halfway across the street, and when Faith did not run it paused, hissing loudly and staring at her as though taking her measure.

"Haversham, what the hell is that?" Faith demanded.

But it was the woman who answered. She had begun to cry, the tears somehow freed by the presence of other people, and she moved in close beside the mute Council operative.

"It's—it was my father. I couldn't reach him and I thought . . . maybe he'd had a heart attack or something. God, Daddy . . ." Her tears came harder then, and she hid behind Haversham. "We've gotta run."

Faith narrowed her eyes. "Screw that." She glared at Haversham. "Buffy said there was some weird crap going on around here that didn't have to do with the Moruach. Whatever these things are, I'm guessing they're related. Two kinds of sea monsters in town? Probably not a coincidence."

She started forward, ready to attack the hissing creature with the jagged looking tentacles on its chest. If it had been a human being, the only thing left of the person it had been was the tattered, bloody clothes.

"No!" the woman cried.

"Get her out of here!" Faith snapped. "She shouldn't have to see this."

As she strode toward the creature, all of its mouths fell silent. Tendrils darted out from its chest, and Faith now saw that it had not been her imagination; there were shiny barbs all along the length of those tentacles. *Fine,* she thought. *Just stay away from those.* Which would have been a lot easier if she had brought a weapon from the trunk of the car. The hell with subtlety, then. She ran straight at it and leaped up into a spinning kick that would snap the thing's neck instantly.

Tendrils snagged her ankle in midair, tearing through the tough leather of her pants and cutting into her leg. It let her fall, dangling her above the pavement as other tentacles darted out and grabbed her around the waist and her left wrist, slicing her skin.

Faith swore furiously and twisted in its grasp. She thrust herself forward, grabbed at its leg with her right hand, and pulled. The creature fell and they tumbled together to the street. Faith rolled away, one of the tendrils ripping and snapping with a spray of dark ichor as she pulled herself free.

She rolled to her feet and the thing was hissing again, louder this time. Faith saw mouths on its arms and its exposed abdomen below the tentacles. This time it did not wait. It had her measure—or so the monster thought—and it attacked, barbed tendrils flashing toward her.

Faith ran to meet it, careful to stay out of reach of those tentacles. She leaped into the air even higher this time, but instead of attacking she somersaulted above the creature and landed behind it, then rammed her elbow hard into the back of its head. She heard the skull crack, bone splintering as it went down on its face on the pavement. She dropped down on top of it, grabbed the reptilian head in both hands, and slammed the monster's face against the road once, twice, a third time.

"I'm bleeding. You made me bleed," she snarled, her raging temper driving her.

Then she shuddered, took a breath, drew it in. *No*. This was not how she was going to handle herself. That was what had gotten her in trouble every other time. She had her knee in the middle of the thing's back and it struggled to turn over, tendrils squirming to get out from under it, to get to her. Calmly, coolly, Faith reached down and took the thing's head in her hands, then twisted, snapping its neck.

Behind her the injured woman who had been fleeing this thing, this monster that had once been her father, wailed in anguish.

Faith stood and faced her, saw the horror in her face, and regretted that she did not know enough to promise that it had been the only way. What if these things could be made human again?

"I'm sorry this happened," she said.

"What? *What* happened? What happened to *him?*"

"I don't know," Faith said regretfully.

"We've gotta get out of here!" the woman shouted at her. "I told you that! We should've run."

Faith stared at her. The fight had taken seconds, literally. Twenty, twenty-five tops. What was the rush? "It's over," she started to say. But the woman wasn't listening.

"We gotta get out of here before the others come."

Others. The word echoed inside Faith's head even as hissing filled the street, echoed off the cottages all around them. She spun and gazed down the way the woman had come and saw them shifting in the shadows, more of these things. Seven, maybe eight of them.

A light had come to life on the front porch of the cottage to their right, and Faith glanced up to shout at the old woman who opened the door to tell her to go back inside. To hide. To call the cops.

The woman wasn't human anymore. She hissed and tore the flesh away from her face to reveal black eyes beneath. Her housedress was soaked with blood, and things moved under the floral-patterned cotton.

More lights went on in other cottages. More doors opened.

The woman Faith had saved at last found her voice to scream again. Haversham grabbed Faith by the arm and tugged, and the Slayer glanced at him and nodded.

"Yeah. Let's haul ass. This is wicked twisted."

The terrified woman between them, they ran back the way they had come. The hissing became a kind of chittering like crickets in tall grass and doors slammed open now. Things swept out of the shadows between cottages, coming toward them. Another few seconds and any escape would have been cut off.

The Mercedes' engine roared as it tore up the narrow street toward them, headlights illuminating the people of this little seaside settlement—revealing them for what they had become. The tires skidded on scattered sand, and then Helen Fontaine was shouting for them to get in.

Haversham stopped inside the open passenger's side door, pulled a handgun out from beneath his coat, and started firing at the creatures that swarmed toward the Mercedes. The report echoed off houses and Faith winced at the noise as she shoved the distraught woman into the backseat, then lunged in after her.

The doors were still open when Helen floored it in reverse, tires burning on the pavement. When she hit the brakes and cut the wheel, the sudden change in momentum slammed the doors closed. Then they were racing along Shore Road away from that strange little maze of homes. Faith looked out through the rear window at the darkened cottages and wondered if anyone human still lived in any of them, and how many other people had been infected.

Then it struck her and she stared sidelong at the woman next to her on the seat before sliding away from her, moving closer to the door. Her gaze ticked from the panting, weeping woman to Haversham and then to Helen, and she wondered what it took to catch whatever it was that had changed those people back there.

"Beautiful," Faith muttered. "Just beautiful. I'm gonna kick Travers's ass."

Off the coast of Sunnydale, far beneath the waves where the light of the moon could not hope to reach, the Aegir lumbered across the ocean bottom with its tentacles outstretched and searching for food, for living things that it would drag into its maw. Nothing sated its hunger, however, for it was not food the Aegir desired.

It was vengeance.

Vengeance, yes. And then destruction and defilement. And worship. Its muddled, ancient brain remembered worship, so long ago. It had been far too long since the Aegir had crawled up onto the sand, forcing the earth to tremble beneath it.

With the ocean churning above, the Aegir reached out with its vile mind and called to all those who had been tainted by its touch, changed and made perfect by it. Its influence had spread among the humans of this land, but it had only just begun. It would change them all, control them all, and they would be its children.

It called to them and felt them stir as they began to answer.

And far beneath the waves the Aegir moved closer to the shore.

Chapter Thirteen

Tuesday came at last.

Tired as Buffy was when she dragged herself out of bed that morning, she was grateful for the sun and the blue sky. Since she had been chosen as Slayer, she had had her share of long days, but Monday had been a contender for the longest. Everything seemed to be happening at once, taking one bad turn after another, too many questions piling on top of one another.

Despite it all, on her walk downtown to the Magic Box, Buffy felt good, and she swung the paper bag with the broken pottery in it at her side. The air was crisp and clean, and though the sun was warm on her arms it was not too hot. A new day. If Spike was right, the Moruach liked the sun about as much as vampires did and would hide away during the day. That bought them some time. Under the light of the sun it would be easier to focus.

Time to find some answers.

She was later getting to the Magic Box than she had

promised Giles the night before, but she figured he was used to operating on Buffy time versus actual time. Not to mention that given what time Xander—and likely Willow and Tara—had gotten home to bed last night, chances were they would all be dragging this morning.

They were expecting her so the door to the Magic Box was unlocked. Buffy walked in—announced as always by the bells above the door—and closed it quickly behind her. Willow and Tara were moving along the shelves, apparently restocking them for a new day's business. They looked tired, but when Willow glanced over at Buffy she made a valiant effort at a smile that was only partially successful.

"Hey," Willow said. "You're not nearly as late as Giles figured you'd be. A big ol' B for effort."

Buffy strode over toward the table at the middle of the shop and set down the bag with the broken pottery. "Only a B?"

"Don't press your luck."

Tara was very carefully placing small icons on a shelf, arranging them as delicately as a glass menagerie. Buffy frowned.

"Isn't that Anya's job?"

Tara nodded. "She and Xander haven't shown up yet. Willow and I thought we'd help out. I don't mind, actually. Sort of takes my mind off of other things." The normally shy witch met Buffy's gaze steadily. "We didn't get very much sleep last night. All these . . . transformations . . . they're spreading, y'know? We've got to stop it before it gets any worse."

She shrugged as though to suggest it wasn't her place to speak about it. Buffy knew that Tara didn't really think of herself as part of the group—that she was a fifth wheel in some way because she was Willow's girlfriend. The Slayer would have liked to argue that. Tara was quiet, yes, but strong in her way and very bright, not to mention a witch. She might never feel quite comfortable around the rest of them, but Buffy was always glad to have her around for a lot of reasons, not least of which was how happy she made Willow.

That was one of the hazards of growing older, really. The people you loved all found mates and you were bound to dislike some of them. It had taken Buffy a while to get to know Tara and even now she didn't know her that well. And Anya . . . that was another story entirely. Xander loved her, so she had that going for her. And she wasn't exactly Yoko Ono.

Time passed. Things changed. Though it didn't always seem that way, she felt that most of the time changes weren't for better or for worse . . . they were just changes.

Tara shifted uncomfortably and went back to sorting crystals and medallions on the shelf.

"We will," Buffy assured her. "We will stop it. It's what we do."

Willow had been watching the entire exchange and when Buffy looked at her again there was a soft smile on her face. It meant a lot to her that Tara had been accepted by the group. Buffy understood all too well. Her relationship with Angel hadn't always been met with cartwheels and the shaking of pom-poms.

The Slayer glanced around the quiet shop. "Okay, so we dragged our butts out of bed to get here. Where's—"

"Good morning, Buffy," Giles said.

He had just stepped into the shop from the training room in back, dressed in a rumpled version of the same clothes he had worn the night before. Once he had wished her a good morning, Buffy waited for the comment she was sure would follow it. "Nice of you to join us," or something like that. But Giles did not chide her at all for her tardiness.

Buffy wondered if that had anything to do with the fact that he did not emerge from the back room alone. His companion was a no-nonsense looking woman with jet-black hair and aquiline features. Her manner and the suit she wore declared that she was all business, but she gazed at Giles in fascination as the Watcher approached the table where Buffy was sitting.

"Long night?" Buffy asked, gaze ticking toward the stranger in their midst.

"Quite. We've got a lot to do and very little time."

Giles rubbed his tired eyes and smoothed his shirt. It was hardly the first time he had spent the night researching, but he was usually cleaned up and shaven by the time the Magic Box was supposed to open for the day. There were still a few hours to go, but Giles seemed in no rush to get home to change.

"You don't want to take care of your customer first?" Buffy asked, nodding toward the woman who now stood near the cash register.

"Hmm?" Giles's brow furrowed and he glanced at her over the tops of his glasses. Then it dawned on him. "Oh. Sorry. Buffy Summers, meet Rosanna Jergens. She's here to help."

Buffy studied the woman again and frowned. "Another Watcher?"

"Sage, actually," Rosanna said as she stepped forward and offered Buffy her hand.

The Slayer stood to grasp it, shook once out of courtesy, and let go. "Xander said something about you last night. So you're a spice?"

"Sage is an herb," Giles corrected before gesturing around the table. "But not in this case. Why don't we all sit? I'm sure Xander and Anya will be along shortly, but I don't know that we ought to wait for them."

Willow waited for Tara to come to the table, and the

two of them sat opposite Buffy. Giles pulled out a chair for Rosanna and then took a seat as well. It was too quiet in the shop in those few seconds and the gravity of the atmosphere among them stole away any good feeling the morning had woken in Buffy. Somehow her rising spirits had been able to combat the dread they had all been plagued by. It returned now in full force.

Yet her determination remained.

"The Coast Guard's probably already towing that freighter in," Buffy said grimly. "Let's get to it."

Giles nodded. "Agreed. Rosanna, would you mind?"

Rosanna, Buffy thought, Giles's voice echoing in her mind as her gaze ticked from her Watcher to the newcomer. *Aren't we all chummy?*

Which was a foolish thing to think. Giles was a man and Rosanna was certainly his type. No way could he have failed to notice her. But Buffy knew the man better than that. They were in major crisis-mode and he wouldn't let flirtation get in the way of business.

For her part, Rosanna took his suggestion as a cue to stand, pushing back her chair. From the expression on her face it was clear she understood that her audience was formidable women. That was a nice change, given that the Council always treated Buffy like a little girl and her friends like useless hangers-on.

"I'll make this quick," Rosanna said. "Then if you have questions, I'm more than happy to answer them. You're all intimately familiar by now with the Council of Watchers. What you may or may not fully realize is that the Council is involved with more than merely monitoring the Slayer and locating and training the dozens of girls who at any one time have the potential to become the Slayer. They study supernatural phenomena around the world, collect arcane artifacts, write histories, send exploration teams into dark dimensions—"

"They what?" Giles asked, obviously taken aback. "You must be joking."

The woman waved his protest away. "Believe what you will. The Council has been involved in numerous other activities over the centuries, including fomenting war between rival factions to hasten their demise—a sort of genocide-by-puppetry."

"Do you have proof of any of this?" Giles inquired.

"We have certain evidence, yes."

The Watcher stared at her. "That didn't sound as confident as I think you'd have liked it to."

Rosanna raised an eyebrow and studied him a moment. "Perhaps what the Council has or has not done is a debate for another day. Suffice to say that there is no doubt that the human world is made safer by their actions, but the Order of Sages questions their methods. We engage in many similar activities, but are not involved in the elimination of non-human sentients from this plane of existence simply based upon their being non-humans. Whenever possible, we capture rather than kill. We try to determine the level of danger presented by various demons and other such creatures and destroy them only when lives are in jeopardy."

"People for the Ethical Treatment of Demons," Buffy said. "And I thought that was a joke."

"Okay," Willow said slowly. "Something is telling me that, hey, you and the Council are not exactly the best of friends."

"Not even close," Rosanna agreed, pushing her black hair away from her eyes. "In fact, you might call us rivals. In our studies and our efforts to capture certain artifacts and to control various archaeological digs around the world, the Order and the Council are very much at odds. It's a rivalry that dates back to the Kludden Conflict of the twelfth century."

Buffy shot a look at Giles. "Which is?"

Giles had taken his glasses off and was tapping the frames softly against the tabletop. Now he slid them on again as he addressed them. "The Kludden were a tribe of goblins from the mountains of eastern Europe. They declared war in 1123 and swept down from their strongholds to slaughter the men, women, and children in every village they came to. They would retreat and then years later it would happen again. The Council sent the Slayer of that time to deal with them, but their forces were too great. In 1147, three Slayers were killed in less than six months.

"The Order of Sages were conducting their own investigation and making their own efforts to end the carnage. The new Slayer—apparently having no desire to become the fourth to die at the Kludden's hands—ignored the Council's orders and joined the ranks of the Order of Sages, along with her Watcher. They remained in the Order's employ for nearly a decade, until that Slayer was killed. Her . . . defection . . . is an episode in its history that the Council has done its best to forget."

Buffy glanced at Willow and Tara, both of whom looked as mystified as she felt. "So what was the Order's solution?"

Rosanna offered Giles a half-smile before replying. "Apparently it was a territorial dispute with the local populace. Humans were hunting on lands the Kludden had laid claim to, and had even desecrated a Kludden burial mound thinking it held treasure of some kind. Once she had come to work with the Order, the Slayer went to parley with the goblins, discovered the source of their rage, and negotiated a settlement and treaty."

"Wow," Willow said. "Slayer as peace ambassador. There's a part of the job description I don't think I've ever heard before."

Buffy raised her eyebrows.

"Not that, y'know, you're not about the peace and stuff," Willow quickly added.

The others were paying little attention, however. Giles and Tara were both studying Rosanna Jergens closely.

"So you're suggesting Buffy try to parley with the Moruach?" Tara asked thoughtfully.

The Sage sat down once more, leaning back in her chair. "Exactly."

Buffy shook her head. "Did I not mention that every time I've seen one of these things they've tried to kill me?"

"Really?" Rosanna asked. "Because from what Rupert said, it sounds like the Moruach are trying to kill the *Aegirie* and you keep getting in their way."

Willow put up her hand almost sheepishly. "Officially lost. What's an ay-zheery?"

But Buffy thought she knew. "Lagoon people. The people who've been changed, like Ben Varrey and those guys from Baker McGee's crew. The Moruach I fought at the Dex and the ones you and Tara dealt with at Hollywood Lanes last night were all hunting them. The Aegirie."

The Slayer glanced at Rosanna and then at Giles. "Confession? I've been wondering about whether or not the Moruach were really evil. You could make the argument that they killed the orderlies at the Dex in self defense, but let's not forget how this all started. Anyone remember those mutilation murders in Docktown? From the size of the bite marks on the corpses, I'm guessing it was the guys with the huge shark-size mouths instead of the itty bitty and yet completely gross multitude."

"I considered that," Giles replied, gaze steady. "Rosanna and I think those people were likely Aegirie who had not reached their final stage of evolution yet.

Monsters about to be born. If so, and tif he Moruach can sense them, it seems logical that they're hunting such people down, rooting out the infection before it spreads, if you will."

Buffy turned it all over in her head. "I don't know. Maybe they're not hunting humans. But there's no way you can tell me they're not dangerous."

"I'm not saying that," Rosanna quickly corrected. "You told Rupert yourself that this vampire, Spike, claims the Moruach don't hunt humans. That they eat sea and land animals, and consider vampires a delicacy."

Willow glanced at Buffy. "You used the word delicacy?"

"Pretty sure I didn't."

"In any case, don't you think it best to find out what the Moruach are doing here, what they want, before going any further?"

Buffy did not bother to explain to the woman that she had said almost the same thing to Faith the night before. Rosanna had left helpful and blasted off into pushy, and Buffy bristled.

"You sure you're not from the Council?" Buffy asked her.

Rosanna flinched, pursed her lips, and said nothing.

"Look, I'm all for not killing anything until I'm sure it needs killing," Buffy went on. "I've been down that road before. But that kind of decision-making? It takes breathing room. And we're suffocating here. We want to save lives—human live—so we're going to have to take control of the situation now. You want to know why the Moruach are here, well, I can tell you that much."

Buffy took the piece of broken pottery from the wrinkled paper bag and slid it across the table to Giles, who examined it appreciatively and showed it to Rosanna.

"The Moruach were trying to open the Hellmouth

last night. I've got pictures of the runes or whatever that they drew on the floor as part of the spell. They're being developed now. I'll have them later this morning. But they weren't there to attack any Aegirie, and they sure tried to kill me and Spike so we wouldn't interfere with their spell. If they're looking to uncap a little Hell on Earth scenario, it doesn't matter if they're killing people one by one here. They open the Hellmouth and we could all die."

Her gaze ticked toward Giles. "You know this song. We've sung it before. Here's what we're going to do. First Willow, Tara, and I are going down to the Coast Guard installation to find out what's going on with that freighter. My bet is it's filled with all of these Aegirie—the entire crew of the ship, probably. It could be a bloodbath. We'll do what we can. When Xander and Anya show up, give them a cell phone and plant them at the high school. We need surveillance on the place to make sure the Moruach don't come back. I knocked down what was left of the walls where they were working, but they might just set up shop in another area of the ruins.

"Tonight, when Spike comes out to play, I'm using him as my bloodhound to track the Moruach. They'll scent him just as fast as he does them. One way or the other I'm sure to run across them. If they can understand me, I'll try to *parley* with them. Who knows? Maybe they just want some more company, big demon party, and some of their invitees are coming through the Hellmouth. If that doesn't work, I can try to get them to leave town. Otherwise we're going to have to kill them."

Giles and Rosanna exchanged a long glance. The Sage looked away, defeated. There was little else the woman could say. Buffy knew that her course of action was the only one that made sense given the circumstances.

"All right. Let's get to work."

Buffy and Giles began to rise, but Willow held up a hand to stop them.

"Wait," she said. "What's with the Aegirie? What's going on?"

Rosanna had been studying the pottery fragment more closely. She pointed to the engraving of the enormous, hideous sea monster painted onto the shard. In her rush to do something, to get moving, Buffy had momentarily forgotten all about that final question.

"The Aegir," said the woman.

"An ancient demon-god of the deepest oceans, probably as old as the world itself," Giles explained. He told them of the myths of the Aegir and its worshippers and how some legends said it had not fled this dimension when the other Old Ones did so, eons past. "The Moruach are tied to the Aegir, but we don't know exactly how."

"And these people, the ones who were changed," Tara said softly, crossing her elbows as though hugging herself for comfort. "You think they're worshippers of the Aegir? That's why you call them Aegirie?"

Rosanna set the pottery shard down with a solid thump on the table. "Actually, we think they've been altered somehow by contact with the Elder beast, or mere proximity to it. They're being infected and the infection is spreading, creating more Aegirie. I'm sure if we did our research, we'd find that every one of those who has undergone this horrible metamorphosis has either been in the water offshore near where the Aegir is even now moving toward land, or has been in physical contact with another Aegirie, probably unknowingly."

"It's like that flesh-eating bacteria or something?" Buffy asked.

"Not precisely, no," Giles replied. "It appears that the speed with which the infection takes over those who have been touched by it differs in its victims. And we haven't been able to observe enough to find out if some people are immune, or less susceptible than others. But what you must understand is that this is not a scientific or medical problem, it isn't a biological infection, but a supernatural one. This is not a disease. It is evil."

"Can I just say 'brr?'" Willow noted. She shook her head as though trying to construct a puzzle in her mind. "What I still don't get is, what's the connection? If the Moruach, our 'dragon-sharks,' are trying to kill the Aegirie, that makes it pretty clear that they don't serve the Aegir. Are they at war with it?"

"Sure, why not?" Buffy sighed. "Sea-monster civil war. And where else would you want to stage it, but good old Sunnydale?"

The door banged open. The bells rang above it and a warm breeze blew in and swirled across the floor, pushing pages of open books that lay on the table. Anya stood on the threshold with her arm beneath Xander, supporting him. The fear and anguish on her face was terrible to see. Buffy hurried across the room toward them, Willow, Tara, and the others following closely behind.

"Xander!" Buffy said. But his eyes were not focusing on her and so she looked to his girlfriend instead. "Anya, what's going on?"

The former demon girl's eyes went quickly from Buffy to Giles and then came to rest on Willow. She reached up and grabbed Xander by the chin and turned his head so that they could all see the strange rash that had developed there.

Only it was immediately obvious that it was no rash. The skin had begun to flake away there and beneath it, Buffy could see scales.

"Do something," Anya said, her voice cracking as tears welled in her eyes. "Help him. That's what you do, isn't it? You witches. Do some magick. Stop it from happening. I know what's going on. He's infected. We're probably all infected. I don't really care if the rest of you turn into octopus people, but it can't happen to Xander, so you just fix him right now."

Buffy turned to the others in the room. "You all know something about magick. I don't know how much time you have, so pretend the answer's none."

All four of them raced deeper into the shop for books. Giles conferred quietly with Rosanna as they climbed the ladder to the Magic Box's loft, where many of the older, more dangerous volumes were kept. Only Anya remained with Xander and Buffy in the shop's foyer.

Buffy kicked the door closed and grabbed Xander by the shoulders. She thought that she could feel something strange beneath the fabric of his shirt, some ridged circular abnormality, and in her mind she saw a round little mouth with jagged teeth.

"Xander, look at me," she snapped. "Focus on me."

His eyes seemed to drift for a second, and then the lids fluttered and it was as though he realized for the first time where he was. If Buffy had not known better she would have thought he was on something.

"Buff, hey," Xander said, voice small and tight. "Sorry. I'm . . . sorry."

"For what?" she asked, her mind racing even as her heart was breaking. "What . . . what are you sorry for?"

His chuckle turned into a frightened giggle and his eyes began to drift again. "You shouldn't have to . . . shouldn't have to slay your friends."

"No," Buffy said quickly, shaking her head.

"They're gonna fix it, honey," Anya said, putting on a hollow pretense of calm and confidence. "Willow's your best friend, right? She'd never let anything happen to you. She wouldn't be able to live with herself."

But Xander wasn't listening. His eyes had begun to glaze over and he collapsed in Buffy's arms. Gently she lowered him to the floor. She grabbed his hand and felt the skin give way like tissue paper, tearing away to reveal mottled green skin beneath.

"Stay with me, Xander!" Buffy snapped at him.

For the first time the horror of the Aegirie really hit her. Buffy had hesitated to kill the Moruach because she was not sure if they were evil. The Aegiric were little more than savage animals. From the very first time she had met one, in the Fish Tank, they had proven to be vicious and evil, willing to kill any human who came into contact with them. Slaying them, destroying them, seemed the only sensible reaction. She had seen what happened to Ben Varrey and that was tragic, but now, with Xander, it was cutting deep.

All of these things she had killed, these Aegirie, no matter what they were now, they had been people before. People with friends and family who loved them.

Xander's eyes focused on her again for just a moment. "Buffy," he whispered, his voice so low only she could hear it. "I'm so scared."

"Willow!" Buffy shouted, rounding on the rest of the shop as though she might trash the place.

"Here," Willow replied, running toward her from the basement door. She gestured toward her girlfriend, who had been wildly knocking over the very same icons and talismans she had been setting out on the shelves earlier. "Tara, do you have it?"

But Tara was shaking her head, muttering to herself frantically. Then triumph lit up her features and she snatched a small, spiny crystal from the clutter, knocking over a dozen little pieces while retrieving it.

"Here!" she said.

Giles and Rosanna had several books in their hands as they rushed back into the center of the shop. Whatever their solution was going to be, it was obviously going to take longer than whatever Willow had in mind.

"See!" Anya cried, voice tinged with hysteria. "Willow has the answer!"

"Well, sort of," Willow said hesitantly, her fear for Xander plain on her face. "We can't . . . we can't stop it. Not yet. Not until we know more. But I'm pretty sure we can keep it from getting worse. We can freeze time around him, just stop him right where he is until we figure it out."

Buffy glanced down at Xander. He had begun to choke, and underneath his shirt his chest rose and fell in a rhythm that had nothing to do with breathing.

"Do it."

Tara stood over Xander holding the spiny, pinkish crystal out in both hands as though it were an offering while Willow recited a spell in Latin. Within seconds a light the same color as the crystal sprang from each of its many spines and showered down over Xander in streaks that shot back and forth over him and around him, like dozens of tiny spiders weaving a web of energy around him.

Seconds passed. The web became a sphere of light that was now more red than pink, surrounding Xander completely.

He stopped moving. Frozen.

For a long moment Buffy stared at him. Then Anya stepped over to Willow, sheepish.

"Thank you. Can you . . ."

The rest of the sentence went unspoken.

"Actually," Giles said, "I think we can. If he's . . . if he's not too far gone we should be able to find a spell to reverse this."

Buffy nodded once. "All right. You take care of him.

I'll pick up the photos on the way back from the Coast Guard station and—" She paused, forgot to breathe for a moment as she played back in her head the things that Giles and Rosanna had said about the Aegirie infection and how it was spreading from person to person with no way to tell who would be infected or not.

She glanced quickly around at those gathered in the shop and she saw in their eyes that they were all thinking the same thing. Any of them might be infected, or all of them. Even now this evil might be growing inside of them. Xander had been surfing out in the deep water. He'd gone under. Swallowed some of it, most likely. *But what if he got it at the Coast Guard station, from someone down there who was already infected?* she thought. The idea terrified her, for Xander had not gone alone. Dawn had been with him.

"Giles, before you do anything else, call and check on Dawn and my mother," Buffy said. "Make sure they're okay. Then figure out how to cure this thing, reverse it, whatever. Figure out how to test for it too, if you can. If it's magick or just evil, there's gotta be a test, right?" Then Buffy glanced at the others. "Willow, you and Tara come with me."

"What?" Anya said. "You're just going to leave?"

Taking a deep breath, Buffy spoke to her as patiently as she could. "We all want Xander to be all right, Anya. We love him too. But if this is spreading, any one of us could be next. We've got to figure out what's causing it and how to stop it or there'll be nobody left to take care of Xander."

"Oh," Anya said, eyes wide. "Well, then go. Don't just stand around. What are you waiting for?"

As they drove into the parking lot of the Coast Guard station, Buffy could hear gunfire. It had begun already.

Tara drove Giles's car across the parking lot to where the chain-link fence that surrounded the rear of the installation joined a double-wide gate blocking their progress. There was no hesitation at all. Tara did not slow down.

Buffy stiffened. "Tara! It's Giles's car!"

But Tara only gripped the wheel tighter and braced for impact. Willow leaned out of the passenger window and shouted a Latin spell. The lock where the two sides of the gate met exploded in a shower of sparks and fell out, and the gate swung wide even as the car careened through. Willow pulled herself back inside just in time, for the opening was so narrow that the car scraped the gate on either side and the mirror on her side was torn right off.

"Open sesame," Buffy muttered.

Willow smiled grimly. "Pretty much."

"Guys," Tara said, voice tinged with alarm.

Buffy peered through the windshield to see that a trio of armed sailors were running to block their progress. But she gave the Coast Guard barely a second thought. It was what lay beyond them that drew her attention. The paved lot behind the Coast Guard station sloped down toward the ocean and the long docks that jutted out into the water from there. It had to be deepwater frontage because there were at least half a dozen ships of varying sizes moored there. Two small Cutters idled just beyond the docks.

The Hendron Corporation freighter had been towed up to the northernmost dock, a huge gray behemoth, unremarkable save for its size. Aegirie swarmed the deck, some leaping into the ocean but others down onto the dock, tentacles coiling like snakes in a basket. There were dozens of them.

From the dock and from the two Cutters in the water, sailors shot at the monsters with weapons generally used for interdiction of drug shipments into the U.S. Bullets struck Aegirie as they dove into the ocean. On the docks, the creatures attacked the sailors. Under that blue sky, in the full light of day, it all looked unreal to Buffy. Most of the horrors of this magnitude she had seen had taken place under cover of night. But this . . . it was Southern California, and the panorama that stretched across her field of vision would have made so much more sense if there had been lighting rigs and movie cameras.

But this was no movie.

Bright red arterial blood sprayed in an arc across the dock and out over the ocean, glittering crimson as it caught the sun.

The guards in front of the car were shouting at them to go back, bringing their weapons to bear.

"Stop," Buffy said, because she wasn't certain Tara would not just keep driving, forcing the guards to get out of the way or shoot them all. There was very little Buffy was certain of at the moment.

The car shuddered as Tara hit the brakes. Buffy jumped out, hands in the air, as the guards ran over. They would have looked sharp in their crisp uniforms if not for the guns and the terror in their eyes.

"You are under arrest for trespassing. Put up your hands!" one of them ordered, a pale white guy going prematurely gray.

Buffy didn't bother telling him that her hands were already up. "Listen, we know what's going on here. We can help. Let us in."

The guy laughed, a little crazy. "Yeah? What can you do?"

Willow stepped out of the car and stood inside the open door. She gestured toward the guard with the graying hair. *"Consurgo."*

The guard began to float off the ground. He dropped his weapon, shouting in a panic a stream of gibberish that

Buffy could barely understand. Something about the monsters, about the whole world falling apart.

The two other armed sailors stepped back and trained their weapons on Willow instead of Buffy.

"Put him down!" snapped a darkly-tanned guy who looked no older than Buffy.

Willow waved a hand and the guard dropped to the pavement.

"What the hell are you, witches or something?"

"Yes," Willow replied sharply. "And your friends are dying down there."

Buffy glared at the man on the ground. "You going to let us pass?"

"Go!" he shouted. "I don't care. You're crazy to go down there. Have you seen those things on the freighter?"

Buffy ran back to the open door of the car and started to climb in. "Yeah," she said as she pulled the door shut.

The three guards were paying almost no attention to them now. They had all turned to look down to the docks where other sailors were screaming and gunfire echoed out over the waves and up against the concrete installation.

"What are they?" asked the one Willow had levitated.

"The crew," Buffy told him.

Then Tara was driving again. It was less than a hundred yards to the end of the dock. The tires skidded in gravel when they slammed to a stop again. Buffy jumped out, popped the trunk, and withdrew a long sword whose blade had been forged in Toledo, Spain, centuries before. It was the sharpest blade she had and would cut through almost anything.

When she started running out along the dock, Willow and Tara were right behind her. Buffy heard them talking to one another, but she shut out the sound. Whether it was the comfort of lovers or the plotting of spells, it wasn't her business. The sun gleamed off her blade as she held it above her.

None of the sailors on the dock saw them coming. There were perhaps twenty men and women in uniform out there who were still standing. Dead and injured officers and other sailors lay on the dock. Strangely it was the Aegirie who noticed Buffy and the witches first. One of the creatures had been running at a female officer who had shot it several times with a pistol. Now it turned toward Buffy, and, almost as though they were all connected, so did two others.

Three of the Aegirie started for the girls. Two more leaped down from the deck of the freighter. Buffy tried to calculate in her mind how many of the monsters had already escaped into the water, how many more people they might infect, spreading the horrible transformation even further.

"Don't let any more get away," she yelled, so Willow and Tara could hear her over the gunfire and the shouts.

The female Coast Guard officer snapped around at those words and stared incredulously at Buffy, Willow, and Tara. But then Buffy wasn't paying attention to anything else but the monsters, the Aegirie, these things that had once been men and women with friends and family.

Then the first of the creatures was upon her, tentacles whickering through the air, barbed edges glinting viciously in the sun. Buffy stopped, crouched, dodging the tentacles, and then she spun around in a single swift motion and swept the sword out, her arms extended. She cut the monster in half and let her momentum keep her going because two others were following immediately behind it. Tendrils lashed out at her and Buffy cut them off. She had been slashed by them before, but not today. The tentacles of the Aegirie were fast, but her blade was faster.

Others came to the edge of the freighter's deck and leaped down toward them.

Willow and Tara held hands and spoke the words of a simple yet powerful spell, and the Aegirie ignited in midair, engulfed by flames before they hit the dock shrieking and writhing. Willow and Tara wielded magick delicately, careful not to drain themselves or go beyond what they knew they were capable of. Fire was simple but effective.

Gunfire ripped the air, tore through more of the creatures.

Buffy lost track of her conscious thought, moving with the sword, dancing elegantly across the dock and killing Aegirie, cutting off their tentacles. At some point amid the spatter of dark ichor from the dead monsters, the gunfire ceased. Buffy did a midair somersault over the head of an Aegirie and lopped its head off almost before her feet had touched the ground again. A loud hiss filled the air above her, and she glanced up to see one last creature falling from the deck of the freighter, coming down upon her with its tentacles and hands all reaching out for her.

The Slayer knelt in place, rested the hilt of her sword on an upraised knee, and ducked her head. Tendrils lashed her back, slicing her shirt and the skin beneath, cutting to the bone at her shoulder. The Aegirie fell upon her sword, impaling itself. A final long hiss escaped its many mouths, and it twitched once and then was dead.

Buffy sloughed it off her, drenched in the dark blood of the creatures, and stood with the sword in her outstretched hand. She glanced around to see if any more of the Aegirie were coming at her, only to find that all those that had not escaped were dead. The dock was scattered with the corpses of the creatures side by side with those of valiant Coast Guard sailors. But all across the dock, those officers and sailors who had survived stood staring at her. Buffy stood in their midst—somehow she had worked her way in among them during the fight—and she was the center of attention. Not one of them raised a weapon to her.

Out on the water the crews of the two Cutters that bobbed on the waves stood on the decks of their ships and stared at the dock.

At Buffy.

Silence reigned.

Willow and Tara stepped up behind her and the three girls glanced around at the faces of the others on the dock, faces turned to them with expressions of mixed horror and awe.

"Who's in charge?" Buffy asked at last.

For long seconds nobody replied. At length a woman took a step toward her. "The group commander is dead. So's the XO. Who are you? Do you know what . . ."

Her words trailed off, but she gestured around her to take in the carnage.

"If I were you guys, I wouldn't tow in any more abandoned ships for today," Buffy told her. "In fact, you might want to keep the waters off Sunnydale clear of any ships for the next twenty-four hours or so."

"What happens in twenty-four hours?" the female officer asked.

"Either it'll be taken care of, or it'll be too late."

Buffy turned, nodded to Willow and Tara, and the three of them started back along the dock past several of the sailors. Others had already knelt down to tend to those who were wounded.

"Wait!" the officer called. "You can't leave. I'm afraid I can't allow—"

"Look around you," Buffy interrupted. "These things? They used to be human. Whatever did this to them is spreading. We can stop it. But not if we hang around here answering questions."

For a long moment the two of them locked eyes. If the senior officers had still been alive, Buffy figured there was no way they'd be allowed to just walk away. But at the moment, with so many dead, and after the help she, Willow, and Tara had given them, she figured the remaining sailors wouldn't be too concerned about protocol.

She was right.

"Go on, then. I have no idea how I'd write up the report anyway."

Buffy nodded her thanks and left the dock with a tired Willow and Tara in tow. After they had all piled into the car, Tara turned around to look at Buffy.

"Where are we going now?"

"To pick up the photos I took last night," Buffy replied. "Then we're going to the Hotel Pacifica. The Council knows something. I want to find out what it is."

Chapter Fourteen

Sunnydale was going all to hell. Not literally—not yet—but the way things were developing that might not be long in coming. It felt like every time they got an inkling as to what was happening it only brought up more questions. Once upon a time, when she had first started out as a Slayer, things had been very black and white. See vamp; dust vamp. No problems. But it just was not that simple anymore. There were shades of gray in everything.

The more she thought about her brief meeting at the Magic Box with that Watcher, Helen Fontaine, and her grim-faced silent partner, the more ticked off she got. They were so damned cavalier about the whole thing. The Moruach were monsters, therefore they deserved to die. Maybe so. Maybe. But there was still something missing from this puzzle, and Buffy had a feeling Quentin Travers knew what it was.

When they left the Coast Guard station, Tara had driven

them to the pharmacy. Buffy had called the Magic Box, and Giles had reassured her that so far no one else had shown signs of infection, including Dawn and her mother, whom he had called. She resisted the urge to call them herself, not wanting to worry her mom any more than absolutely necessary. Inside the pharmacy, the girl behind the counter had spent fifteen minutes insisting that there were no photos under the name Summers, and it was not until Buffy asked to speak to the manager that anybody noticed that there were *two* bins for the letter S. One labeled SA–SL and the other SM–SZ. Like a lot of people's names started with *Sz*.

By the time they had gotten it sorted out and Buffy left the pharmacy with photographs in hand, Sunnydale had already begun to fall apart. She had heard a thousand times that bad news traveled fast, but never seen it illustrated quite so effectively. As they pulled out of the parking lot, police cars and ambulances were screaming down the road in the general direction of the Coast Guard station. A number of other cars seemed in an equal rush to reach that destination, and Buffy wondered if they were reporters or merely spectators—she also wondered how many of them would be effectively barred from the area and how many would be infected, would become Aegirie.

The thought made her feel sick to her stomach. People were dying. Every second they wasted more people were infected, more people were transformed, and were destined to die.

"You really think Giles and that Sage woman can reverse what's happening to Xander?" Buffy asked from the backseat.

Tara glanced at her in the rearview mirror. Willow turned in her seat as they slid out onto the highway and headed toward the Hotel Pacifica.

"Probably," Willow said. "I wish I could say for sure. But . . . probably."

There was a deep ache in her voice, a kind of weariness that Buffy understood completely. They'd been so focused on the Moruach at first and the Aegirie had seemed somehow less important. Now they were forced to wonder how many people could have been saved if they had approached things differently. But it was no use thinking about it. They had figured out what the real danger was; now they just had to find out if they had figured it out in time to do something about it.

"If they can reverse it in Xander . . . ," Tara began, but her words trailed off.

They passed more police cars and shops and parking lots that seemed strangely empty. A news van from Channel 9 flew past doing about seventy.

Willow reached across the front seat and took Tara's hand. "What I thought, too. Maybe the Aegirie can be cured. Maybe the process can be reversed."

"And every single one of them we've killed—," Buffy began.

"Don't go there," Tara said, suddenly emphatic. Though she kept her eyes on the road, she bit her lip, brows knitted. "We can't think like that. We didn't know—we still don't know—if they can be helped. They're savage . . . completely overcome by bloodlust. They frighten me more than vampires because there's no thought in it. Just pure cruelty. We've done what we had to do to protect ourselves and other people. If we figure out a way to change them back, that'd be great. But up till now, we've done what was necessary."

The car fell silent. Buffy wanted to believe Tara was right, but she could not accept the words completely. Where demons were concerned it was act first, think later. But sometimes that was the wrong way to go. What she wanted to know, what she *really* wanted to know, was when she would learn how to make that call, how to judge what reaction was appropriate in a given situation.

Until then Buffy would have to do her best. Sometimes that meant she would make mistakes.

But right now she could not afford to make any more.

Half a mile before they reached the Hotel Pacifica, they passed a small convoy of military trucks heading into Sunnydale. There was a National Guard installation in El Suerte, just up the road, so Buffy figured that was where they had come from. She wondered if it had gotten worse back at the Coast Guard station, if something else had happened, if more Aegirie had shown up. But she didn't tell Tara to turn around. They didn't have time for a lot more one-on-one fighting.

The hotel was in a huge parking lot beyond an industrial park, the perfect place for men and women traveling on business. When Tara had parked and they got out, they could hear more sirens in the distance and Buffy wondered where they were all coming from. Sunnydale did not have that many police cars.

"As soon as I'm done with Travers, we're going back to see Giles. I want to show him those pictures, but hopefully he'll know what else is going on in town."

Buffy took the lead as they strode into the lobby and across to the check-in counter. The bespectacled man behind it smiled as he glanced up at them.

"Can I help you?"

"What room is Quentin Travers in?"

The man frowned. "I'm sorry, miss. We can't give out that information. If you'd like you can ring Mr. Travers's room from a house phone." He gestured toward a white phone at a small kiosk built into the wall in the lobby.

Buffy tensed. Her nostrils flared and she was about to grab the guy by the lapels when Tara laid a hand on her arm.

"Thank you," Willow quickly told the man behind the counter. "We'll do that."

The witches led Buffy toward the house phone. Before they had reached it a reed-thin man wearing a turban rose from a chair in the lobby and walked over to them.

"One of you is Miss Summers?" the man asked.

Buffy stopped, rested her hands on her hips. "I am. Which team are you batting for?"

The man smiled, but there was nothing kind in it. "I am Tarjik. Mr. Travers thought you might pay us a visit. Please follow me." He walked toward the elevator, but as soon as they fell in behind him the man stopped and turned and looked at Willow and Tara with a supercilious air.

"Only the Slayer."

"You know what?" Buffy began angrily, ready to pop the guy.

"It's fine," Willow said quickly.

Buffy shot her a questioning look, troubled.

"It's fine," Willow reiterated. "We're big girls. Besides, we can check in with Giles, get the ol' lowdown on Xander and, y'know, assorted other bits of chaos."

"We're good," Tara reassured her. "Give 'im hell."

Anya was torn between tears and terror, between the urge to kneel by Xander's side and wring her hands, and the urge to run like hell as far and as fast as she could. She stood against the counter, watching from across the shop as Giles and the Jergens woman hustled around gathering up ingredients for an elixir they believed would reverse the transformation that had begun in Xander.

Out of the way. She had told them that she wanted to stay out of the way, to let them work. It was a horrible lie that she tried and failed to make herself believe. The truth made her quake inwardly with sadness and doubt.

She loved Xander not in spite of how silly he could be, but because of it. That and a hundred other things. They might not realize it, Buffy and the others, but he was the soul and conscience of their little ensemble. And as the only one among them who could truly claim to be nothing other than ordinary, he was also the bravest.

You're awful, she told herself. *Evil. Go and sit with him. Whisper to him and tell him he's okay, that it's going to be all right.*

But Anya could not do that. Her conscious mind had attempted it, had tried to drive her legs forward, but her subconscious resisted. She had seen those rough, scaly bits of skin where he had started to change. Frantic, she had gotten him here as quickly as possible. But once she had had a chance to think about it, to dwell, the terror had taken her over completely.

As a vengeance demon she had been immortal, or near enough. For thousands of years she had visited horrors upon human males. She had not only seen but been responsible for absolutely repulsive physical deterioration.

She was mortal now. In time she would grow old and die. But not right away. Anya had looked forward to a great many years of coming to terms with her mortality—a great many years in which she would remain beautiful . . . her body firm. The idea that whatever contagion or curse had befallen Xander might pass to her—might already have passed to her—had unhinged her almost completely.

But she hid it. She giggled at the most inappropriate moments and held her hands to her mouth to hide the quiver of her lips, and she watched Giles and the Jergens woman work and she prayed. Strange as it was, she prayed. For Xander as well as for herself.

And in her mind she whispered over and over again an unspoken apology to the man that she loved for her fear, for her cowardice. Anya had been a lot of things in her very long life, but the one thing she had never been was ashamed.

"Anya!" Giles snapped.

Her gaze had been locked on Xander, who lay on the floor in the crackling sphere of magick Willow and Tara had placed around him. Now Giles's voice tore her attention away from him. The Watcher crouched on the floor beside of the woman from the Order of the Sages. *Jergens. What's her first name, though? Rosanna. That's it.* Giles held a small jar in his hand—the sort of thing in which human children might capture small insects they wished to admire or torture or both—and in the jar was a dark sludge-like liquid that bubbled as though dish soap had been a primary ingredient.

"What? I'm sorry, what?"

Giles's gaze softened as though he thought her distraction was solely her anxiety over Xander's condition. Anya felt even guiltier.

"In the small refrigerator in the training room there's a quart of milk. Bring it here, would you?" the Watcher asked.

"Milk?" she replied, on edge. "Xander's skin is . . . is flaking off . . . he's turning into some kind of freak-fish, and you want—"

"It's for the elixir," Giles interrupted. "The smell of this potion is vile, Anya. The last thing I want is a glass of milk at the moment. It's an odd ingredient, but it's what's called for. Would you mind?"

She stared at him, then shook her head. "Sorry. Sorry."

As fast as she could manage she ran back into the training room and opened up the small fridge Giles kept there. It was mostly soft drinks and bottled water, along with the bag lunch Giles had brought himself that morning and never touched. But the milk was there. She grabbed the quart and returned to the main shop. Now that her strange paralysis had been broken she was able to approach Xander.

But she did not look directly at him for fear of catching sight of that reptilian skin again, and she went no farther than where Giles and Rosanna concocted their elixir. The woman took the milk from Anya, checked the book propped open on the floor in front of her, and poured just a little bit into the glass jar Giles held so gingerly.

A sudden stink emanated from the jar as though the milk had gone sour upon contact with its contents—and perhaps it had. All three of them groaned at the smell and Anya took a step backward.

Away. Again, she was moving away.

Suddenly determined, she crossed the shop and knelt beside the sphere of energy that surrounded Xander. Still she would not look at the blemishes on his skin, but she was not going to leave his side again. She loved him. For better or worse.

And this is worse, she thought. *So bring on the better.*

"Just do it already," Anya snapped. "Fix him."

Giles and Rosanna both raised their eyebrows and looked up at her. Anya fixed them with a steely glare.

"We're ready," Giles told her. "Anya, you're going to have to hold his shoulders, make certain his mouth is open." He cast a glance at Rosanna. "You can eliminate the suspension field whenever you're ready."

The woman smiled, her black hair framing her face so that even after hours of concentration she looked attractive. It was annoying.

"You're going to owe me a watch," Rosanna said.

Giles smiled in return. "Of your choosing."

Anya had noticed the energy between her and Giles, especially the way Giles admired Rosanna. It pissed her off. Both of them should have been more focused on helping Xander instead of the sexual tension that was being whipped up between them. But it was time now, and the rest of it didn't matter anymore. The woman took the watch from her wrist and let it dangle from her fingers. She passed it through the sphere of time-freezing magick and the watch stopped, and then its glass face shattered.

The magick dispersed.

"Anya, now!" Giles said.

She bit her lip and tried to suppress the shudder of revulsion that swept through her as she fell to her knees at Xander's side. He had begun to writhe again and something was moving under his shirt with a wet, tearing sound. Anya grabbed his shoulders and Giles put a hand on his forehead. Xander's mouth was open and an unsettling gurgling sound came out of it.

Giles poured the elixir down his throat.

Xander choked and shook, and his eyes rolled back in his head. But the shifting beneath his shirt stopped. Anya watched him for several long, almost unendurable seconds until at last Xander took a long, hitching breath and a tiny sound came from his lips, the sort of small sigh that escaped those lips while he slept. Anya had watched him many times while he was sleeping, trying to see what it was about him that fascinated her so.

His eyes opened.

"For the record?" Xander rasped. "That stuff tastes like—"

"Xander!" Anya cried. Forgetting all about herself, about her own skin and the horrible contagion that had been going around, she threw her arms around him and held him, cooing happily.

He hugged her tightly and a low, contented rumble came from inside his chest. "My plan? We bottle some of that and save it for the being alone time. Uncap that bottle in the boudoir."

Anya purred. "Did you just say boudoir?"

"Pretty sure I did. Should I say it again?"

"Please God, no," Giles interrupted with a groan.

Anya and Xander looked up to see Giles and Rosanna standing over them.

"How are you feeling?" Giles asked.

Xander itched at one of the dry, scaly spots on his cheek and it flaked away, revealing pink new skin beneath. "Kinda brittle. But otherwise? Like I slept for a week. Who's the babe?"

Anya batted him on the arm for even noticing Rosanna. The phone rang and as Giles went to answer, introductions were made between Xander and the woman from the Order of Sages. They talked for a few minutes and Xander seemed very pleased with her hostility toward the Council.

"Hate those guys. Bunch of pompous Englishmen—" He shot a quick look at Giles, but the Watcher was on the phone and had not heard him. "Not that there's anything wrong with being pompous and English. Guess some guys just carry it off better than others."

Rosanna crossed her arms, nodding wisely. "That much is true. The Order has been at odds with the Council for centuries. Really, it's all pride on their part. A bunch of arrogant fools too fast on the draw, too quick to resort to bloodshed when a bit of investigation and understanding will often do. They're Neanderthals really. What's happening in Sunnydale now is an opportunity for us, I think. These Moruach are exactly the sort of creatures we clash over. I'd like to teach the Council the error of their ways once and for all."

"I'd pay to see it," Xander observed as he stood and started tucking in his shirt, wincing as his fingers gingerly touched his belly. "Ooh, kinda sore there. Gonna just choose not to think about it."

Giles cleared his throat. All three of them turned to look at him. "That was Willow. They're at the hotel where Quentin Travers is staying. From what Buffy has said, Faith is likely there as well. Buffy believes Quentin knows more than he's telling, and I must agree. Though what she thinks he'll reveal to her I have no idea. I've known him too long to think he can be easily intimidated. Out-thought, yes, but never intimidated."

The Watcher's eyes narrowed behind his glasses and he studied Rosanna a moment. "You know, Miss Jergens, from your tone I'm forced to wonder if trumping your rivals is of more importance to you than finding out how to stop the Aegirie contagion from spreading."

The woman stared at Giles, lips pressed together in a thin line. "I resent the implication," she said coolly.

"I hope you do. While I was speaking with Willow, your supervisor, Miss Johannsen, beeped in. She informed me that other members of the Order will be arriving in several hours and will meet with you here. In the meantime, while I'd like to do more research on the Aegir, I think our time is best spent attempting to make this elixir effective for fully transformed Aegirie."

Giles glanced at Anya and Xander. "Before we all start sprouting tentacles."

Still obviously annoyed, Rosanna tucked a lock of hair behind her ear and raised her chin. "Let's get to work, then."

"I'm in!" Anya said quickly.

"Me too. My stomach got all squiggly and I'm really hoping to avoid a repeat performance." Xander put his arm around Anya.

"Actually," Giles said, turning toward them, "I have a job for you two. If Xander is feeling up to it."

"Me? I'm peppy as a newborn pup. And kinda hungry, actually. And . . . never mind." He glanced sheepishly away.

Giles went across the shop and reached under the counter to retrieve a small cellular phone. He brought it to Anya.

She held it in her hand and looked at it quizzically. "We're ordering Chinese?"

"You're going over to the old high school," Giles began, gazing at them each in turn. "You're to find a place to hide where you might observe any comings and goings. If there's any sign of Moruach activity, call me here immediately and I will get word to Buffy or come myself. If they truly are attempting to open the Hellmouth, we cannot allow it, no matter what their rationale."

He slipped off his glasses and rubbed tiredly at his eyes. "Oh, and do hurry," he added as he put them back on. "Given what Willow told me of the situation at the Coast Guard station, I suspect it won't be long before our ability to freely move around town is severely curtailed."

Anya looked regretfully at the phone. She took no pleasure from this sort of thing. The idea of coming into contact with a sea serpent was less than appealing. But at least she had her Xander back, and he wasn't sprouting new appendages.

As long as they were together, she knew they'd be all right.

Buffy rode the elevator with Tarjik in silence. The arrogance of the man in the turban made her want to slap him, but that was sort of par for the course where the Council was concerned. Tarjik led her to the end of a fourth floor corridor and rapped loudly on the door to room 401. The door opened almost instantly to reveal the face of Daniel Haversham. The operative looked about as happy as Buffy's current escort as he stepped out of the way to let her pass.

Room 401 was a suite. Two computers were set up on a round table on the far side of the sitting room. Helen Fontaine stood by the sliding glass door that led onto a balcony, cell phone cradled against her ear, her delicate features compressed into an anxious frown.

Quentin Travers was seated behind a desk, studying some paperwork. He looked older than when she had last seen him, his hair thinning a bit more, dark circles under his eyes revealing just how tired the man was. It only reinforced the impression in Buffy's mind that he knew something she didn't. Travers had been involved with and connected to a lot of royal screwups since Buffy had become the Slayer, and somehow he had avoided getting the ax. He had blamed Giles and Wesley Wyndam-Pryce and whoever else he could, and had managed to shield himself from any fallout.

But when he looked up at Buffy now, there was a haunted sort of desperation in his eyes, and she had a feeling Quentin Travers was worried that maybe this time, he wouldn't be able to protect himself.

"Hello, Buffy."

"Wow," Buffy said. "No animosity. No veiled threats. No trying to pull my strings. I'm almost disappointed."

Tiredly, Travers removed his glasses and studied her. "Only because I haven't the energy to devote to how deeply your performance continues to disappoint. Now, unless you've come to your senses and decided to be a team player again, I'm going to have to ask you to—"

"You are one cold-blooded freak, aren't you?" Buffy interrupted. "Makes you wonder who the monsters are sometimes."

Travers narrowed his gaze and at last put his papers down. He rose to glare at her from behind the desk. The room had fallen silent. Helen held the cell phone away from her face, staring at Buffy. Haversham had his arms crossed, but the way he stood it was clear he was prepared for a fight if one was in the making. The man who had escorted Buffy into the room stood just inside the door, glaring with open hostility.

"Miss Summers," Travers said, almost amiably. "Of all of us here in this room, you seem to be the only one uncertain of who the monsters are. The truth is, for that alone I don't want you on my team. You'd only be an impediment."

"So you have Faith instead," Buffy replied dryly. "Because she's always been such a team player."

"She has a great deal to make up for," Travers allowed. "What sort of people would we be if we did not try to afford her the opportunity to do so?"

Buffy shook her head. "I'm sorry. Aren't you the ones who tried to kill her? Looks like we're all about forgiveness this week. Y'know, I gotta wonder how you convinced the other members of the Board to go along with it, bringing Faith into this. I would've loved to have been a fly on the wall for that conversation."

Travers flinched slightly, but Buffy saw it. And she understood.

"Oh, wait." A smile blossomed upon her lips. "They don't know, do they?" Buffy shook her head in amusement. "Oh, you really stepped in it this time. If it works out for you, great. Extra credit for the initiative. But if it doesn't . . ."

"If what doesn't?" a sleepy voice asked.

Buffy glanced toward one end of the suite, where one of the two bedroom doors had just opened. Faith stood just inside the sitting room in a pair of jeans and an oversized T-shirt. She stretched and yawned and then leaned against the wall, crossing her bare feet.

"Hey, B. Glad you came by to visit. You two burying the hatchet?" The sarcasm in her voice was sharp and cutting.

Buffy smiled. "Didn't bring my hatchet."

"Actually, Faith," Travers said, turning his attention to the other Slayer, "Buffy was just leaving. And I'm glad you're up at last. Our situation has begun to escalate and we have a great deal of work to do."

The Watcher ticked his gaze toward Haversham, who stepped in close behind Buffy. Then Travers glanced at Helen.

"You should go, Buffy," the American woman said. "If you're not working with us, you really are in the way. It's a shame, really. We could accomplish so much more as a unit."

"More slaughter, you mean," Buffy replied without even looking at her. She took a step toward Travers. Haversham grabbed her arm—about to try to get her into a headlock, probably—but Buffy just shot an elbow into his gut, cracking a lower rib and dropping him, coughing, to the floor.

Buffy glanced up at Faith to see if she would intervene, but Faith only nodded appreciatively.

"Please," Helen Fontaine said. "There's no time for—"

It was as though the words were coming out of Travers's mouth. The smug, disdainful expression on his face enraged Buffy. She strode up to the desk and faced him across it.

"Maybe instead of just brushing me off you should listen to reason, you pompous ass. There's a war going on in Sunnydale and it isn't the one between you and the Moruach, it's the one between the Moruach and the Aegirie."

When she uttered that last word, Travers flinched again. A surge of triumph went through her, for he had just confirmed that he knew more than he was letting on. But the triumph was erased instantly by renewed anger.

"Look," Buffy said, gaze ticking from Travers to Faith and back again. "Instead of obsessing about killing the Moruach, maybe you should be trying to figure out how to stop all these people from being turned into monsters. If the Moruach are left alone the only people they're going to try to kill are vampires and the ones who've already started the bizarro metamorphosis. Deal with them later. Stop this Aegirie infection from spreading."

Expressionless, Travers stared at her for a long moment. Everyone else in the room was staring at him, awaiting his response. At length he sighed.

"You always think you're so far ahead of the rest of us," Travers said. "A trait you've inherited from your Watcher, I think. Mr. Giles was always a bit self-involved."

Buffy dug her fingers into the top of the desk, her whole body tensed as she fought the urge to knock Quentin Travers on his butt.

Travers cleared his throat. "You're missing a vital connection, Miss Summers. The Moruach are demons. A threat to our world. They must be exterminated. But if that isn't reason enough for you, think on this. If you destroy all of the Moruach in Sunnydale, there will be no more Aegirie here."

"Damn it, Travers!" she shouted, slapping the desk. "What are you hiding?"

Faith stepped deeper into the room, gracefully moving toward her. "Hey, B. Maybe you should take off now, huh? We all want the same thing. Don't you think all that healthy, hot-blooded rage could be put to better use on the bad guys?"

Buffy stared at her, stunned and infuriated to find that Faith had a point. Travers wasn't going to tell her anything.

Buffy was just spinning her wheels, wasting time, and it had taken Faith of all people to set her straight.

"You're just loving being their fair-haired girl, aren't you?" she muttered.

Faith grinned and threw back her hair, hands on hips. "Well, yeah. It doesn't suck."

"Trust me," Buffy said. "It gets old."

She turned and strode to the door. Tarjik stepped out of her way. But when Buffy opened the door, Willow and Tara were standing in the hall, just about to knock.

"Buffy! We need to talk," Willow said.

"What's going on?" Buffy asked, all thoughts of who else was in the room driven from her mind by the sight of the anxiety on her friend's face.

"Kind of a good news/bad news thing." Willow began, fidgeting warily as she realized the size of their audience. "Good news being that Giles reversed Xander's . . . problem. And might be able to do the same for more serious cases. He's working on it."

"The bad?"

Willow took a deep breath.

"The town's been quarantined and no one's allowed out on the streets until further notice," Tara said reluctantly, putting an arm around Willow. "We're stuck here."

Inside Travers's suite, several voices began speaking at once. Buffy wasn't listening to any of them. She had given up hoping that any answers would come from the Council and tuned them out. With a single glance back in at Faith, who looked like the whole thing was one big party, Buffy stepped out into the hall with her friends, pulling the door closed behind her.

Willow started to speak almost instantly, but Buffy shushed her. Anything they said to each other now she wanted to be out of earshot of any of the people in that suite. Whatever her feelings of resentment and disappointment regarding Faith, the other Slayer seemed to be out for herself and just glad to be out of prison for a while. But she was working with Travers, and so for now Buffy had to think of her as . . . *how did Travers put it? An impediment. Just like the rest of them.*

Once they were on the elevator headed down to the lobby, Buffy turned to Willow and Tara.

"How did you find me?"

Tara smiled softly. "It's the mojo."

"Also, we have an idea," Willow said quickly.

"About how to get out of here?" Buffy asked, as the lights above the elevator door clicked from the third floor to the second.

Willow frowned. "Well, no. I'm thinking you with the Slayer-y stealth and us having the witchy mojo, the ol' martial law curfew doesn't pose too much of a problem."

"I'm confused," Buffy said. "What's the idea then?"

Tara lit up. "We were talking about Baker McGee. And . . . and all that happened to his crew. We need to get to him. Get to the hospital. When you were talking about Ben Varrey you said he kind of babbled . . . Not that there's anything wrong with babbling."

"Nope," Willow agreed. "Babbling is actually kinda sexy."

"Not when stinky old sailors do it," Buffy corrected.

"Eew," Willow replied, nodding grimly. "True."

The elevator reached the lobby and the doors slid open.

Tara blushed as she went on, lowering her voice as they entered the lobby. "But when he was babbling, he talked about the Children of the Sea or whatever. He was talking about the Moruach. Or maybe about the Aegirie. But the thing is, it was like he was . . ."

Her hands fluttered as she searched for the word.

"Communing," Willow provided. "Like Ben Varrey

was communing with the Aegir. And if he could do it, and Captain McGee's infected, maybe *he* can do it too."

Buffy stared at them. "Which would mean he might be able to tell us if it's really here . . . how it's changing people . . . and what it wants."

Willow nodded. "Not even mentioning the all-important *where* the sea monster is, and if it intends to eat Sunnydale."

Buffy scanned the lobby. There was a single National Guardsman in front of the concierge desk. Through the glass doors at the front of the lobby she could see a gray-green military Jeep parked outside.

"Should be interesting to see what kind of spin they put on this," Buffy said. Her tone was light, but inwardly she was chilled by the sight. In the back of her mind there loomed an image of what Sunnydale might become if she failed in this.

Tunguska. Roanoke Island. Area 51. Chernobyl. It occurred to her, not for the first time, that these places of disaster and mystery might have had origins other than those ascribed to them. If a military solution was necessary—or even possible—in this situation, Sunnydale would be turned into a ghost town.

Steam enveloped Faith so completely that she could barely see the shower door. The water arced down upon her, almost scalding. Of all the things she appreciated about this brief furlough from her prison sentence, she relished a truly hot shower most of all. The smell of the soap, the shampoo. It was the typical hotel crap, but she never got French milled soap behind bars, so Faith wasn't complaining. Her shoulders were stiff, so she let the hot water course over her back for a while, easing the muscles.

Nearly three quarters of an hour after she had stepped in, Faith reluctantly emerged from the shower. The bathroom was filled with steam, the mirror above the sink completely obscured. She toweled off, enjoying the feel of the heat in the bathroom, the moisture adhering to the tiles. Already she missed the needles of hot water on her skin. But any longer and Travers would be pounding on the door, and that was the last thing she wanted. Old man probably would have loved a free show, though.

Faith smiled to herself, and in the steamed mirror she could barely make out her own Cheshire grin. She wrapped the towel around her body and turned to the mirror again. A silhouette wasn't going to help if she wanted to be able to see her hair while she dried it, so she opened the door just a crack to let the steam out.

And she heard them. Travers and Fontaine. They were arguing, or as close as two people could come to arguing when one of them worked for the other and didn't want to get her ass fired. Fontaine had an issue with the way Travers was handling things. Buffy was mentioned. So were the Moruach. And something called the Aegir.

Faith listened.

She slumped back against the sink.

After a minute she reached forward and clicked the door shut as quietly as possible. Then she turned on the hair dryer and faced the mirror, paying no attention at all to whether or not she could see her own features or how her hair looked.

"Son of a bitch," she whispered through gritted teeth.

It looked like she would be headed back to prison sooner than expected.

Chapter Fifteen

Crouched low, Buffy ran across the roof of the Magic Box, careful to stay out of sight of the street. She dropped to her stomach and crawled to the edge of the roof to look out over downtown Sunnydale. There were plenty of cars, but none in motion save for a couple of ambulances that swept through town without sirens, silent as ghosts. A Jeep and two green-gray troop carriers were parked in front of the Sun Cinema—illegally, Buffy noticed, though she didn't think anyone would be giving out tickets today.

Soldiers stood scattered on various street corners, some conferring with one another, others just looking bored. This was not where the action was. *Yeah,* Buffy thought, *but try telling that to the people who'll be living at the Espresso Pump until this thing's over.* For there were people in the Espresso Pump, pressed against the plate glass windows and peering out at the soldiers and the otherwise deserted streets. They reminded Buffy of the lonely-looking puppies in the window of the pet shop.

The whole quarantine business was more than a little inconvenient, but it would be dark in a few hours, and then it would become much easier for her to escape notice. Meanwhile, Buffy knew it was for the best. If they could keep people off the streets that would slow the spread of the Aegirie infection. She tried not to think about how many people might already have been tainted, might already be starting to change. Almost all of the people she cared about had come into contact with the Aegirie in some way. She shuddered to think about any of them becoming one of those things, about what would happen to their bodies and minds. And she wondered if being the Slayer would prevent her from becoming infected herself.

With a final glance at the quiet street below she turned around and scuttled along the roof to the rear of the Magic Box. A narrow alley ran back there from which she could reach the door to the training room at the back of the shop. Her first stop had been home, to check on Mom and Dawn. Everything seemed all right there, with no signs of amphibi-acne on either of them. Buffy had hesitated before leaving—she would much rather have sat with them and watched a movie and pigged out on microwave popcorn and ice cream while the chaos was being dealt with—but that was part of the Slayer gig. She was the one who had to deal with the lunacy. The snacks would have to wait.

Though it was quiet in the alley behind the shop, she paused at the rear edge of the roof to make sure no one was around. Then she dropped over the edge and landed with a grunt on the pavement below. Swiftly, stealthily, she went to the door that let into the training room and knocked. It was loud, but that couldn't be avoided. Buffy pressed herself against the building and glanced around for anyone who might have heard.

After a few seconds the door swung open. Giles looked a bit tired and disheveled, but he smiled with obvious relief when he saw her. Buffy slipped inside and Giles closed the door behind her, locking it. Only then did the Slayer notice Rosanna Jergens standing in the open doorway that led to the front of the shop.

"Isn't this cozy?" she said, as she handed Giles the packet of photographs she had picked up at the pharmacy. "You two enjoying the quarantine?"

Giles looked at her balefully. "Hardly."

Buffy let her smile fade. "Not much with the funny right now, are we? But at least you two have found a way to get rid of that nasty skin rash people keep getting."

"It's a beginning, but it won't help if no one will listen to us. We'll have reached the point soon where we will be able to protect your friends and their families, but otherwise the Aegirie infection will continue to spread," Rosanna said.

"What do we do about that?" Buffy asked grimly.

"Not to worry," Giles said, frowning at Rosanna. "It's only a matter of time, really. I've made several calls to the mayor's office, the governor's office, and the National Guard command in El Suerte. Someone's bound to call back sooner or later."

Buffy stared at him. "And you're going to tell them you have the magick spell they need to cure people? So what about after they lock you up?"

"It's not magick, really," Rosanna replied. She strode further into the room and sat on a chair near the heavy bag Buffy often worked out on. "Certainly the components might sound a little odd in layman's terms, but it all depends upon how you describe the ingredients. We're breaking down the chemical composition so that they can experiment with it."

"Experimentation will still be necessary," Giles

added. "We managed to cure Xander, but we'll need a bit more time before we can begin inoculating people. Soon, though, Buffy. At which point we must be ready to act. You'll have to take the cure to Dawn and your mother at that point."

"I'll keep checking in from the chaos," Buffy promised. "Soon, though, right?"

"Yes, soon."

"Well, that's a relief," Buffy said, patting her stomach. "No sprouting extra appendages for you." Then she frowned and glanced at Giles. "What about the Aegirie, the people who are already changed?"

The Watcher ticked his gaze toward Rosanna a moment, then looked back at Buffy. From his pallor and the set of his features she could tell the news was not quite as good. "We're not quite sure. At a certain point in the metamorphosis it must become irreversible. But without experimentation it's impossible to know how far gone is too far."

"It's the best we could do, I'm afraid," Rosanna said.

Buffy looked up sharply, surprised by the genuine remorse in the woman's voice. Though she was more inclined to side with the philosophy espoused by the Order of Sages than with the Council these days, she had still mentally lumped them all together as a bunch of clinical automatons. For the first time she saw Rosanna as a person instead of one of a parade of Watchers and Sages and Initiative soldiers and scientists more interested in dissecting evil than defeating it, people who were in the battle for the righteous glory, instead of in it because it was the right thing to do.

"Thanks," Buffy said. "It's a shame the Council doesn't spend more time looking for answers instead of assuming they know them all already."

Rosanna looked pleased. She nodded. "My pleasure.

It's an honor to work with you, really. I've always wondered how much more the Order could accomplish with a Slayer on our team. We wouldn't squander your abilities the way the Council has, that much is certain."

Buffy felt slightly uncomfortable with the praise, but it got her thinking. Whatever the Order's agenda was, it did not seem anywhere near as petty and controlling as the Council.

"Yes," Giles said dryly, "and given it's been more than eight hundred years since the last time it happened, I'm certain that the Order would relish the humiliation the Council would suffer in the world's sorcerous community should another Slayer join their ranks."

Surprised, Buffy glanced back and forth between Giles and Rosanna. Her Watcher certainly had his own bitter feelings regarding the Council, but she had no idea he harbored any ill will toward the Sages. Rosanna stiffened slightly, but from her reaction Buffy realized she was not particularly stunned by Giles's thinly veiled accusation.

"You may think what you want, Mr. Giles. I wasn't recruiting. Just wishing aloud. Is that a crime? Travers and his trained monkeys think they're involved in some sort of jihad. They're on a crusade to blot anything nonhuman from the face of the world. The Order wants to study the so-called demon races, to learn from them, to find a common ground so that we can all stop killing each other."

"Um," Buffy ventured, "hoping I don't really have to point this out to you, but it pretty much *is* a crusade. There's a reason the job title is 'Slayer.'"

Rosanna sighed. "Yes, I know. And more's the pity."

"You make it sound like it's Northern Ireland or something," Buffy said, bristling. "Okay, not all monsters are technically monstrous, not all demons are real demonic, but most of 'em? I'm gonna go out on a limb and say 'evil,' which is a word I haven't heard you use."

"There are warring factions of the human race who commonly refer to their enemies as 'evil.' Your own country does it. It's not exactly new."

Buffy stared at her, then shook her head. "You've gotta be kidding me," she muttered.

Giles moved up beside her, both of them staring at Rosanna.

"You realize, of course, that we have seen firsthand the efforts of a great many demons and others of . . . evil persuasion . . . to eradicate humanity from the face of the earth? That we've dealt with countless murders and so many other horrors they would be difficult to catalog? The implication that we're mindlessly slaughtering things that are not evil but simply sad and misunderstood is not only baseless, it's offensive."

Rosanna stared at him, her fine features no longer seeming attractive at all. "And the approach the Council takes is vastly superior, I take it? Admirable, even?"

Giles faltered. "That isn't what I said."

"Mr. Giles, Buffy, the Romans said the same things about the Carthaginians that you're saying now. Byzantium said it about the Turks. The American Colonists said it about King George, and the Native Americans said it about the Colonists. It's all about territory. Conflict over a stretch of earth. The demons used to control this world. Now humans do, and the original proprietors want it back. So we are at war. That's what the Council spends their time at, though they don't always call it that.

"Humanity and the demon races are at war. We kill. We grieve. We fight over every inch of land. Why? Because they do not understand our culture and we do not understand theirs."

Buffy threw up her hands. "Or, maybe 'cause they're, y'know, *evil*!"

Rosanna only looked sad. "There are many demon races who are very peaceful and wise. There are others who are more barbaric. The Order of Sages wants to study them all in the hope that one day all races can share the world peacefully. We choose wisdom, Buffy.

"And there is no wisdom in war.

"Admittedly, even we are sometimes forced to violence. But it is never our first choice. I doubt the Order could make poorer use of the Slayer's services than the Council has done."

"You know what?" Buffy replied sharply. "The only one using the Slayer's services is the Slayer. If the Moruach aren't generally dangerous to humans—if the people they killed here *were* in self defense—and they feel like going back to their little undersea caves or whatever, great. I'll hold the door open for them on their way out. I don't kill for the fun of it.

"It's nice that you're all sixties idealistic and stuff, but out here in the real world, monsters are killing people or turning them *into* other monsters. And I'm sorry if it isn't PC enough for you, but I'm gonna side with the people every time."

For several seconds Rosanna stared at Buffy and Giles, then she turned without another word and went back into the front of the shop, leaving them alone. Buffy turned to Giles and saw that his forehead was creased with contemplation. He was obviously very troubled.

"Where'd you find her?" Buffy asked.

Giles sighed. "She has a point."

Buffy blinked. "We all do. They don't all make sense." She went to the heavy bag and struck it several times in quick succession, her frustration pouring out with every blow.

"Hers does. In a perfect world—"

"It isn't," Buffy said, her fist colliding with the bag

again. Then she glanced at him. "It isn't a perfect world. Pretending it is only sets us up for disappointment . . . and possible dismemberment. We just do our best, Giles. And we watch out for each other."

A wan smile appeared on his face. "That we do."

With a grunt, Buffy struck the bag again, spun, and kicked it hard. Giles had finally opened the packet of photographs she had brought and was looking through them. He quickly flipped through half a dozen or so, then paused to stare at one of them, studying it closely.

"Oh my."

Buffy paused and looked over at him. "Lions and tigers and bears?"

"Not exactly," Giles replied. He did not take his eyes off the photo. "As I suspected from your description, the strange geometric symbols painted here are a summons to the Great Old Ones. The Moruach are likely an offshoot, some species descended from them. The markings or runes around them are part of an incantation."

"To open the Hellmouth?" Buffy asked.

"Indeed," Giles replied. Then he looked up at her at last. "But they're not trying to bring about the apocalypse or bring the Great Old Ones back to Earth."

The Slayer lowered her fists and stared at her Watcher quizzically. "Then why open the Hellmouth?"

Giles glanced back down at the photograph.

"They're trying to go home."

Spike shifted uncomfortably in his sleep, drew up his knees into a fetal position, and moaned softly. In his dreams, dark figures slithered through shadows, emerged gleaming and dripping from dark rivers, and constricted around him, their scales rough against his naked skin.

Even asleep the combination of terror and arousal was almost more than he could bear. He wanted her, wanted the Queen to wrap herself around him and crush him until his bones snapped and were ground down to dust, wanted to sink his fangs into her filthy flesh even though he knew the taste of her blood would sicken him.

Revulsion drove him up out of sleep and into consciousness.

His eyes flickered open and she loomed there in the darkness above him. Spike cried out and rolled away from her, fell off his bed, and rose up with his fists clenched, ready to fight her, to tear her apart, to take her . . .

He blinked. What had seemed in the confusing moments of waking to be a huge, looming figure, a Moruach, was not at all. It was human. Petite. Female. His eyes adjusted to the dark.

"Bloody hell, Slayer," he hissed. "You about gave me a heart attack."

Buffy crossed her arms and cocked one hip in that way she had that always seemed to dare him to do anything but submit to whatever it was she wanted at the time. Made him want to rip her head off. He might have done it, too, except for the small problem of the chip in his head that would have sent pain tearing through his own head.

"Cardiac arrest, pretty much impossible if you don't have a heartbeat, Spike. Why so jumpy? Bad dreams?"

Spike glared at her. "Not that it's any of your business, but yeah."

"What do vampires dream about, anyway?"

A grin split his features. "Wouldn't you like to know?"

"Not especially. Now that I think about it, not at all."

"You couldn't handle a night in my dreams," Spike said slowly. "Probably break your sanity up into tiny pieces."

"Pretty much," Buffy agreed. "All those sweaty half-naked soap opera bimbos'd drive me batty."

The vampire sneered and rose, wrapping his sheets around his naked torso. "You've already outstayed your welcome and you've only been here two minutes. What do you want, Slayer?"

"We had a date, remember?"

A tremor went through Spike, and he turned and walked to a chair to pick up his pants. He let the sheet drop and Buffy turned to look away quickly.

"Do you mind?" she snapped.

"Yeah. I do," he sniffed. "But you're here anyway."

Spike knew full well why she had come. All during that long, too-warm day he had slept only fitfully, tossing and turning as images of the Moruach Queen had whispered across his dreams, sinister and cruel and dangerous, and yet somehow also seductive. He wasn't sure whether to be more disgusted by his fear of her, or by the allure he could no longer deny. Spike tried to tell himself that maybe that was how the Moruach got the better of the vampires they hunted. Maybe it was a pheromone or something they exuded that aroused vampires, lulled them into complacency.

"A lot of people are dying, Spike. The Moruach aren't killing them, but I think they may know what's causing it, and what to do about it."

The vampire zipped up his jeans. At the sound, Buffy turned to regard him again and he stared at her.

"You really think these things'll help you?" he asked.

"Maybe. Maybe there's something we can do to help them in return," the Slayer said. "But the only way to know is to ask them. To do that, I have to find them. And you're the only bloodhound in town."

He wanted to tell her to get out, to leave him alone. Or that he'd help her find the Moruach, but then she was on her own. But Spike didn't say either one of those things. The time he and the Queen had communicated, if it could even be called that, it was a kind of low-level telepathy. He figured they didn't have a spoken language, or if they did it wasn't something Buffy was going to be able to understand. The Slayer needed him.

Not that he cared.

When it came down to it, the Moruach and the other sea monsters could eat as many people as they liked—make it a regular Sunnydale buffet—and the only thing he'd feel was jealousy. But he needed to see the Queen again, face to face, if only to prove to himself that he could do it. If he could work it the way Buffy wanted, fine. If he had to kill the Moruach Queen, well, that was fine too.

"Right, then." Spike grabbed a shirt, slipped it on, and began buttoning it up. "Let's saddle up, then. Unleash the hound."

Tara sat quietly in an aluminum chair with fake leather on the seat and back and wondered how anyone endured the discomfort of the thing for any length of time. Only love for a patient or absolute desperation could have kept her in that seat. At the moment, it was the latter, for the chair was set beside the hospital bed of Baker McGee. The aging fisherman had been placed in a private room in the security wing of the hospital, wrists bound by padded straps apparently in use to keep him from harming himself.

Or from tearing off his skin.

McGee's epidermis was peeling off. Beneath it Tara could see the scaly, fishlike skin that was growing to replace what had made the man human. There was no movement at his abdomen yet, nothing that would indicate the growth of tentacles, but she knew it was only a matter of time.

So she sat at the bedside of the heavily sedated man and she wept for him, tears of regret for the unfulfilled potential of the years that ought to have remained in the life of a kind, gentle man. Tara had barely known him, but McGee had struck her as a good soul. Several times as she sat there she reached out to take his hand but pulled away at the last moment. She wasn't infected yet. At least she did not think she was. If there was a way she could comfort him, that he could be aware of her presence there, she would have tried to offer him that solace.

But what if she caught it from him? Just how contagious was it? Sure, Giles and the woman from the Order of Sages had figured out how to arrest and even reverse it in early stages. They'd done it for Xander. But that did not mean Tara wanted to experience even the first stirrings of metamorphosis.

No.

She sat with her hands in her lap and watched him, a new regret in her now. This time for herself, for the reluctance that she felt, and her fear. From time to time she glanced at the small, square window in the door to the room. It was high up and crisscrossed with wire, just like the windows in all the doors in the security wing. Orderlies, doctors, and nurses needed to be able to look into the room before entering, just in case a patient had gotten out of hand. Nobody had looked in, as far as Tara could tell.

Not that they would have noticed her if they had.

It wasn't that she was invisible. Willow had come up with a spell when they had left the hotel that would make them . . . inconspicuous. It didn't mean people couldn't see them, only that they wouldn't notice. It was sort of like opposite magnetic poles. When they walked by, people would just look away. People *could* see them. They just wouldn't.

The weird irony of it was that Tara had felt that way almost her entire life. Not invisible. Just *unseen*.

Willow had changed that. A smile crossed Tara's face

just thinking about her. Somehow just by being her friend, by loving her, by noticing her, Willow had brought Tara out into a world it felt like she had never been a part of before. It was like the sun had started to shine on her for the very first time. It was wonderful, but it had its drawbacks as well.

Being in the world meant participating in it, and she had been unprepared for that. She'd never been required to participate before, to have an opinion, to contribute. Tara wanted to contribute, of course. But she had spent so many years being quiet and still that it took effort to speak up, to draw attention to herself. She was still working on it.

Willow was giving her all the time in the world. And though it had taken a while before she felt like Buffy and the others had noticed her, that was okay too. She was used to it. Now that they had, they were giving her room to grow as well. When she was in elementary school—she couldn't remember what year—the teacher had planted a flower bulb in a cutoff milk jug filled with dirt and left it on the windowsill. Every day when the kids arrived they would walk past the window to see if the bulb had begun to grow. Tara felt a little bit like that flower bulb.

It was good.

She frowned now, though, suddenly troubled. The image of that cutoff milk jug, the tiny sprig of green poking up out of the earth, had been a pleasant one. But now she stared at the dry patches of flaking skin on Baker McGee's face and it took on a new and ugly significance. Her stomach roiled with nausea and Tara turned away.

Baker McGee was becoming something new as well. And here she was, just sitting by, watching to see what might grow.

Tara shuddered and hugged herself and wondered

what was taking Willow so long. She had gone down the hall to call Giles and—

"It rises," Baker McGee whispered.

She jerked upright in her chair, heart hammering in her chest, and stared at the man strapped to the bed. His voice was a dry rasp that called to her mind images of what changes might be occurring inside his mouth, his throat, down within his body. But there was a smile of ecstasy on what remained of his face.

"What does?" Tara asked, leaning ever so slightly closer. "Is it the Aegir, Mr. McGee? The Aegir is coming?"

The old man twitched at the sound of her voice. He knew she was there, in spite of the sedatives and his delirium.

"It . . . rises . . . ," McGee rasped again. "It calls to us. Yes. We come. We gather at the shore where the spawn of Kyaltha'yan hide. We must kneel in the surf . . . we must pay obeisance . . . offer ourselves. Then it shall rise and command us."

Tara hesitated. Swallowed hard. "Command us to do what?" she asked.

"The spawn of Kyaltha'yan will be destroyed."

Baker McGee opened his eyes as though the lids had been forced back. His gaze was dead and glassy . . . and his eyes began to bulge out of their sockets. He did not so much as twitch as his eyeballs burst in a splash of vitreous fluid and their remains were pushed out from below and sloughed off like snakeskin to reveal huge black, gleaming orbs below.

And he *looked* at her.

Tara screamed, shaking her head, hands waving in front of her as she backed up against the wall. It was too much . . . all of it just too much, and she had been driven over the edge. Hysterical, she turned her face to the wall and tried to catch her breath, to slow her heartbeat.

When she looked back at McGee, there was blood soaking through his hospital pajamas at the chest, and things were squirming underneath. He began to buck against the restraints the held him on that bed, and one of the electronic monitors attached to him began to squeal in alarm.

Seconds passed and the door banged open. An orderly rushed in, stared in terror at the blood and McGee's eyes and the tentacles tearing their way out of his pajamas, then turned and ran back into the corridor, shouting for help.

Biting her lip to stay silent, tears threatening at the corners of her eyes, Tara slowly made her way to the door and out into the hall. She passed within two feet of the frantic orderly, but he did not notice her, not at all. The deflection spell was still working perfectly. No one would see her if she cried. No one except—

"Tara!"

Willow's voice echoed off the tiled walls. Tara looked along the corridor to see her hurrying up from the bank of pay phones, a smile on her face. All around her the nurses moved rapidly. Two orderlies brushed past Willow on their way to McGee's room. But just as none of them noticed Willow, she paid no attention to them.

"I talked to Giles," she said breathlessly as she ran up to Tara and took her hand. "They were right. The elixir they used to cure Xander will work on anybody who's infected, as long as the metamorphosis hasn't finished. He already talked to the National Guard. 'Course they're gonna analyze the elixir to make sure he's not some fruit-cake, but then—"

Tara stared at her wide-eyed, but Willow had been so excited she had not seen it right away. Now her enthusiasm faltered, her smile evaporated, and she stared at Tara, clutching both of her girlfriend's hands in her own.

"It's too late, isn't it?" Willow asked softly.

Tara nodded. "For Captain McGee. Yeah. It is."

They embraced then, there in the hallway of the hospital with nurses and doctors and orderlies rushing around them in a panic. The two witches held one another close while the world went on around them as though they weren't even there, unaware of their grief, unmoved.

Tara felt cold, despite the warmth of Willow's body against hers. She wanted to remove the spell, wanted to be seen. Though she knew they needed to remain inconspicuous to move freely around Sunnydale, in that moment she wanted more than anything to be a part of the world again, to be forced into the flow of life around her, to participate. Even with Willow in her arms, she felt terribly alone.

"I . . ." She swallowed hard, fought back the sadness. "I think I know. Where the Aegir's g-going to come up. It's c-calling to them. The Aegirie. They're all . . . all . . ."

She shuddered. Willow shushed her and stroked her hair and whispered softly in her ear, covering her face with tiny kisses. Tara melted into her and suddenly it was all right that even in that busy corridor they were essentially alone. More than all right. Willow could not erase her sadness and her horror, but she could make it better.

And she did.

A tropical breeze blew off the Pacific, cutting across the top of the bluff overlooking the ocean. Buffy tasted salt on her lips. Her hair was tied back, but a loose strand whipped around in front of her face. She ignored it, barely even noticed it. Her attention was focused entirely on the enormous, sprawling mansion that loomed above her.

"Here?" she asked doubtfully.

Beside her, Spike tipped a cigarette out of the pack, drew it out pinched between his lips, and sparked up his lighter. He drew a long drag off it before replying.

"Here."

The Slayer shook her head. "It doesn't make any sense. Look at the place. It's gotta be worth millions. The property alone—"

"Yeah. Looks like a hideaway for some twenties movie star," Spike agreed. "But you think I'd ramble across this town like a bloody prat if I didn't have the scent? I do. And it leads here."

Spike sucked on the cigarette again. The embers at its tip glowed in the darkness, a tiny beacon in the night, casting strange orange shadows across his face. When he lowered it again, his hand was shaking. Buffy stared at the vampire, who twitched and sniffed and shifted his weight from foot to foot like a kid afraid to ask his dream girl to the prom. The words were out of her mouth before she had a chance to even consider them.

"You're afraid," she said in astonishment.

The snarl transformed his face in an instant, lips curling back to reveal his fangs, nostrils flaring in fury. "Bollocks," he said, and he flicked his cigarette at her face.

Buffy caught the burning cig in her hand, unmindful of the ash searing her skin. She dropped it beneath her heel and ground it out, staring at him. Any other time she would have knocked him down for tossing the butt at her, but she was taken aback by his fear. Spike had told her the effect that the Moruach had on vampires, but it was unsettling to see it.

He glared at her mercilessly, too proud to look away. At length it was Buffy who lowered her gaze, then glanced back up at the house.

"What are we supposed to do? Just knock?"

"I don't think she'd answer. You want in, you go in,"

Spike drawled, lifting his chin as though in defiance of the looming house itself.

She, Buffy thought. *Not they. I don't think* she'd *answer.* Any doubts that might have lingered in her regarding the veracity of Spike's stories about his past run-ins with the Moruach Queen evaporated.

"Then let's go."

But when she started up toward the house, Spike didn't move. Buffy glared at him. "You coming?"

"Right behind you," the vampire replied, but he stuffed his hands in his pockets and studied her. "Just want to clarify a little something first. You know the people who own this house are dead, yeah? I mean, it's a safe bet the soddin' Moruach didn't check around to see who was on vacation before moving in. If they took the place, it was out of convenience."

A hard knot began to form in Buffy's gut, but she nodded. "They're probably dead, yeah."

"And they killed folks at the Dex, didn't they? The Moruach."

Again, Buffy nodded.

"So why are you goin' easy on them?" Spike asked. "Not turnin' soft on me, I hope?"

She looked up at the house, all of its windows ominously dark. "The people who died at the Dex . . . that might have been self-defense. Sure, a little over-the-top self-defense, but the Moruach aren't human, are they? It's like a couple of lions getting loose at the zoo. They're dangerous, but they're not evil. Not like the Aegir and all the people it's infected, killing everything in sight just for the sake of killing. *That's* evil. But the Moruach are just animals. There's no malice in it. They don't want to turn the world into Hell on Earth; they just want to go home. Just keep it in mind, Spike. We're not here to kill these things. I just want them out of Sunnydale."

Spike stretched, rolled his head a bit, muscles popping in his neck as he prepared for a fight. He smiled at her. "Or maybe it's just that the idea of doing what the Council wants you to do pisses you off."

"That could have something to do with it."

Buffy strode up toward the front of the house. This time she did not pause to see if Spike was following her. To one side of the door, a plaque announced the place as THE WILLIAM TALISKER HOUSE, 1881. She'd never heard of Talisker, but she suspected that if he still haunted the magnificent old house, he had fresh company, that the Moruach had killed the current owners. How was she supposed to parley with the Moruach if that were the case? The answer came back to her the instant the question crossed her mind.

I can't. If the Moruach had slaughtered the owners of the Talisker House, no one could tell her that it had been done in self-defense. That would change things.

The problem was, she was certain the Moruach held the key to stopping the Aegirie. An image of Quentin Travers rose up in her mind. He'd said the Aegirie would be stopped if all the Moruach were killed and he was probably right. If the Aegir was after the Moruach and creating these other monsters to hunt them, it was simple. Kill the Moruach. The Aegir goes away. But that might not stop the spread of the Aegirie infection. And it wouldn't provide the answers she was looking for.

"Well?" Spike prodded, his voice a rasp.

Conflicting emotions continued to swirl in Buffy's mind, but nothing would be accomplished just standing there. On the front steps of the Talisker House she took a deep breath and kicked the door in. It crashed open, lock splintering the frame, and Buffy strode into the shadowy interior of the house with Spike at her heels.

The foyer was dark and silent, save for the echo of

their violent entrance and the tick of a grandfather clock that stood against one wall. The carpets were unruffled, the walls unmarred. The place seemed abandoned, right down to a kind of musty smell that accumulated in houses that had been closed up too long in warm weather.

Buffy shot a questioning look at Spike, who shook his head.

"They're here," he whispered, a quaver in his voice. But this time she thought the quaver sounded more like hunger than fear. "I can smell them."

And now Buffy thought she could as well. There was a dank, salt odor in the air that she had smelled before, and beneath it all the vague aroma of something rotten. Yet the room was empty, the house silent.

The silence was broken by a chorus of high-pitched screeching and the shadows came alive. From every room the Moruach slithered into the foyer, moving so swiftly that Buffy could not count them. Several more came down the grand staircase and, impossibly, a huge serpentine shape unfurled from the chandelier above, crystal tinkling softly. Their massive flat heads darted at the air as they hissed, sliding toward her, eel bodies moving low to the ground. Quartets of black eyes glared at her and Spike.

The Moruach attacked.

There was nowhere to run. Buffy launched herself at the nearest of the sea serpents. Even as it opened its massive jaws and lunged toward her face she ducked low and drove her fist into its chest. The Moruach squealed that tortured wail as it crashed into the banister at the bottom of the stairs, long body whipping back and forth as though it might find purchase. Others were moving on her, too many, too fast. She lost track of Spike but could hear him shouting somewhere off to her right, toward the front parlor of the vast house. Something crashed. Glass shattered.

"I thought you could talk to these things!" Buffy shouted at him.

But no response was forthcoming, and she had to wonder if Spike had already been dragged down by the monsters. Vampires were a delicacy to them. Spike had said so himself. Buffy cursed silently. All she'd done was play pizza-delivery girl to these things.

They had come without weapons, fearing that the Moruach would not believe they had come in peace if they arrived armed. *Stupid,* Buffy thought now. But it was too late for self-recrimination.

Three of the Moruach moved on her at once. She dodged the snapping jaws of a monster that lunged at her from above even as she snapped a sidekick into the head of one that came in low, belly to the ground. Its teeth shattered.

The third one raked its talons across her back, and Buffy cried out in pain, stumbling away. Another of the creatures waited for her, and in her mind she tried calculating how many of them there might be in the house. The only thought that came to mind then was *enough*—enough to kill her.

Buffy thrust out her hands and grasped the jaws of the Moruach who had caught her in its razor-sharp talons, but it shook her loose. Its tail whipped around and cracked across her back hard enough that had she not been the Slayer, the blow would probably have shattered her spinal cord. She slammed into the grandfather clock and it chimed loudly in her ears as its glass face shattered, and the whole, heavy encasement tipped to one side and crashed to the ground. She went down with it, landing on top of the thing, her palms sliced up by the broken glass.

She looked up just in time to see a Moruach darting toward her. Buffy rolled away across shards of jagged glass that stuck to her clothes and skin and drew a dozen beads of blood from her flesh.

Then she was up and facing them again—backed into a corner, but that was the safest place for her. There was nowhere to run. The Moruach had paused in their attack, seeing that she was trapped. Now they began to surround her, some standing tall and others coiling low to the floor. Horrible silhouettes in the dark, shadows upon shadows. Even as her eyes adjusted, the Moruach seemed like liquid darkness moving in and out of the shafts of muted moonlight that came through the curtained windows. Buffy counted at least eighteen, and there were more coming down the stairs. A lot more.

She stood up straight. *What are you holding back for?* she thought wildly, angry at herself. *Get clear, get outside where there's room to fight, and just kill them.* As fast as they were, and as much as that dread and terror still tickled the base of her skull, she knew she could fight them. They might kill her, but it was possible she could take them all.

Long minutes passed—though she could not have said how many with the grandfather clock in ruins on the ground. Was it five minutes? Ten? She could no more answer that question than she could figure out what was keeping them back, why the Moruach hadn't just swarmed in on her and torn her to shreds. Buffy had no idea what the creatures were waiting for, but she used the time, every second, to examine her options. Like chess, she tried to plot out her actions as far ahead as she could, tried to figure a way for her to take them all on with no backup and no weapons, how to use the house and its rooms and furniture to her advantage.

No matter how she approached it, the answer was the same. If she stayed in the house, she was screwed.

The Moruach gathered in a half circle around her.

Buffy tensed, ready to leap over them, head for one of the tall windows in the foyer. She'd throw herself through one of them, take the fight out onto the bluff. Maybe drive some of them over the edge. If she could just get out of the house, she had a chance.

In sudden unison, the Moruach opened their huge mouths wide and wailed that horrid sea-song. Buffy winced, narrowing her eyes and drawing back, wanting to cover her ears but not daring to lower her guard.

It stopped, and she felt a small trickle of blood run down her earlobe and drip onto her neck.

Something heavy bumped down the stairs. More than one something. The Moruach began to move back, clearing a path for several new arrivals, serpents that dragged with them two thick bundles of bed sheets. And wrapped in the bed sheets, squirming, eyes wide with terror, were a human man and woman. The man was twisted away from her, but the woman's eyes widened as she saw Buffy and she started to scream.

"Oh Jesus, oh God, do something! Help us! They're going to eat us!"

Buffy drew in a long breath, staring incredulously at the woman and then around at the Moruach. Her gaze ticked back toward the captives. "Y'know, I don't think they are. Who are you?"

"Polly . . . Polly Haskell," she stammered, face streaked with tears and sweat and dust from wherever the Moruach had been storing her during their stay.

"This is your house?"

The woman gave no sign that Buffy's words lent her any comfort, but she nodded, eyes darting back and forth with every slither and snort of the Moruach.

The Slayer shifted uncomfortably. "Sorry about the mess."

Once again the Moruach shifted suddenly, all of

them turning at once toward the parlor. The creature that emerged from that room was larger than the others, yet thinner. Its eyes were somehow both more intelligent and more savage as it opened its maw wide, rows of razor teeth gleaming in the muted moonlight. The way the creatures all shifted, their flat heads bowing low, Buffy knew this was the Queen.

They hadn't killed the owners of the house. The only human lives they'd taken had been the security people at the Dex who had tried to stop them from killing Ben Varrey. They'd killed. But they weren't killers. It was a fine line, and in war, maybe it wouldn't have mattered.

But this wasn't really war. It was survival.

"Your majesty," Buffy said, straightening up.

Which was when Spike followed the Moruach Queen into the parlor, buttoning up his jeans. His shirt was ripped and he was bleeding from gashes on his arms and chest. There were scratches on his face and his hair was mussed.

He smiled as he looked at Buffy. Then he pulled out his cigarettes and lit one quickly, slipping the pack and lighter back into his pocket.

"Parley's over, Slayer. What next?"

Buffy barely had time to register what had gone down here or to channel her revulsion at the horrible images in her mind, for outside the house an engine roared and tires skidded to a halt and car doors opened and slammed closed.

For a moment she stared at Spike, then her gaze fell again upon the Moruach Queen. The monster reached out and dragged its talons along the line of Spike's jaw as though she might tear his head off any second, but there was something tender in that gesture as well. Then the Queen gazed at Buffy, that dark intelligence commanding and brutal, and she slithered toward the Slayer on her powerful serpentine trunk.

The Queen waved toward the door, and the Moruach cleared away. Buffy hesitated only a second before moving swiftly to the front of the room and peering out through the open door. In the moonlight she could see five figures walking up toward Talisker House from an SUV parked sideways across the drive. They were silhouettes only: two female and three male. One of the men wore a turban.

And she recognized the walk of one of the females.

Faith, Buffy thought.

All of them were armed.

They had come for war.

Chapter Sixteen

A car drove by out on the street, some classic-rock anthem or other grinding out of the speakers at window-thumping volume. Even this far from the road, Xander and Anya could hear the music clearly. Night had fallen, and Xander had always felt that sounds carried farther after dark. There wasn't any science to it—or if there was he didn't know about it—but there it was: Xander Harris Theory number 417.

From their vantage point, it felt like he could hear every noise for half a mile around. Every dog barking, every argument, every door slamming, even the unmistakable clacking of a couple of kids trying skateboard stunts a block over. The wind had picked up and it shook the chain-link fence that ran around what was left of Sunnydale High—what Xander thought of as the school's corpse. Even from a distance he could hear the creak of the ruins as the wind rushed through them.

He and Anya sat in the highest row of the bleachers

in the abandoned football stadium next to the school. They had a clear view of three sides of the school. The fourth side—the one they could not see—was clearly visible from the road that ran in front of the school, even through the chain-link fence. They had reasoned that if the Moruach were going to come, they weren't likely to come from that side.

It was a risk Xander was prepared to take, given that there was literally nowhere else they could hide. Not only nowhere that would give them a decent view of the school, but no Dumpster or copse of trees or generator box that could provide them cover from which to do this little surveillance errand Giles had sent them on. The only other option was to wait inside the school for the Moruach to show; inside the crumbling, burnt-out wreckage that could bury them alive at any moment. Whatever the crisis, Xander doubted Giles expected that of them.

"Kind of weird, isn't it?" Anya asked, voice low.

Xander was leaning over the rear wall of the stadium, looking down at the remains of the school, his back to the field. His injured shoulder seemed almost numb, but he still kept the arm in the sling close to his body. Anya was beside him, her crossed arms resting atop the wall, chin propped up on her arms.

"What is?" Xander asked, searching the ruins for any sign of movement, ears attuned for any sound other than that eerie creaking as the wind blew through the devastated structure.

"Not that long ago, everything was different. The school was still a school. There were actual sports games here. You were a loveable loser instead of the manly and durable stud muffin you've become. Not long before that, I was still a demon."

Troubled, Xander glanced at her. "Okay, please tell me you're not feeling nostalgic for the good old days.

'Cause, me? Singing Hosannas that the eternal torment of high school came to an end."

Anya's expression softened. "Not at all. They weren't the good old days. Though some of them were good." Her gaze turned back toward the crumbling, blackened ruins. "I was only thinking that without Sunnydale High, we would never have met. And how it's sort of sad you all had to blow it up."

Surprised, Xander smiled. "An, you're being wistful. You're wistful woman."

A tiny pout turned down the edges of Anya's mouth. "You're teasing me," she said petulantly. "You know how it irks me, the teasing, when it isn't sexual."

"Not. No teasing here."

Her gaze lifted and her eyes met his. "So wistful is a good thing?" she asked, doubtful.

"Absolutely. It's sweet and romantic and girly—in that, 'Yep, I'm a tough, former demon-chick with a secret need to be cuddled' kinda way."

Anya raised an eyebrow. "Will the cuddling be accompanied by more strenuous and sweaty expressions of mutual love and attraction?"

Xander smiled. "Vixen. Always with the verbal seduction."

He grabbed her and pulled her toward him with his free hand. Anya wrapped her arms around him and embraced him tightly as she kissed him, nibbling gently on his lower lip. Despite his recent ordeal—or perhaps because of the elixir Giles had used to cure him of it—he felt better than he had in days. A rare energy coursed through him and he was looking forward to Buffy figuring out how to vanquish the latest evil so he and Anya could—

She shoved him away. "Xander. Your shoulder."

A frown creased his forehead for a moment, and then he understood what had alarmed her. Curious, Xander glanced down at his left arm and the sling he wore. He reached up with the fingers of his right hand and gingerly explored the collarbone that had been broken in his surfing accident over the weekend, and his eyes widened.

"Hunh," he grunted. Tentatively, he moved his shoulder around and then slipped his arm out of the sling. Xander flexed his fingers and slowly stretched the arm out all the way, rotating his shoulder.

"It doesn't hurt?" Anya asked, staring at him in amazement.

Once again he stretched. "Actually, I'm feeling pretty great. Must be some side effect of the cure Giles gave me. Not that I wanna start turning all black lagoon-y again to test it out, but, pretty cool."

He took the sling from around his neck and made to toss it down among the bleachers, but Anya grabbed it from his hand.

"Wait," she said, all business as she folded it and stuffed it into the back pocket of her beige pants. "We may find a use for this later."

Xander shot her a dubious look. "Ya think? What use could that thing possibly—" He cut himself off and gaped at her. "Oh. Ooohhh."

Once more they were smiling. *Grinning at each other like a pair of idiots,* Xander thought, though he did not mind in the least. But even as he slid both arms around his girlfriend this time, a sound caught his attention. He glanced around, roughly in the direction from which it had come, and waited for it to come again. Skateboard kids were still out practicing, but that was not what he had heard. A woman shouted for her dog, which had apparently run away. The low drone of cars was ever present in the distance.

Then it came again and a chill went through him. *Clink, clink-clink.*

"The fence?" Anya whispered.

Xander nodded and crouched low, moved back to the wall at the rear of the stadium. The healing of his collarbone was a surprise, but it was also an extraordinary blessing. If they had to fight . . . or, more likely, if they had to run . . . he would be able to move more quickly now.

They stood together in the darkness at the top of the bleachers and looked down upon the school lawn. *Could be kids,* Xander thought. *Skateboard punks moving off the street, looking to try something new.* Once upon a time he'd been one of them, though he'd never been as good on a skateboard as he'd hoped to become.

His eyes searched the darkness, but Xander saw nothing. In his mind he began to count, a silent tick-tock of seconds from when he had last heard the sound of the fence being jostled. It wasn't the wind, that was for sure. But he supposed it might have been merely someone walking by, idly pushing on the fence as they passed. It could have been anything, really.

Anya jabbed a finger into his ribs and Xander flinched but kept silent. He looked at her, saw where her attention was fixed, and glanced that way. Almost right beneath them, and slightly off to the right, things moved in the shadows of the night out across the moonlit lawn. Buffy had described them after first running into the Moruach at the Dex, but it was still chilling to see them slithering across the grounds, their lower bodies undulating to propel them forward even as they gestured toward one another and toward the ruins of the school with their talons. One of the creatures carried a plastic sack but Xander could not tell what was inside it. The others went to a collapsed wall among the ruins and begin to clear debris from the spot.

For several long moments Xander and Anya merely

crouched there side by side and watched them. A chill went up the back of Xander's neck and the little hairs stood up. Many of the demons Buffy had fought were relatively humanoid—hell, vampires looked like humans most of the time. But these things were just so completely inhuman that they unnerved him like nothing else. A dread crawled all through him then, but it wasn't manufactured, the way it had felt in the past couple of days. This was real, and the reason for it was right below.

He waited until the last of the Moruach had begun sifting the ruins—there were five altogether, including the one with the plastic bag—before he reached into his pocket and slipped out the cell phone Giles had given him. Xander glanced at the ghostly green glow on the digital readout, then quickly dialed the number for the Magic Box. With every soft beep of the keypad he saw Anya glance over the edge of the stadium wall to be certain they had not been heard.

The phone was answered on the second ring. "Magic Box?"

"Giles, it's Xander," he whispered, afraid even that would be too loud. He stared at Anya, watching to see if she would react to some activity below. "They're here."

"I was afraid of that," the Watcher replied. "I haven't heard anything from Buffy yet. No way to know if she's made contact with them yet."

"Well, no sign of her *here,*" Xander said, anxiety rippling through him. "Just a bunch of eel-men digging out some chunks of high school for souvenirs."

Anya glanced down at him, and he could see that she was on edge, but there was no alarm in her eyes. That was good.

"So what now?" Xander asked.

"Can you tell what they're up to?" Giles asked. "If they're digging out the library area, they may be making another attempt at opening the Hellmouth."

"Hang on," Xander whispered.

He inched up and glanced over the wall. The Moruach were working perhaps sixty yards away, farther along the outer perimeter of the ruins. The one with the plastic sack was still hanging back from the others as they cleared more debris.

"They're just making room right now. But the spot they're in might have been the library. It's hard to tell from outside."

"Are they carrying anything?" Giles asked. "Buffy said there had been animal and human sacrifices. A sea turtle, I believe. And then—"

"Just a plastic bag. Like from the supermarket," Xander cut in. "It'd have to be a small turtle or maybe Mini-Me. And now I'm thinkin' too small even to be Mini-Me."

"I'm not going to ask what that is," the Watcher said dryly. "Can't you get a better look at what they're carrying?"

"Gee, maybe I should just go and ask them?" Xander replied, more than a little edge to his voice.

Giles did not seem to get the humor, or he chose to ignore it. "No," the Watcher said. "You don't speak their language. They'd probably just kill you."

"Oh, well, I'd better not then." Xander sighed and shook his head. His sarcasm was wasted.

"Xander!" Anya hissed.

He snapped his head back to gaze up at her. She was motioning for him to look over the edge. When he did he saw that the collapsed walls of the library had been somewhat cleared and the Moruach were moving into the ruins. The one with the plastic bag followed the others and they disappeared inside.

"Giles, they went in. I can't see them from here."

"We need to know what's in that bag, Xander," Giles

told him. "If they're going to try to open the Hellmouth again, it may be up to you to stop them. Rosanna and I will leave here now, but we'll never get there in time. If there's any sort of blood sacrifice involved, you're going to have to stop them. Try to get a closer look. We're on our way."

The line went dead. Xander held the phone out and stared down at it, as though he could make the phone feel guilty for leaving him hanging, then he slipped it back into his pocket. When at last he stood and turned toward Anya, she was looking at him sternly.

"What?" he whispered.

"Don't go."

"What?" he said again.

"I got the gist of that conversation," she told him, her demeanor that of an aggravated schoolteacher. "Giles is sending you into the jaws of doom. That's just not going to happen. It's Buffy's job to stop the apocalypse. It always is. That's part of her whole deal. Not yours. You're my mate. My hard-working man. You're not the hero. Nobody chose you to be some champion for freako cosmic powers that can't lift a finger to help themselves. You're just the . . . the side dish."

"The side dish?" he repeated, not liking the sound of those words. "So in the restaurant of danger I'm, what? The vegetable medley? The French fries?"

"I was thinking pilaf."

"I'm the pilaf?" Xander felt deflated.

"Don't be upset," Anya told him. "Heck, I'm just the pilaf's girlfriend."

Xander took a long breath and let it out, shaking his head. Then he stood up a little straighter and faced her. "Anya. Buffy's not here. Willow's not here. Giles is on the way, but he's not here either. It's just you and me, honey, and though going down there is about as appealing to me as having all my teeth drilled to the nerve, Novocain-free, if they're trying to open the Hellmouth, I can't *not* try to stop them."

Her lips were pressed together so tightly they were white, and her arms were crossed as though she were trying to stop herself from slapping him. At length, Anya sighed.

"All right. But if you get killed, don't think that's the end of it. In my vengeance demon days, there were guys I made suffer even after they were dead."

Xander forced a wan smile. "What a comfort."

Then he turned and started down through the stands, careful to remain as quiet as possible. It took him a moment to realize that Anya was following him. He considered telling her to go back, and then thought better of it, unwilling to dare her wrath further. Instead he paused for her to catch up to him, and then together they made their way out of the stadium. At the outer gate they paused and Xander poked his head out to look across the stretch of yellowed grass between the stadium and the corpse of Sunnydale High. It had not been cared for, of course, and so where it still grew at all the grass had been burnt by the sun. It crunched softly beneath Xander's feet as he crept away from the stadium. Anya followed a moment later.

They moved alongside the stadium, keeping in the shadow of the bleachers, hoping to get a vantage point from which they would be able to see inside the remains of the library and still have room to run if it came to that. He held his breath and started across the burnt lawn. Anya was with him every step. The air felt electrically charged with their fear and with the peril they were placing themselves in. Even if Buffy had not told him how fast the Moruach could move, all he would have had to do was take a single look at them and it would have been obvious.

With every step he moved more slowly until he

thought he would just freeze there in place, too afraid to go any farther. But he had to see, had to find out what they were doing in there, even if it meant going . . . inside.

What are you doing? he thought to himself. *You're the pilaf!* Xander wanted more than anything to just turn around and hide until Giles showed up with reinforcements. But what he had said to Anya had not been merely because of his hurt feelings. He had to do this. They had to do it. At the moment, there was no one else. And this moment might be the last one, the only one that mattered.

Xander took a deep breath, and stepped to within a few yards of the collapsed outer wall. He could smell a briny odor that had to come from the Moruach.

In his pocket, the cell phone rang.

He froze, glanced at Anya, then stared down at his pants. It rang again and then he was fumbling for it, trying to retrieve it from his pocket, glancing frantically into the shuddering moonlit shadows in the depths of the ruins and then down at his own shaking hands.

"Oh sh—," he began.

His words were cut off by an earsplitting, high-pitched screech from within the corpse of the school.

Quentin Travers had offered Faith a gun.

She had declined.

That wasn't the way this sort of thing was done. She had tried to explain that to him, but the aging Watcher had brushed her off with a look that told her exactly what he thought of her opinion. He could be all honey-sweet when he wanted to be, but Travers was a cranky old creep whose hair seemed thinner and whose eyes looked more tired with every passing hour, as though he were withering away in front of her. Magick could have done that, certainly, but Faith had a feeling it was simpler than that. Travers had a lot riding on what happened in Sunnydale tonight, with the Moruach and the Order of Sages and with Faith herself.

Stress was a killer.

She hoped he had a hell of an ulcer.

Travers had been busy earlier in the day. With the information Faith had gotten from Willy about Buffy's exploits at the nuthouse, the old man had done a little back-alley dealing with the local authorities and gotten himself the corpse of one of the Moruach. It had been simpler than Travers had expected, since the plan had apparently been to incinerate the remains of anything that was obviously non-human. The Council hadn't pushed the issue too much, but Faith had gathered from a brief conversation with Helen Fontaine that the authorities in Sunnydale disposed of strange carcasses by cremation on a fairly regular basis rather than risk bad press that might kill tourism.

So the people in this town aren't stupid after all, Faith had thought. *It's just another handy conspiracy.* But it was going to take a lot more than the mayor and a few town officials to cover up what was happening now . . . especially if the Aegir came ashore. And that was Travers's ammunition, as it turned out. He told them that with the remains of one of the creatures, he might be able to make all their troubles go away.

Tarjik had taken one of the dead Moruach's hands and burned the flesh off it. There was no smoking in the Hotel Pacifica, so he had done it out on the balcony of the suite, but the stink had still permeated the place so much that there were two calls from the front desk inquiring after the smell. Travers explained that he had burned some incense on the porch as part of a religious observance, and there had been no further complaint. No one wanted to infringe upon anyone's religious rights . . . and it was on the balcony, after all, not in the room.

The burnt flesh of the Moruach had gone into a metal dish with the bones from its hand, several teeth pried from its jaw, a black candle, several drops of Tarjik's own blood, and some other ingredients Faith had not recognized. She'd never paid a lot of attention to magick. Whatever it was, the spell had allowed Tarjik to track the Moruach's kin with its own finger bones.

And here they were.

Tarjik's dabbling in the black arts had led them to this majestic house overlooking the ocean, but the man was obviously no sorcerer. A minor magician, maybe, but without any actual magick of his own. Otherwise he wouldn't have been holding the nine-millimeter Walther MPL submachine gun in his hands.

Travers and Fontaine had guns as well, though the latter had tried to demur, complaining that she was a Watcher, not an operative, and that the wholesale slaughter of *anything* with any weapon was outside of her job description. Travers had not responded well to that, pulling the woman aside and whispering to her fiercely. Whatever it was he had said—Faith suspected something about her job with the Council, maybe even about the books she had said she was writing—Helen had reluctantly taken one of the weapons as well, though when she folded out the metal stock and held it against her shoulder, it had been with a look of such repugnance that Faith knew she would be useless with the thing unless something was about to bite her head off.

Which could happen.

Haversham—though mute—had managed to make his own disdain of such weapons very plain, despite Travers's lecture on the quality of the German armaments and how they had to use whatever tools were available in order to achieve their goals.

Faith had winced at those words. *Whatever tools are*

available. They made her angry and a little . . . soiled. Which was almost funny, considering the life she had led up until recently.

But she was glad Haversham had refused to take a gun. Faith herself had taken a sword from the back of the van that they had driven up here, and Haversham followed suit, though the blade he used was quite different from her own. She had chosen a modern claymore, a beautiful and deadly blade, long and thin, made to be wielded with two hands, while Haversham had taken an antique *cinquedea,* an Italian blade that was narrow at the tip but extremely broad at the base. Both were excellent killing swords, perfectly suited for decapitation.

Faith did not know a damn thing about the guns except what Travers had told her, but she had made it her business, once upon a time, to learn about blades.

The five of them stood shoulder to shoulder now as if that moonlit, windblown stone bluff with the salt of the Pacific in the air was actually Tombstone, Arizona, and they themselves the Clanton gang. Travers took the lead by several steps, studying the house carefully. Faith thought it was an unlikely place for marine demons to be hiding out, but had no reason to believe Tarjik's magick had been unreliable.

"Do you see anything?" Helen whispered, her voice barely audible over the wind.

Faith glanced over to see that the woman was talking to her, and not Travers. She shook her head. Travers ushered them onward, and they all began to move toward the house. Faith strode quickly ahead so that she was abreast of him, and Travers did not chide her for it. As they drew nearer she kept her focus on the house. The curtains were heavy and it was dark inside. Were it not for the fact that the door had obviously been forced open recently, she would have begun to second-guess Tarjik after all.

Then she saw it, just the slight rustle of a curtain inside. An instant later, a pale, almost ghostly figure moved past the open door, so indistinct it might have been her imagination. But she was sure it was not.

"Something's moving," she said.

Haversham appeared suddenly on her other side, *cinquedea* brandished in his right hand. Faith had the claymore held in both hands as though she were carrying a flag. Travers tensed, the barrel of his Walther rising, scything back and forth as he studied the front of the house. For a long moment they all waited for an attack, but none came.

"Faith—," Travers began.

A figure appeared upon the doorstep from within the deeper shadows of the house. Travers raised his Walther, the motion caught Faith's eye, and she saw that he was about to fire. So quickly that her hand was a blur, she reached out and grabbed the barrel of the gun, pushing it toward the sky. Travers shot her a withering glance, but by then he had seen that the figure at the top of the steps was not a Moruach at all.

It was Buffy. She stood there, unarmed, just on the threshold of the old, dark house and stared at them as though they were murderers sneaking about in the dark. And, Faith thought, perhaps they were.

"They're gone," Buffy said. A dangerous smile crossed her lips as she stared at Travers. "The Moruach."

Travers shot a dark look back at Tarjik who shook his head emphatically. The aging Watcher stared at Buffy again.

"You're lying. Step aside."

"Can't do that," Buffy replied. Her gaze ticked toward Faith and there was steel in her eyes. "Sunnydale's got other issues at the moment. We've got a truce with the Moruach. They're not going to open the Hellmouth, and we're not going to try to kill them. Meanwhile, they're gonna help us with a bigger problem."

"The Aegir," Helen Fontaine said quietly.

Travers looked as though he would have struck her if he had dared take his attention away from Buffy.

"Exactly," Buffy said.

Her arms were crossed in defiance and her clothes were torn and stained with blood, which somehow made her look all the more formidable. It was easy for people to underestimate her, this little blonde thing with big, sad eyes and a heartbreaking smile. But that was one mistake that Faith had never made. She had never underestimated Buffy.

"I told you how to stop the Aegir—"

"Yeah, you did," Buffy agreed. "We're not going with that, but thanks for the suggestion."

"She's stalling," Tarjik snapped. He glanced down at the Moruach bones in his hand. "They're moving farther away."

Haversham tensed at Faith's side. Helen shifted awkwardly, the gun still clutched in her grasp as though it were too hot to hold. Travers swore under his breath but continued to glare at Buffy.

"Faith. Get her out of the way. We're going in."

The cell phone rang a third time as Xander pulled it out of his pocket. His skin prickled with fear, and adrenaline rushed through him with such force that he was shaking. He gripped the phone tightly and punched the talk button, more to stop it from ringing than to actually answer it.

"Xander," Anya whispered at his side.

The tone of her voice was enough to freeze his blood. They stood between the former Sunnydale High football stadium and the ruins of the school itself, just outside a massive hole in the burnt and blasted wall of what had once been the library. Inside, the Moruach had been in the midst of . . . something.

He looked up, and through that huge hole in the crumbling structure he could see dark, oily things moving in the moonlight that strafed through the wreckage from above. He could see their eyes—too many eyes. Debris shifted and one of the Moruach moved to the opening in the wall, the moonlight falling upon its shark-like head and huge serpentine body.

"Good plan," Xander muttered furiously.

He grabbed Anya's arm with his free hand—cell phone still clutched in the other—and they turned to run back the way they had come. With a screech that pierced the night and made him wince even as he ran, the Moruach darted out of the ruins of the school and set off across the burnt grass after them, covering the ground twice as fast as Xander and Anya could run.

"Great plan! If monkeys had come up with it! Xander, how do you stop the sea monsters from opening the Hellmouth? Easy! You use yourself as bait and lure them away!"

The ear-splitting wailing had ceased, and now there was only the shush of the Moruach's horrible bodies against the ground as the things pursued them. Xander did not dare turn to look, but he knew they were closing the distance quickly. The fence on the other side of the stadium seemed miles away.

"Xander, we'll never—," Anya panted.

"Just run!" he said. "Get back to the stadium! Maybe there's someplace in there we can hide."

He could picture it in his head. They'd never make it around the other side of the stadium to the fence, that was certain. So maybe they could find a locker room or a restroom and lock or jam the door. Something. Anything.

Before he could stop himself, he risked a look back and nearly faltered in his gait when he saw the silent, monstrous things bent low over the dead lawn, bearing down fast upon them.

A distant, tinny voice was calling his name.

The phone. Still held tightly in his hand. He pressed it to his ear as he ran.

". . . der," he heard, the tail end of Giles's voice.

"I'm here!" Xander said, terror drowning out his anger.

"I called to tell you not to approach the Moruach yet."

"Well, aren't you just Mr. Sucky-Timing?"

There was a sigh on the other end of the line. "You're being pursued, aren't you?"

Before he could respond, Anya lost her footing. She let out a shrill, sharp cry and tumbled to the ground, her momentum rolling her over. Xander whipped around and ran to her, standing over her as the Moruach rushed at him.

"Not anymore," he said grimly.

The phone slipped out of his grasp, but he was hardly aware of it anymore. He faced the Moruach with his fists in the air, knowing how foolish he must look and yet not caring. If he had to tear their eyes out with his fingers or choke them with his own arms, he was going to keep the things away from Anya. The five serpentine creatures slowed as they approached, and Xander found that though his chest was rising and falling rapidly, terror arcing through his mind and racing up his spine, he could barely breathe.

Three of them came low to the ground, circling around them, hemming them in to keep them from fleeing. The other two stood tall and proud on the gleaming, oily, black trunks of their bodies. One among them, its four eyes locked on Xander, raised its arms, talons glinting in the moonlight, and uttered several quick, guttural noises that reminded Xander immediately of the sea lions down on the beach.

They did not attack.

Slowly Anya got to her feet. Xander shot her a quick glance and saw that her brow was furrowed with concentration.

"Say that again," Anya muttered.

The Moruach let its head loll back and let loose an ululating, rolling cry that was part bark and part squeal. Yet there was a pattern to the noises, sounds cut off in throaty grunts and clicks.

"He's talking to us," Anya whispered. "I've heard the language before. A long time ago. It's a chaos tongue, totally archaic. Native to demons of the Pacific islands."

"Can you understand him?" Xander asked in a low voice, a broad smile on his face as he looked around at the swaying, coiling creatures that surrounded them. Any moment he expected to have his throat torn out.

"Not a word," Anya said.

Xander swallowed hard. Slowly he began to crouch. A Moruach hissed and darted toward him, gnashing its jaws. Xander cried out and froze, but when the monster did not try to eat him, he snatched the cell phone off the ground and slowly rose to his feet once more.

"You still there?" he asked Giles, putting a happy tone into his voice, keeping that smile on his face.

"Yes, thank God. I thought you were both dead. Xander, listen. I called to tell you that Willow and Tara are on their way. They should be there any moment now. If you can evade the Moruach for just a few more moments—"

"Giles, do you by any chance speak any chaos languages?"

"Chaos languages? Why do you . . . oh, God. They're standing right there, aren't they?"

"Yep."

"Well, at least you're not dead. Perhaps they truly aren't savages after all."

"There's that. Meanwhile, though, some help? Anya thinks its some Pacific island demon talk. Sounds like the dry heaves to me," he said quickly, smiling even more broadly and hoping that the Moruach were as clueless about his language as he was about theirs.

"Hang on," Giles told him.

"Kinda stuck here."

Xander heard muffled voices on the cell phone, and then Giles was gone and the woman from the Order of Sages came on the line.

"This is Rosanna Jergens. I think I can help. Please put your girlfriend on the phone."

His smile stretched even wider and he imagined himself grotesque, like the Joker in the Batman comics. Xander handed the phone over to Anya.

"It's for you."

Then he stood frozen as Anya spoke quickly to the woman on the other end of the phone line. A sudden flash of terror went through his mind as he wondered what would happen if they had a moment of typical cell phone frustration. But after a few moments, Anya cleared her throat and howled into the night, completely confident, as if it were something she did regularly and was often applauded for.

The Moruach were troubled and they began to move closer, lower to the ground, huge shark jaws opening and snapping quickly shut. The one that had barked at them before stayed upright and began to yowl at them again. Anya held the phone out so that Rosanna could hear it on the other end of the line. Then she clapped it to her ear again, frowned, and responded in a voice that sounded to Xander as though she were trying to cough up a fur ball.

"Xander!"

He turned quickly to see Willow and Tara running toward them from around the side of the stadium. The Moruach shifted uneasily and one of them whipped around to face the two girls, who slowed carefully. Willow and Tara joined hands and a deep purple glow—like a black-light bulb—began to emanate from their twined fingers.

"Anya, Xander, pay attention," Tara called, no trace of the usual hesitation in her voice. Xander had always found it remarkable that any kind of tense conversation would rattle her, but Tara could bravely walk into a horror like this.

"When I say go, run toward us!" Tara told them.

Anya brushed it off. "Oh, please. We're just starting to communicate here. We're fine."

"You're . . . fine?" Willow asked.

Xander grinned. "Aside from the cardiac arrest and the need to change my pants? Well, nobody's eaten me yet, but the night is young."

Willow and Tara hesitated but stayed where they were. Anya continued to choke and bellow like a lunatic, apparently translating a conversation between the Moruach and Rosanna Jergens. After several more minutes of this, she hung up the phone and looked at Xander.

"Okay, we're set," she told him, as the Moruach expectantly eyed her every move.

"Set as in?"

Anya waved her hand in the air like the whole episode had been no big deal and they hadn't been fleeing for their meager existences just minutes before.

"Set, set," she insisted. "They weren't trying to open the Hellmouth again. Well, they were kinda planning on it, but apparently the Queen cut a deal with Buffy and Spike that I think may have involved sex, but for some reason Rosanna wanted to avoid following up on that.

Why is everyone so weird about sex? Especially sex with demons. Obviously *you* don't have any problem with it."

Anya rolled her eyes. "Anyway, I'm getting all this sort of third-hand because the Moruach are interspecies telepaths, which is how our slimy ambassadors here knew the truce was on. The Queen ordered them not to open the Hellmouth, but told them to come down anyway and do a worship ritual, just to cleanse all of their spirits before the battle."

She looked wistful and took a deep breath before sighing. "I remember worship rituals. Nobody pays obeisance to me anymore."

At last Willow and Tara had realized it was safe to approach, though as they walked over they watched the Moruach carefully. They were close enough that they had heard most of what Anya had said, and it was Willow who spoke up now.

"Battle?" she asked.

Anya nodded enthusiastically, apparently very pleased to find herself able to help. "Yes. Their ancient enemy, the Aegir, has pursued them to Sunnydale and could rise from the ocean any time now to destroy them. I gathered it was sort of a long story."

Willow and Tara exchanged a very uneasy glance and Xander noticed immediately.

"What?" he asked. "What is it?"

"We were hoping we were wrong," Willow said. "'Cause we got the news too. About the Aegir? Only it isn't any time now. It's now. He's leaving the ocean now.

"And we know where."

"Faith," Travers said, voice low and dangerous. "Get her out of the way. We're going in."

Buffy turned to look at Faith, her eyes narrowing as she moved into a battle stance. In that look Faith saw all of their shared past, the good and the bad, all the resentment and frustration and disappointment, all of the anger, every blow traded or laugh shared.

A shadow seemed to fall over Faith's heart and mind in that moment. She punched the claymore sword into the hard dirt so that it stood upright, blade gleaming in the moonlight. Then she shifted her body slowly into a stance similar to the one Buffy had taken, every muscle in her body prepared for combat. She sensed the moves, acted them out in her head, even before she was in motion.

Then she moved.

Faith leaped up into a spinning kick that took Daniel Haversham completely by surprise. Her boot connected with his temple and the operative went down hard, unconscious before he even hit the dirt, his own sword thumping uselessly to the ground.

Tarjik was faster than she had expected. Swift as she was, he managed to drop the Moruach bones and swing his weapon up, but he never got to pull the trigger. Faith grabbed the barrel in both hands and shot a sidekick up into his abdomen, snapping a couple of ribs and probably breaking several of his fingers as she yanked the gun from his grasp. With another kick she broke his leg, and the man went down roaring in pain.

Faith had never liked Tarjik.

In his youth, Travers had likely been quite intimidating. But age had no doubt slowed him. It had taken him a couple of seconds to really understand what was happening here, and by then she was ready for him. Faith rushed at him, slapped the gun from his hands and drove him to his knees with a firm grip on his shoulder. Idly she tossed first one gun and then the other onto the ground a few feet in front of Buffy, who stared in wide-eyed disbelief at the spectacle before her.

Faith grinned. "What's the matter, B.? Cat got your tongue?"

"Helen!" Travers was shouting. "Shoot her, damn you! Don't just stand there!"

But Helen Fontaine, who had been staring at the proceedings with a look not unlike the one on Buffy's face, folded up the stock of her gun, walked to Tarjik, and knocked him unconscious with a single blow of the butt.

"All right, Watcher-girl!" Faith said gleefully.

Helen stared at her. "How did you know I wouldn't shoot you?"

"I didn't," Faith replied, a frown creasing her forehead. "But I figured you hated this pompous ass as much as I do. I get the idea you're not interested in killing anyone, Helen. That what you really want is to go home to your writing and your husband and pretend you never heard of the Council or the Slayer or any of this crap."

There was something in the look Faith and Helen exchanged then, some kind of understanding, though Faith doubted she would ever have been able to put it into words.

"I don't blame you," Faith told her, voice low. "I'd walk away if I could. I wish you luck."

Travers fumed, but none of them spoke a word as Helen Fontaine walked back and climbed into the SUV, started it up, and drove off, red taillights receding into the distance.

"You've made a terrible mistake, Faith," Travers spat. "You'll be treated like you escaped from prison. When they find you—and they will, with the help of the Council—years will be added to your sentence."

Her nostrils flared angrily as she shoved him to the ground, pressed his face against the dirt and bent over him.

"You son of a bitch. You don't understand anything about anything, do you? If it doesn't fit the way you see the world, you force it. Well, guess what? Tonight we're doing things my way."

"Let go of me, you—"

"Uh-uh." She cut him off, gripping his thinning hair more tightly, tight enough to hurt. "No name calling. Sticks and stones may not break my bones, but they'll do a hell of a job on yours. Here's the deal. Tomorrow, I'm going back to prison. You *borrowed* me, Travers. And I'll go back, because I said I'd do my time, and I'm going to. As far as the Council's concerned, you're not going to say a freakin' word, you absolute and total loser, because you weren't supposed to come near me in the first place. It'd be bad enough if they knew you brought the prodigal back into the fold, but if you *lost* me? If you screwed it up?

"Let me tell ya from firsthand experience: The Council aren't all that forgiving."

Buffy came down the front steps of the house. She no longer seemed stunned by the turn of events, but she was obviously still uncertain of exactly what was happening here.

"Faith," she ventured cautiously, those sad eyes wide now with sincerity. "Don't do anything—"

"Stupid?" Faith asked. She laughed softly, maybe a little sad now herself. "You're just not getting it, are you, B.? Travers used me. Just like always. You oughta know how it feels. Well, don't worry. Maybe once upon a time I didn't see that line, you know, the one you don't cross? But I see it now. So nothing stupid."

Then she leaned hard on Travers, grinding his face into the dirt. "Just the truth," she said grimly between gritted teeth. "Tell her, old man. Tell her why killing the Moruach would stop the Aegir from coming. Explain to her how it's all your fault."

Faith glanced up then and was surprised to see that Buffy did not seem shocked by this revelation at all. The other Slayer's features were grave, and angry, but far from stunned.

"What did you do?" Buffy demanded.

"Go to hell," Travers snarled.

Faith ground his face into the dirt harder, but it wasn't her physical force that would sway him. She knew that much. "Quentin. You can tell her, or I can tell her. But if I have to tell her, I'll also explain it all to the other members of the Council. Giles will help, I'm pretty sure. I'll tell them why you pulled in an American Watcher with absolutely zero field experience and a couple of operatives loyal to you. Why you got me this little jaunt from prison. How you're responsible for dozens of deaths here in happy little—"

"It wasn't my fault!" Travers snapped.

All the amusement left Faith then. She let go of the man and stepped back from him, crossed her arms, and waited. Travers sat up slowly. His face was cut from small rocks in the dirt, but he merely brushed off his shirt and stared up at the two young women.

When he spoke, there was a kind of faraway look in his eyes, along with a glint of anger he held in reserve for someone else, for whomever it was he really blamed for his predicament.

"The Council have been researching the Moruach for years. Or trying to, at least. They have some small history of sorcery," Travers explained, "but it's a kind of magick we don't really understand. Our primary interest was in magickal imprisonment."

Travers smoothed his hair, wincing as his fingers touched the back of his head where he must have been tender from Faith's ministrations. His eyes ticked back and forth between them.

"Thousands of years ago, the Moruach managed to capture the Aegir. It had been the enemy of their species for eons, fed by the worship of the Aegirie, humans it had changed with the taint of its presence. We wanted them to teach us how to do it, but the Moruach refused."

Buffy stepped up beside Faith. The Slayers stared down at him.

"What did you *do*?" Buffy demanded again.

The Watcher shook his head. "It wasn't me. But the Watchers responsible were following my instructions as best they could. I told them to find a way to convince the Moruach to share that knowledge with us, that it was their only task and that they would not be able to move up within the ranks of the Council until they had solved it.

"They improvised," Travers confessed, and the weight of that one word was heavy on him. "The Moruach were intractable, and so the idiots—unable to figure out how it had been caged—found a way to set it free instead."

Buffy stared at him in horror. "They thought the Moruach would just do the spell over and they could figure it out that way, by watching," she said, a bit hoarse.

"Bingo," Faith put in. "I heard them talking about it back at the hotel. But, see, what the moron parade apparently didn't realize was that the Moruach had done the spell so long ago that they'd forgotten how it was done."

"The Aegir was free," Travers said, seeming almost eager to complete his confession now that it was begun. "Like modern humans who do not understand how the pyramids were built, the Moruach had lost the knowledge that had originally held it captive. They could not fight the Aegir, so they had to flee. They came here to attempt to open the Hellmouth, to return to the dark dimension of the Great Old Ones, which had spawned them at the beginning of time."

"And the Aegir followed," Buffy said, shaking her head. "The sea lions were afraid of the Moruach or the Aegir or both. So the Aegir attacked ships and infected the people on board. Maybe even some fish that people ate. And the Aegirie infection—the metamorphosis—started to spread. And it can control them, the ones who are changed, and it made them hunt for the Moruach, out for revenge."

Faith was watching Buffy as she spoke, as she put it all together. When Buffy looked up at her, Faith nodded once.

"And now it's here," she said.

Buffy closed her eyes a moment. When she opened them again, she turned her back on Faith and Travers and began walking toward the house. After several steps she paused and looked back at Faith.

"You coming?"

Faith smiled. Ignoring Travers, she went to where Haversham had dropped his *cinquedea* and snatched the fat-bladed sword up off the ground. She offered it to Buffy, and the other Slayer took it with a quiet nod of gratitude. Then Faith pulled her claymore from the dirt, and together the two of them started up the front steps of the old house.

"You're both going to die," Travers called to them, a bit of the old arrogance creeping back into his voice. "You know that, don't you?"

"No, we're not," Faith replied calmly, without turning. "If we die, then you get a brand-spanking-new Slayer to toy with and twist around. And we're not gonna let that happen."

When she cast a sidelong glance at Buffy, Faith saw that she was smiling.

The two Slayers went into the house. Faith's eyes adjusted quickly enough that she had a few moments to appreciate the interior of the place, and to notice the damage done by whatever fight had happened here. Then Buffy led her into the back of the house, to a corridor that took them into a wing whose walls and floors were in serious need of maintenance. A section of the floor had been torn up, and a breeze wafted up out of the darkness.

It smelled of the ocean.

Something shifted in the depths, hissing low, and Faith saw a quartet of amber eyes peering out at her. A Moruach raised its head, uncoiling the length of its serpentine body from a rocky ledge down in that hole in the floor, as though it had been waiting for them.

Then another figure moved in that stone well, platinum hair gleaming in what little moonlight slipped in through the cracks in the boarded up windows. Pale and lithe, the vampire gave her an appreciative glance and then looked at Buffy.

"Took you long enough, Slayer," Spike said.

"Slayers," Buffy corrected him. "Slayers."

Chapter Seventeen

The crack that descended down through the otherwise solid rock of the bluff was remarkable. In some places it was angular enough and had enough stone outcroppings that if one were careful it was simple to travel through that strange, natural chimney in the rock. Not all of it was natural, though.

There were crevices furrowed in the cave through which the dim glow of the moon reached small fingers of light. Buffy put her eye to one and found that she was looking through a kind of peephole that showed a view of the horizon, where the sea met the starlit sky. These certainly seemed to have been made for that purpose, though she had no idea who would have made the effort or why they would have bothered. Whoever had done it, however, had also provided some manmade aid to their descent in the form of wooden handgrips and even—in several places—stairs.

Someday when she had the time, she thought it might

be interesting to find out. At the moment, she was merely grateful for the gloomy light and the extraordinary passage down toward the sea.

"This is wicked cool," Faith muttered, as if to herself.

Buffy glanced at her, pale face almost ghostly in the gloom, and saw Faith stiffen. The sentiment was unlike her, revealing a different Faith, a less cynical woman unafraid to feel enthusiasm . . . or perhaps only harkening back to younger days, when she was a girl, not yet the Slayer. Wherever within her the words had come from, they had obviously made her self-conscious, for she hurried ahead of Buffy now in pursuit of Spike and the Moruach tribe, who had found their way much more easily down through the cavern. Like the demons who dwelt in the depths of the ocean, the vampire's eyes were better attuned to the darkness.

Despite her convoluted feelings where Faith was concerned, Buffy was glad to have the other Slayer fighting at her side. It might not change things between them, but it felt as though they had reached a point they could both move on from. In the gloom of the cave, Buffy smiled softly, realizing that Faith probably had not put nearly as much thought into it.

There were things that the other Slayer had done that Buffy doubted she could ever forgive. But for the first time, she felt content to forget about them while Faith sought out the atonement she claimed to desire. And after the proof she had seen tonight, Buffy did not doubt that she wanted to redeem herself. As for whether she believed Faith would be capable of it, she would keep her opinions to herself.

Carefully they continued their descent, a journey made more difficult by the strange sword in Buffy's hand. Faith at least had a crude scabbard with which she strapped the long claymore across her back. From time to time Buffy could hear Spike swearing to himself, likely wondering how he had gotten into all of this. *Blaming me,* Buffy thought, though she had had nothing to do with his past encounters with the Moruach Queen or—and now she shuddered in disgust—what he had chosen to do to settle the matter between them.

The roar of the ocean seemed to fill the very air around them, thrumming in the walls as though they were already beneath the water, in the heart of the sea instead of above it. The air was heavy and damp, and she could taste the salt with every breath.

"Hey," she said, her voice sounding dry and distant as it rebounded off the stone walls of the cave.

Faith glanced back at her.

"I guess I should thank you," Buffy said. "For what you did up there."

"Nah. You don't have to." Faith turned her attention back to the descent, carefully stepping down to a plateau of stone that was barely visible in the little light available to them. "I didn't do it for you."

"Okay," Buffy said lightly. "Well, never mind then."

A moment later, without turning, Faith spoke again. "I was outta control for a lotta years, y'know? I'm not talking about here. I'm talking about before. Before I was Chosen. I guess mainly because nobody cared enough to stop me.

"Maybe by the time the Council came along . . . by the time my Watcher told me what I was . . . maybe I was looking for something to be part of. For a while the Council offered that. Then, in a way, I guess it was you and Sunnydale. Didn't work out too well. I hadn't had any practice, y'know? Fitting in, I mean. Then the Mayor came along. It was all pretty dumb, but I let myself fall into it 'cause it was easy, too. After a long time on my own, it was good to *matter* to someone."

As she spoke, Faith had continued to work her way down, reaching out for sharp stone outcroppings, lowering herself deeper, stepping across the very chasm through which they were descending. Now she arrived at a place where someone, long ago, had installed a set of seven steps built at odd angles and widths into the cave. She paused there and looked back at Buffy.

"Problem is, when you care too much about that, you stop looking in here for answers," Faith said, and she rapped her fist against her chest. "You start letting other people decide what's right. And that's no way to live. No way at all. Cost me a lot to learn that."

Without waiting for a response she turned again and continued on. They were coming closer to Spike and the Moruach now. Buffy could hear them hissing low, and the slither of their oily skin as they coiled and uncoiled their thick bodies.

She let Faith go, staring after her, unable in that moment to continue. With every word Faith had spoken Buffy had realized that in the last few days she had done the very thing the other Slayer had just cautioned against. She had been looking for someone else to lead the way, to impress one's own philosophy upon her, to make sense of the world so that she wouldn't have to do it herself. Despite her feelings about the Council, she had considered their arguments. And the Order had swayed her greatly, to the point where she had wondered if it wouldn't be better to just throw in with them full-time like the Slayer whose defection had caused the rift between Watchers and Sages so long ago.

An image flashed across her mind of the sea lions massing on the beach that day when Xander had hurt himself surfing. The sunlight on the waves, the controversy up on the sand, the protesters and the media. And the poor creatures gathered on shore in terror of the thing that had driven them from their ocean home. The shipping and fishing companies had been unwilling to address the marine animals' safety in favor of the bottom line, and the protesters were demanding someone take action to protect the sea lions. Even then, Buffy had let her friends play out the debate so that she could choose among their points rather than making up her own mind about the situation.

As these thoughts all came together in her mind, she shook her head. *No. On the Moruach, I did choose a philosophy. "Wait and see" is as good as anything else.*

Faith had disappeared into the murky dark of the cave below. Buffy took a long breath and let it out slowly, then she followed the other Slayer, grimly determined not to win the war between Aegir and Moruach, but to end it.

Sword in hand, Buffy followed Faith down those few steps and around a small turn in the natural rock formation, and then the cave leveled off. The roar of the surf grew louder, the sound almost taking on substance as she moved forward. She imagined now her place in that cliff and the path they had taken, as though the earth had swallowed them whole. Several strides farther along, the cave grew brighter, the moonlight casting the stone around her in a sickly yellow hue. The path ahead dropped off once more but when Buffy reached the edge and looked down, what she saw astounded her.

The cave was larger there, opening into a chamber perhaps fifteen feet high and twenty wide. A narrow cleft in the far wall of the cavern was open to the ocean, the moonlit waves clearly visible even from Buffy's vantage point. She wondered if the cave opening could be seen during the day by passing boats or beachgoers on WaveRunners, or by surfers a bit out of the way. Reason suggested it was unlikely or it wouldn't have remained a secret—and this place certainly *felt* secret. From outside, with the sun shining above, she suspected it would look like nothing more than a crevice, a dark slash in the rock face of the cliff.

The reality was extraordinary, especially now. There were so many Moruach twisted into that space that the cavern felt more like a hive. Quartets of slitted amber eyes studied her as she crept carefully down the slope to that cavern. Dragon-snakes, as Giles had said they had once been known, and Buffy could understand the definition now better than she ever had. Like snakes, they pressed against one another, moving over and beneath each other with a chilling intimacy.

Her heartbeat sped momentarily as she looked at them, and she was happy the Moruach were her allies at the moment.

Spike and Faith stood on either side of the cleft in the cliff face, their exit from this stovepipe cavern, and one by one the Moruach slid up to them and out through that hole. Buffy moved down among them, trying not to recoil at the feel of the creatures' oily skin against her own. They made way for her as best they could and in moments she stood beside Spike.

With a hiss, the largest of the Moruach slid up to her, its serpentine body curling across the rock floor of the cave. It was the Queen, and she hissed as she bumped Buffy backward, dark eyes burning.

"What was that?" Buffy demanded, glaring at Spike. "Hello, allies?"

"Maybe she's jealous," Faith suggested, a low snicker escaping her lips.

Spike made an obscene gesture at both of them, but he said nothing. Buffy realized that Faith was probably right, and Spike knew it. At the moment, however, she wasn't about to tease him herself. Not with the way the Queen bared her rows of jagged little teeth and slid closer to Buffy, nudging her away. The Moruach were flooding out of the cave now, slipping down to what Buffy now could see was the shore of a narrow, rocky cove below, and then into the water.

She moved away from Spike. "Trust me," she told the Queen, whose chest rose and fell with each breath, and whose claws were hooked into talons as she studied Buffy. "No interest. He's all yours."

"Isn't *that* a relief?" Spike sneered. But when the Moruach Queen looked at him, he smiled. "No offense to you, Your Majesty."

"Majesty?" Faith said.

Though Buffy was sure some whipcrack sarcasm was to follow that up, Faith said nothing more. Buffy figured she had thought better of it given the stakes at hand.

The last of the Moruach were slipping through the cleft in the rock, down to the cove, and into the sea. Buffy stared out at the water and realized that there were things moving upon the waves. Dozens, perhaps hundreds of dark figures bobbing up out of the ocean only to sink below again a moment later. She understood immediately what she was seeing.

"The sea lions," Buffy said, barely aware she had spoken aloud.

The Moruach Queen let out a low hiss and peered out through the hole beside her, then glanced at Spike. The vampire shuddered and touched the side of his head, as though the sound hurt him.

"They're runnin' off, cowardly little—," Spike said. "Queenie says they can sense the fight coming, figure they'll vanish before they end up somebody's victory feast."

The Moruach Queen slithered out through the hole in the cliff face and landed on the rocky shore with her talons digging at the ground, her serpentine body slapping the earth. Then she was off, sliding into the ocean after the rest of her tribe, disappearing beneath the water, arcing off to the left, headed south.

Faith cocked her head to one side and stared at Spike. "You understand that lisp? That a demon language or something?"

With a roll of his eyes, the vampire sighed. "Not too quick on the uptake, are you? The Moruach are telepaths. I'm not exactly on their wavelength, but I get the gist."

"Guess you're down on her level," Faith replied, flashing a savage grin.

Then she bent forward and looked out at the ocean. Buffy saw the expression on her face change, that smile fading in an instant, draining from her face. Faith stared out at the ocean as though entranced.

"You gotta be freakin' kidding me," she whispered.

Buffy turned to look out through the opening to see what had inspired those words, though she knew even before she saw it.

Perhaps half a mile from shore something had broken the surface. It slid across the water in the moonlight and Buffy realized that this huge black thing with its jagged edges was but a single tentacle, only one limb of the horrible creature who might well have inspired many a sea monster myth. Behind it and slightly south, the top of the creature emerged from the water like a small island being born, and even from this distance some of its eyes were visible. They glowed with a pale green luminescence that sent shivers of unease through Buffy. All the dread that had filled her in days past had been fought off—her body had adjusted to it. Yet now the force of it was so great it took her breath away.

"What is that?" Faith said through gritted teeth.

Buffy knew that she did not mean the Aegir, for what else could it be? Faith was referring to what she felt, to the malignant presence in the air that had gotten under her skin just as it had Buffy's. She almost said fear, but that would not have been precisely correct. The sick dread that roiled in her gut was not fear, really. It was more than that.

But it was Spike who named it.

"Evil," the vampire said, lips pressed together as though he were savoring the very thing that the Slayers found so disturbing. "What you're feeling is pure, unadulterated evil. Don't get that much on this side of things. In this world, I mean. That thing's a throwback to the way the world was, once upon a time. Y'know all those times you stopped the apocalypse? That feeling? That thing out there? It's just a little taste of what you've been fighting all along."

Buffy's gaze ticked from Spike to Faith and back. "We have to hurry. Where are the Moruach going?"

"South, for the beach. The metamorph freaks—what'd you call 'em? Aegirie? They're already there."

"How do you know?"

"Queenie told me. The Moruach can smell 'em."

Faith stared at him, then gazed a moment at Buffy. At length she turned, went to the exit, and leaped out fifteen feet above the rocky shore of the cove, claymore still strapped to her back. Faith waded into the water then dove under, the heavy sword weighing her down. She surfaced a moment later, her black hair slicked back across her head, and began to swim after the demon Queen.

Buffy stared out at the ocean, where the Aegir continued to rise, continued to move closer to shore, several other tentacles breaking the surface. She had no idea how they were going to fight the thing, but in the back of her mind an echo was building—an echo of something she had heard earlier—and she hoped it would resolve itself into a plan before long.

She started for the opening, but Spike stopped her.

"What's the point of all this?" he asked. "You know the whole story now, right? It's their war. Why not let them fight it out, just wait 'til it's over?"

She stared at him. "I told you what Travers said up there at the house. After all the time it's been caged, do you really think the Aegir's going to go away if it destroys the Moruach? It's coming ashore, and it's not going to stop at the beach."

With that she went to the opening in the cliff, stepped forward, and then leaped down onto the shore below, holding the sword above her like some marauding pirate. As she was wading into the surf, Spike followed, grunting as he hit the ground and rolled on the rocks. He swore as he got to his feet again. Buffy wondered if he was coming along because he was afraid of her, because he wanted to maintain the strange détente between them that allowed him to live in Sunnydale, or because of whatever bizarre fascination there was between him and the Moruach Queen.

Then she realized she did not want to know why.

Purposefully keeping her gaze away from the horizon where the Aegir slowly moved toward shore, making its own waves, the Slayer dove into the ocean and began to swim.

Police sirens slashed the night. Blue lights splashed off the interior of Xander's car and the engine screamed as he accelerated, speeding even faster along Shore Road. In the passenger seat, Anya was speaking to herself in a quiet counterpoint to the roar of the car and the tension of the moment, her words filled with self-recrimination as she reminded herself for the hundredth time that she ought to have stayed at the Magick Shop.

The road curved and Xander cut the wheel too hard,

the rear tires squealing as the car slewed off course a moment before he brought it back under control.

"Xander!" Willow snapped. "Slow down if you have to. We're almost there."

"You drove better when you had one arm in a sling," Anya told him curtly.

"Why is now the time to have that conversation?" Xander retorted, voice almost shrill with tension as he pushed the car even faster. The road was rough and pitted beneath them, and the shocks were not the best; they all jostled around in their seats.

"Tell me again why you couldn't have done that pay-no-attention-to-the-man-behind-the-curtain spell on the car?" Xander asked, glancing into the rearview mirror.

"That charm is all about the subtlety," she replied. "Speeding car, not big on subtlety. Tara and I would've been useless by the time we got to the beach."

"Not gonna be all that helpful if we don't get to the beach," Xander reminded her.

"We'll get there," Tara said.

Her words carried a strange weight in the car, and all of them fell silent. The engine roared and the wind whipped in through the open windows and the siren ripped the night. Willow glanced at Tara, saw the blue lights strobing her face, and she grabbed her girlfriend's hand. In the time they had been together Tara had become her stability. Willow didn't know what she would ever do without her. Anya's mutterings about staying back at the Magic Box made her wish now that Tara had stayed behind.

It was a foolish wish. Tara would not have stayed behind and let Willow put herself in danger. And that was the way it ought to be. Together, come what may.

Xander navigated another turn, though this one with a bit more finesse, and Willow held onto Tara's hand and stared ahead, through the windshield, watching for the beach to come into view. After the situation with the Moruach at the ruins of the high school had been defused, the demons had slipped off into the shadows and they had been left to figure out how to get to the beach without getting caught. The town was under quarantine still, and the Sunnydale police department was working with the National Guard to keep it that way. Willow and Tara might have been able to cast their "attention-deflection" charm on Xander and Anya, too, but it would take too long to walk down to the beach. There was really only one choice: Get to Xander's house, take his car, and make a run for it.

Which had brought them here, with the police in pursuit.

"Company!" Xander snapped. "Lots of it."

Willow craned her neck to get a better view as Xander swung the car to the right. They were headed north on Shore Road and the beach was coming up on their left. But they were never going to reach it in the car. A pair of National Guard vehicles were blocking the road ahead. Beyond it several police cars sat with their lights spinning, throwing a blue hue over everything, including the people out on the sand.

Except they weren't people. At least not anymore.

Dozens of Aegirie milled about on the beach in tattered, bloodied clothes. Most of them bore no resemblance now to the human beings they had once been, scaly green-black flesh and huge indigo eyes having replaced their features, barbed tentacles squirming from their chests, and tiny, vicious little mouths gnashing the air where they had opened on the creatures' arms and legs, necks and torsos.

As if the cue had been the arrival of Xander's car, chaos erupted. National Guardsmen and police officers opened fire on the Aegirie. Gunshots echoed like fireworks through the air, and just like the Fourth of July, Willow could feel the report of every shot in her chest as though the sound had come from within her. It was possible that by now the National Guardsmen knew that these monsters had once been human, knew that those who had not been completely transformed might still be saved. For their sake, she hoped not; she hoped that they were completely ignorant of the horror they were perpetrating.

"Oh, goddess, no," Tara whispered.

Willow's throat was dry, but her eyes were moist.

Xander hit the brakes hard and brought the car to a skidding halt twenty feet from the National Guard roadblock. The police car that had been pursuing them killed its siren and coasted to a stop, but none of them was paying any attention now to what was behind them. Only to the grotesque scene that was playing itself out before them now.

Willow got out of the car and the others followed suit, but none of them moved any closer to the chaos, to the gunfire. There was nothing they could have done to stop what was unfolding there. Bullets tore inhuman, twisted flesh. Dark blood flew in arcs that spattered the sand. For several seconds it seemed that the Aegirie would be slaughtered.

But there were more of them than it had seemed at first, perhaps as many as a hundred. Perhaps more. A sound like static on a radio turned up much too loud reached them, and Willow looked to the right, away from the water. More Aegirie were there and they ran across the road to attack the police and the Guardsmen from behind, tentacles snapping and lunging out from their chests. The Aegirie who had been targets attacked as well, and soon the night air was filled with the screams of their victims.

The cop who had been chasing them forgot all about them. Gun drawn, he ran past Xander's car crying out to God. Then he started shooting, and several of the Aegirie turned his way. Willow saw bullets tear into them. One of them went down, half of its head torn away. The others lunged for the cop.

"We've got to do s-something," Tara said, shaking her head.

Willow did not hesitate a moment longer. She ran to the sidewalk and onto the sand, muttered an incantation, and passed her fingers through the air. A vibrant golden light exploded above her, showering down around her. Among the police cars and National Guard vehicles, all along the Shore Road, the Aegirie stopped in their attack and looked over at her.

Tara shouted her name, but it was too late. The damage was done.

The Aegirie pulled themselves away from their victims and started across the beach toward Willow, hissing. Their voices sounded like the crash of the waves upon the shore. Or like that radio tuned only to static, turned up even louder.

Willow heard Xander fumbling to open his trunk, to get at the battle-axes stored there. Tara ran up beside her, breathing hard but saying not a word as they faced the creatures together. So many of them. So very many.

Some of the police and Guardsmen were surely dead, and many wounded. But not all. She had saved some of their lives. Shouts could be heard on the street, and it was only a matter of time before the slaughter started again, the killing of humans and of those who had once been human.

Another car skidded to a halt behind her. Willow didn't dare turn around, but she heard Giles's voice and knew that somehow he and Rosanna had avoided the quarantine and made it down here. She heard Giles call to her, but still she did not turn.

Not with so many dark, unblinking eyes staring at her.

She held her breath as they came for her, saw the tendrils like Medusa's snakes upon their chests and those tiny mouths. Willow reached out and grasped Tara's hand again, and she felt the connection between them, felt the circuit completed, felt the surge of magick that always happened when they were linked. It might have been only her feelings for Tara rather than any actual symbiosis, but it certainly felt as though they provided each other strength.

Eldritch energy crackled between them.

Then the Aegirie simply stopped. Wherever they were on the sand they stopped and turned away, toward the ocean, and began to make their way over the beach to the surf, to fall to their knees.

The remaining police and Guardsmen opened fire immediately, now that the creatures were away from Willow and Tara. Demon blood splashed the sand again and many of the Aegirie were torn to shreds by the gunfire.

"Stop!" Giles began to shout. "Stop it, you fools! Save your bullets! Cease fire! Save your ammunition."

Miraculously, it stopped. Willow spun away from the Aegirie to see that Giles had begun to move in front of them, to block their line of fire. One of the men shouted at him.

"Out of the way, idiot!"

"I said save your ammunition!" Giles yelled.

"What the hell for?"

But Willow had seen the Aegirie fall to their knees. Tara had told her what the transformed Baker McGee had said. She knew.

"For that!" Giles shouted, and he pointed.

All eyes turned to the sea.

Beside her, Tara whispered a prayer to the goddess again. Willow felt nausea roll through her and nearly threw up on the beach. They had all become inured to the dread and fear that had been permeating the atmosphere of Sunnydale for the past few days, grown used to it. Now it crashed over her again and threatened to overwhelm her. Behind her, she heard Xander and Anya both swearing.

The Aegir was not far off shore. In the chaos of the battle it had somehow risen unnoticed. Tentacles splashed the water, making waves of their own. Its huge bulbous body was covered with eyes glowing sickly green, and its single enormous maw was just like those on the bodies of the Aegirie, round and filled with needle teeth. It was revolting to look at, even in the dark under the pale moonlight. Its tentacles were lined with sharp protrusions like hooks, and its flesh looked rotten, even from this distance, as though it was riddled with disease. A stench rolled off the beast and rode the wind up onto the sand, and Willow's stomach twisted again, so foul was that odor.

But the worst of it was the strange shape of the thing, like nothing she could describe. It had odd angles that simply seemed wrong, a vile nightmare even Picasso could not have drawn. Her head hurt to look at it, to try to make sense of the lines and edges of the thing, of the shifting, putrid hues that the moon brought out upon the sheen of its pustulent flesh.

It was twice the size of a house even without the huge tentacles that even now burst from the waves and slammed back into the water again, drawing it forward. She got the sense that its massive upper body was supported from beneath, and in her mind she saw the drawing Giles had shown them, the thing like a snail's body that must be sliding across the ocean bottom even now.

"Will," Xander said weakly.

She glanced at him, wondering if she looked as stricken as he did.

Giles and Rosanna came running over, leaving the National Guard to talk among themselves, no doubt on the radio that very moment calling for a cavalry made up of army, navy, air force, and marines, none of whom could possibly get there in time. And after what had happened earlier, the Coast Guard wasn't going to be any help either.

Then they were all there.

"How do we stop that?" Xander asked as Anya clung close to him.

Willow shook her head. "I don't know."

They all turned to Giles and Rosanna.

"So, Sage-lady," Xander said, strained levity in his voice. "Any advice?"

Rosanna shook her head. "I wasn't trained for anything on this level. And my supervisor . . . she left it on me. There isn't any help coming."

But Giles was no longer looking at the Aegir. His attention was on a place nearer to them.

"I'm not so sure about that," the Watcher said.

A short way down the coast where the beach stopped and the shoreline turned rocky, the Moruach had begun to emerge from the surf. And they were not alone.

Chapter Eighteen

It had been worse in the water. The dread that had overwhelmed her, that overriding sense of evil, had saturated her as completely as the sea had soaked her clothes, seeping into every pore. Buffy tried to focus on swimming, only on swimming, but it had not been easy. Not with the Aegir moving closer. They swam at an angle to its approach and it seemed to gain speed. Or that might have been her imagination—it might have been that they were moving too slowly.

Now she rose from the surf with Spike and Faith awaiting her on the sand. As Buffy emerged she scanned the beach, took it all in. The police. The National Guard. The blue lights flashing against the sky. The figures up near the road off to the south; Willow and Tara, Xander and Anya, Giles and Rosanna. All alive.

Silently, she thanked God for that.

Then the Aegirie, who had been on their knees in the waves just up the beach, their attention on the ancient demon, the Great Old One whose tentacles tore the waves perhaps a hundred yards from shore . . . the Aegirie, its children, turned as one to face their enemy.

The Moruach attacked. Faster than any human could have run, the dragon-snakes sped off along the wet sand, tiny waves lapping the shore, their serpentine bodies twisting to propel them forward. And the Moruach began to bark and screech in those wailing voices. For the first time, Buffy did not wince at the sound.

But the Aegirie did. The things that had once been human paused and clapped hands to their ears, though they were farther away than Buffy, Spike, and Faith. Their tentacles seemed to fall limp a moment before lashing out again.

"Spike!" Buffy snapped. "Tell the Queen to wait."

The vampire called to the largest of the Moruach, Queen of the tribe or the brood or perhaps an entire species. More of the Moruach had joined them underwater, though where they had come from Buffy had no idea. She had lost count but thought there were forty or fifty of them.

Spike shouted at the Moruach Queen, but Buffy thought it was his intentions that stopped her, the thoughts that were radiating from his mind. Whatever it was, the Queen turned in the surf, sand driven up by her powerful body twisting to face him. Then Buffy ran after them.

"What?" Faith asked, following her. "You know something. I can see in your face. What've you got, B.?"

"An echo," she replied.

For that was truly all it was, the echo of words resounding in her head. Quentin Travers's words, to be exact. When Buffy reached Spike and the Queen, the demon rose up on its torso so that she towered over the Slayer. Buffy spoke to Spike, but her eyes were on the Queen's the entire time.

"I was told that a long time ago you captured the Aegir," she said. "That you held it that way for a very long time. That your kind has some sort of magick you used to do that, but that you've forgotten how to use it."

Spike glanced back and forth between Buffy and the Queen. After a few moments he flinched and swore and blood began to flow from his nose. He wiped at his nostrils, stared angrily at his red fingers, then looked up at Buffy and Faith.

"They didn't forget. She was pretty emphatic about that," he snarled, looking up at the Queen before returning his attention to the Slayers. "They just don't have the numbers they used to, yeah? Population, I mean. Once the bloody enormous bugger was free, they didn't have the strength to trap it again."

Faith shook her sodden hair back, slicked it to the back of her skull with both hands. She moved next to Buffy, obviously catching on now.

"But what was it?" Faith demanded. "The spell or whatever? If they could still do it, even stop the thing long enough for me and Buffy to get close—"

"And do what?" Spike scoffed. "You see the size of that thing?"

"Ask her!" Faith snapped. "And ask her where its heart is!"

Spike did. The blood flowed more freely from his nose, but he only grimaced now, forcing himself to just take the pain. When he turned to them again, streaks of blood had run down over his lips and chin, and he did not bother to wipe them away.

"Bitch is killing me," he muttered, eyes narrowed. "You owe me big, Slayer. Not just for this, but for all of it. What I had to do."

The Moruach were still screeching, and they battled the Aegirie talon to tentacle now, there on the beach. The

Aegir drew closer. One of its huge limbs shot up out of the surf less than thirty yards away, and when it splashed down again the water sprayed far enough to wet them all again.

Buffy glared at Spike. "Whatever you did, it wasn't for me. *What did she say?*"

"Well, as for a heart, the thing doesn't have one. But she says if you cut off its tentacles, it'll probably die. As for the magick . . . it's their voices. That soddin' racket they make every time they open their mouths. There's magick in that. Like a chorus, you understand. Together, they could bind it, if there were just enough of them."

Stunned, Buffy looked between Spike and the Queen, staring in horror at the bloody combat on the sand, at this war in which Moruach and Aegirie were both dying. But with every Moruach that died, it was getting that much more impossible to defeat the Aegir.

"Spike, I'll make you a deal," Buffy said quickly. "Tell the Queen to try. To get the rest of them to try, even while they're fighting. Hit that high note, get in harmony, whatever. But now! Then get to Willow and the others. Tell them we need to amp up what the Moruach are doing. They've gotta figure a way to tap into it, to add to its power."

"Yeah. What's my end of the deal?" Spike asked.

"I don't tell anyone what happened up in that house."

The vampire sneered at her and then turned to the Queen. He clapped a hand to his temple as they communicated, but then the huge Moruach matriarch was off across the surf so swiftly it was as though she moved on top of the water. Spike took off up the sand, running toward Willow, Giles, and the others.

Buffy turned to Faith. "You with me?"

Faith reached over her shoulder and drew the long claymore sword from behind her. "I didn't swim all that way with this hunk of steel just to be a spectator."

* * *

Willow saw Spike running up the beach and she started down toward him with Tara, Xander, and Anya in tow. Giles and Rosanna were nattering back and forth to each other, apparently trying to figure out what magick might be brought to bear against the Aegir—obviously physical strength wasn't going to be enough. Buffy and Faith were never going to be able to get close enough to the Old One to do it much real damage.

"What's going on? Does Buffy have a plan?" Willow asked as Spike came to a hard stop, his feet spraying sand up to pepper her legs. The vampire was breathing hard and it unnerved her; dead people did not need to breathe, but most vampires kept up the pretense, apparently just as much for their own benefit as for others'.

"Not much of one, but yeah, there's a plan," Spike replied. "Hope you girls aren't bloody tone deaf. See, the Moruach? Their magick's in their voices, like the sirens outta ancient myth, only nastier. That's how they trapped the Aegir in the first place, but they're not strong enough to do it now. Buffy thinks you lot'll be able to magnify the effect, take their magick and give it a boost."

As Spike was talking, Giles and Rosanna had come down to join them all, and their conversation had broken off as they listened to the vampire's words. Now Giles shook a fist in the air in punctuation.

"Yes!" the Watcher said. His gaze ticked toward Rosanna. "Are you familiar with harmonic refraction?"

Rosanna nodded, a faraway look in her eyes. "Vaguely, yes. It's an amplification spell."

"Um, not to interrupt, but me, here, witch-girl? Without a clue," Willow informed them. She glanced at Tara. "Any clues in your vicinity?"

"Not a one," Tara replied anxiously. "Maybe you can share the knowledge?"

The Sage glanced regretfully at Giles and then turned to the witches. "It's simple enough, I suppose. At least conceptually. It's a mischief spell, really. The sort of thing you're never taught when you're being trained in the use of magick, but that the more troublesome witches and sorcerers in training discover on their own. Ensorcel some door so that when it slams the sound is loud as thunder, enough to shake a building. Or curse a radio so that its volume increases by—"

"So in other words," Willow interrupted, gaze ticking between Giles and Rosanna, "exactly what Buffy wants."

"Precisely," Giles agreed.

"Oooh, the Watcher comes through in the ninth inning," Xander crowed.

"Xander," Giles chided him. "People are dying. We have a bit of a crisis on our hands. We're hardly keeping score."

"Pffft," Anya muttered. "I am."

"And you can be sure she is," Spike added, pointing to Rosanna. "It's all a big chess game for you people. Well I'm out of the game, hear?"

Willow glared at him. "Spike, look at that thing! You can't just walk away. Well, okay, you could. But you can't!"

All of them turned to look at the Aegir. Willow felt sick to her stomach again, nausea roiling in her gut as she saw that one of its huge tentacles had reached the sand. Though it had dozens, even hundreds of eyes, she felt that the thing was looking at *her,* right through her, that it could see down inside her and knew she was imperfect— that all humans had a seed of cruelty in them and that it could exploit that seed, make it grow. She tore her gaze away, let herself see the tentacles, the slaughter on the beach with the Slayers and the slithering Moruach locked in battle with the Aegirie . . . but she would not look at those eyes again.

Spike patted his pockets in search of his cigarettes, then apparently remembered that he was soaking wet, and even if he found them they'd be saturated.

"Let me guess. You're gonna tell me it's evil. Big ol' nasty thing. Needs to be scrubbed from the face of the earth, yeah? Problem is, I'm a tad smaller, but also evil. Seems I have to keep reminding you people 'bout that."

Tara slapped him.

Spike snarled, baring his fangs, and his face erupted instantly into the savage countenance of the vampire. "Don't push me, witch."

"Screw you," Tara snapped, no trace of a stutter in her voice. "What are you going to do? Get a nosebleed on me? We know you're evil, okay? But until now I wasn't sure you were this stupid. Now we know."

Xander shook his head like a disappointed father. "Ah, Spike. Tara's right. Not paying attention. We all know from past experience you don't want the world to turn into just another demon dimension any more than we do. You really think if the Aegir does the Godzilla Tokyo-stomp through Southern Cali there won't be more to follow? The other Old Ones'll notice, and if the Aegir's successful, they'll get in on the act pretty damn quick."

Spike glared at them, then ran his hands through his sodden hair before spinning on the sand.

"I hate you all," he said, as he ran back the way he'd come, back toward Buffy, Faith, and the bloodshed, back toward the abomination that no longer had a place in this world.

"The feeling's mutual," Xander called after him.

But Willow wasn't paying attention to Spike or even Xander anymore. For the Moruach had begun to scream. All along, their screeches and barks had been assaulting the night air, the ocean breeze. But now they began in earnest, their huge shark mouths opening to release a kind of ululating howl that grated on her ears like fingernails on a chalkboard. There was agony in it, but she could summon no sympathy. Each Moruach voice was like sound transmuted into shards of broken glass.

She shot a hard look at Giles, and had to shout to be heard. "We're supposed to harmonize with that?"

The windows in the police cars and National Guard vehicles splintered, some shattering. Xander swore. Anya clapped her hands over her ears. But Giles and Rosanna only flinched and moved to Tara and Willow.

"There's power in that sound," Giles said. "The Latin words to the harmonic refraction spell are simple enough. Anyone could cast it upon a radio or a barking dog. But to amplify magick . . . only those with natural magickal abilities could use the spell for that. You've got to be able to tap into the same magickal . . . frequency, I suppose, of the thing you're augmenting. You've got to find that harmony in your mind, reach out to it, and cast the spell."

Willow shook her head. "Giles, I don't know."

"What's the incantation?" Tara asked, shouting to be heard.

Rosanna Jergens looked at Giles. "You do remember, don't you?"

The Watcher frowned. "Let's just say I did more than my share of mischief once upon a time. *Consensius cum sonitus, exclamo. Consensius cum sonitus, exclamo.*"

Together Willow and Tara repeated the Latin phrasing several times to memorize it. Then they turned toward the Aegir again. The Moruach had moved away from the water now as two of the thing's massive tentacles coiled and reached for them on the sand, and it slid its lumbering, hideous, putrescent mass closer to shore. Its round mouth gnashed, and even over the scream of the Moruach Willow thought she could hear the noise its teeth made as they crashed together, a sound like rending metal.

She pushed the sound away. Almost unconsciously, the two witches joined hands. Willow barely felt Tara's fingers in her own as she cleared her mind of everything, every sound, every image, even the dreadful gaze of the Aegir and the evil that emanated from the thing and sat heavy on the air like the stifling humidity just before a storm.

Willow ignored it all. There was magick in her. She did not know where it had come from, but innate within her was the potential to become a powerful witch. Whatever it was, she could feel it there inside her. Now, somehow, she touched that part of herself and used it to sense, to *listen,* in a way, to the voice of the Moruach.

"I th-think I've got it," Tara said hesitantly.

Without opening her eyes, Willow nodded. "Me too."

As one, they began to speak the incantation.

When the last syllable had left their lips, the horrible wailing of the Moruach exploded through the air in a tidal wave of sound that made Willow cry out in pain and clap her hands to her ears. She felt warmth there, tasted copper inside her mouth, and feared that her ears were bleeding.

Eyes wide with pain, she spun around, saw that all of the others were doing the same thing, hands over their ears. Anya had fallen to the sand and pulled her legs up beneath her in a fetal position. Xander was beside her on his knees. Willow was terrified that they would all be deaf, that their eardrums had all been ruptured. As Willow watched, Giles went to his knees as well. Rosanna slumped to the sand, unconscious. But with her hands over her ears, Willow began to think that though the decibel level might deafen them if it was sustained for too long, they would probably recover if it could all be ended quickly.

Then she turned to search for Tara, who had been by her side a moment before. She glanced down and saw her girlfriend sitting on the sand as though someone had just shoved her down. Her hands were not over her ears. Rather, Tara had her hands held out in front of her face, staring in gape-mouthed horror at her palms.

Her skin had begun to flake in places, on her cheeks and on her hands and arms, to reveal a rough, greenish new flesh beneath.

Willow started to go to her, but Xander grabbed her from behind and Willow spun around to see that the same thing had begun to happen to Anya, and to Giles. And when she glanced over at the police and the Guardsmen—many of whom had also been driven to the ground by the decibel level of that scream—she saw that they too had begun to change. One of them was already tearing the skin off his face; perhaps, she thought, he had begun the metamorphosis before any of the others.

So this was the Aegir fighting back. She knew it, absolutely, had never been more certain of anything. Furious, she spun again, this time to stare out at the multitude of eyes on the body of the Old One, and now she saw that it had stopped moving, stopped that snail-like forward motion, its tentacles slipping under the water and lying dormant on the beach as though it had fallen asleep.

It was dazed, even paralyzed. Only yards away from its motionless tentacles, the Moruach were slaughtering its children, the Aegirie. The battle raged, flesh was torn and blood flew and was washed away in the surf or soaked into the damp sand, but even incapacitated, the Aegir was fighting back . . . spreading the taint of its evil . . . infecting them all. Making more Aegirie to fight and die for it.

There was a cure, of course. Giles had figured a way to reverse it if the metamorphosis was treated in time. But the hospital was so far away, and the Magic Box no closer. Buffy had to destroy it. That was the only answer. She and Faith and Spike had to stop the Aegir, to kill it, and pray that would save all of them, or give them time to save themselves.

Up on the road the police and the Guardsmen—horrified at the transformation they were undergoing—began shooting once again. Some of them were firing toward the ocean, but others among those afflicted men, in their terror, turned their weapons upon one another, or upon themselves.

Willow sank to the sand beside Tara and took her hands, and she felt that circuit between them again, that connection they share, but this time the emotion that surged through it was pure fear. For when Willow looked down at their clasped hands, she saw that her own skin had begun to flake as well.

It itched. Goddess, how it itched.

Every time a Moruach died, Buffy winced, knowing their chances had become that much more remote. Spike had come back to the fight. Though he seemed to prefer to look human, his face was that of the vampire now, and he attacked the Aegirie with a savagery she had rarely seen before in any creature. It was a disturbing reminder of what a dangerous animal he truly was.

The thought crossed her mind in an instant and was forgotten as an Aegirie tentacle lashed her across the neck and face, slicing deeply into her skin. Blood ran freely from her wounds and the salt air stung them, but Buffy took that pain into herself, let it focus her, wake her up from the despair that had begun to close its darkness around her.

She stood on the wet sand ten feet from where the tide rolled up the beach. All around her the melee unfolded, Aegirie and Moruach killing one another, both of their numbers dwindling. There was no way she and Faith could attack the Aegir unless the Moruach worked their magick—not unless they ended up with no choice. For now they fought the Aegirie, fought to keep the Moruach alive.

All around her the Aegirie were swarming, their tentacles darting and slashing. To her left, three of them leaped upon a Moruach, one of them grabbing its lower trunk and holding on tight, trying to force it to the sand, tentacles wrapping around the creature.

Buffy leaped instantly into action. The sword Faith had given her was unlike any she had ever seen, its blade narrow at the tip and nearly as broad as the hilt at its base. But it was heavy and sharp enough to slice bone, and the weight was perfect in her hand. She ran at the nearest Aegirie—praying every time she attacked one that she would see nothing in its clothes or its bearing that would reveal its human identity, who it had been before its metamorphosis. As she brought the sword around, decapitating the thing, she grieved for the man it had been and for whatever family it had left behind.

But the others had seen her, and her mourning for these things that were long past mourning had slowed her. Tentacles lashed at her from behind, slicing up her back like a half dozen bullwhips. Buffy cried out, but she could barely hear her own pain over the barks and screeches of the Moruach.

She reversed the sword in her hands, drove it backward past her waist, and impaled the creature behind her. In a single swift motion she slid the sword out of the dead Aegirie and spun as a third came after her. The blade cut into its neck, cleaving diagonally down through its body, and then stopped with a clang of metal upon metal.

Buffy tugged the sword back, the Aegirie falling in pieces to the ground, and stood facing Faith over its corpse. The other Slayer held her two-handed long sword tightly, though its blade was nearly black with the blood of these monsters. But the Moruach they had both tried to save, the one that had been driven down by the three Aegirie, had been eviscerated on the sand, its organs strewn across the beach.

"We're running out of screamers," Faith shouted to Buffy, her eyes wild, her face flecked with blood. Her hair was still wet and stringy, and tendrils of it were pasted to her forehead.

She looked to Buffy like some ancient warrior or the goddess of the hunt. It was a truth that Faith would have liked to escape, but Buffy thought that this was the other Slayer's element. She was born for this.

Nearby she heard Spike shouting and turned to see the vampire rip the throat out of an Aegirie and spit the revolting scaly flesh and dark blood to the ground.

"Spike!" she called. "We can't give Willow any more time! Tell the Queen to start!"

Without even acknowledging he had heard her, the vampire ran across the beach, shot an elbow into the face of an Aegirie that tried to stop him, and reached the Queen in seconds. Buffy could not hear what he was shouting, but she believed that the Queen wasn't hearing his words anyway. She was hearing his thoughts.

Then the Moruach Queen rose up as high as the thick trunk of her long serpentine body would allow, opened her huge, vicious mouth, and began to screech louder than ever before. Some of the other Moruach continued to fight even as they followed suit, their voices rising to match the intensity of their Queen's. Many of them just stopped to join the horrible, cacophonous harmony.

The Aegirie began to scream as well, but theirs were horrid, rasping voices that had once been human—choking, strangled cries. They faltered weakly, covered their ears, and yet tried to continue their attack.

Buffy, Faith, and Spike cut into them, the Slayers

with their swords and the vampire with his bare hands. For a minute, no more, they just killed. Buffy was only a few feet away from Faith, but she saw the other Slayer's eyes widen and Faith pointed past Buffy.

Too late she turned and the Aegir's tentacle unfurled toward her, splashing up a wave that blinded Buffy a moment. Then the tentacle struck her and slapped her to the ground. Though along most of its length it was as thick as a Sequoia, the ends of those tentacles tapered to the width of Buffy's thigh. It wrapped around her, snatching her up from the beach, and she felt the black razors at the tip cut into her pelvis, grating against the bone.

Buffy screamed and nearly blacked out from the pain, darkness closing in around her eyes.

But the Aegir was rolling her up in the tentacle, and in a second she would be dragged across a much larger barb, this one big as a guillotine, and it would cut her in half.

Or it would have, had Faith not brought her blood-encrusted sword down to hack off the end of the Aegir's tentacle. The flesh sliced easily with a wet slurping noise that could be heard even over the Moruach's screaming. The part that was wrapped around Buffy dropped away as she fell toward the sand.

Spike caught her. The vampire lay her down on the sand and stared at her hips even as Faith ran to join them.

"Oh, hell, B.," Faith muttered furiously, Buffy reading the words from her lips more than actually hearing them.

Buffy weakly pushed herself up to see her wounds. Her pants were still soaked, but no longer with sea water. The Aegir's barb had cut her at the hip, sliced down to the bone, but there was nothing vital there, nothing she could not live without. Except the blood. If she lost too much blood, that would be bad. The Slayer healed faster than normal humans, that was one of her gifts. But Buffy did not want to test the limits of her durability, did not want to find out how much blood she would have to lose before she died.

"Where's my sword?" she demanded.

"Buffy, you can't—," Spike began.

"The sword!" she shouted.

Faith handed it to her, then gave her a hand up. Buffy rose and the two Slayers stood nose to nose.

"We can't wait."

"Nope," Faith replied.

They turned and began to wade into the ocean, Spike shouting at them from behind. But they had gone only a few feet when the air suddenly exploded with sound, the night thundering with the screams of the Moruach, now so loud that Buffy stumbled forward and Faith had to catch her. They held each other up, trying to cover their ears without dropping their swords and then surrendering to the sound, their weapons far more important than their hearing.

Behind them on the beach, the Moruach were arranged in a strange ellipse, drawn up to their full height, their shark mouths open so wide Buffy could not see their eyes. The Aegirie had fallen to the sand, and while the two Slayers watched, one of them simply exploded, showering viscera into the surf. Spike was on his knees, hands clamped over his ears.

"It's not moving!" Faith shouted, her face inches from Buffy's.

Buffy whirled to look at the Aegir—nearly losing her balance from loss of blood—and saw that Faith was right. The Old One, this ancient demon from the beginning of time, swayed and rocked with the pull of the waves, tentacles rolling in the water, but it was not moving under its own power. With the help of Willow and Tara's magicks, the Moruach's scream had disoriented the Aegir enough that it was helpless.

Whatever her thoughts over the past few days about war, Buffy was long past choosing sides. No matter what anyone else thought, one fundamental truth was clear to her: The Aegir was not merely the aggressor: it was evil incarnate. She felt it in every pore of her skin, seeping through the air and the water, she felt it in her blood where the eldritch horror had sliced her.

This wasn't war. It was survival. For all of them.

Her lower body practically numb in the water, from exhaustion or blood loss or some combination thereof, she forced herself forward, sword raised high. Faith was beside her, and together they waded the distance to the body of the towering sea monstrosity. The slug-like body beneath it was no concern to them, nor were its eyes. The Moruach Queen had said that without its tentacles it would die, so vital were they to its biology.

Buffy was up to her shoulders in the water when she drew up beside the Aegir. Its tentacles drooped down all around the two Slayers. Buffy and Faith raised their arms out of the water, clasped their swords, and began to slash into the jellied, pustulent flesh of the creature. An unholy stench like nothing Buffy had ever smelled poured out of it, and she turned her head to one side and threw up. Quickly she drew a hand across her mouth and then set to work again, hacking gracelessly at the thing.

In moments they had each severed a tentacle. But as Buffy went to work on yet another, the night fell silent.

The Moruach had stopped screaming.

Buffy tried to turn to look back at the shore, but the waves lifted her and she could not see. Then she caught a single glimpse of the Moruach. They were coming into the water, slipping under the waves and striking out toward the Aegir.

"What's going on?" Faith shouted.

Her ears were ringing so loud Buffy could barely hear the muffled words. But she got the gist. Unfortunately she had no answers. She set to work again, slashing her sword down at the Aegir's tentacle.

The moment the metal struck its flesh, the gigantic demon began to move. It shifted, the wave knocking Buffy back, and began to rise up on its thick snail body. Weakly it lifted its tentacles, slipping them under the water to defend itself, for now the Moruach were moving in to attack. The tentacles that Buffy and Faith were cutting into began to rise as well, and Buffy screamed to Faith, wondering if the other Slayer could hear any better than she could.

Buffy hacked at the disgusting rotten flesh with a fury born of terror, ignoring the vile filth that spattered her face and arms. She cut and slashed until she was almost inside the tentacle, and at last it stopped twitching, cut all the way through, and fell away into the water.

The Slayer turned to look for Faith and saw that she was already finished with the other tentacle and had moved on. Faith had buried her sword in the body of the Aegir and was scaling its body even as it surged forward now, moving toward shore at last. Buffy followed suit, using the tentacle lolling in the water as a step to leap up and ram her sword into one of the demon's eyes. It punctured and she got her boots lodged in the socket, used that as leverage to climb farther.

The Aegir lifted its remaining tentacles, and rolling in its grasp were Moruach, twitching and flailing but no longer screaming, their voices having given out. Their blood poured into the ocean like black rain. The rest of the Moruach tribe followed the Queen in an attack that Buffy herself might have inspired. They swam far too swiftly for the Aegir to catch them all, and they leaped up from the water and clung to its flesh with the talons, raking its eyes with those claws, blinding the Aegir, this thing that had once been worshipped as a god.

It twitched, there on the sand, for now it had slid its

bulk up onto the beach at last. With its remaining tentacles it lashed at them, tearing at its own flesh.

But it could no longer see.

Buffy and Faith, working together, severed the rest of the Aegir's tentacles one by one. All through the process it surged farther up the wet sand, trying to shake the Slayers and the Moruach loose even as it was torn apart. While working on the last of the tentacles Buffy looked south along the beach to where the sand ended and the coastline became nothing but rocks. Upon the highest of those rocks sat a single sea lion, grimly observing the horrific proceedings below.

The last of the tentacles was severed.

The Aegir shuddered once and then fell still, never to move again.

The sword slipped from Buffy's hand and fell to the sand beside the disembodied tentacle. Then the Slayer herself collapsed, sliding from the body of the ancient horror to land on the sand at the ocean's edge amidst the gentle surf.

She fell unconscious there, with the tide rolling in around her.

EPILOGUE

Shortly before dawn Spike stood at the end of a wharf in Docktown and stared out at the Pacific Ocean. The tip of his cigarette glowed a pale amber against the rich cobalt of the lightening sky. He was not supposed to be on the streets—no one was during the quarantine—and so he was keenly aware of his surroundings, of every sound from the ding of a buoy on the water to the distant rumble of trucks rolling through Sunnydale.

Unmarked trucks.

Military trucks.

From his vantage point he could not see the beach where that final battle had taken place only hours before, but on the horizon to the north the sky was brighter, lit with orange flame. He was glad the wind had shifted, for when it had been blowing down the coast toward him the stench was enough to make his stomach churn so violently that he had simply stopped breathing to avoid smelling it.

It.

The army—or whatever silent, stealthy fragment of it had infiltrated Sunnydale tonight—was burning the Aegir. If the thing had bones, Spike figured whatever remained of it would be trucked to some Area 51-esque location for research, for study, or maybe just so that nobody else would ever see it and the world could pretend that sort of thing didn't exist.

What a bloody mess, he thought. It was the kind of carnage that had been common in his life once—hell, usually it was he who caused it—but it had been a long while since this much death and destruction had come his way. A hundred locals dead—maybe a hundred and fifty total, counting Coast Guard and crews of some fishing boats and freighters, most of whom Giles had figured were from out of town. All turned into vicious monsters.

No way to tell how many more would've had to undergo that metamorphosis if the Aegir hadn't been killed. Giles and that Sage woman, the witches, Xander and his little ex-demon girlfriend, all of them for sure. But when the Aegir died, the transformation had just stopped. That elixir Giles had whipped up would reverse the process for them, but in the next couple of days the whole town was probably gonna have to be inoculated. It'd be interesting to see what kind of story they cooked up to explain it all.

All of it. The death and the metamorphosis and the military presence. Never mind the dozens of cops and National Guard who'd died on Shore Road in all the chaos.

It was freakin' anarchy. There'd been a time when anarchy had been the sole purpose of Spike's existence.

So why aren't you giddy about it, eh? he wondered as he took a long drag from his cigarette. *You used to live for this sort of action.*

Spike did not have an answer to his own question, and it made him bitterly angry. He blew a stream of cigarette smoke out of his nostrils and then flicked the half-gone butt off the dock into the surf below.

The burning ash was snuffed upon contact with the water. But something else beneath the waves drew his attention. A quartet of narrow eyes stared up at him. The Queen of the Moruach lifted her head above the water and bobbed there, watching him.

"Oh, sod off," Spike muttered.

But the words masked the confusion that swept through him. The dread he felt at her presence still lingered. He was a predator, the Big Bad, but around her he always felt like prey. All the Moruach looked at him like he was the tastiest morsel they'd ever set eyes on. It was unsettling but there was also something about the Queen that fascinated him, a kind of death-urge, like standing on a balcony of a tall building and feeling the tug of gravity and knowing how easy it would be to just let himself fall.

Thanatos, it was called. *Yeah, the death-urge.* So maybe that was why the thoughts about the Queen were all tangled up in his head. No matter how terrifying she was, there was also this strange allure, this temptation to just let her take him.

'Cause the next time it might not work out the same way.

Spike winced suddenly, and put his fingers to his temples. He swore under his breath, and tasted the copper tang of his blood once again. The Queen was inside his head, talking to him. Not talking exactly, but *thinking* to him. It never came to him in words, her communication. But the images and impressions were simple enough to understand.

The Moruach were leaving. They were going home, not through the Hellmouth, but into the ocean, back to the place they had lived for millennia. They would have to begin again, but it would be worthwhile. Though their ancestors hailed from another dimension, a world of dark and ancient oceans, they liked it better here now. This was their home.

He understood.

The Queen let him know in no uncertain terms that she would think of him often and that she would find him again some day.

Spike had no idea how to respond to that and she sensed his equivocation. The pressured in his head eased. His nose stopped bleeding. For several moments she just swayed there, tall and proud in the water. Then she slipped beneath the waves and was gone without a trace.

"You owe me, Slayer," Spike muttered. "You owe me big."

Then the wind shifted again, and the stench of the burning Aegir wafted south toward him and Spike shuddered in revulsion. The sun would rise soon anyway and so he retreated along the dock, watchful in case anyone in authority might see him. He would hide away in his crypt for the day, resting while the conspiracy to obfuscate the truth of what had happened wormed its way through Sunnydale.

When it was over, and the quarantine was finally lifted, he would have to buy himself a new coat.

Well, perhaps *buy* was the wrong word.

"Lighten up, you two. B.'s gonna be fine."

Faith stared at the back of Xander's head, then at Anya's. Neither of them even responded to her. It had been a hell of an awkward car ride. Mostly for the two of them. Not that Faith didn't understand. Her track record with these people wasn't pretty; they weren't her friends. Then there was the fact that she'd been there first with Xander. It hadn't meant anything to her, but she figured maybe it had Anya's nose out of a joint a little.

The tension in the car wasn't improved by the fact that they were all worried about Buffy. With the Aegir dead, Giles had been able to concoct enough of that nasty-smelling tea or whatever to make everybody's scaly growths go away. But Buffy and Faith hadn't been affected by the bacteria or whatever it was the Aegir used to transform people. Neither had Spike. Faith figured it had to do with Spike being dead and them being Slayers, but it could have been just luck. She wasn't going to waste a lot of brain time worrying about it. That was Giles's job.

Buffy had her own troubles, though. The Aegir had hurt her bad. Faith knew firsthand that being the Slayer didn't make her invulnerable. Some wounds were too much even for the healing gifts of the Chosen One.

"Trust me," Faith said into the silence of the car.

Anya snorted laughter and turned at last to face her. "Trust you? Do you have any idea how funny that is? I barely know you. But I know enough not to trust you. The rest of them weren't willing to say it because you helped Buffy last night. But do you really think that if you just pretend you never did any of the horrible, cruel, evil things you did, that they'll just go away and everything will be all right? I know you're deranged, but are you *that* deranged?"

Faith narrowed her eyes and glared at Anya. "No one's pretendin' here. You don't pretend to like me and I don't pretend to like you. That's the way it oughta be. I don't make believe I'm something I'm not. But how about this? How 'bout you don't act like the only bitch you've got with me is about the people I hurt, instead of—"

She cut herself off, shook her head, and smiled. "Whatever."

The sun had been up for less than half an hour when Xander at last pulled the car up in front of the prison. Though Faith was pretty sure Travers would not report her slipping the Council's custody because of the trouble he'd get in back home, she couldn't be sure. That meant she had to get back to her cozy little cell before he had a chance to let anyone know she was a fugitive.

Xander and Anya reluctantly agreed to take her back to Los Angeles. They found a series of back roads that would take them south out of town and managed to slip quietly through the net the government was throwing around Sunnydale before it could close completely, before the chaos calmed down.

Now here she was.

Home. Four high walls, bars, and barbed wire. It had occurred to her more than once that if she served her whole sentence she would end up living here longer than she had ever lived in one place. Home.

"Thanks for the lift."

Xander's window was rolled down and he glanced at Faith as she stepped out of the car.

"No problem."

Faith stared at him a moment. At length she nodded. "Buffy's gonna be fine, Xander. She's strong."

"Yeah," was all he said.

Then the car was rolling away. Faith watched it until the brake lights went on and it turned right to head back toward the freeway.

"Faith?"

She whirled, tired and bloodied but ready for a fight if one was to come. Helen Fontaine stood fifteen feet away, not far from the main entrance to the prison. Despite the blue sky above and the warmth of the day, the sun shining down, Helen looked cold and pale, almost ghostly.

"What are you doing here?" Faith demanded.

Helen pushed a lock of blonde hair behind her ear almost demurely, but she did not lower her gaze. "Travers and the others are already gone. I . . . I quit."

"I think that was pretty clear to him already, don't you?" Faith asked.

A small smile flickered across Helen's face.

Faith softened. "Listen, thanks."

"For what?"

"For not being like them."

Helen nodded.

"You never answered my question," Faith told her. "What are you doing here?"

The former Watcher shrugged. "I spoke to Rupert Giles on the phone earlier and he told me what your plan was. I just thought it would be easier for you if I was here when you came back. I wanted to make sure you didn't have any trouble with the prison administration."

Faith felt her throat tighten. She blinked several times, and for a few moments she found herself unable to respond to that. Helping the Council out had seemed to her at first an opportunity to redeem herself, not in the Council's eyes but in her own. She had come close to making a mistake, to thinking that if she played along, she could hurry things along, be the hero, wipe the slate clean. But in her heart she knew it was not something that could be done quickly.

Time. It was going to take a long time.

"Thank you," she said softly, and Helen Fontaine nodded in return.

Faith started toward the prison entrance, determined that the next time she walked free of this place it would be because she had found the atonement and the peace of mind she sought.

Buffy's eyes fluttered halfway open and she moaned

softly. Her vision was blurred and her eyes burned in the sockets. Her entire body ached except for her left hip, all the way down to the knee on that side, which was completely numb. If not for the fact that she could wiggle the toes of her left foot, she would have been worried that maybe numb meant *gone*. But no. Toes meant foot and foot meant leg and she couldn't have the bottom of the leg without the top.

"So that's good," she mumbled to herself, the words sort of sliding out, and her fuzzy brain realized that she had been sedated.

"Buffy? She's awake!"

The voice belonged to Willow, but it took Buffy a second to realize Willow was talking about her. She tried to lift her head and instead had to be satisfied with lolling it to the right. Willow and Tara came into view. They were a bit blurry, but Buffy's eyesight was improving every time she blinked.

"Hey," Willow said softly.

"Hey," Buffy rasped.

"You had us worried for a while," Tara said.

Buffy might have smiled. She tried to, but she wasn't sure her brain was sending the right signals to her muscles just yet. "Everyone else all right?"

"Almost turned into sea monsters," Willow replied. "But we're good. Xander and Anya took Faith back to L.A."

A wave of sleepiness left over from her sedation made Buffy close her eyes a moment, but then it passed and she felt suddenly more awake.

"My Mom? Dawn?"

"They're here," Willow assured her. "Talking to the doctor."

Tara smiled. "They're trying to figure out how you could lose so much blood and not be dead."

But Willow's expression faltered at her girlfriend's

words. "We were pretty worried, Buffy. You had us all scared. The Aegir nearly took your leg. You were in surgery for a while—they had to close up the wound on your hip. Even with the way you heal, I don't think you would've made it if Giles hadn't gotten you here in time."

Buffy let the words sink in, understood the truth of them, but at the same time she did her best not to remember what it had felt like when the Aegir had picked her up and the razor edges of its tentacle had started to cut through her. It was a memory she hoped she would one day be able to block out completely.

"Giles," she said. "Where is—?"

"Here."

By now she was able to raise her head and she saw him coming through the door, Rosanna Jergens in tow. She frowned as she gazed at the stiff-looking woman, who wore a clean, crisp, brown pantsuit. *Raiding Scully's closet,* Buffy thought.

"So what's going on?" Buffy asked him.

Giles uttered that little chuckle he always reserved for particularly ironic moments. "That would depend upon whom you ask. Officially, a shipment entering Sunnydale on a freighter from Argentina carried aboard it beef infected with a flesh-eating bacteria, the sort of thing we've seen on the news several times these last few years. Only this was a much more virulent case that cost the lives of dozens of Sunnydale residents. If not for the swift action of the governor and the National Guard, the entire nation might have been at risk. There are medals being given out, lots of patting on the back. I suspect a lot of people's silence is being bought and the surviving National Guard soldiers and police officers who were at the beach last night will take early retirement with enormous pensions. The town remains under quarantine and likely will continue as such for several days."

Buffy stared at him. "That's incredible."

"Not really," Rosanna said quietly. "You'd be amazed by some of the things various governments have kept quiet over the years."

Everyone in the room turned to look at her. Rosanna shifted awkwardly under the attention.

"I'm sorry," the woman said. "I know I'm intruding. And I'll go now. I only wanted to be certain you were all right, and to tell you that should you ever tire of the war, ever think there might be more to do with the gifts you've been given—"

"The Order of Sages will be there," Buffy finished for her.

Rosanna nodded.

"Thanks, but no thanks," Buffy replied, sitting up even further in the bed. Her gaze ticked from Giles to Willow and Tara, then back to Rosanna again. "Nothing personal, but your Order isn't as different from the Council as you like to think. See, it takes two sides to fight a war, but only one to start it. Sure, you're supposed to turn the other cheek, but what if you do and they hit you again?

"We're in a war against enemies who don't just want to conquer us. They want to burn us all off the face of the earth. I'm with you guys in that we need to try our best to avoid the fight if possible. Nobody wins. Last night's a perfect example. But if you think you can avoid war just by wishing it away, you're kidding yourselves."

Buffy shook her head. Willow came to her side and put a hand on her shoulder. Giles crossed his arms and lifted his chin, a proud sort of smile on his face.

"It's really tragic, y'know?" Buffy said to Rosanna, who looked as though she wished she had never come into the room. "I wonder what the Sages and the Watchers could accomplish if you all tried working together for once."

A melancholy expression appeared upon the woman's face and she met Buffy's gaze now without wavering. "So do I," she said sadly. "So do I."

Then she turned without another word, for there was nothing left to say, and walked from the room. On her way out she passed Dawn, who peeked inside, great concern on her face.

"You're awake!" Dawn said happily.

"Yay me," Buffy confirmed.

As Dawn hurried into the room to bend over and gently hug her sister, Willow, Tara, and Giles moved just a bit closer, gathering almost protectively around her.

"Hey, Dawnie," Buffy said, "anybody heard anything about the sea lions? Are they all gone? Back where they belong?"

"I don't know. The news is all 'Hot Zone Sunnydale' flesh-eating bacteria and stuff."

"We should find out," Buffy told her, eyes locking on her sister's. "Somebody's gotta look out for those little guys."

The smile on Dawn's face warmed Buffy, and she returned it with one of her own. All the talking made her feel sleepy again. Her eyes began to flutter once more, and then to close. Somewhere, coming nearer, out in the hallway perhaps, she heard her mother's voice as Joyce Summers spoke to the doctor. The others began to whisper to each other, and slowly to slip away. But she knew they would not go far.

Buffy felt very much at peace.

ABOUT THE AUTHOR

Christopher Golden is the award-winning, *L.A. Times*–best-selling author of such novels as *The Ferryman, Strangewood, Of Saints and Shadows, Prowlers,* and the Body of Evidence series of teen thrillers, which was honored with an award from the American Library Association as one of its Best Books for Young Readers.

Golden has also written or co-written a great many books and comic books related to the TV series *Buffy the Vampire Slayer* and *Angel,* as well as the script for the *Buffy the Vampire Slayer* video game for Microsoft Xbox, which he co-wrote with frequent collaborator Tom Sniegoski. His other comic book work includes stories featuring such characters as Batman, Wolverine, Spider-Man, The Crow, and Hellboy, among many others.

As a pop culture journalist, he was the editor of the Bram Stoker Award–winning book of criticism, *CUT!: Horror Writers on Horror Film,* and co-author of both *Buffy the Vampire Slayer: The Watcher's Guide* and *The Stephen King Universe.*

Golden was born and raised in Massachusetts, where he still lives with his family. He graduated from Tufts University. There are more than six million copies of his books in print. At present he is at work on *The Gathering Dark,* a new novel in his Shadow Saga series. Please visit him at www.christophergolden.com.

. . . A GIRL BORN
WITHOUT THE FEAR GENE

FEARLESS™

A SERIES BY
FRANCINE PASCAL

FROM SIMON PULSE
PUBLISHED BY SIMON & SCHUSTER

3029